ir

Captivity

Captivity

❧❦

DEBORAH NOYES

UNBRIDLED

BOOKS

Unbridled Books

Library of Congress Cataloging-in-Publication Data

Noyes, Deborah.
Captivity / Deborah Noyes.
p. cm.
ISBN 978-1-936071-63-0
1. Fox, Margaret, 1833–1893—Fiction.
2. Spiritualism—Fiction.   I. Title.
PS3614.O975C37 2010
813'.6—dc22
2009053813

1   3   5   7   9   10   8   6   4   2

Book Design by SH · CV

First Printing

For M.G.

Captivity

PART ONE

Fate

The twelvemonth and a day being up,
The dead began to speak:
"Oh who sits weeping on my grave,
And will not let me sleep?"

· TRADITIONAL ·

I ❖ Machinations

March 31, 1848
Rochester, New York

A bell is tolling for me, Clara thinks, awakened in her chair by the wind. *Or in spite of me.* For weeks now she's listened into the creaking strangeness of the old house she shares with her father, a roused house. She's tracked footfalls and merry whispering behind closed doors. But tonight, in the clamor of dusting and meddling downstairs, she hears at last the death of something. She understands that to be as she was before—to barely be—will not be tolerated.

The same rude wind that seized her curtain with a snap, startling her awake, holds her at the window. She rests her forearms on the sill, her nose twitching like a fox's. Out there, all is bluster and agitation. Flailing laundry haunts the lines, and if carriages are arriving round front, she can't hear them for the wind; beyond alley rows and back gardens, it propels anything light and loose along the roadways. Ash-can covers clank, and a raccoon makes its furtive, clumsy way down the neighbors' rain vent. Clara watches with delight as the animal shimmies, curling like a flag at low mast before lighting on its haunches in Matilda Frye's winter garden. Then it pads out of sight into the outer wilds of Rochester.

It was unseasonably warm earlier, almost sultry, so she let the fire die, opened her bedroom windows, and drowsed in her chair, soothed by the good smells of river and thawing mud. She forgot for a time the mean truth: that the parlor downstairs will soon be full of strangers.

Father has broken their pact. He's betrayed her to that Widow Bray, who now "advises" him on domestic matters, it seems, though Clara has managed to run their modest household these twenty years past. Worse, by requesting her presence at his gathering, he has forced Clara to refuse. He has made his grown daughter publicly defy him, an agony for both.

Delicacy is not the widow's strong suit.

Clara wouldn't begrudge her father a companion, a helpmeet, but let him steer that helpmeet—machinations and all—away from *her*. Isn't that understood? Clara's never had with maids underfoot, and Father eats at his club; no need for a cook. In fact, since the unpleasantness in Philadelphia, they haven't hired in at all.

How then is this house, Clara's only refuge, lately, incredibly, crawling with strangers?

Closing the shutters, she turns her thoughts to horses. If carriages must intrude at the front gate—and by now, they must have—there will be horses. *Black and bay, dapple and gray, all the pretty little horses,* swinging their glossy manes. But there will also be coachmen setting out carriage steps for ladies in ringlets and hoops and shawls. Doors will open and close, and open.

And they do.

Little by little, the lower story fills with voices.

Clara knows how sound inhabits every room of this house. She knows what board squeaking signifies what stance and where her father is at any given moment and whether he's in boots or slippers.

Her ears are like spies and travel out, fan out an army and return with intelligence.

But this is cacophony.

Clara smooths the folds of her wrinkled morning gown and slips out into the upstairs hall, easing the door closed behind her.

She moves slowly at first, calmly, until her hip bumps a table, knocking some knickknack to the carpet, and she spooks like a horse in a narrow stall. Her bare toes curl in defense, but she doesn't pause. Her hands trail over oval frames and carved wainscoting.

If she could she would stop the voices, the laughter, rising round her like bars. Her breath is feathery, her life a crushed bird. Who are these people? Who's playing the square piano—unplayed all these years? Who thought to tune it and unseat the dust? Not Father.

Why has he exposed her this way? He owes Clara her privacy, and more. What else does she have? What more could she want? To die, maybe, or live. *To leave the place between.*

For nearly two decades, her entire adult life, the place between has served. It has been Clara's habit and shelter, her home, and now it's under siege by progressive ladies in clip bonnets and cross-barred silk. She knows the crowd well enough, if secondhand; to keep his recluse up on the world's passing, Father gives regular updates on the doings in his social circle. Clutching the banister, Clara listens, but she can't distinguish voices in the cheerful din or find her father's. He speaks so softly.

As if she might yet descend and make her entrance, Clara smooths her simple skirts—no hoops for her, no boning, no bother—and plunks down on the top step. She lurks long in that dim stairwell in a gown the same tired shade as the marmalade cat (a feral tom who sometimes graces them . . . like her, he's found himself exiled upstairs) now purring and stabbing his front paws lustily into her thighs. Wild-haired and bare-footed and with Will at her back— near enough to feel but never near enough—Clara gives the tom the rough strokes he craves. Spotting a dribble of tea on her bodice, she sees herself as her father's guests might now, given a candle and a chance, as a mad, furtive creature, a truth best hidden.

She cranes into the gaping air, and the dark is dizzying. Strains of conversation emerge, now that the tinkling piano has ceased: someone has been to a thrilling lecture by Margaret Fuller . . . Seneca and abolitionism . . . capital punishment . . . prejudice against the poor and the Irish . . . asylum conditions and hygiene . . .

Clara hears her name amid the worthy clamor like a strange bird's song. Her listening sharpens. That vile woman's asking after her health again as if Clara is an invalid . . . perhaps she is, in her way, but would the widow raise that specter in polite company? No. They've absconded. Father and his Mrs. Bray are out in the hall now, hovering between the drawing room and Clara's realm above. She sees the widow, or her reflection, in the glass of a heavy walnut hall stand heaped with coats and top hats on pegs. One gloved hand grazes the multitude of umbrellas in the stand as if to assess their quality.

"Your daughter has so much to offer." The voice drops to treacherous, flirtatious. "As you yourself attest. Why let her live like a recluse?"

Clara can scarce make out the words now. She has to strain and imagines how her face, poised between the banister bars, would appear from below. An apparition. Were they not so absorbed in each other, they might sense her up there spying, but they don't; they won't, Clara knows. For one with so little social care or opportunity, she's learned to read people precisely.

Father remains out of view, but the widow—or her reflection—moves in accord with him, speaking with her hands. "I know a capable physician. . . ."

Does he love her? Say he's invited Mrs. Bray and the others here to announce his intentions. What then? Submitting to the will of a busy housemistress (someone like Aunt Alice, perhaps, who lived with them throughout Clara's youth in London—a woman with bold opinions about how Mr. Gill's dependents ought conduct themselves) is beyond humiliating at Clara's age, even if her temperament allowed.

". . . a gentleman who attends nervous conditions . . . sensitive to the artistic, in women especially . . ."

"One doesn't 'allow' Clara anything. . . ." Father laughs uneasily. "Goodness."

Well that he remembers how to speak, how to salvage for his child the smallest dignity.

But the widow's intent is obvious, monstrous. "You've sheltered her well, sir. It does you much credit and your daughter no good." The hand in the mirror reaches. "Now, then. Who heads this household?" Clara has a glimpse of trimmed whisker as he tilts his head to receive her caress, all obedience. "Let us go together and fetch her."

Clara stiffens, and the disapproving cat leaves a chill. The upper hall is full of shadows that she, like the rangy tom, might dissolve into.

As the widow in the looking glass peels off a glove, Father appears in the mirror, trying almost playfully to detain her. Instead, she steps out into full view. Striding the length of the hallway below, she runs her plump hand, loosed and creamy, over framed rows of zoological drawings: Clara's.

Sometimes Clara can desert her senses the way the cat did her lap, absent herself from nubby carpet and waxed wood of banisters and chiming clocks. But however expert her stillness, they'll spot her and say (sternly), *What are you doing out here? What do you want?* As if they hadn't set out to find and disturb her. As if they were not in the least responsible.

"She's in frail health," Father says with such grave patience that Clara loves him again.

The widow considers, accepting the lie as she might a satisfactory bolt of fabric from her dressmaker. Father scoops her glove from the floor, she accepts his arm, and they return to their noisy party.

Mine, Clara thinks. *This is mine.* But a peal of laughter behind the drawing-room doors rebukes her. *Tell me again, Will,* she pleads. *Why have they come? All these strangers?*

Clara listens for an answer.

Clara listens.

2 ✢ Mr. Splitfoot, Do As I Do

Here is how the Fox sisters teach the dead to speak.

Maggie and Kate are giddy with fear on the mattress when Ma comes running with the candle. "We've found it out," they cry, and Ma's monstrous, flickering shadow rounds the bedroom wall. She nods hard, poor soul, hefting the candle higher, and her hand shakes.

"It" is the rapping that's robbed them of sleep and peace for so long, a hellish business, and who can bear it? Not Ma, surely.

She'll have to, thinks Maggie, who is filled with fate as a sail is for going. Yes, they'll go, she understands, from Wayne County with its brittle fields and trees—an unrelenting patchwork of brown and white to which spring takes its sweet time coming—and it won't be long. Even Ma's weary, pious face can't prevent it.

As if reading Maggie's thoughts, her younger sister, Kate, springs out of bed and snaps babyish fingers. "Follow me," she orders, and how can Maggie not? Who can take their eyes off Katie Dear, so like a blithe spirit herself, all hush and mischief in her threadbare shift? *Snap snap*, and then, in the shadow of Kate's trailing hand, *rap rap*, audible as a heartbeat, deep inside the house.

"Here, Mr. Splitfoot." Kate claps milky hands three times. "Do as I do."

Rap rap rap.

The phantom makes the very walls quake, it seems.

Beneath the spectral racket, Maggie hears the usual soft sounds of night, the ordinary unease of their little rented saltbox cottage: mice scrabbling in the walls, moaning March wind, creaking cold floorboards. These were lonely sounds before and chilled her, but now and suddenly she misses them. Almost. Their empty promises.

She watches the shadow-flicker of branches dreamily. They've not been in the cottage—meant to serve till Pa gets the new farmstead built—long enough to inhabit it, really. Ma hasn't hung their few gilt-framed pictures. The walls, paperless and water-stained, are bare but for the cameo of Grandmother Rutan over the washstand.

Maggie would sooner leave "Mr. Splitfoot" out of it. Already, in just these few days' time, she finds it hard to unravel the sounds she makes or imagines from those without—from her sister, from the earth or the air. It's like when you're rapt with your chores and hear a voice humming but only later, an instant later or an hour, recognize your own voice. Now's no time for the Devil to come calling.

"Three raps mean yes." Kate's voice rings like a rifle shot, and Ma might be a mouse caught in the flour barrel for all her astonishment. Even dour Father has been reeled in now, the hand scarred with old burns from the forge supporting his weight in the doorway, his eyes unreadable behind a candle-glare of spectacles. *Yes, our ghost is still here. Did you really think he'd go so easily?*

Maggie can't but take a certain pride in having disarmed the man who's so cheerlessly charted their collective course. Until tonight.

Rap rap rap.

They are all wild-eyed for lack of rest. Should Maggie scold Kate or applaud her—treacherous girl—for taking it this far? Too far. Her sister won't meet her gaze. They have no plans. They know no allegiance in this game, if indeed it is a game, and now for once Maggie's unwilling to say that it is or isn't, to ask it, to know. But it's *theirs*, whatever it is, and Kate's sport is catching.

"Now do as *I* do!" Maggie waves her arms, signaling three times like a mighty hawk flapping phantom wings or a hell-bent angel. Her winged shadow swells, shivering inside the black dance of branches on walls and wardrobe and the graying old quilt Ma spent a whole season of evenings squinting over by the hearth, stitching and squinting.

Rap rap rap, replies the ghost.

"It can see as well as hear!" she exults, but Ma hears only their visitor now. Maggie looks to Kate, smiling with her eyes like Mona Lisa. Kate does not look back, but Maggie smiles anyway. Their ghost commands what they cannot.

"Are you a disembodied spirit?" Ma sways in the balance. "Speak now! I'm so broken of my rest I'm almost sick."

Rap rap rap.

"Tell me my eldest child's age."

A torrent of rapping, on and on till Maggie loses the will to count. First for Leah, and then Elizabeth, Marie, David. Her mind wanders through the storm of noise, a steady thumping as of some giant come to tread their roof, but Ma is breathless, vigilant, counting along. Fifteen raps for Maggie. Eleven for Kate.

"My youngest now," Ma demands mysteriously, and Maggie thinks, *It's one patient ghost to weather such a taskmaster.* Besides which Kate is their youngest. But the visitor raps thrice, faintly, and Ma swoons. So there was another child once. Did Kate know?

Why not Maggie? Father's lips flap in prayer, and Maggie wonders at the secret, mortifying world of adults. What more unspoken? What else?

"Will you continue to rap if I call my neighbors in?" Ma trembles. It's a terror to see her this way. And a thrill beyond reckoning. Pity and fear catch like a bone in Maggie's throat, but she has no shame, evidently. It's too late for that.

"That they might hear it also?" Ma pleads.

Maggie imagines the men and boys out night fishing by Mud Creek. They'll mill and murmur with eyes full of moonshine. They'll listen intently, blow into strong hands with icy breath. She will have them in thrall.

Rap rap rap.

Ma stamps out into the darkness of the hall, clutching her shift close round a spacious bosom, Pa stumbling at her heels.

Kate leads their visitor up and back in a hypnotic square, the walls resounding. Doesn't she see there's no one left to impress now? Where has she gone to in mind? Her eyes shine like ice.

Rap. Rap. Rap.

Had the river burst its banks and come swirling in under their roof this night, Maggie understands, the Fox sisters could not have seen their way clear.

We were born for this, she thinks.

❀ The first to arrive is candid Mrs. Redfield, meaning to have a laugh at their expense. Indulged city children (the Fox family has only just relocated from Rochester) scared silly in their beds.

But when Ma enlists the clever spirit to rap out her neighbor's age, Mrs. Redfield promptly fetches Mr. Redfield. His ripe old age is likewise disclosed. He, in turn, sends for Mr. and Mrs. Duesler, who summon the Hydes. Before the girls know it (always "the girls," as if deprived at birth of Christian names), the house swarms with eager Methodists in various degrees of undress demanding audience with the spirit. For shame! Ankles on view everywhere, even the ladies', and this is something. This is grandeur.

"Is it a human being that answers us?" prompts Duesler in his righteous baritone. His morning beard shadows a doughy jaw. His bare feet with their revolting horny nails—he alone politely removed snow-crusted boots at the door, woolens or no—rivet Maggie. The only sound in the now overheated room is squeaking-wet soles. The occasional dry cough. "Is it a spirit? If it is, make three raps please."

Rap rap rap.

"Are you an injured spirit, then? Make three raps if you are."

It does, and it's deafening.

"Were you injured in this house?"

Yes.

"Were you murdered?"

Yes.

"Can your murderer be brought to justice?"

No comment.

"Is the person living that harmed you?

Yes.

Everyone in the room seems to shrink, for the only expedient way to finger the assailant is list each luckless person they can think of and hope for a match, which is cause for murmuring and downcast eyes. Who will be named? On what grounds? Who will do the naming—offending whom? With a lofty sigh, their leader, Mr. Duesler, proposes, "There are twenty-six letters in the alphabet. Will you

rap out the number that corresponds with each letter? One for 'A,'
two for 'B,' and so on?"

Yes.

With this tedious method, their ghost, identified as a Mr.
Charles B. Rosna, formerly an itinerant peddler, narrates its violent
demise. Five years earlier, for his worldly wealth of five hundred
dollars, his throat was cut with a butcher knife in the east bedroom,
his body dragged down through the buttery to the cellar and left
lying the night long. In due course, he was buried ten feet below the
earthen floor.

❧ The population within the little house, meanwhile, has surged.
Men up from the creek move with fishing poles slung over shoulders, a threat to life and limb, though a thoughtful few have lined
them up outdoors. Too exhausted to navigate the forest of ripe
bodies, excited to the point of collapse by clamor, Maggie prays for
sleep under the stairwell crawlspace. She wishes Mr. Hyde would
take out his fiddle, that for a change they might roll up the ratty rug
and dance as they did in Rochester, instead of milling about rooms
where a dead man got dragged, his blood streaking the boards.

When Charles B. Rosna intrudes on her thoughts, her rest under the stair is broken. Maggie crawls out, slapping spiderwebs off
her dress, to search for Kate, who's retreated to the empty room
upstairs, their room before the rappings began. Kate is wound tight
in a blanket, a dead weight that Maggie can't unravel; nor can she
pry her way in, so she lies alongside her sister's mummified shape,
Kate's breath soft on her cheek and faintly stale in the sweet way of
childhood. Maggie watches her sister's chest rise and fall and the
flicker of her pulse at the hollow of her freckled neck. She buries

her head in that warm space under Kate's chin a moment, marveling at their sway over and invisibility among so vast an assemblage of neighbors.

A low roar of voices fills the house as even the spectral rappings did not.

But the thing in the cellar commands her. Even if she and Kate and their joint imagination have planted it there—and she can't say for certain anymore—the peddler's ruined body has swelled, spread like a foul demon vegetable in the nether regions of their farmhouse. Maggie can't long keep it from her thoughts.

When the rappings began, Marta Weekman, who's nine but seems younger, told Maggie and Kate matter-of-factly that she once lived in their house and suffered there. It knocked, Marta said, and when her father answered, there was no one. Her pa raced round in bare feet to see was the knocker here concealed or there, and this—her befuddled father's evident lunacy—terrified her worst of all. One night she felt a hand trail over her sheets as fingers play on water or a harp, and when the hand reached her face, it was cold. She lay rigid till dawn, too stricken to speak or cry out, and refused to enter her room again after dark. Not long after, her family moved out.

Maggie hopes it won't touch her.

On the other hand, what might it feel like, being touched by a hand from Beyond? Wondering—like when she wonders about God or the devil—makes her feel light and unpinned from her body, wide-awake and willing to a fault.

She curls tight, listening to the swell of voices. Safe among her family and neighbors, Maggie wonders, is Marta Weekman downstairs with her parents? Or have they had their fill of the spook house? She wonders about the rappings, about herself and Kate, whose breath now warms her wrist. All these people milling about in the strangeness of night, including the peddler with limp head dangling over a great gash. *Who are we? How have we come to be here? Now. Together.*

꙳꙳ Maggie lurks outside the parlor next morning, holding her shadow back from the threshold.

Inside, in full morning sun, Mrs. Redfield kneels, surrounded by a hushed assemblage—more arrive every hour—of villagers. She asks in a voice unfamiliar and soft, urgent enough to make a blacksmith blush, "Is there a heaven to attain?"

In broad daylight, the question floats down among the farmhouse congregation like a feather. It rocks on the air like a baby's cradle. Each word a creaking prayer. Is. There. A heaven. To. Attain.

Right on cue, Mr. Charles B. Rosna arrives with comfort.

Rap. Rap. Rap.

"Is Mary there?" Mrs. Redfield, on her knees, bows her head. Her shoulders shake, but only just. "Is my Mary in heaven?"

However petty Mrs. Redfield is, she deserves an answer. But it was a poor night's rest, and already Maggie's weary of the work and the day. She saunters off, trying not to imagine the rueful silence in her wake. Does their bold new world exist when she's not present? When she and Kate step offstage? Who was it said the world's but a stage? Mr. Shakespeare. She thinks fondly of Amy Post reading aloud from a leather volume while she and Kate lazed on their stomachs, bicycling back the air with stocking feet, their skirts in an unladylike sprawl. Amy's a Quaker and can't approve of the plays, which Maggie's managed through her own cunning to borrow from her pastor's library, but Amy makes an exception for the poems.

After that, the spirit is reticent. People come and go, and it doesn't please them to go. They linger by wagons, stamping with the horses. They murmur into their gloves. Kate is young yet to rate the lash for immodesty, so after they procure a furtive lunch of bread and too-ripe cheese, she climbs the attic ladder to view it all from the rafters.

By evening, men and able boys have commenced digging in the cellar. Debate rages among them and floats up through floorboards.

"We can't lower this water."

"I never have seen or heard a thing I can't account for on reasonable grounds."

"Account for it, then."

"I see no human agency at work."

"Rats. None but rats in the walls."

"The Fox elders never seen any rats."

"There's that cobbler fellow down the way. Might be an insomniac hammering his leather all night."

"He's outside now, taking his nips on Obadiah's wagon while we dig."

"Waste of a night's rest."

"Why does the spirit rap only with those girls present? It's fine sport for them."

"These children were the first to befriend it. Maybe it trusts them."

Maggie wonders if Kate feels the same excitement she does with some two dozen strong-armed men in sweat-stained shirtsleeves laboring just below the floorboards, or is Katie too young for that?

The men dig and dig, metal picks ringing on packed earth, until a great, violent scraping sounds and one man barks, "There! You've done it again. Here comes the water racing."

The men stamp mud up the stairs, their spirits dampened. They emerge singly and in pairs to convene round the kitchen, mutter, and warm their hands with Pa's coffee.

There is no rapping that night.

Long past bedtime, youngsters sprawl under tables, whispering with ears pressed to the planks. They kneel and play at jacks as big frighten little with grotesque, silent pantomimes of the dead man, heads dangling limp on boyish necks. The house smells of warm cider. Mr. Hyde slyly kisses Mrs. Hyde behind one ear. A dog barks far off, and keeps barking. But gradually, the good neighbors trickle out. Ma leaves the men and the stragglers to it. She steers her girls out after Mrs. Hyde, and the Fox women sleep on a hard bed in strange bedcovers, dreaming of phantoms. They sleep straight through their morning chores.

3 ❖ A Candle and a Chance

They've gone. Clara hears his voice from a long way off, waking with her head on her father's shoulder. His thin arm in lint-specked dinner-jacket sleeve folds Clara close, prevents her drooping forward and toppling down the stair. He has removed his tie and looks uncharacteristically rakish for a man of his years, smiling sideways with his ruined teeth. Clara smiles back fuzzily, lulled and small.

She feels and looks, she supposes, exactly like a child who's surrendered to sleep whilst spying on the grown-ups downstairs. Except she's nearly forty years old and aching soundly, the grown-ups have gone home, and the smile on her father's lips is not one of exasperation or bemusement but concern.

"Well, then." A voice behind them startles her out of her wits— or into them. It belongs to the Widow Bray, seated at the same narrow table Clara collided with earlier. "You nodded off in mid-entrance, Clara. At least we two waited for the dessert tray to arrive." The widow and her vast shadow set the candleholder on the table, tame ample skirts into submission, and join the other two on the step. O cozy horror.

Clara lifts her father's sheltering arm away and stands with a palm on the wall to steady herself. She sidles past them, crossing to the abandoned chair. To retreat outright would be unforgivable, and she and Father have very little but forgiveness left to offer one another.

"Clara," he tries, not unkindly, as they gape at her. "Please."

She looks them over, looks away.

Life as Clara knows it is ending. The widow has found her slipper-hold, clearly. She'll have ideas and advice. Tidy wisdom. Even now, her small hand rests on Father's sleeve, enlisting him for the sake of a unified front.

Floundering in her skirts again, the widow struggles to her feet with Father's help. The wretch can't kneel in all those layers—Clara doesn't suppose the widow *would* kneel—so strides forth with hand extended as to a child. "Come, join us downstairs for tea. Your father will look fondly on your willingness."

Clara knows that when it comes to guarding what's dear, enough is never enough. Ferocity is not enough. She winces to make the widow disappear, but plump fingers close round her bony wrist. Clara feels a fluid buzzing in her body, a riot of blood and nerves. She is unused to being touched or coerced. Unused to many things. Unused.

"Up, now, and spare his mind, won't you?"

Who is *this woman?* The question roars in Clara's eyes, but her father won't meet their gaze. *Look at me.*

The widow is a member of Amy Post's circle, not a Quaker but a reform-minded sort with a mind to do good at any cost. Her husband, much respected and many years dead, was a physician. This Clara knows. *But who is she?* Clara would demand if she could. *Who is she to us?* And, *What have you told her? Answer me.*

Forsaken, she admits a surge of the same bloody reel that soothed her the last time meddling women influenced her father . . . eyes craving glass, fists resolved to rake her own flesh with willing shards. Clara never acted on it, of course, this or a thousand other petty acts of violence. But like a magic-lantern show, like any good diversion, the reel gave her pause. It gave her rest. The insurance of youth: that when the time came and no amount of subterfuge would do, she might act against her own flesh to free the unhappy spirit.

Look at me, old man.

The widow lets go Clara's wrist almost gently, but her words keep like a clamp. "You must rally, Clara. You're no longer a young woman . . . quite. I don't like to say it, to press a wound, but you're approaching an age . . . we might say that with your habits, you're unlikely to marry or bear children."

Father purses his lips, not quite nodding.

"A woman in your circumstances must care for her elders, not tax them. You're neither frail nor a fool. Take responsibility for your life. I beg you. Relieve him."

"I thank you, mum, but I believe we endured very well before . . . without you."

The widow sighs, her interest waning. "Enough drama now."

Even this deep in dismay, Clara must credit her opponent: Mrs. Bray will have the last word. She will have her way.

She turns once more and desperately to Father, who keeps his back to her, facing away as he ever has when a strong woman has hold of him. Clara speaks to the back of his head, to the vulnerable neck nicked by his barber's shaving blade, in a voice quietly savage. "The only consolation I require, sir—you know this, and you know why—is solitude."

4 ⚜ Outwitting Death

Night again, another haunted night, and Maggie glimpses the whites of eyes shining like moths in the long black bar between the curtains. Boldly she throws open the panels, an actress taking the stage. She finds at least one eyeball pressed very near the glass out there, and a mashed, waxen cheek or two.

Raised candles make shifting fragments of it all, grotesque half-masks. There are other figures, a great many others fanned out behind, and a huge flickering bonfire in the east meadow. These are not drifting phantoms or witches' rites but pilgrims, legions of them, come from Newark and farther still to an otherwise unremarkable farming hamlet to get a glimpse of the girls who raised the dead.

When at last Mr. Charles B. Rosna and his audience taxed her beyond reason, Ma removed her girls from "the spook house" to brother David's farm two miles away.

But soon David's roof and walls resound with rapping also.

The theory arises that the spirit isn't one but *many* spirits, craving the receptive company of the Fox sisters, who needn't be magnetized—two different newspapers have taken note—to converse with them.

This theory is championed by Leah, the eldest Fox sibling, who arrives some weeks into the affair with trunks and lady friends and her daughter, Lizzie, in tow, exclaiming, *What's all this?* and *Why didn't you write me?* Leah learned of their trials when a friend saw page proofs of a report soon to circulate in Rochester in pamphlet form. "I came at once," she pronounced.

Bet you did, thought Maggie.

But no matter. It's clear to everyone that Maggie and Kate Fox are at the center of this strange affair. Spirits are resolved to be where they are, and when the rapping followed to David's so too did half of the crowd, even with investigations and excavation still ongoing at the cottage.

The migrant squatters have wreaked havoc on David's property. With his fields trodden, he makes a poor host. His patience is daily and sorely tested, and his wife, Elizabeth, when not trekking back and forth to the well or sating neighbors grim with controversy, spends thankless hours plucking chickens and crafting puddings, pies, and cakes for the diggers, who return jittery, soiled, and hungry at night.

David and Elizabeth's little daughter, Ella, is in bliss, though, running wild in plain sight with the neighbor children and the gypsy hordes. It's a topsy-turvy world, and Maggie vows not to let the rare if barely contained aggression of disbelievers, or muttered words like *chicanery* and *witchcraft*, distract from the fun that she and not a few others—for once in their tedious lives—are having.

"Come look, dimwits," she commands when Kate and Lizzie stray in, nibbling sweetmeats. "It's like All Hallows Eve out there—"

The other two approach the teeming window but reel away in a rapture of giggling. Emboldened, Maggie plays indignant, lifting her arms like Moses poised to part the waters, aware of being watched by multitudes. It's a novel feeling, and Maggie likes it rather too well. "That's enough now."

When she snaps the curtains closed, a muffled cry of disappointment erupts behind the glass. One child even raps on it, though Maggie—pleased that good Christian country manners are adhered to, even in strange days—hears the mother scold him for it. Many things about her community she finds trying. Others are as warm and familiar as her favorite shawl, and she'll miss them.

Some dozen transient females in that house have laid stake to Ella's bedroom (men, as many or more, have claimed the master bedroom). Bedsteads have been stored in the attic, and top and bottom mattresses crowd together like rafts on a sea of hardwood. A tangle of doled-out bedding lies over it all like ship's rope. Kate leaps deftly from raft to raft, pausing to bounce in place. Lizzie, likewise bouncing, bites the cookie out of Katie's hand, and they laugh like crazies.

"How will we sleep?" Kate laments, falling still, her bodice specked with crumbs. She seems melancholy all of a sudden, genuinely perplexed, and Maggie vows in mind to protect her . . . always. But then Kate and Lizzie are sidling out of the room, murmuring into each other's shoulders, already bored.

Alone with closed curtains, apprehensive in a way she can't name, Maggie feels a strange surge of relief when Leah comes in. She hopes her sister won't make her tidy up. The room's in chaos, and with Elizabeth put-upon, lamenting and enlisting all over the house, it's a wonder Maggie has eluded labor this long. Ella's is the only room not teeming with people, and Maggie has discovered she needs her peace. *Entitled or not*, she thinks, following Leah with her eyes.

Striding to the window with her steaming teacup, Leah peeks between frayed curtains at the horses, wagons, and humans beyond. She lets the curtain fall, setting her saucer on the floor and settling beside Maggie on the mattress with a flick of her hand. "It's a perfect plague of flies in here."

Leah begins to plait her thick hair (who can say anymore what's public time and what private . . . when it's safe to unlace a corset or loose your mane . . . what's immodest and what isn't) but soon starts in fussing and smoothing Maggie's instead, her expression at once stern and tender. "Everyone traipsing through all day."

Her silence grows unnerving. Leah isn't around much, but when she is, Maggie thinks of her as a second and inferior mother more than a sister. Twice Maggie's age or more, Leah is a will to be overcome. *And about as willful as they come*, Maggie thinks. *Go on, then. Say it. Whatever it is.*

"Have you any idea what you've started?"

Maggie bristles, though she's steeled herself. Is this prelude to a scold—or congratulations disguised? Leah won't waste her time if there isn't something to be had. She sips her tea with agonizing slowness, sets cup in saucer on the floor, and reaches again, annoyingly, for Maggie's hair. It was coming loose from its bun, despite Kate's best efforts, which are never very good. Pa won't hire a girl when his two are "healthy young mares in their own right, fit to be farmed out elsewhere," so all day Maggie and Kate clean and scrub and husk and card and can and quilt and knit shawls and mend sun-bleached bonnets till their eyes ache at the dim hearthside; but to break the routine, they attend to each other like queen's maids, bind one another up in corsets, fashion and flaunt jewelry of berries and seedpods, curl and recurl the hair round their ears just so.

It's a dull life in the country, to be sure, though Ma's good for a laugh behind Pa's back. ("She's the better horse in the team, by far," Maggie overheard one farm wife snipe. She knows it's true, though it hurt to hear an outsider get on about it.)

"Of course I know."

"And what do you mean to do about it?'

"Do?"

Leah stops stroking Maggie's hair, but her idle hand looks twitchy in her lap. Leah likes to be busy, Maggie knows, likes her fingers racing over ivory keys and her strong hands trained to such useful tasks as orchestrating a human circle round men digging for bones in a basement. (Ma boasted about it all afternoon: Leah saw to it that none got through, even the most abrasive and demanding, who weren't welcome.)

"You've unearthed something here in Hydesville," Leah says. "Besides your Mr. Charles B. Rosna, I mean." She speaks the name snidely, drawing out each syllable, though it's been on everyone's lips all day.

Those diggers elected to stand watch at the cottage overnight reported gurgling and strangling noises. With digging scheduled to resume at dawn, the murdered peddler reenacted his own demise on the hour, choreographing the crunch of breaking crockery, the repeated *thump* of a great weight being dragged across the floor, other urgent noises . . . ugly dripping, wasp-like sawing.

Leah's expression changes, growing serene and strange. "They found lime down there this morning. Bits of teeth and bone. Did you hear? Strands of reddish hair. While they were digging, the floor above creaked with the weight of so many. I felt sure it would fall in and crush us all. People are poised for something more."

"A show?"

Leah takes her chin firmly and turns her face up like a child's. "Listen to me, Margaretta—"

It's the name Leah uses when she means business, which she mostly does. Maggie relents when her chin gets sore from her sister's squeezing. "I'll listen, but I can't work miracles. I can't, to suit you, walk on Mud Pond or make shillings from pinecones."

"You'll do something better."

For the first time, Maggie meets her sister's gaze freely.

"You'll open a passageway between the mortal and spirit worlds," Leah adds, nodding as if to reassure her, *This is true.* "Know what you've been given. You and Kate. Me. The Fox sisters," she adds slyly. "We'll outwit death. We have that *duty.*"

Maggie laughs again, nervously. There's nothing especially funny in the notion (is it morbid or the opposite? Holy somehow? Lifelong Methodist teaching's done nothing to prepare her for this), and already, in that early moment, the burden begins to wear on her. She senses that she'll keep the invisible dead like an anvil round her neck her life long, but she's grateful, too, and ready. Maggie Fox is ready.

"Our brother's fit to tear out his hair. 'Better to die together,'" Leah mimics, "'than live so disgraced.' He's been carrying on all day—"

"Well, they've stomped all over his plantings—"

"Till Chauncy called in and agreed to help dig, I thought David would send everyone away. I felt sure he would. But he didn't, Margaretta. He didn't."

Maggie hears another wagon arrive. The bodies of neighbors and eager strangers bat against the glass of the bedroom window; a dog barks; and a moth circles the lit tallow candle on the nightstand, singeing its wing. The little hiss is audible even under the groaning of David's crowded house, the comforts of laughter and clinking glassware, the muffled fray of Ella and visitors' children issuing threats and challenges (goaded, no doubt, by Kate and Lizzie) and scrambling under furniture.

Maggie nods her consent, and Leah smiles, laying a hand on her sister's head, as in benediction.

❧❧ But there is more to Leah's plan, it would seem. A great deal more that Maggie doesn't know about. She hears Leah down there in the relative quiet after the children are in bed—pleading, extolling, bending Ma's ear in that nasal voice of hers. *The girls should be separated*, Leah advises. *Let's see how the spirits fare then. I'll take Kate with me for a time.*

All winter long, Maggie dreamed of returning to Rochester, of strolling beside the windy Genesee in warm weather, in big bell sleeves and a brand-new lace bertha bedecked with ribbons while gulls wheeled on high and great flocks of geese came over pointing their hopeful arrows south, of attending lectures and shows, of taking tea with the Posts and their lively circle of reformers.

But look, she and Kate managed to bring the excitement home instead. How clever!

Why would Leah thwart that—if not to please herself? What does she want? Maggie can't sleep for wondering. Long after Leah and the other women settle around her in faint moonlight, she lies there rigid, seething with the injustice of it.

Kate and Lizzie sleep back-to-back, joined at the fold like the wings of a butterfly. The youngsters doze at lanky angles, breathing jaggedly. At the rim of the sprawl lie stouter frames: Ma and Leah, Elizabeth and Maria, Mrs. Post and Mrs. Capron and Jane Little . . . here and there, snoring and twitching in the night, other wives and daughters stationed at David's while their men commute to and from the cottage. Maggie listens, charting the dwindlings of human concern, sensing at length—within that lullaby of not-quite stillness—some other, unseen presence.

Fate is in your favor, it assures, relaxing Maggie out of anger, soothing her into sleep.

❧❧ She half-wakes in the dark of early morning in a tangle of limbs. Kate, of course, is cocooned in the only nearby quilt, and Maggie shivers herself conscious. The world is all unaccountable silence.

The breath of the girls and women has steamed the window near the bed. In the other bedroom, some half-dozen men sleep soundly. Outdoors, the pilgrims snore in their cold encampments.

Looking out into a blue half-light, Maggie smears her hand across a pane twice and for a peculiar moment imagines her brother's trampled fields swarming with the dead. Spirits traipse here and there, tufts of light, farmers and farm wives, soldiers and babies and old ones—some marked by their style of dress and half-familiar. They are made of light mostly, and ride lightly over the earth, treading no soil. And they are everywhere.

She blinks her eyes, suspecting her own mind has planted them like a strange crop in the field. The strangeness of seeing them is new, but Death itself is no stranger, surely. Not a day goes by in

Arcadia when one among her community isn't lost to fire or drowning, typhus, yellow fever . . . a mule's kick. These deaths are real and ever present, reported daily in neat columns of newsprint along with farmers' reports of stray pigs, sentimental poems, ads for patent remedies, or word of the war with Mexico, the abdication of the French king, Whigs battling Democrats.

But what if they aren't gone over Jordan after all? What if they are just across the way, a hand's reach, waiting to be seen and heard from?

Now, that's strange, and she will seize the strangeness in her hands and shape it. She will not be afraid. In truth, Maggie Fox *is* afraid—how vast a thought it is—but not of the spirits themselves, who seem to her just strangers full of secret need. Out she goes into the blue dawn and passes them in the field, holding out her hands to feel them streaming through, to fancy their shuffling woe crowding close round her like cattle. Too close. She breaks away and strides past a stand of crooked trees under which bruised apples have lain all winter long, frozen many times over.

The sun rises as she walks and warms her. She comes out on the cart road again and dips back into the dappled wood, thinking ahead to the sweet smell of the battered peppermint fields, which sport their pink flowers like finery.

Maggie wanders without a thought, and when a thought does come, it stops her in her tracks, and her eyes brim with tears. Here she is, out on a muddy track ruining her good boots—when all she wants is to mill about in city drawing rooms in a lovely big-bustled gown and be admired. Kate will get there first, it seems. Without her.

Recalling the harmonious tangle of limbs back in Ella's bedroom, and Kate and Lizzie asleep with their foreheads touching,

Maggie is already lonely. *Katie . . . stay.* But Katie won't. She can't, Maggie knows, not once Leah has her hooks in.

Maggie spots a perfect little basket near the crook of a young tree, an oriole's nest, brittle and fine. Pinching it down, she cradles it carefully, as once it cradled eggs.

She walks all morning with the nest on her palm, and the dead do not follow. They are gone when Maggie enters David's kitchen, where the women are assembling breakfast. Even the murdered peddler two miles away at the cottage lies asleep, she expects, soundless in his mud-and-limestone bed below the floorboards.

5 ❖ Difficulties

The Widow Bray might be a general for all her strategy. It's weeks before she insinuates herself again, with Clara's guard down.

When her father knocks, he finds her sketching. Her room is open to the elements, honey-lit, all breeze and bird chatter. He enters tentatively, crossing to a seat on the edge of her bed, and Clara feels the point of her fountain pen straining on the page, her fingers pinching hard. Father never intrudes this early in the day. When at last he states his purpose, his voice sags with apology. "You'll recall the girl we hired on to help with the party?"

Clara regards him blankly.

"Elizabeth, the younger of the two—daughter of Mrs. Fish?"

"I wouldn't know Mrs. Fish from Mrs. Fowl." Clara's disdain for the architect fast closing in on her father's affections is vast. Best keep mum, she thinks, or risk slandering Mrs. Bray. "I wouldn't know one girl from another," she manages. "I didn't employ them. I never saw them."

"This Elizabeth," he continues, "'Lizzie' . . . apparently her relations are experiencing . . . difficulties in Arcadia. Mrs. Fish's maiden name is Fox. I thought I'd catch you up, as you may hear of it when young Lizzie returns this week."

"*Difficulties*," Clara says vaguely—though her real concern is *when young Lizzie returns*—"is a euphemism for scandal, in my experience." Her hand speeds over the page. By now Clara's avian subject has long eluded her, like everything else. She looks up, and her father seems so earnest, so hopeful that she can't but smile back at him. "And how would such gossip find me?"

"I'm an old squirrel," he admits, lifting her chin, "eager for chatter. But you *are* curious?"

Her jaw tenses, and Father's palsied hand settles at his side again. To admit curiosity is to admit defeat. Clara mustn't relax her guard. She'll lose, but gracefully, with her pride intact.

"It's said these girls can communicate with the dead," he adds wryly.

Clara replies with deathly silence, and he doesn't press. She can be as vile and childish as she likes these days, and Father, a man made audacious by secrets, intolerable ones, carries on unmoved. She'll tolerate. She always has.

"This leads me to other business." He clears his throat. "I've decided to keep her on . . . hire Lizzie Fish on permanently if very part-time . . . and perhaps her young aunt, too, when the girl arrives. It's been discussed. Mrs. Fish supports the idea."

Clara needn't ask who else supports it. Who discussed it with Mrs. Fish.

"Both girls come highly recommended by the Little family and the Posts. I guess in that few short days I grew reacquainted," he adds, "with . . . domestic niceties."

"Did you."

He leans in collusion. "You'll grant we're an austere pair, you and I."

How he can afford to transform the household this way with commissions scant and his "sabbatical" extended through the fall is not her concern. It's not her place to ask. "They won't fix a decent cup of tea," she complains. "Americans don't, you know."

He smiles back at her. Patiently.

Clara opens a drawer in her writing desk, and the sketchpad vanishes inside. Lacing pale hands in her lap, she sits back resolutely. "As you please." Her pencil rolls to the floor.

"You disapprove?"

"Is it within my rights to?"

Silence. The widow's influence, then, is certain, insidious. There is no undoing it. First will come the servants, Mrs. Bray's personal selection. A housekeeper to boss and batter Clara with lists and expectations courtesy of the incoming mistress. The trunks will follow, chintz and frippery, and of course the wedding dress, well dusted for a second run. At length, Clara will be shipped off to strain plums for a great-aunt she didn't know she had. "So be it," she almost croaks, for her throat has screwed up, cutting her breath.

"You might find their young company amusing. Given the chance."

"And bless you and Mrs. Bray for giving it to me."

"Clara?"

She looks at him directly, mournfully, and away. Down at her folded hands. "Sir?"

"Trust me now."

"I will not." Her voice is a fierce whisper, and when she lifts her eyes again, her father's shine with the sting.

6 ❧ The Invisibles

Ma and Maggie arrive in Rochester the day after Leah's household relocates to Prospect Street. The piano movers are on hand. They've positioned the instrument wrong, and with Leah noisily redirecting them, and Kate trying to keep the cat from underfoot, and Lizzie hollering for the sake of it, and Ma and Maggie and the hired coachman lugging bags and parcels indoors and tracking in mud, the reunion is unceremonious at best.

No sooner has Leah hustled the piano men out again than she turns to interrogating Ma, who has yet to remove her shawl. Maggie feels a terrific urge to race out after the coachman and have him see her home again. But where is home? Sobered, she helps Ma with her overclothes as Kate and Lizzie stand stupidly by, tormenting the cat.

Leah nods over the piano keys, tapping out tuneless notes and wincing. "What news at home?"

Hanging Ma's things, Maggie glances up under her lashes at Kate, her favorite person in the world, and her look goes unanswered.

Ma seems pleased that much-older Leah—twice married and twice estranged—speaks easily of "home" when the cottage in

Hydesville never was her home, but she's having trouble gathering her thoughts.

So Leah intrudes on them: "What more have the men found in the cellar?"

Ma begins to gush like a stuck pig, like the cellar floor when the men first took their picks to it. She wails of the crowds at both the cottage and David's; of the digging that just goes on and on, weather allowing; of the mess and disorder and Ella running wild in the thick of it all; of David and Elizabeth with their weariness and worn nerves; and of the fickle ghost and the baffled investigators.

The more panicked and weepy Ma becomes, the more roused seems Leah. Maggie can almost feel her circling, assessing the story's edges, searching for a place to turn her claws in.

Chilled to the bone from the canal ride, Maggie sits on her hands to warm them. She's trying to keep still, marveling at her sister's composure.

Now and again Leah taps out a note with her thumb—C, E, F, A—that wilts on the air. To call in a tuner will be an extra expense, but Leah makes her living teaching piano. She can teach even the dumbest brat to master Mozart because her patience never flags.

If Leah was upset that no one sent for her when it happened, that she had to hear the news like a stranger from neighbors and journalists, she didn't let on. Instead she hurried to Hydesville and made herself useful. "Don't cry, Ma." She stands now and crosses to their mother, taking her hand, patting it like a puppy. "You can stay here as long as you like." Leah takes them in one by one, all beneficence. "You all can. But you believe in this spirit? These *spirits*?"

Maggie stares forward blankly. With Kate and Lizzie like strangers, there is no safe gaze to seek refuge in.

On the other hand, their ghost has made Maggie brave. Always, in the past, she was the cautious one, the one who planned and recorded, who said but rarely did. *Tell me a tale*, Katie begged when they were children in Canada. *You have a secret, Maggie! Tell it now. . . .* And Maggie told, in grave whispers, for it was one way to hold her sister still and present. Kate was ever in motion, whooping, chasing crows from the fields. She ran whirling and the birds seemed not so much afraid as under her sway. They rose thundering together into the slate-gray air, and Maggie half-feared her sister would rise with them, but Katie only laughed and mocked her care. Kate was and is the most careless, uncomplicated creature Maggie knows, and Maggie loves her well for it.

At the cottage and at David's, "the girls" rarely spoke of the spirits or planned their path but moved together like dancers, *step step turn*. The music became a thing outside them, spectral music with a life of its own, and whosoever might stop the music could be damned.

When Leah came and took Kate away to Rochester, leaving Maggie behind with Ma to suffer the tedium of David's farm, Maggie thought her heart would burst, but she rallied, soldiering on alone. Thanks in part to "A Report of the Mysterious Noises Heard in the House of John D. Fox, in Hydesville, Arcadia, Wayne County"—the very document, penned by a Mr. E. E. Lewis, that alerted Leah in Rochester to their predicament—western New York was alive with speculation. Whether born of trickery, fear, superstition, or the lot, the pamphlet held, "if any one has been able thus to deceive a large, intelligent, and candid community for a such a length of time as this has been carried on, it certainly surpasses any thing that has ever occurred in this country or any other." The Fox sisters were on everyone's lips, but their own family—Pa now deferentially referred to it as "David's household"—didn't speak of the cottage, even in rare moments of privacy round the kitchen table. It was as if Maggie and Kate and their parents had never lived there, had never been the people in Mr. Lewis's pages.

While investigations ensued and everyone and his mule whispered of her exploits, Maggie Fox, down on the farm, had none but the impersonal dead to confer with. Ma's lip quivered when she tried. If Maggie so much as hinted, Ma wept morosely and groped for her Bible.

In spite of all, Maggie got by, and so did Mr. Charles B. Rosna—by no means loquacious but present just often enough to keep his audience on edge.

When Leah wrote to say that she'd secured rooms in a two-family house on quiet, tree-lined Prospect Street in Rochester's fashionable Third Ward, and that Ma and Maggie were welcome to join them there, Maggie's joy was fierce. So was her passion to be with Kate again, to hold her sister and giggle and fall again under the spell of *them*.

But it's instantly clear that things won't be the same at Leah's.

Ma kneads an embroidered hankie—one of Kate's, full of jagged lightning stitches—in one raw, red farm-wife hand. "You know me, girl. I'm sorry for this trouble. It's our grave misfortune to live in such a house. I believe only what I've heard and what these here and your father and our good neighbors have heard, and I pray for deliverance."

"Margaretta," Leah barks, riveting them all. Kate even stops toying with the cat's tail. "What do *you* say?"

"Marta Weekman—"

"I don't care what Marta Weekman says. I'm asking you."

Maggie keeps her eyes on the ginger cat in Kate's grasp, which emits a noise between a snarl and a belch and flicks its tail. Her gaze darts north in desperation, and at last Katie meets her eyes with a flickering smile. The world is instantly warm and wide again, as if the sun, withholding, has consented to rise. "I told you," Maggie counters. "Ask the ghost. He keeps few secrets, it would seem."

"And very late hours!" Leah says with altogether too much satisfaction. "Tell them, Katie." She nods brightly at Ma, giving Kate no chance to do as she's told. "We've had . . . a few visitors of our own. Sit. We'll say all about it."

❧❧ The place in Rochester's Mechanics Square, it turns out, is as haunted as David's house, and the cottage before that. It only took the right residents to notice.

"We were scarce out of Hydesville," Leah begins, swollen with self-importance, "and still on the canal when the trouble began. There we were, minding our business, dining with the other passengers, when the spirits went to town with a great show of rapping. Then and there. The table jumped, and water came splashing from our glasses, but with the noise of the boat going through the locks, no others noticed. Thank heavens."

Ma frowns determinedly.

"We got home to Rochester around five P.M. Kate and Lizzie went straight out to the garden, I remember. They weren't gone long when I heard a noise." Leah sighs, gathering strength for the telling. "Like a pail of bonny clabber being dumped from the ceiling onto the floor. There was a terrific jarring after that, and the windows rattled—I'll never forget it—as if we were by a battlefield. As if someone had fired off heavy artillery. It shames me, but I was paralyzed by fear. The girls rushed in, all wonderment, and walked me to my bed. There we huddled under the blankets, much alarmed, trying to sleep, but the moment the candle was extinguished the children screamed. Do you remember, girls?"

Both nod, a bit too dutifully, Maggie thinks.

"Lizzie said she felt a cold hand over her face and another stroking her shoulder and her back."

Maggie looks to Lizzie, who can't check a self-satisfied smile. The poor housecat has given in to its fate and gone limp and tender in Kate's arms. Perhaps to hide that gloating smile, Lizzie mimics the cat, jabbing her forehead into the crook of Kate's neck, craving affection. Kate again seems as distant and mysterious as the moon.

"So I took out the Bible and read a chapter, and while I read, the girls continued to feel touches. I never did, I confess. Finally we slept—I won't say easily. We woke with the sun to the smell of roses. The birds were singing in the trees of the public square. The night now gone seemed unreal. I kept my own counsel but had my doubts, and toward evening, Jane Little and other friends came in to spend an hour. We sang and I played piano—" She looks around for impact, lowers her voice. Lizzie's eyes widen as if she's hearing this for the first time. "And while the lamp burned, I felt the throbbing of the dull accompaniment of the invisibles keeping time to the music, though the spirits remained kindly concealed so as not to alarm the company. We retired at ten," Leah concludes—at least Maggie hopes this is the end—"and slept quietly for two hours."

"And then?" Maggie demands, predicting an encore.

"And then . . ." Leah draws out her words in agonizing fashion ". . . woke with the house in a perfect uproar."

Leah rises out of her chair. She starts stomping about with her hands moving like a mime's to narrate how doors opened and closed in the dark. "Someone, followed by a great many others, walked up the stairs and into our bedroom, jostling and whispering. All I can figure is that it was some kind of show . . . with pantomime and clog dancing and raucous clapping . . . and then their footfalls moved away and downstairs again, the doors thumping closed behind them.

"On it went," Leah says, "night after night, the whispering, giggling, and scuffling of this spectral assembly. There were death struggles and murder scenes of fearful character—I dare not describe—but in time it was as if we dawned on them, slowly, and they included us. They gathered in strong force around us."

Ma listens, transfixed, and Maggie can't but wonder: *Why would Leah lie?* She isn't the better part a child, as Kate and Maggie are. Despite Leah's wry pragmatism and occasional inclination to wink or stoop to child's play, she's a grown woman, dour with her days' burdens. *Why would she lie?*

Maggie must conclude that Kate and Lizzie have carried on without her, which leaves her feeling even more out of place and out of sorts than when she arrived. These spirits are not Maggie's. They are no part of her design.

"It's useless," Leah sums up grandly, "to record all that's come to pass these last few weeks. At length I engaged these rooms. This is a brand-new building, I'll have you know. Construction's just completed. There were no former tenants, so it harbors no history, no crimes. Come," she says brightly, "let's have a look around and see you settled. Ma, you look exhausted."

Is it any wonder? Maggie thinks expansively. Lonely and tired in view of Kate and Lizzie, their tittering and giggling, Maggie lags behind on the tour. Things were difficult and dull at David's, and then that long journey in on the packet, and here they all are, competing warily for some prize she can't name.

Leah points out that the house is really two houses on a single foundation. "The cellar's there, and this kitchen staircase leads up to the second floor and the dining and sitting rooms. On the third floor, we've just the one long room that runs the length of the house. We put three beds there and curtained off a space for storage."

Maggie hears Leah's tour voice, traveling along with their footfalls upstairs, but she's stopped short in the pantry. It looks out on the fenced back garden, but beyond that, plainly visible from the pantry window, are the bleak stony tips of monuments. Her mind reels and orients itself. Prospect Street. That must be the Buffalo Burying Ground. So much for "no history," she thinks, a smile twitching on her face.

She'll have to work quickly, she knows, and with great energy to draw Katie back from Lizzie's sway and Leah's. It's always the way: when the other two get their hooks in, she has to lure and coax and charm Katie back.

But yes, Mr. Rosna has made her brave. If Maggie could navigate David and their parents and the never-ending flow of curious strangers, reporters, and investigators back at the cottage, she won't be cowed by Lizzie now. Lizzie's no match for Maggie Fox, even if Leah is.

Now that Maggie is home again—home will ever be with Kate—she'll lie awake nights studying what she can make out in moon- or starlight of her sister's turned-up nose with its spray of freckles, the sweet mouth with its habit of holding untruths, and feel an awed pulse of gratitude.

Home.

All is quiet until midnight, when distinct footsteps are heard moving steadily up the stairs and into the little green-curtained storeroom. From within, sounds—shuffling, giggling, whispering—

the spirits, muffled in chintz, anticipating their own mischief. Out they come and give the beds a shake, lifting the sleepers off the floor, letting them down with a bang, patting them with cold hands before retiring again to what the Fox women will dub "the green room."

"Can it be possible?" pleads Ma, in the dark. "How will we live and endure it?"

7 ❧ In the Fever of Not Trying

It's said these girls can communicate with the dead. How to reconcile Father's blunt words with the ridiculous monologue ensuing downstairs in the drawing room?

With her closet door open, Clara hears the whole thing through the dumbwaiter shaft: the widow braying like a tiresome donkey, like the wife she isn't yet, like the busybody she's doubtless always been. Shall it be a Tuesday/Thursday schedule for Miss Lizzie and a Monday/Wednesday/Friday for the other—Margaretta, presumably, though the elder, Leah Fish, has yet to confirm which of her two younger sisters she'll farm out for labor and which she'll keep at home—and will you have them for three hours each day or four? And would it be better to include one weekend day, and if so, Saturday baking day would be better, would it not? And do you take an ample afternoon tea and a light high tea, or the reverse? Surely you won't subsist on bread-and-butter sandwiches for the former . . . perhaps some more inventive recipes? Chicken curry? Cucumber mint? Radish-poppy seed?

If sound and silence be indicators, Father is winningly defiant, pausing between questions and sometimes not responding at all, at least not that Clara can hear. Nodding, no doubt—or nodding off—over his news sheet as the widow prattles on in her grievous, well-meaning way. Clara can only hope good Mrs. Bray drives him past his point of no return, an arduous if not unreachable destination. Clara, meanwhile, is a ghost in her own home, neither awake nor asleep, aware of her own transparency.

There will be plans galore, more and grander plans, and the endless, tedious discussions that go with them, discussions she will be expected to partake of. The widow's voice will echo round the walls, tomorrow and again and the next day and the next, seething with intent, and then will come other voices, servants and strangers, each with her will, her agenda, her own wills and won'ts. Those same walls seem to be pressing in on Clara, inching closer. The inevitable beats on them with blunt fists, and she can't devise a way out or a defense from within.

The light is failing. Heavy-lidded, she wakes and sleeps and wakes again. Once this pattern was as peaceful as a lapping tide; now it rises and falls like floodwater, all damp chill and promised destruction. What will she wake up *to*? There is a continual sense of things changing, disassembling, reassembling outside her view. If only she could glimpse that stubborn future now, once and for all, and know the degree of the problem.

All is eerie silence when next she wakes. It seems moments ago the question of To Radish-Poppy Seed or Not to Radish-Poppy Seed ruled the world. Now stillness blankets everything, and Father's curious words fall softly there, like snow: *It's said . . . it's said . . . the dead.*

Who says they can do it? Who claims this knack for them?

Idiots? Fools? No. Amy and Isaac Post are not fools. Nor are the others in Father's circle, even the more credulous among them, like the Widow Bray. Overhopeful, perhaps—unlike his friends in London who would laugh such claim into submission—but not fools. America is full of sunny, hopeful people, despite all evidence to the contrary—but are hope and folly *necessarily* the same thing?

Clara opens a window, breathing hard, closes it again. She is a vile, dependent thing, and not since London has this rude certainty been more present; she has no place to go once Father abandons her to the wolves of domesticity and society, and no one to go there with. For years Clara has been allowed to be indolent, inviolate, hidden. She's needed and longed for nothing, and nothing has been expected of her.

If she could see far enough into the future to know what the widow will make of her life, Clara might find cause to end that life quietly, gratefully, taking the only initiative she has left. But she can't see. She doesn't know, and she is frightened and angry for it.

To ease her panic, she fumbles for sketchbook and pencils. Tonight she peers down into the well where her heart still lives in search of a story. As a rule, the past repels her, but the best stories belong to childhood, and her best to Artemus and Mary.

Artemus favored the classical, the Greeks and Romans. Mary drew on changelings and other fairy mischief. To honor them both, Clara fishes from her dark well the myth of Proteus the sea god; to elude captors who would have him tell their future, Proteus shifted shape.

Clara sometimes tires of drawing animals, but for better or worse they're her subject of record, and every picture, every story commands them. Her pencil begins, then, with a wild eye, a wing and a claw, with flashing fur and diamond scales. She sketches furiously as wily Proteus takes many forms, but she outlasts him, and at length he must assume his right form and gift her with her future.

And so appears, like a wolf loping out of a fog, a man's face. Not the gnarled old sea god—eyes sunk in their webs of flesh, the stained ivory of a foot-long beard—but a beloved face unfurling against her will, frightening for its likeness. Did she trust she had forgotten?

There is William Cross, unprecedented on the page and unwelcome, unapologetic. The eyes, truer than any human eyes she has ever fashioned, even in the fever of not-trying, stare back at her, noncommittal but intense, as if he isn't certain how he got there or what to make of her. And could he be? Would he know her now? He's an agony and an outrage: beautiful, young, unchanged—and she a puffy wretch of questionable appearance (when did Clara last consult a mirror? Vanity is the first to die, followed by curiosity, and hers left her years ago). She slaps the sketchbook closed.

Do you frighten yourself? For a moment she applauds her own skill, though it feels less like craft or genius now than some reckless imposition. She has sketched Will—or her memory of him—from every possible angle year after year and never found a likeness, quite, and never tired of trying. She's concocted him hair by hair and heartbeat by heartbeat, over and over, that ceaseless task of unrequited lovers, grieving mothers, fathers of sons who commit unspeakable acts, abandoned children. Will is a locked door for which there is no key, and he can neither satisfy nor disappoint.

In the spirit of foolishness, why not take up that bit of tripe father has left on her side chair, a penny-press account of the haunted doings in Hydesville? A hook for a dull fish.

Clara reads intently, her brow furrowing. What would her old friend Marianne Pratt conclude? Is this why Galileo faced the Inquisition and died a prisoner, or Diderot labored over his encyclopedia? Why Wollstonecraft dissected Malleus? So that a pair of farm girls might arouse ancient superstitions in a credulous public?

Father left the pamphlet conveniently by because he wants to engage with her on this point, clearly—his strategy whenever a new book arrives or a lecture incites enough controversy to be written up in the morning papers. So many of Father's influential friends have been taken in by this spirit ruse that Clara has to give him, give all of them, the benefit of the doubt. She reads through to the end, sits a long moment, and feeds the pamphlet to the fire, transfixed by the leaping flame.

Rousing herself, she takes up her sketchbook and thumbs through to Proteus transforming, shifting closer to the truth. How often has she spoken the words in mind: *Tell me, Will. Tell me?* What would he tell her, if he could?

She pries the page from the book and systematically begins shredding the deathless lips, the sad, scarred sweetness of expression, until only his accusing eyes remain. These she tears also, first one and then the other, flinging him toward the ceiling, letting the confetti of Will Cross rain down on her feet and her furniture.

Here's a mess for you, Clara thinks.

Let that silly girl clean this. Give her real work to do. Let her fall on her knees in vain. Let her see that neither prayer nor wish nor trickery makes it so.

The dead are silent.

The dead are gone.

8 ❖ Mad Clara

Soon, as at the cottage and David's house and Leah's former home on Mechanics Square—anywhere the Fox sisters hang their bonnets—the new apartment on Prospect Street resounds with rapping. Nightly there is scuffling and shuffling, shuddering and malevolent snickering. Ma despairs and takes to bed red-eyed, complaining of curses. Merry with malice, the spirits lift the mattress she shares with Leah, letting it fall with a great, jarring thud that leaves Ma howling and Leah grim and shaken, massaging her lower back.

If, during such antics, Maggie strays in mind, conjuring the Posts or other solemn persons she respects, she chafes and softens her stance, but shame can't outshine the thrill for long.

Dozens of press inquiries and investigator requests and beseeching tracts from mourners arrive weekly. Their lives have swollen to twice their natural size, but Leah, whom Ma has entrusted with the administration of their fortunes, persists in promising something larger still.

The excitement is hard to bear, but in its midst, ordinary life must go on. There is never enough money, fame and popularity notwithstanding. Ma and Kate keep house while Leah traipses about teaching piano (and spreading word of wonders). Maggie is elected to join Lizzie, who cooks and does light housekeeping for pay in the home of a neighboring family. "He's an old English gentleman," Leah assures. "A friend of Amy Post's. Lizzie's done very well with it."

Maggie doesn't care for being a servant or for being away from Kate. She doesn't fancy the idea of things happening at home without her, not one bit, and hems and haws, but Leah is adamant.

"Another student quitted me last week." Leah glares as if it were Maggie's fault, as if Maggie might have done something to prevent it. "You'll fix lunch and do a touch of cleaning after is all. It's three days a week. Lizzie will see to it the other days."

Kate can't resist the chance to speak a truth no one else will. "So we're serving-class now? I thought we were *improving* our prospects, not . . ." She winks at Maggie, warming her through.

Maggie holds Kate's gaze, playing along. "Won't he make his daughters cook?"

"He has one, all right. But she's mad and won't leave her room," Leah complains. "Our second day there, she scratched Lizzie like a monkey on her face. I thought to put the wretch over my knee, but now we leave the tray outside her lair. Mr. Gill is too mild to punish her."

The notion of a madwoman draped over Leah's broad lap, crushing her petticoats, is delicious. "Does he beat her?" Maggie begs. "And does she run all up and down the river at night with flowers in her hair like Ophelia?"

"I've said, haven't I? Mr. Gill's the mildest kind of gentleman. But you remember Mrs. Bray? She's hinted, in strictest confidence of course, that the Gills have suffered and leave behind some scandal in London. . . ." Leah sighs, adding with barely concealed satisfaction, "Now, go introduce yourself. See what Mr. Gill has for you. Lizzie has an errand for Mrs. Little, but she'll come along tomorrow and instruct you fully."

Leah marches Maggie to the door, facing her toward Sophia Street. "It's just six doors down from the Posts'. The Gill residence. Ring, and they'll let you in and show you your work."

The Gill house smells of must layered under lavender. Master Gill answers the bell himself, and his teeth, the worst Maggie's ever seen, recall the doomed peddler moldering in the cellar in Hydesville. But he's otherwise sober in appearance, high-collared with neatly trimmed mustache and sideburns. With his mouth closed, he looks the perfect gentleman, and he scarce notes that she isn't his lately hired help, not loud-mouthed Lizzie but a stranger off the street, and a newly famous one at that. Come to it, Mr. Gill seems to notice very little. Waving her in, he has the aspect of a mole.

He leads her to the kitchen, pointing her amiably here and there as she inspects columns of bone china in the cabinet. The front row sparkles, but all else sports a fine fuzz of dust that Maggie wagers is tacky to the touch.

The wallpaper is formerly grand, grim, you might say, if not for the pictures. Some are fine and delicate, ink-and-watercolor in gilt frames, others just pencil sketches tacked up at random and tending—like that baboon with the murderous shine in its eye—toward morose.

By the time Maggie finishes her inspection, Mr. Gill has a tea tray all done up for service and is shakily portioning out his own sandwiches, shifting his plate off to a sideboard. "Come," he says, waving her to the doorway.

They stand side by side in musty shadows, and he gestures down the long hall, then back at the tray, watching her face anxiously as if she might object. "Third door on the left. Clara likes a whole pot. We'll make me another when you've done with her. Find me in the drawing room."

Does she, now . . . and will we?

Maggie can't abide being addressed as a servant, especially in view of her newly elevated status. She imagines a girl like the baboon from the drawing leaping onto her back, but curiosity wins out. It usually does. "You'd like me to pour it for her?"

"Please. If she'll allow."

Not *if you please* but *if she'll allow.*

Flashing that frightful smile, he returns for his plate of bread-and-butter sandwiches, heading down the hall with it in the opposite direction. Maggie looks warily after. Mr. Gill seems unduly satisfied about something, brave in his mild way, which bodes ill. But Maggie remembers Lizzie—fearless here before her—and won't be bested. Lizzie can't triumph, especially with Kate in the balance.

"And you'll see she opens the drapes if needs be?" he calls over a bony shoulder.

For the fun of it, Maggie dips into a dainty curtsy. "I will, sir."

❖❖ The figure hovers between velvet curtains as if to slip through to another world. She's slight, facing away, and her stance slippery, but there's little else worth remarking on, little at least that smacks of madness in all the melodramatic forms Maggie enjoys. Maggie lives not far from the State Custodial Asylum for Feeble Minded Women, after all, the gabled recesses of which fund the best sort of gossip.

A shock of silvery hair hangs in lank splendor down Mad Clara's back, but her satin gown is simple and clean, old-fashioned, nearly the shade of her skin. It's a color like absence. She's all watery insubstantial, it seems, till she hears Maggie and turns, leveling those shocking eyes on her—fierce, intelligent eyes in a gaunt face. *That'll cut glass, that look.*

"Hello, miss. Your father said to open the drapes."

Mad Clara only stares as if to say, *Try.*

"I won't if you prefer not."

"I prefer . . . not."

"Where will you have this?" The tray's a strain on Maggie's wrists, but she won't sigh in complaint.

"There on the table. Push those papers aside."

Maggie does with her elbow, and drawings float to the floor like leaves. Birds, mostly. Lovely ones. Maggie recognizes a thrush, a catbird, others that are mere skeletons, spare and shining as spiderwebs. She sets down the tray and kneels to gather up these strange likenesses, which invite the same dazed ingratitude live birds do when Maggie chances to notice them. They might be hard at work stitching the world together with their beaks, for all she knows, holding the stuffing in, but such work is theirs to do.

Setting the drawings down, Maggie crosses to the window. She has no wish to be scratched and already knows to forgo pleasantries. She jerks the curtains open to a tangle of garden, remembering the flawless nest she found on David's lot, now concealed in a hatbox in Leah's closet.

Mad Clara's too self-possessed to wince or protest, but some scarce-visible part of her stiffens in a crouch.

Maggie has an overwhelming urge to clap in this stranger's face. Everything about the woman orders Maggie out, as if a return to solitude is the one thing that will mend Miss Gill's evidently measly life.

But charity isn't Maggie's strong point.

She waves at the streaming twilight, the jumble of books and papers, abandoned watercolor washes, inkpots, pens. "Won't Lizzie dust in here? It's choking." She has no business berating an elder—her "better," at that—but the week's events have made Maggie Fox bold. They've shown the world for what it is, a sham of vast proportions. Maggie holds it all by a thread, and she never knew. Never dreamed how simple it would be to reach out and gather the world in like spring flowers.

Clara Gill seems feral and strange and possibly entertaining, and if Maggie has to endure being away from Kate and from home with all its haunted doings, from a citizenry buzzing with her name on its lips, the least she can do is craft a day's amusement. Never again will she suffer an instant's tedium. For the world has split like an old scar, and leaping underneath is her own heartbeat, the bright pulse of her future.

Maggie feels such impatience these days to cut through the sludge of manners, to slice and stab with wit and candor, to arrive at once at the heart of matters. She's changed—her experience with the spirits, because of the spirits, has changed her—but the world *hasn't*. Not a whit. People are as meek and dogged as ever; they bow and lower their eyes and take her hand limply and speak of tedious things much as they ever have; meanwhile, every minute, Maggie is spilling out, barely contained.

A craving to confide in someone older than Kate, kinder than Leah, wiser than Ma, and blunter than Amy Post—someone unusual enough to be useful—now overwhelms her. Maggie can't resist. She must know and know quickly, and so parks her hands on her hips, tilts her head rakishly, looks straight into the madwoman's face, and sticks out her tongue.

Mad Clara only stands there, stubborn, shimmering with the soft violence of a rain cloud.

"You *want* to smile," Maggie all but whispers, looking away—half-mad herself with presuming. *(Say something. Be unlike the others. Be as I am.)* "I see you do. Why won't you? If I have to be here, let me amuse you. Amuse *me*."

Clara walks to a chair beside her narrow spinster's bed, silver mane rocking like a pendulum. She sits, straight of back, folding her hands slowly in her lap.

A moment passes and another, heavier still, and Maggie waits.

"You're amusing," the woman concedes in a faraway voice—looking up and then down at her bony hands again, elegant hands—"if one is partial to monkeys."

Maggie feels her face rearrange itself into a grin. Mimicry is one of many games she excels at in league with Kate, and she's sore tempted to retort in Clara Gill's good British accent, but she breathes a hard breath instead, turning to lay out the contents of the tray with great deliberation: Mr. Gill's bread-and-butter sandwiches, a hard-boiled egg on a dainty ceramic pedestal, ragged-sliced pears on a willow-pattern plate, a potbellied teapot. She looks at her handiwork, tugs discreetly at the old right-tending boning in her corset, seeks out that gaunt face again, afraid.

Mad Clara's stare unsettles without censoring. She may be as impatient as Maggie is to get on with it, whatever it is for her, and for a moment more seems partial to surprise, receptive; but then something changes in her face. Crossing briskly to the tray, Clara ours out dark, reddish tea, her expression blank. Her cup rattles in the saucer as she strides back to her chair, which abrupt action must have set her mad, mute heart beating like a drum.

"Say if you take milk," Maggie offers, weary now on her companion's behalf as the clock ticks on the mantel. *Tick tock. Tick tock.* She wonders are the men and boys back now, digging in the basement in Hydesville? Are birds dropping into the trees around the cottage, lured by fuss and sunshine? Are ladies in drawing rooms all over Rochester whispering her name?

Her companion's face is implacable again. Maggie wants the last word and means to have it, but Clara's eyes *are* a bit mad, a bit hawk-like. Maggie is no mouse, and she's the sane one in the pair—at least as likely to be believed in a skirmish—but she's also outside her element. Crazed or no, Miss Gill is a grown woman whose now cold stare reminds Maggie of her life before the rappings—a child's life that wasn't much to speak of. She resents the setback.

"I'll be going, then."

Her feet haven't crossed the threshold when a voice barely perceptible, rusty with disuse, says, "Wait." Like a white flag waving.

But the world is calling now, the waiting bustle and murmur back at Leah's, the house in Hydesville with a story larger than Maggie's own life, the spirits who've followed and will not now abandon her. News is spreading all over New York State, and wouldn't Solomon Beecher, home in Hydesville, beg to kiss the famous Miss Fox behind the woodpile now?

Maggie waves at the tray, feeling tall in the doorway. "I'll be back another time," she promises.

9 ❧❧ Pixie-Led

The beast keeper murmurs something to the parrot on his shoulder and thumps his own chest with a fist.

"Be still, my heart." The bird's tone is smug and oddly soulful, a world-weary old man's. "*Squawk!* Still."

From a corner of her eye, Clara watches it nuzzle the keeper's ear, as if in caress. She does not lift her head nor stop her hand, charcoal racing over the ivory page, though she wants nothing more than to look at him straight on, has been wishing it for days since first she glimpsed his comings and goings with shovel and pail in the big circular hall. She longs to memorize the outline of him, work her way in from the shadowy edges with a bit of color, breathe him back on the page through her restless right hand.

But he might catch her at it, and with sketches due for Sir Lever's approval Friday, it won't do to digress. Clara settles instead on the young man's portable shoulder ornament.

Usually the parrot is caged in the aviary in the other building, where it taunts more majestic inmates—golden eagle, griffon vulture, secretary bird, none of whom Clara has sketched yet. If the bird's comely perch sets it down, Clara will know where to find it.

Father is off in search of this boy's employer, Mr. Cops, a family friend who has given Father and his assistant—Clara, that is—leave to stay on at the menagerie after public hours. They come almost every afternoon, but Father never seems to note the young man at work with shovel and rake, spreading fresh shavings; sneezing as he hurls hay bales here or there; and sometimes, to her well-concealed dismay, disappearing through the door of the keepers' apartments. Like the animals, which are ever hopeful of a scrap of meat or a snatch of song, Clara can sense where he is at any given moment.

Unless the public—prone to hanging on the lead gates, hooting at the inmates and disturbing the garrisons—clamors for the spectacle of meat flung to the carnivores, Clara remains in the hollow aisles into evening, sketching by gaslight while Father loiters in Mr. Cops's library. Locks clanging, the keeper moves among those beasts that will not maim him. Gruff and tender, he barks, "Shove off, fool, if you want a chop" and other husky endearments. If they are favorites, he coos to them.

Motherless Clara has aunts who live to parade her before men of a certain status. Mostly they watch in mounting despair as she neglects them. But Clara's virtue is a commodity, prized, so where are her guardians now? His voice, so easy and present, seems dangerously close at hand. At times it might be echoing inside her.

They banter back and forth, bird and boy. (Not a boy, exactly—older than she perhaps, but with an air of play about him.) The phrase ricochets on stone, dazzling her with indirection. Once she catches him regarding her with those eyes—a shocking blue, they are—and not regarding her too, as servants do and don't regard their betters. He can absent himself. He has that gift, it seems, which explains Father's willingness to abandon his socially vulnerable daughter in the dank recesses of a house of beasts with a loping boy-stranger. Father does not see the beast keeper any more than he takes note of individual beasts.

Besides which, Clara is notoriously sensible. This and her skill as an artist give her a degree of domestic liberty little duplicated in other households. Their first day at the menagerie, for her sake, Mr. Cops made a great show of the leopard's predilection for seizing and destroying parasols, muffs, and hats almost before the astonished visitor knew to miss them. Father only smiled, well assured. His Clara would not flaunt her finery before a leopard.

But here she is, left feeble-minded by the lean curve of a boy's back. She's a honey hive full of bees, all distraction. They have no history, she and this boy, no memory in common, but—and this is ridiculous—she seems to recognize him. His voice, ringing from all directions and none at all, soothes and bewilders, and she envies the bobbing, mangy bird balanced on the plane of his shoulder, gnawing his ear.

Clara won't lift her eyes from her charcoal sketch but uses deft knuckles and thumb to smudge, deepen, enrage the white space. It's spiteful, the ivory page, sworn to see her fail. But caring little lets her succeed where her father, who in his quiet way cares so much, fails. She sometimes imagines her talents come of a spell cast by some benevolent spirit on behalf of her dead mother.

Clara draws as well as any scientific artist in London, and the older and more marriageable she becomes, the better she understands: this is her breath and barter.

He'll be in this gallery, Clara knows, for at least an hour. It's evening mealtime, and now she knows his habits as she knows those of the other residents of the menagerie, of which there are fewer and fewer each day, with the king and Cops gradually surrendering them to the Zoological Society of London's more scientific venture at Regent's Park.

The cats will pace and sleep at intervals and then crowd with tensing muscles by the slat door a quarter hour before their meat arrives. Old Martin the grizzly makes three long paces and then rubs his back against the stone and, turning, flings his upper half into the air before beginning the pattern all over again. She knows when the singing birds will sing, if at all. The hyena and a gaunt American black bear share a den, and while neither actually succeeds in killing the other, relations between roommates are daily tested. When they have a bone to squabble over, squabble they do, in a ludicrous manner, and the devious hyena always wins the day.

"Which of my lovelies are you drawing today?" His voice seems almost shy, though she knows a glamour when she meets one. She doesn't make the mistake of looking at him.

But it's a bold gesture. They're alone and he at least remotely in the Crown's employ; he couldn't know who she is: the daughter of a great man? An old friend of the royal line? A courtier's child? Her clothes are plain but fine, the product of doting aunts who pity her prospects. He can't know whom he might offend, or that she is only her father's daughter, here because her talents have proven useful. Thanks to the charitable impulses of Sir Artemus Lever, an old family friend, she and Father have secured between them a major commission. Father has redemption and she respite from the tedious topic of matrimony.

"I'm sketching that one." She motions to his parrot. "Since you've been so kind as to display him for me."

He smiles, and his teeth are gently crooked. "*Display* is a fine word for old Mettle." He breathes deep and begins a litany that dizzies her. "*Psittacus erithacus erithacus*, native to Africa. He's a fine mimic, easily bored, with a tendency to growl, except at me. He's a vocabulary to rival most men and fancies himself a humorist. Marie Antoinette had a grey like this. So did Henry VIII, one as ill-mannered as his master. That one amused himself by crying out by the river, 'I'm drowning! He fell in the Thames!' Or he'd hail the boatmen over from Hampton Court Palace. Across they'd row thinking to be paid for their trouble, but inciting royal chaos was all in a day's entertainment for the rogue. Mettle's vain about his dress, drab though it is, so your favor's a great conquest."

Clara steels herself to look at him. "Is that the speech you give everyone? *Psittacus erithacus erithacus?*"

"You're not impressed, then?" He feigns disappointment. "With the Latin, at least?"

Her lips purse and her nose twitches. It isn't right. It won't do. What would Aunt Lucretia advise in such a crisis? Defy flattery. Pray for grace.

She prays but finds him closer. He's loped closer, and she can see now that he has a slight limp, so slight as to go almost unnoticed, and she can't breathe. Clara drops her charcoal, and the crayon rolls off down the stone, right to him. Mesmerized. Even a dumb piece of coal knows what to do. But instead—to spare her complexion, as the advice columns trumpet—she practices self-restraint. She feels his furtive gaze, unbearably lit from behind with a hard light, slipping from her face to her hand. Slipping.

"I'd hoped for a nod, at least, from an educated specimen like yourself."

She looks up and catches him teasing his lower lip with his top teeth to check his smile. "All right, yes." She lets her breath out. "I was impressed." *Now you've done it.* "Very."

He reaches down for the charcoal but doesn't close the space between them to deliver it, folding it circumspectly in his fist. "'Very' because I'm a mere beast keeper and a buffoon, probably, or because the facts were of use to you?" His gaze, now unabashed—and it's as if she's never been looked at before this moment, really looked at by another human soul in all her endless nineteen years—is terrible in its brightness, his eyes endearingly ringed round with sun and laugh lines. *It hurts,* she thinks, *hurts,* for it does, sweetly, to be seen, and who could have warned her? "I don't look for charity, as a rule, but I like to be of use."

She watches him swallow, noting the shadow on his hard jaw—no elaborate mustaches for him—watches him await her verdict. The Adam's apple travels in his fine-muscled throat, such a lovely sun-kissed throat the color of honey, and for one agonizing instant she's not in the stony heart of her nation's capital but lying with this wildly beautiful, clever but no less inappropriate boy in a fall orchard full of goldenrod and smashed fruit and drunken bees, her favorite sort of place. A paler bit of flesh winks under the collar, and perhaps he feels her eyes on it, for he shifts a bit, pulls his cap down lightly, and this is a relief since it shadows those eyes so like the sky over an orchard on a clear day with the white clouds billowing by fast and senseless as dreams, and she can't look away on her own.

Though he seems frank and foolish as a child, he compliments her somehow, without a word. He makes words redundant. Lord knows words have her in a thicket now.

Mere. Beast. Buffoon. Very.

"A little of both, I confess, sir. But I thank you for your knowledge. My father's illustrating a scientific catalog," she adds quickly, to justify her gratitude, "and I assist. He and his sponsor hope to expand their findings into a book."

"Looks to me that you're illustrating it." He smiles with his eyes alone—fearful witchcraft. "I say so humbly, of course, with all respect due your father."

"You have no obligation to respect him . . . a stranger." She busies her hands, packing.

The keeper clears his throat, motioning gravely toward her sketch. "Mettle will fault me if you don't finish his portrait." He glances round and speaks furtively into his curved hand. "He's vain as any courtier." The keeper reaches out an arm, and the bird side-steps up it. "Here, Mettle. Stay or face my wrath. Perch." He unloads Mettle onto the back of her chair. "Too close for you?"

Isn't it? He draws back the dirty, strong-veined hand, but "No," she says. *No.*

He motions toward the relative quiet of the semicircular exhibit hall, where animals in their cages snuffle and shift, warm bodies settling not in content or resignation but some other rhythm they understand, which all captive creatures understand. "Work's a solace, ain't it?"

He doesn't wink before he goes—that would be impertinent, even for a beast keeper with no grasp of English grammar—but he does reach out almost sadly for her hand and close the charcoal in it. You might suppose they've known each other for years and none would think the worse of it. The warmth of him causes a riot in her skin, though his voice calms it again, and in her mind she's pleading, *No,* but he lets go, and she breathes him out, and the beast keeper goes his merry way, humming and speaking softly to his charges.

10 ❧❧ Wicked Games

I've called on Calvin," Ma announces at breakfast one day, stabbing her biscuit in gravy.

Calvin lived with them as a teenager after his mother died, and while Maggie and Kate adore their good-natured foster brother, they know this for the ruse it is. The spirits are not pleased.

They let go a volley of brisk raps that leave Ma cringing over her plate. Ma has dark circles under her eyes, which should chasten but instead irritates Maggie. Why must their mother take every little thing to heart? She turns to Leah, who only shrugs. "Pa's building the new farmhouse," the eldest says, "and David has the farm. Ma wants a man around here."

"He'll arrive next Sunday," the matriarch adds in the voice of a defiant child, crossing knife and fork over her half-eaten breakfast, laying her napkin over like a shroud.

❧❧ If the idea is to muffle the spirits or muzzle them, the opposite holds true. It delights Maggie and Kate to have a new mark and to practice and perfect their skills on a discerning new audience. Calvin's an earnest sort, and that first night, after a loud rattling wakes the household from sleep, drowsy Leah, intent on aligning herself with the youngsters before she loses too much ground, smiles and directs the visitor to dance the highland fling. The room explodes in raucous shuffling, and Ma shrieks for Calvin, who arrives rumpled and endearing. Holding a manly pose, he scolds them all for giving in to and so encouraging—he looks hard at Maggie, Kate, and Lizzie—the "spirits."

Back in his bed, Calvin suffers a volley of slippers. "They're up to some deviltry now!" he calls. "I hear them by me. . . ."

What's this?

He's *thwack*ed in the dark with his own walking stick and—*ack!*—pummeled with a candlestick. He fumbles after nimble attackers, reporting every move. Arriving back in the women's quarters tangled in bedsheet, he trips and careers into a wardrobe, proclaiming the spirits a solemn malediction. "Devils!" he cries, over and over, and the girls laugh at his calamity while Ma and Leah struggle not to.

⁂ But under his bulk and bravado, Calvin's as sweet-tempered as they come, and because the nightly tricks and taunts seem mostly in a spirit of fun, he soon gives up active pursuit.

The invisibles now make themselves known day and night, gleefully raiding the basement's winter stores, relieving barrels of apples, potatoes, and turnips; these rain down at random or plop singly into Ma's soup. The "imps," as Calvin calls them, remove chairs from under backsides just as the victims would sit. They make water dance in glasses and pluck Ma's cap from her head.

Ma no longer sees the humor and prays nightly on her red

hands and knees. "What have we done," she pleads, "to be so tormented? Pray, children, for God's mercy."

"I can't pray," Kate goads. "I feel like swearing."

It's next to impossible, from Maggie's point of view, to know who's crafting what mischief and what's real and what isn't and which innovations will take and which will fail.

The spirits are with them and of them and too willful to predict. All is silent improvisation, cooperative, suspect—like the circus in that you don't know which ring to look at or whom to blame or credit or what will come of any of it. Kate won't say. Leah won't, either. Lizzie, who lacks talent, knows only that it thrills and frightens her. How Ma feels Maggie can't say, but the question inspires a passing pity, a moment's mercy.

Night after night the high jinks continue. The spirits rap on the roof, and the family implores them to stay outside. "Leave us be," Ma wails (she's later slapped in her sleep for her trouble). The spirits still favor the curtained "green room" and often congregate within to plan an evening's larks.

But one bleak incident gives even Maggie pause. Calvin and the Fox women are seated in a ring with candles, making to-do with the spirits, when Katie gets that look in her eye, a glazed weariness that reminds Maggie how young she is—a little girl, really, deserving of comfort.

Kate reaches her pale hand into the nothing and lays claim to a dying man wound in white sheets. His death rattle is so intense, she reports in a distant, terrible voice, that it makes the mattress shiver under her like water. She feels the dread of someone drowning.

In great distress, this spirit—all gurgle and vibration—and Kate falls into a sympathetic trance, looking as if someone has pulled the plug and drained her dry.

"Kate!" Calvin feels her forehead, scooping her head into his hands. Lifting her waxen face, he demands a mirror. "Katie?" Maggie fetches one, and Calvin holds the looking glass over her perfect heart-shaped mouth. "She's breathing." He looks from one to the other and back to the fog dancing on the mirror.

Ma huddles and mutters while Leah looks stern and Lizzie whimpers with her back to the rest. Maggie feels a desperate need to dash to the outhouse to retch or buckle over laughing. Not quite sane. Understanding this, she remains there rigid for Katie's sake. They've come too far to be frightened now, though Lizzie clearly is. Maggie's niece keeps her back to them, covering her ears against the sound of Kate's eerie voice.

More or less revived, Kate sits up and begins rocking to the chant of "To be with Christ is better far," which alarms her audience even more. Maggie sits silently by, stroking her sister's freckled arm.

When it's over and the elders are asleep again, Lizzie sits up in bed and announces that she will no more invite "the invisibles" or play such deathly games. "I don't care what either of you says. Or Mother, either," she hisses, glaring at Maggie before she turns toward the wall. "They're wicked."

꧁ What *does* Maggie say? What is her real stance regarding the spirits?

Even or perhaps especially in the deafening silence that Leah grows more and more determined to fill, Maggie means to keep her options open. Despite her occasional mischief with Kate, and Leah's focused interest therein, Maggie seems to see—every now and then, at the corner of her eye—a flare of invisible matter, a shimmering rip in the air. Just often enough, when she isn't trying, she'll glimpse some thing unaccountable to others. It's a kind of beckoning, isn't it? The same you feel when you're walking home across the fields after dark and pass a lighted window. No one prompts you to look in, and you know it isn't right to peer into the glow of another family's privacy, isn't respectable, but the busyness inside, the very square of light against the cricket-roaring black, invites you.

A shimmering rip in the air or a simple certainly; if it isn't exactly possible, then it's easy enough to conjure—like the crowd of spirits back in the field in Hydesville—with feverish intensity. And what's the difference, after all, between real and unreal when people react precisely the same way to either? Doesn't the Bible say somewhere, *Ask and you'll receive?* Well, Maggie's asking, and since this spirit game started, no one's told her no. Her whole life before the peddler was one agonizing *no*.

II ❖ No Wish to Be Right

Clara isn't surprised when the girl bursts in again without warning. The other one was just as brash till Clara grabbed her wrist one morning and warned in a tone of seething civility, "You will not enter this room again without knocking. Do you understand?" Clara never bit or scratched the hand, as rumors had it, but she might have done, and that was enough. Lizzie—the other one—has been timid and quiet ever since, though it taxes her nature, clearly.

Father insists these girls be treated with respect. "These aren't ordinary servants, Clara, but the beleaguered daughters of friends in our circle." By *our* circle, he meant *his*, of course. "They've been under tremendous pressure and require our support and tolerance."

"And for this we pay them?" she asked.

Clara does her best, but she can little tolerate—much less support—some bright young body flitting about her room every day, *her* room, like a trapped hummingbird reeking of nectar.

But this Maggie Fox does seem a rare species.

Clara sits unnaturally still in her corner chair, squinting over a book, and it takes the girl a moment to ferret her out. She throws open the curtains again, all insolence, and the room blooms with dusty light. "You'll ruin your eyes."

Clara feels her own wrath, even if the child doesn't. "I may have mentioned that my mother died when I was born. . . ."

Maggie Fox looks up woefully under dark brows as if to say, "No, you didn't."

"I got on rather well without her."

"I doubt that—"

"I'm saying, of course, that if I wished the drapes to be open, I would open them. I thank you, but I'm not an invalid. Not yet."

"You're welcome," Maggie Fox says gamely, and it's only for her father's sake that Clara protests no further. She's spent her lifetime reining herself in, not for society's sake but for her own; she has a knack and a preference for revealing next to nothing about herself.

But this girl can communicate with the dead, people say, with those dead and gone and gravely silent. And now this same witless creature is trailing plump fingers over the line of seashells formerly concealed on Clara's windowsill. "They're pretty," she croons. "Did you collect them?"

"*Pretty*"—Clara crosses her hands stiffly over her lap—"is a cheap word. Worthless. I'd advise you to relegate it to the cupboard with your dolls. Together with *nice* and *good*. People will expect more of you from now on."

But words don't sting this one as they did the other. Maggie Fox stares back at her—curious, expectant—and then lifts a shell and peers into it as if it were not dry and barren, as if there might be life there yet.

"I collected them years ago." Clara's not sure why her voice, persistent as grief, issues like a stranger's from her hoarse throat.

Casting back hurts, as green leaves hurt in springtime because they are too loud and bright. It was her nature, as in Mudeford with Will, to pluck up the downed feather, slip the smooth pebble in her cuff, a habit that bound her to him in memory, but she came to scorn the impulse to collect. It became tiresome as fashions do: fern cases and seaweed albums; parties of earnest ladies armed at the seaside with jam jars, prying up anemones from rock pools. "But I'm glad to have them now." *Glad because the door is too far away for me to reach. My arm is a weight. My fist is clenched. Because there you see every trace of him, all that's left.*

"Because they remind you of England?"

Clara fixes Maggie Fox in her hard gaze. "I need little to remind me of England." She taps her forehead. "I've hardly left it."

Did that sound pitiful? Despondent? She draws back. She will not give herself away if it can be helped—especially with the Widow Bray on the premises, as she lately is on Mondays, helping Father with his books—and it can always be helped.

"Well," the swaying other says, concealing something behind her back, "this isn't from England. I found it lately on a walk. I thought of you when I unpacked it this morning. Close your eyes."

Why are her lids closing? Perhaps she's sleepwalking again, as she did as a child. The girl lifts Clara's two hands, her two cold hands, and it seems they will crumble and collapse to dust, for she is rarely touched. No servant cinches her into a corset or brushes her hair with the rough strokes of girlhood. Clara wears antique dresses from her mother's trunk, the empire cut that doesn't beg support—for why bind herself to sit alone? She brushes her own hair now. It helps the time pass.

"Now, don't look," the girl cautions, and how to bear it, both the waiting and the willingness to wait? Clara trembles, cannot but tremble as the plump hands set into her bony ones a perfect brittle oriole's nest, delicately knit, smelling of the three seasons it has accumulated like shiny coins. Though she's been peeking through slits anyway, Clara opens her eyes.

"I thought of you." The girl motions toward drawings marking every free space on the walls, table, shelves.

Is Maggie Fox so guileless as that?

"I like it because there's a girl's hair ribbon stitched in."

Whatever can she want?

"See there, a bit of red? It's faded now, but you can still make it out. It might be mine. I rather think it *is* mine—"

Clara winces back tears. No. She won't weep, not this far from caring. There's no route out, no safe passage. She manages to mutter a thank-you and sets the nest on her little table heaped with books and sketches. It instantly belongs there as if it never was anywhere else, never nestled eggs at its soft heart or rocked in a cruel wind. Perfectly formed and petrified. This room does that.

Clara nods dumbly, remembering Will's tale of his mentor, the limber old gypsy, "seller of nesties" at Smithfield. She hears for an instant, and with a clarity she had thought gone, Will's teasing voice.

"You're welcome." Maggie Fox has the sense to leave then, but the door doesn't click shut just yet. She opens it a crack and lays her words in cautiously, as Will once hurled meat to the lions in the Tower. "They all say you're mad, you know."

Of course she knows. On some level, they've whispered it since she was born: *Poor wretch stopped the world on her way in, killing her own mother.* Wise early to the benefits of bed rest and solitude, Clara didn't discourage them. Being a sickly, boyish, and "artistic" child was her best revenge against a meddlesome world. The "mad," in her estimation, are routinely treated to the spectacle of people in all their plainness. Like children, they rate human pettiness, cruelty, and longing in the extreme, which, if you're idly curious about human nature, makes for interesting study. Besides which, it is no one's business whom she killed or did not kill.

"Why don't you set them right?"

Already Clara has forgotten who's speaking, whom she's speaking to. Her head is full of other times and, faintly, other voices. Once a sneering suitor, complaining to the aunts, called her *otherworldly*. Ridiculous, of course, since where else would she be but here in the world, waiting, in the cage of her own body?

Clara dabs at the nest with her finger to assure herself that it's real. "I have no wish to be right." She plucks a bit of down from the straw bowl and presses it, wiry-soft, to her cheek.

She catches sight of a grinning eye and one corner of the girl's mouth before the door clicks shut: "They say a lot of things about me, too."

❧❧ Father brings tea when Clara rings her bell. She's taxed. He must know it, for he sits by without a word. She takes up her book, nodding thanks while he pours with tremulous hands.

Before the Widow Bray took to detaining him five days out of seven, this was a routine well established. Clara hardly remembers when it began. When they first settled in New York, it was difficult to speak, to dodge the anger—hers, hard as a bitter blade—reawakened by gossips in Philadelphia.

But Father's a deal more patient than most. He's like an old tree, and they value each other, so they staged a truce, even in the face of hardship.

Their conversations now sound the same. "Won't you take your health outside?" "I won't today, thank you." Murmurs of appreciation for the buttery touch of twilight on the east wall or the corner carpet where the feral cat sleeps. Polite protestations about the weather or the sensationalism of certain journalists bent on running stories about boys falling into vats of molasses where they're promptly licked to death by hogs. This talk is diverting without cost, and less dishonest than their forays into progressive or political subjects—Universalist doctrine, temperance reform. Father would rather enjoy these at ease over a pipe with his companions. She would rather avoid significance altogether, since the one significant thing she might say or ask would destroy their fragile peace with a stroke.

After Will came between them, they learned to be together but separate, to sit and read or sketch or be lost in thought, and to this day her gratitude knows no bounds. Not a bold man, Father has devoted his life to sheltering her, and she, too, shelters him.

Clara won't admit it to Maggie, but she does prefer the drapes open. She can occupy herself at the window for hours. To starved senses, the back garden is better than a magic-lantern show: oak leaves languid and falling, glossy crows heavy on branches, bats wheeling and snapping at dusk. She can almost recall what it feels like to be out among them where the Genesee winds blow hard.

The natural world she loves above all else goes on working its endless circles, full of phantoms and scurrying small things that keep out of sight to survive, as she does. Larger things, too: the gray fox leaping over an ice crust, the "devil cat"—at least in legend—with its woman's shriek. Their house borders the edge of the city, and these and more are all alive in her head.

When they first came to the States, to Philadelphia, they learned quickly that it wasn't far enough from London. The relative wilds of western New York, on the other hand, might be another universe. Whatever healing she's managed to do she did here, in the gardens, on woodland paths, in the meadows around Rochester.

When Will's voice did not go from her head and couldn't be unraveled from the wild world he knew so well, that world began to seem for the first time unwelcoming, and she unworthy. It's ever what it was, beautiful and shining and full of wonder, but the more she dishonors it, denying what it will have from all who care—curiosity and the body's cooperative engagement—the more unworthy she becomes, and the more conscious of failure. Sometimes she feels she is nothing now *but* consciousness, unmoving in her chair, tracking the ever-changing light, the astonishing clouds flying past, the fat fly that circled and circled inside the shade of her reading lamp, knocking like a drunken fool at her thoughts. She forgets she has a body, and when she remembers, grief rests like lead on her chest, in which her heart still beats in its old frame, stubborn as rain. Sometimes she traces her lips absently with her fingertips, marveling at their softness, like the inside of a lamb's ear, and is struck by the great waste she's made of an earthly life. But apologize?

Before this room swallowed her whole, she did her best to make do in the world, on ships and trains, in drawing rooms and corsets, lecture halls and tearooms, but the conversations there failed to rouse her, and she felt that she was sleeping through them, dreaming in their midst. Even the best exceptions, the moments that stood out, could never match the joy she had felt in a single furtive afternoon with Will or lying on a hill of heather alone with a dog circling her feet. It isn't right to hold them, everyone, by his light or against the bee-loud quiet of a grove of trees twisted and heavy with fruit. But she never understood why not. She neglected no vows. She's taken none.

There's something about Maggie Fox that teases and troubles her. She can't reel back the way she can with others, whose faint concern, even tenderness—vulgar curiosity certainly—are of no use to her. Clara doesn't require friendship. She's a grateful recluse and believes that many others feel this way but without courage to act on it. Half the women she knew in London suffered "sick headaches" on command, usually when faced with intolerable social tasks, and those with the prerogative of wealth relinquished their children to the household.

But this Maggie Fox has wares for barter, though Clara is too skeptical and sensible to believe. It's a lovely hoax, of course. The continuity of life. It has the farmers whispering across their fields from Newark to Rochester and the ladies in their drawing rooms too. Clara reaches out for the bird's nest. *It might be mine, for all I know.*

Maggie Fox, unexceptional farm girl, has pinned her to a board, recalled her to the human race, enslaved her anew with longing.

12 ✥✥ And Then You Will Be

May 1835
London

"Which would you be?" His voice, all innocence, echoes through the empty halls. Empty of public but never empty. "If you were an animal." There are bodies all around, furred, scaled, writhing, rolling on coarse hay, scratching, snorting, preening, grunting. Everywhere is the warmth and rich stink of them. Clara resolved today to finish her sketch of the Barbary wolf. It's her biggest disappointment so far, and reviewing the week's sketches in light of their printing schedule, Father concurred. It was neither anatomically accurate nor satisfying in a stylized way. There was nothing of the animal's essence there, and she can't say why.

She motions to the wolf, and the beast keeper asks, strangely, "Are you a Methodist?"

She hesitates. Religion is such a personal thing, divisive in England now as ever, but it will do to be honest to a point. She shakes her head. "Why?"

"The founder of that sect, a Mr. Wesley, once came here to the tower to play his flute for the lions. He wondered did they respond to music in the way that a soul will. The way we do."

She feels her pulse leap, for it is, again, as if he's speaking inside her own head, insinuating himself into the weave of her thoughts. "And did they?"

"Accounts are mixed, I fear . . ."

"Pythagoras," she cuts in absently, "the Greek . . ."

"I know him, miss." He smiles grimly. "*Of* him, I mean. I rate I look a wreck and smell like these others here"—he motions to the animals, laughing—"but I've read a thing or two. Mr. Cops has a fine library . . . you wouldn't know it to look at him, but natural philosophy's his passion. He lets me skulk in when I will."

"Pythagoras believed souls migrated after death between humans, animals, and birds," she goes on, guarding her advantage, however slight. "Plato, too, I think. 'Metempsychosis' was the term."

"Well, legend says one of the five lions came forward to hear the flute and sat rapt while a tiger leaped over him and squirmed under, and leaped over again, and kept at it on and on. Round and round." He shrugs and blinks his gaze from her. "But who can say it was a dance or the music done it? And for every five men who hear a tune, four won't tap a toe. I *like* to believe it, but belief's a funny thing. I can linger in a belief only so long before another, equally formed and fine, presents itself. There's too much probability in our world. Have you noticed?"

"Then you hold no creed? You're an atheist?"

"I never said that. But you've watched a hawk hunting in a field?"

He waits for her to assent, and she does, nodding.

"The way it veers and tips, and you know death is there—you feel its wings beating. You pity the soft little thing in its sights, but the fact is you're cheering the hawk. You're far from mercy, but it takes your breath, don't it? There's beauty in it."

Beauty. Who but poets use that word? It doesn't seem real or respectable somehow, in the workaday world. It seems ridiculous. "Yes, but sir—"

"Will, miss. Will Cross." He leans on his rake and reaches out a hand in a brotherly way, leveling her with those eyes. "And you are?"

She looks down at her sketchpad.

He waves the scandalous hand like a magician, smiles wryly, and withdraws it unshaken.

"Clara," she says without lifting her head, and the wolf on the page torments her. "Clara Gill."

"My point, Clara Gill, is that it's wise to choose your allegiance in this world, take a side or a story or a creed, but you might be wrong. You might be dazzled."

"But it's no life at all not to choose. To devote yourself."

"Well, that's a choice, isn't it?"

"You speak in riddles."

"I like a riddle. My mum, I well remember, used to sing a ballad about a maid on the roadside who meets an elfin prince, and she'll have him for her lover. . . ."

Now Clara feels her jaw clench. She must be in jeopardy, truly, for what man of virtue would speak so to a young lady unattended? Does she not look a lady? Does she not hold her back straight like one? What about her screams out lust and damnation?

"Which is to say," he presses on, "that mothers are fine ones for sentiment and sometimes fill their sons' heads with rot. I had no father to teach me a man's way. My brothers had their work."

Clara shrinks inside, for his voice cranes so, and so gently. How could such a voice mislead her?

"They didn't spare the rod, though, so I know to apologize

when I've gone too far. I am sorry, Clara Gill. Your attentions fish words from me I'd never sensibly part with."

He bows low, and though she'd like nothing better than to gather in his charms—just a glamour born of a boy's lust, she tells herself—she casts about for caution. Her maiden aunts weren't good for much in childhood, but she took in all manner of lore and wisdom from servants over the years, and she knows this moment in her own story. She's being pixie-led into a wood where he'll feed her treats with lovely long fingers and she'll forget her name and how to get home again, for perfectly virtuous and otherwise clever girls are led astray in just this way and ruined daily. She apes a modesty she doesn't feel, or not in the expected way, crying out, *Fool, fool* in her thoughts till he pities her enough to turn off down the corridor with his jagged gait and his pail swinging.

Clara tries to seize what it is in the wolf she needs, that spark, that craning toward form, and hears far off now the trace of a ballad she knows. She can't say where from—a moment when Mary was brushing her hair, teasing out the fairy knots Clara fashioned in her sleep with twirling—about an elfin prince who bade the maiden make him a cambric shirt without a stitch of seamster's work. *Wash it in a well,* he said, *where never was water and rain never fell. And then you will be a true lover of mine.*

Clara blushes, watching Will Cross whistle his way down the aisle. He disappears through the door of the keeper's apartment, and she looks at the live wolf—which will not look back, as no self-respecting wolf will—and finds herself humming (she remembers the tune now) the maid's reply:

Go tell him to clear me an acre of land
Between the sea and the fine sea sand.

Tell him to plow it all with a thorn,
And plant it all over with one grain of corn.

Her hand moves on the page, and she smiles.

Tell this young man when he gets his work done,
Come to my house and his shirt'll be done.

13 ❖ Collective Spirit

Day by day it's clearer that Leah means to have her share. Lately she's been threatening to confide in their soft-spoken Quaker friends Amy and Isaac Post, to explain that the spirits are not confined to the cottage in Hydesville and seem to require a sympathetic audience.

Though the Posts were on hand for the summer digging, Maggie hasn't seen them since she returned to Rochester. Amy and Isaac have long been like surrogate parents to the girls, so gentle and good that Maggie bristles to think of them misled in *any* way.

Some stubborn part of her won't see the thing forward, though it laps like a tide at her ankles.

But Leah will not be deterred. Scrubbing their three faces as if they are infants, she hustles them into clean gowns one morning, sets them to work tending each other's hair, and assigns herself the task of brushing their visiting capes. "It's time," she pronounces, holding aloft for inspection Lizzie's much-mended specimen, "that we see how our friends fare in society."

When the Fox women infiltrate the Posts' drawing room to relate their doings, they're met with polite laughter. But Leah's persistence is solemn. Amy at last leans close, taking Leah's hand, her voice slow and soft with regret and tenderness. "Perhaps you three and your good parent suffer under some psychological delusion?"

Leah counters by inviting them to tea, together with Mr. and Mrs. Bush, at which occasion a lower bass note on her piano tolls a death knell in the room next door as if played by an unseen hand. The party files in, murmuring, and Leah makes a show of closing and locking the piano. They resume their visit—poised awkwardly, expectantly, over teacups—only to hear the somber noise resume.

Trooping in once more, they wait, breathless, as Leah unlocks the piano and opens it. They stare at the leaping yellowed ivory as if the key is the very mouth of God. In due course, Henry Bush sinks to his knees and in fact evokes the Almighty. "Sustain this family," he urges, "if, in Your great wisdom, You have chosen them as instruments through which mankind can be benefited."

The piano tolls on dully, and at one A.M., the mystified party disbands.

❧ After a dinner engagement with the Posts, Maggie bids Kate lead Amy and Mr. and Mrs. Bush into a bedroom at the back of the house to make the acquaintance of the spirit. These approach slowly, looking as if they stand before the judgment. Amy in her gentle voice questions the presence, and as she and the Bushes exchange thoughtful glances, distinct thumps sound under the hardwood. Leah explains the family's rap-yes-or-rap-no mode of translation, and the spirits dispatch Amy's mundane household questions swiftly.

The Posts have lost two of five offspring to illness, and while Amy doesn't at first relent, before long and inevitably, the Posts ache to communicate with these lost ones, and the dutiful spirits do their bidding.

Dizzy with success, Amy and Isaac Post become the first in Rochester to proclaim belief in the sisters' "spiritual manifestations" and in what Leah—who's busily staking claims and crafting a vocabulary to suit—has christened the new faith of spiritualism, a product of "collective spirit," that beneficent force that calls to and empowers each of us to right the wrongs of the world.

In days to come, the well-respected Posts explain to any and all who will hear them that they have conversed with the spirits. As have their children and Dutch servant girl. "But we only get answers with the sisters present." For progressive Friends like the Posts, these goings-on promise, or at least hint at, the communal, a universal brother- and sisterhood; they are a very cure for intolerance.

Despite Leah's early-interrupted education, she expertly exploits Quaker concepts in service of a new "faith" positing, in place of heaven and hell, an idyllic Summerland for *all* souls, exclusive of race, religion, or history of sin.

Early on the spirit of Isaac's mother manifests at a séance, confiding, "Isaac, my son, a reformation is going on in the spirit world, and these spirits seek the company of honest men like you."

Why *not* draw on their otherworldly influence for the benefit of all, Amy agrees, in service of social reforms?

By June, the Greek revival homes and clapboard cottages of Rochester are abuzz with spiritualist gab and gossip. The sisters, sometimes all three—to Maggie's mounting irritation—but more often just "the girls" with Leah conducting, hold frequent sittings for the Posts and their friends.

Leah has slowly been taking possession, crafting her séances (they *are* hers, after all, increasingly) after established patterns of religious service, urging sitters to join hands and recite the Lord's Prayer in opening, sing "Hymn of the New Jerusalem," or partake of a moment of silence as at the opening of a Quaker meeting. Visitors fall easily and thankfully into such patterns, which both alleviate anxiety and discourage absurdity.

Only then can they enjoy the spectacle of Maggie and Kate being magnetized and slipping, with closed eyes, into a half-conscious trance state. Soon faint, eerie raps resound. The guests shift soundly in their chairs, anticipating "manifestations." The raps grow louder, questions are called out, and Leah painstakingly translates the raps of reply.

❧ In November, at the insistence of his wife, skeptic Lyman Grainer hosts a séance in his home. Leah directs the assembled to gather round the table in the parlor.

After a long indignant silence (these are intellectuals, after all, and will not subsist on a diet of *rap rap rap*ping about the weather and lost hogs, though word of an imminent marriage proposal triggers grateful sighs), Leah announces, "The spirits have a message from Harriet."

A stunned murmur travels like electric current round the circle; most know that Grainer's daughter died recently after following her physician husband to Michigan.

There and then Maggie fathoms the breadth of Leah's vision. Having stumbled upon the power to give and withhold what is most ardently desired, Leah will not relinquish it. With mounting despair, Maggie watches the hushed assembly process this latest development, damp fingers clasped in awkward intimacy.

Leah's adult life has been riddled with hardship. She struggled as a child bride and, later, as a single mother and must relish this power, Maggie knows. Perhaps Leah deserves what power she can wrest—but she'll master its shadings and enslave her sisters in its name, and there isn't a thing in the world Maggie can do about it.

Harriet's rapping grows increasingly urgent, and Leah takes her time interpreting. She's begun to wax publicly philosophical about the significance of the trance state. This all-important entry point eclipses for a time the medium's own awareness, she'll boast, eclipsing her very identity in readiness for possession by spirits from a higher plane.

These artful trances leave Maggie emotionally exhausted, as does remaining alert and present before an audience to Leah's every expression and action, to a faint flutter of lashes, a flaring of nostrils. And such is the greed and selfishness, or simple forgetfulness, of most sitters that this aching, overtaxed state of clairvoyance goes unnoticed or ignored.

She and Kate barely have time to recuperate their mortal strength, see their vitality returned, before the regimen begins again, though Kate minds it less.

Kate, in fact, is slipping away again. Maggie no longer frets over or vies with Lizzie, who lacks talent and has been consequently reduced to the status of bystander, but Katie seems confidently in thrall to Leah's direction. Her eyes never meet Maggie's anymore but turn always to Leah for approval or instruction or assurance. Fickle child. Kate's a sucker for a leader with a capable plan, and Leah has made them famous, after all. Leah *impresses* Kate, while Maggie only adores her.

If only Maggie *knew* what to do. But she is better at doing what she's told.

Translating Maggie's trance and the raps that follow, Leah makes taffy of Harriet's urgency until it seems tonight's audience will stamp and chant for expediency. It finally emerges that the unfortunate Harriet, so lately taken, was poisoned by her physician husband.

Her father scoffs, breaks the circle of damp hands, pounds a fist on the table in uncharacteristic fervor, and condemns the affair as the worst sort of fraud. Chair legs scrape on hardwood, and with bowed heads, the visitors take their leave.

But in the end Mr. Grainer is roused enough to consent to another séance, as Leah knows he will be—few can resist such insights, Maggie's learning—at which time Harriet recalls minute details about her life.

Mr. Grainer is "overcome by the evidence" (no matter that his wife, Adelaide, and Leah are friends and confidants). Like the Posts, he becomes vocal, enlisting Reverend Lemuel Clark to attend a séance, during which he poses a practical challenge to the ghost. "Will the Spirit please move the table to Brother Clark," he commands, adding also that Kate and Leah, who are conducting—and everyone else, too—should raise their hands. And still the table moves.

In due course, Isaac's cousin George Willetts is also won over.

As are the Thomas McClintocks.

And Elizabeth Stanton.

"If it's humbug," Willetts trumpets about town, "it spreads fast."

14 ❦ A Treacherous Relation

May 1835
London

How easily Clara surrenders him.

"You know you'll have to relent sooner or later," Alice argues, her brushstrokes slow and nimble, almost languid. As a rule, it's Mary who rakes without preamble or ceremony at Clara's hip-length snarls, but today is market day, and with Mary and the other servants out, Alice seizes the chance to steer her captive niece toward the subject of matrimony.

Clara relaxes in spite of herself, bending her head to the tug of the brush. "I'd like to believe," she admits, forgetting herself for a moment—all three aunts find Clara's aversion to the subject of marriage worse than suspect, and she rarely engages—"that I'm *known* . . . before I—"

Alice pauses, holding the hairbrush still. "Clara?"

Clara hesitates an instant too long, and that's all it takes.

"You're in love!" Alice's gray eyes glint like a blade. "Is there someone I don't know about? Tell me."

Clara's prospects, or the lack, are a household joke, though the aunts take it more seriously than they let on. She entertains the occasional suitor for her family's sake, but Clara is careful to discourage him beyond any reasonable doubt. The older men endure with wry good humor, as if both parties are in on a joke that has no bearing on either of them; if the aunts don't insist with lemon cake, a pleasant afternoon will pass. Younger men think more of themselves and their time. These look once into Miss Gill's implacable eyes and curse the cousin or great-aunt or misguided friend who proposed the association. They no sooner arrive than they plan an exit, and rightly so.

Just when youthful luck is beginning to wane and Father to relent to the aunts, Clara's lessons reveal that her artistic eye is matched with a flair for anatomical exactness that makes her more than an able colorist. To her own surprise, she's proven an inventive draftsman—or -woman. Father gives in to her pleadings and begins teaching her in the field, with support from family friend and lately patron Sir Artemus Lever, "Uncle Artemus" to Clara.

"What will become of her when you're gone?" demand the aunts. " She'll die a governess."

"It would seem," Alice hints later that day over her embroidery, "that our Clara believes in *love*."

Never did a word sound so soiled and small.

"Surely," rails Lucretia, "we're no advocates for improvident marriage. Love in a cottage is charming indeed, but it must be a cottage *ornée,* and if with a double coach house, the love will endure all the more."

"These days," Tilda puts in dolefully, "any gentleman can join a club and enjoy the benefits of matrimony without a bride. Think what—for a handful of shillings and an annual subscription—he has at his disposal. Every possible amenity. Fine meals and a library and manly chitchat all safe from domestic intrigue." She deflates with a sigh. "I knew we were done for when Artemus sneaked off to Cornhill and joined that Jerusalem Coffee House."

"These are dark days indeed." Alice winks at Clara, who by now stands sipping tea in the drawing-room doorway, bemused. "With potential husbands vanishing like shy animals into the wilds of the Athenaeum." She fixes Tilda, the middle sister, in her sights. "But it's well to remember, Clara, that one is never tempted to offer in her own person those advantages of matrimony *not* available in his club. These, too, he's likely to obtain elsewhere than at the domestic hearth."

Tilda reddens, and a wave of titillation breaks over them all, causing Clara to snort tea through her nose.

"Subtlety," says Lucretia, restoring order, "is paramount. If a ponderous suitor can keep you in the condition to which you aspire . . ." Looming over Tilda's chair, Lucretia plucks a gray hair at the root from her sister's head with an air of triumph. "You must wait, and wait gracefully."

"Correct!" Tilda slaps the offending hand away. "Every hunter suffers the occasional setback. And if all else fails, pray you have a beneficent brother. If you learn one thing from our mistakes, dear niece: do not waste your charms on the unendowed."

᪥᪥ Word has reached Sir Lever, through a certain treacherous relation, that Clara's fabled resistance has weakened. Just days after her talk with Alice, Artemus corners Clara in Father's parlor, alone.

He tells her that with the sketches nearly ready for the engraver, he's planned a fund-raising dinner to generate advance interest in the auction, at which the printed catalog containing Father's (and her own) art will circulate.

"I have money to spare," he confides or rather reminds her, pacing before the hearth in a way that makes her fidget, "despite my collecting 'habit,' but little of it fluid."

Her uncle's goal, he's already explained, is to fund an expedition to the East Indies by selling some of his extensive private holdings. "Robbing Peter to pay Paul," as he puts it. Luckily for her, he heeded her advice that they follow Leonardo da Vinci's example. They worked from live "models" wherever possible, rather than from the specimens (however expertly stuffed and preserved) in his collection, since from there, they might expand into a broader book of natural history for popular consumption, such books being all the rage.

The Tower menagerie isn't long for this world, her uncle is quick to remind anyone who will listen; the more progressive zoological society will keep Mr. Cops and his ilk out of business once and for all. "He may be well-intentioned and a sound trainer, but he's behind the times, little better than his cronies at the old Exeter 'Change."

Artemus insists yet again that his own effort is to educate as well as entertain. He's consulted leading scientists, many of whom will attend his novel dinner, and he means to streamline his collection and strengthen it thematically. "What enlightened person would see animals shut up in dank dens with no natural context anymore?"

He regards Clara with fierce attention all through this tirade, as if she's somehow personally responsible for the failings of Mr. Cops and the unenlightened public. "I'm grateful," he adds as an afterthought, "that he's giving us such ready access to the Tower collection—don't mistake me—but it's a means to an end. They're coming apart over there. The king has already moved his portion of beasts to Regent's, and no one at the Tower needs Cops clinging like a mussel to a stone. "

"The dinner?" Clara tries, eager to direct her patron away from the walls containing Will.

With a sigh, her uncle settles into the facing chair, his thick legs shifting against striped silk.

He can no more sit still than a schoolboy, Clara thinks, bewildered.

"The dinner, yes. This leads to my point concerning you."

Still he will not get to it directly. Instead he prepares a pipe, considering her with dark hazel eyes in that candid familial way. He's almost handsome, she decides, and certainly distinguished with his salt-and-pepper hair and long sideburns, with his heavy, not inelegant features. Artemus is well-groomed and -mannered but with a furtive quality that might unnerve if she didn't know him as well as she did. She doesn't trust him, not exactly, but she does take for granted his support as she would any member of her family.

"Clara," he says, regretfully, settling back to smoke, and now she is nervous. To avoid his eyes, she sinks deeper in her chair, like a child grateful to be seen and not heard, the child she has always been allowed to be.

Her mind seeks ease in wandering. Not an hour ago she was at the Tower, furtively sketching Will as he moved from cage to cage among his charges, humming his muffled tunes with hands purposeful as birds, and she's still flush with him. There will be no impropriety unless she initiates it—this she understands. It surprises her that safety is always complicit in the vast confusion of what she feels in his presence. While he's nearby, she's so engaged in talk, in conversation (like talking to God, unmeasured and ill-tuned to decorum) about her curiosities and passions, that she sometimes forgets to feel any sensations at all. It's when she's away from him, ironically, outside his presence, that her thoughts turn physical. She conjures him then, vivid and intense, the lean look and imagined smell of him, his seeing eyes on her, the vibration of his hoarse, boyish voice against her ear, her hair loose and looped round strong fingers.

In his presence, she does not dare.

Clara.

"I've been working with a Mrs. Peat of London Tavern on the guest list and menu. Both have taken an ingenious turn, if I may say so. We'll have an exotic edible theme. I've had Asa Buckland's promise to attend, and he's led me to interesting fare. Strikes me as a bit repulsive, some of it, but it's the kind of thing that brings people out and livens them up, loosens their purse strings.

"As for the guest list, you won't be surprised. I've allowed for a wife or two—and select others of your gender in the field, to put you at ease. I wouldn't dream of excluding ladies of sound scientific mind. I've also"—he paused for what could only be dramatic effect—"invited someone off the beaten path. I understand he may have charmed you. When I heard this rumor, I took the trouble to meet him myself, as he's a disciple of Mr. Cops."

Clara looks up suddenly, horrified and embarrassed, and sees not Artemus gazing back his challenge but Alice, her soft voice coaxing. Clara feels again the bristled tingling of the hairbrush near her scalp, the warmth of the hearth fire on her face, and understands that she has betrayed Will, relinquished him like a wild neighbor to a trophy hunter.

With Artemus studying her, gauging her reaction, Clara knows not to give him one. She must deny and undo before it's too late. But as she prepares to dissemble, her "uncle" cuts in. "He performed admirably during our interview, a right self-educated youth, though his clothes reveal him—as clothes and manners do. I gather he's taken a fancy to a young lady beyond his means, which seems unfortunate given his promise. He's certain to suffer for it."

Clara feels in this moment every bit as young and naive as she is, damning herself for it. "It isn't true!"

"Clara," he says again, softly, leaning forward, "you treat me like a stranger when all I've ever asked, all I've ever wished, is that you accept my regard for you, for your family, and that we be honest with one another in dishonest days. Social pressure is a vile thing, but it fuels the machine that is our world. Do you think I haven't had unlikely notions myself? Do you think I was never young? Do you imagine I would use my influence with your father for any but your truest welfare?"

"Artemus, please—"

"When you speak my name that way"—he holds up her chin—"you so rarely do, Clara—it makes me recall that little pact we had when you were a sprite on your father's knee. Do you remember, when I told you about the Greek goddess of the hunt and of the animals, a wild thing who begged her father never to make her marry? She would traipse through the forest with her lop-eared hounds and never answer to a soul. I said you were far more like her than I who share her name. You loved that story, and you smiled and begged me to plead with Papa Zeus on your behalf, and to get you a puppy besides."

Clara feels tears crowding in, for he did just that, gave her a puppy named Hound, now dead a year. Artemus has acted for her all these years, influenced her father to her autonomy, encouraged her talents, seen her as more than a mere marriageable young relation.

But he is no relation, really, and it occurs to her now that he may have labored not to shelter but to indebt her, keep her in reach, in view. He leans closer, and she rights her slump, back straight to get her distance. Her one advantage is that she really didn't tell Alice very much. Just Will's name, and that he is not what Father would hope for her. That he is everything. And not nearly enough.

"As for your young Orion. Your beast keeper. Do you imagine he'll exhibit such undying affection when he has you in his humble home? What he'll do, of course, what all men do when they marry but especially those without means, is attempt to squash down every trace of the thing he found alluring, of that which signaled to him, like a bird or a butterfly, and which, once captured, becomes contemptible. Here it is—a paradox to make any sane woman subversive in her own defense—assuring a union of treachery. He'll truss you up."

Artemus makes a sweeping gesture with his hand that takes in the stiff, still specimens dotting his drawing room, their beady eyes catching the gold of what little twilight finds admittance to this dim room. "Make a trophy of you. Trust me as a collector in this." Leaning forward again, he almost whispers, "And there is no more dangerous thing than a man accustomed to nothing who at long last gets his hands on a thing of value. Beauty, no less. He'll live to crush in you what life has crushed in him, or will before his drawn lot is done."

Clara shakes her head, but he's moved nearer still now; he's at the edge of his seat and angry. This is an Artemus she doesn't know and yet recognizes in some dim corridor of mind in a thousand furtive glances past, in machinations that at the time seemed boyish. She was so naive always—intent on her freedom. So intent she didn't realize how little she had. Artemus has never hurried in his life. But what if "no" is no longer her prerogative?

"I at least can promise you finery," he says in an alarmingly soft voice, "and time and presence of mind to paint. You do lovely work, Clara. Why give that up for any man?" He reaches out to touch her arm, and she starts back, sick and astonished by her own innocence.

Was that a proposal?

Clara sinks back in her chair, eyes fixed on a dusty column of light spearing velvet drapes, on the ghost of her freedom.

She has always imagined, taken for granted in some condescending way, that one of her aunts would win his difficult affections. Alice, probably, though her busyness vexed him. It had never crossed Clara's mind to be wary of Artemus. Uncle. Bringer of puppies. What's more, why would Alice, wanting him for herself, aid in the day's treachery? What use had she for a young rival, or had she sacrificed her niece, exposed her misbehavior, to plague Artemus and please herself?

Clara seizes her teacup, finds it empty, and sets it shakily in the saucer again. Artemus will watch and study and wait—the soul of patience. It's his way. She feels his fury, muffled by tenderness, and knows that her time has come to think hard about her own future and the politics required to secure it. Or else forsake it.

"It's the longing you love, Clara." His voice is hushed and terrible. "But you must know that consummation is the least of it. The very least. And unretractable."

"Sir," she pleads, "Uncle"—relying on past success—"you mistake me. Please. Let this rest."

"You won't object, then, to encountering your young admirer in my company and your father's at the dinner?"

"Object? If you'll waste a seat coveted by every fashionable and endowed scientific type from here to Bath on a penniless beast keeper, why would I discourage you?"

He smiles grimly. "You flatter me well, Clara. But I won't be trifled with."

Nor will I, she vows in mind, but the vow troubles her. She's a spoiled girl, really. Spoiled not with finery but tolerance—both doted on and, until today, left largely to her own devices—and she's never had cause to object.

15 ⚜ Sweet William

The next time Maggie Fox enters without knocking, Clara turns her back on the girl. She first waves the tray away, then like a petulant child swivels her desk chair abruptly, its legs scraping on the hardwood.

The room is dank after rain. Rain drummed her to sleep with her head on her desk, and she woke in her chair to find the girl standing in the lighted doorway clutching an overlarge tray. It's raining still, and Clara is mute, her tongue a dry weight in her throat. Her face streaked with tears, she's dying of thirst and plagued by water. *I am too old for this*, she thinks, all sullenness. *Shut me in my coffin*, and she can almost feel the sweet william growing over, roots insinuating themselves into the earth she's become, and it's a feeling like no other.

The girl doesn't go as directed or fuss with the drapes as she's wont to do; instead she's patient. She floats a wordless question on the air, and her silence roars in the clutter of Clara's head.

"What do you want?" Clara wonders aloud, her back still turned, though she sees the girl with her side vision. "Do your work. And why do you look at me that way? What are you waiting for?"

"I don't know."

"It's a bit odd, you'll grant. To press on this way without encouragement?"

Maggie doesn't slink out as Clara wills and expects her to. A long, brazen silence ensues. The girl busies herself with the items on the tray, moving them about. "I figured you were odd enough not to notice."

Unthwarted and all-consumed, Maggie resumes Thursday's outlandish monologue.

Spirits have infiltrated every nook and cranny in her home, it seems, an army of mischievous hobgoblins that do everything but spoil the milk, and since the sabbath, they've been "insufferable."

"I wouldn't choose to keep going," she says. "I would've stopped weeks ago, but they have all manner of plans for us. We have a mission. 'Make ready for the work,' they say, and we devote much discussion to their demands. But night before last I wanted nothing to do with them. All I wanted was a good night's sleep, but the wretches seemed possessed of all kinds of tools."

Amusing though Maggie Fox's accountings can be, Clara doesn't solicit them. She doesn't have to.

"All night they sawed at boards and dropped them, and there were jarring and planing and jointing noises. . . ."

Clara won't abide the other one, but in spite of herself, she enjoys this girl. Maggie Fox is oblivious and self-absorbed, and in this, they are alike and succeed very well together.

"It sounded like—" She looks up as if reading Clara's mood for the first time—"someone screwing down a coffin lid." Maggie pours a cup of tea and sips voraciously, forgetting herself.

"And guess what we found yestermorning in the kitchen? Four coffins drawn on the floor, life-sized. One each for Mother, myself,

Leah, and Katie. We scrubbed them away, but now this morning . . . do you know what we found this morning? On the ceiling?"

Clara is desperately thirsty. Maggie's morbid tale has begun to grate on her thoughts like a saw.

"Drawn handsomely in black-and-white, with the lids thrown back to show how well they pinked the white linings . . . each had its plate drawn on with our names and ages perfectly and correctly written . . . and marked below was 'If you do not go forth and do your duty, you will soon be laid in your coffins.' Devils! Leah's in an uproar (and did I say that all her music students have stopped their lessons?), for Ma still resists them."

The girl will wind down like a clock. In time. Clara has observed this over the course of several visits.

"Katie won't speak at all. Pa would have us home, but . . ."

Clara is patient for as long as she can be, but a warning pulse in her head has grown deafening. She can no longer hear what Maggie Fox is saying. "Whatever it is you want," she snaps, turning full around, "I don't have any."

Maggie's eyes, ever round and liquid, are wild now—perhaps that look has been there all morning—and Clara turns briskly away again, back toward the curtained window. "Go home," she snaps, "to your mother."

Clara hears the clink of spout against teacup, and her thirst burns, but she doesn't clamor. She waits, absorbing the silence as a plant does light.

But then she feels the lightest touch on her head from behind, as of near-weightless hands cradling her scalp, gently tracing its outline. It's how she's imagined, year after absent year, Will's hands might feel in the night if he ever did what she half-expected he could do and found his way back to her. Some nights, even now, she is startled into believing it, and it lulls her now for what she wouldn't give—or believe—to have him there.

But it's only this: the stubborn brat has presumed to brush her hair. It's the hand lifting and the teeth of the brush sweeping.

"It's dreadful tangled," Maggie murmurs. "Won't anyone care for it? How can you stand to be alone so much? I *hate* being alone—"

Clara slaps the brush out of the girl's hand. It wheels across the room and clatters in a corner, the pewter plate snapping free and spinning like a top on the hardwood.

She swivels round, and they lock eyes. Maggie looks stricken, which shames Clara. But lines must be drawn. Rules declared. "I take great comfort in my own company. And who gave you permission to do that?"

The girl's lip trembles. She seems genuinely stung, which is at best out of character and hard on Clara's resolve. "Not today, please," she relents.

Maggie Fox curtsies, tears brimming in those round brown eyes. She takes the tray, walking out with her back painfully straight, and all Clara can think to do is watch her go.

16 ❖ Captive in Me

May 1835
London

That last week, with the catalog drawings due, Clara spends every afternoon at the Tower.

Once the public is hustled out for the afternoon, they call to each other, freely, from one end of a yard to the other. She knows the feeding schedule and when to park her little portable chair in what corner.

The animals are confined in two yards in a double tier of indoor dens, strongly barred. In the first, the dens are disposed in a semi-circular building faced with brick, the remains of an ancient tower, Will said, its back wall at least seven feet thick. There was a large room forty feet in length for the birds and gramnivorous animals, while carnivores were housed outdoors. He feeds the meat eaters last, as a rule, luckily for her, since the light holds longest here.

That last day, the day after Artemus Lever's startling reproach, Clara finds herself revising her sketch of the Siberian tiger, a mangy specimen and a lonely one—for a scuffle with the lions has landed her in isolation—but no less terrible in her loneliness, pacing in Will's absence. This afternoon Clara can't locate him by listening. Usually she picks up his humming or whistling, the clang of his gear, moments after settling in with her supplies. What if she misses him today, after all, and for that goes without him always? This is a fate too grim to contemplate.

The increasingly influential zoological society has already absorbed the king's collection, and Mr. Cops has been forced to part with a portion of his. With animals going, Will explained, in cover of night in horse-drawn trailers, part of his job these days is to groom his charges for their arduous crossing to a better life at Regent's Park. "They have their ways and rites here," he confessed last week. "A move won't go easy with most of them."

But now she hears the scrape of metal, and his hand appears at the grate within. He flings what looks to be a whole haunch into the enclosure, and the tiger sidles to it as if she had never paced in anguish. She seems calm now, proud, and won't be rushed, even by hunger. Clara erases the shoulder on the page, adds height and resolve.

"Do you know who else came here to sketch the tigers?"

She jumps at his address behind her, mis-shades. "How did you get there so quickly?"

Will bows in apology as she turns, and everything in her cranes toward his voice. By the time she finds her own, he's already moved off toward the far dens.

The excuse of looking over her shoulder at her sketches often brings him tentatively near, tantalizingly, but for an instant at a time, as if he doesn't trust himself to linger. Perhaps he's guarding her reputation, though Clara has long since abandoned all care for it.

"It wasn't this tiger, of course," Will resumes from a fair distance, engaged again with his chores, "but around 1789, I'd guess, William Blake made his way downriver from Lambeth to paint one of the two tigers in residence then."

"'Tiger, tiger, burning bright,'" she calls back dutifully.

"That's right." Now he sets his rake against the wall and strides toward her again, and he's at her side so quickly it almost frightens her. She can smell him even among the other animal smells. She can feel his shadow in the late, slanting light.

He peers down at her final sketch for the catalog—much improved, she thinks, since this morning—saying, "You have your own way of seeing."

To hear that she has a vision, a comprehension unique to herself, is a gift beyond measure. Would he seduce her with such a gift? Did it matter? Gratitude aside, she wills him to touch her. *Do it now please, while no one's looking.* She imagines his hand rising to stroke the hair from her face—those loose gold strands that seem a sign of disrepair to come, like milkweed fibers bursting, like bruised petals. *Please* and what delicious panic, for she is here and willing and Father elsewhere and no chaperone to speak of, despite Artemus, despite everything, and there is no more time to promise or retract, and she takes herself for a lucky girl and knows that luck is borrowed from a negligent world.

When he won't comply with her thoughts, when he doesn't reach for her but stands awkwardly aside like someone waiting to hand her bags up on a carriage, she whispers, "Do you believe what Blake said?" and he has to move closer to hear her. "That everything that lives is holy?"

He nods at once. "I do."

"Then does this pain you? To see them here."

"Here with me," he says cheerily. "It might be worse. They might be here without me. They might be here anyway." He laughs, abashed. "I realize how that sounds. What I mean is that they might be furniture or toys to the one lords over them. We had a keeper here who fed an elephant so much beer she tipped over and near choked in her own vomit. They're going to be shut up anyway," he explains. "The world runs its course."

"And you run yours." She smiles without meaning to, and there's no discomfort in the way those fierce blue eyes hold and behold her, uncannily. What she won't give to stay in his sight, for this is where she belongs.

"You would've loved old Tom," he says, looking fast away. "He taught me all I know about them . . . when I was a boy . . . if I can be so bold as to say I *know*."

"And?"

"It's a long tale devised to keep you."

"Keep me."

He nods, crouching by with a hand on the stone floor to steady himself. "Once a month, Mother sent one of my brothers off in the cart with me in tow to Friday market at Smithfield. Have you been?"

She shakes her head.

"I reckon not. Proper girl like you. But the blocks between St. Bartholomew's Hospital and Long Lane were the Costermongers' Exchange. John or Henry—it was usually one of those—went in quest of old baskets and nets, wheels and springs, scales and measures. The crowds were such that with nowhere to lay them down, sellers stood with bridles and rope dangling from their beefy arms. All strung like Christmas trees with secondhand goods. There was always a boy there, no older than me, hollering, 'Ginger beer, ha' penny a glass! Ha' penny a glass!' while his mam handed down bottles from a painted wagon. It was better than a trip to a sweets shop, Smithfield, for you never knew what you'd find on offer. *Oysters! Penny-a-lot . . . Cherries! Try my fruit pies!* The fair had everything to eat."

Every now and then she feels Will sway a little in his precarious crouch until at last he tires of balancing on his heels and settles with legs folded like Buddha on the cold stone floor beside her chair. To have him below eye level in her peripheral vision is a rigorous distraction, but she keeps her senses trained on the pictures in his words.

"Fried fish and plum dough, pea soup and whelks, ham sandwiches and hot eels. Even oranges. This was more than enough to occupy yours truly, but invariably a lady friend caught the attentions of brother-minder of the day. I was purchased a raspberriade and sent on my way with a slap on the bony backside.

"By age ten I knew the fair like I knew my island home. I spent those free hours in the alley of the live animal sellers, where you had a wonderful stink," he says, smiling his crooked smile, "as here in our Tower. You had your vagrant types peddling rats and dogs or sparrows tied at the leg, exhausted with flopping about. But it was Tom with his dirty smock-frock full of pockets and ragged Italian hat I looked for. Tom had black curling hair like a gypsy, his feet were bare and black with mud, and he always clutched in one hand a basket of nests, each with its varicolored eggs. In the other he kept a writhing snake or the knotty tree bough he used for a walking stick.

"When first I spotted him, I stood a long while by—too long, I wager, for he finally broke down and gave me his spiel. A proud one was Tom in his shifty way." Will puffs out his chest, his voice rising in character. "'I am a seller of birds' nesties,' he'd say, 'slow worms, adders, and effets (lizards is their common name), hedgehogs for killing the black beetles (these I gets in Essex . . . they take bread and milk and'll suck a cow dry in their wild state). I find frogs for the French to order (they eats 'em, you know, the yellow-bellied) from ponds and ditches up Hampstead and Highgate way, and I got snails to strengthen a sickly child's back. I'll fetch roots and snowdrops and what that grows, bulrushes in summer. The young birds generally dies of the cramp before you can get rid of 'em, so I leave those alone. You buying, boy?'

"I'd look pensive and poke dirty fingers in Tom's nests till he took pity and resumed. The same spiel every month, and I never tired of it. 'The linnet she has mostly four eggs, they're 4d, the nest. A threepenny nest has six eggs (halfpenny an egg). Moorhens wot build on the moors has from eight to nine eggs, chaffinches has five (and they're 3d). The woodpecker, I never see no more nor two, a great curiosity and seldom found (6d the pair). The kingfisher has four eggs (6d) and makes a nest of sticks and bones coughed up of its supper.

"'You're one a' them that loiters, well.' He'd scowl and pluck a bit of straw from a nest to pick his teeth with. "Most of my customers is stray boys in the streets. I sells now and then to a lady with a child. I sold three partridge eggs yesterday to a gentleman said he'll put 'em under a bantam he's got to hatch 'em, but the boys of twelve to fifteen is my best friends.'

"'How do you get them?' I troubled to ask one day, and a friendship was born.

"'The snakes and adders and slow-worms,' says he, 'I get from where there's moss or a deal of grass. Sunny weather's best for them. I'm heading out. You come along if you like.'

"Needless to say, I went missing after that. My keeper that day was Henry, and he had to cry defeat at sundown when the fair cleared out. He skulked home without me and earned himself hell's wrath from the parish and a whipping from our mam, grown man or no.

"I was at the fair with Tom every Friday after, though my brothers weren't. It didn't much concern me—foolish, faith-filled boy that I was—but after the month had passed, I thought to wait by the painted ginger-beer wagon at sunup, which fetched me my own thrashing over John's knee when he found me. 'That's for Henry,' he panted, wiping his own snotty nose on his sleeve. 'Ignorant boy.'"

"I took my public punishment without tears, as you can imagine, for the relief in John's eyes . . . well . . . let's say it was a fright."

"Where did you go?" Clara looks askance at him for the first time since he began his story. "That whole long while your family thought you were dead under a wagon's wheels?"

"It was summer, so after a nap in a squat Tom knew, we set out very late at night for the coolness and walked for hours. We skippered it under a hedge if we needed rest, and, well, we climbed. Some dozen trees a day. If there was nothing in a nest, we climbed back down, had a pipe (I didn't take to it much, though I puffed once or twice for politeness), and started all over again." Will glances over to see if she is with him. She is. "'After I take a bird's nest,' Tom'd warn, 'the old bird comes dancing over it, chirruping and crying and flapping about. They wander when they lose a nest and don't know where to go. I wouldn't take the nesties if not for want of money.'"

"You loved him," Clara interrupts, like a proud child solving a puzzle.

"I did, and that open-air tramp's freedom, too. In time my brothers approved our affable seller of nesties, and I guess you'd say old Tom became my mentor. By the time he died, a year after

we met—facedown in a drainage ditch outside a Cheapside inn—
he'd taught me all you could wish about wild things and their
haunts and habits. He was a good man, giving to a fault and scarred
for it."

That is all, Clara realizes as the familiar noises of the menagerie
resume, rushing into the silence Will's voice has occupied. He has
"kept" her as long as he can, and they turn in tandem, their eyes
locked in something like surprise.

"Do you really mean to accept that dinner invitation?" she
pleads.

"Dinner?" he asks coyly. " I'd love to."

"Sir Artemus Lever is my father's oldest friend." *Toys to the one
lords over them*, Clara thinks vaguely, and has to look away. "He's
like an uncle to me. A meddlesome one, at that."

"I do mean to." Will's voice, so sure and steady, calls her gaze
back. "It's just the ticket for a young naturalist of ambition and
modest means, wouldn't you say? All those great men of science in
one room."

"I would say—"

He puts his forefinger to her lips, or not quite to, almost touching them. It sends a charge straight through her, and she nearly
gives in, shuts her eyes, but his hold her.

"*Don't* say, then, Clara Gill. You look as if to warn me off. But
you should know I'm a determined sort, and patient, too."

"They—"

"Are no better than I am. Just born to it. Just lucky, really.
You'll see it."

"I need no convincing."

"Everyone needs convincing." He draws back, urgent and distracted, and kneels by her. "I'm no alchemist, but listen, now. I've

been sifting through my thoughts all day a scrap I found in one of Cops's old books. Ready?"

She nods with what she hopes is great dignity.

"'Understand that thou hast within thyself herds of cattle . . . flocks of sheep and flocks of goats . . . understand that fowls of the air are also within thee. Understand that thou thyself art another world in little, and hast within thee the sun and the moon, and also the stars. Thou seest that thou hast all those things which the world hath.'"

All this, captive in me.

"Do you see it?" he demands. "Do you understand?"

She looks away, though she does and can hardly bear it. Surely they'll disappoint each other. Is that tragic in a world that harbors plague and war and poverty? *Yes.*

Smiling faintly as he nods his cap, she stands and begins to order her supplies while he, his face unreadable, starts toward the keepers' apartments.

The sprawling tiger wrestles with her bone, huge bloody paws owning its stringy pinkness almost tenderly. Clara steadies herself. How to let him pass through that door and out of range of what requires him? "Speaking of Blake," she calls brightly, "every holy thing is going to be *served* at that dinner, Will Cross. Fair warning. Eland, wildebeest, puppy dog . . . you name it."

He turns on his heel, looking up and down the aisle to assure they're alone. Addressing his muddy boots, he shrugs, smiling crookedly from that now vast distance between them: "How else do I get to see you in a party dress?"

17 ❖ A Dam Broken

1849

Rochester

When old Mrs. Vick, their kindly neighbor, dies, a new tenant moves in next door, a sickly man with a badger's humor. As much to spite taskmaster Leah as master the Badger and his timid family, the spirits grow restive. By summer, the tidy building overlooking Buffalo Burying Ground is a constant storm of noise. Calvin must again be summoned to defend against furniture moving (and blocking doors in alarming fashion) of its own volition, hurled and scattered books, and music playing at all hours.

After months of "unchecked racket," the Badger threatens to involve the authorities.

Not only do the spirits, in league with Maggie and Kate, not check the clamor, they upgrade to what Leah calls "heavy artillery." They're no mere nuisances now but submit the unfortunate household next door to a savage and continual barrage of discord. They even go so far as to steal into the family's dark rooms one night and pluck the oily pillow out from under the sleeping father's head, which report quickly reaches his church elders and, before long, the landlord.

Leah is served a summons.

The "ladies" will remove at once.

Leah's friends rally and by September secure the family a pleasant cottage on Troup Street. Maggie and Kate earn a whipping each for their antics and a fortnight's moratorium on spending money. In company, Leah urges them toward gentler visitations. The messengers signify, after all, a loving, all-forgiving divinity with Leah now single-mindedly devoted to their cause.

Before, sitters questioned the spirits directly, inviting a simple yes or no. But during a small séance among their circle, Isaac Post points out, "Leah, you remember that your brother David conversed with the Hydesville spirits using the alphabet? Perhaps these also will adopt that method . . . in the spirit of Mr. Morse's telegraph." Isaac Post lifts his head, expectant. "Have you something to say to us?"

Encouraged by a flurry of raps, Leah painstakingly and repeatedly recites the alphabet, matching her way to a simple message.

They settle on five raps when the spirits require the board, and over the course of several meetings, a fateful missive emerges: "Dear Friends, you must proclaim these truths to the world. This is the dawning of a new era; you must not try to conceal it any longer. When you do your duty, God will protect you and good Spirits will watch over you."

It is, Isaac and Amy offer ecstatically, the new "spiritual telegraph," one that will change the world, letter by letter. Word by word.

The spirits are bursting with words and advisings, and Leah has the audacity to hint that the work is progressing too slowly to suit. Ma continues to dig in her heels. Neither Leah's assurances nor Calvin's stoicism ease her mind.

What does ease her is the spirit child who comes one night when they're conducting a private circle at which Leah is magnetized.

"We must permit the little angel"—so Leah calls it for Ma's sake—
"to do as she wishes. Don't anyone move or shrink away if she touches
you. She has entered the world to prove to us that she lives and still
loves us." Leah shudders, collapsing forward in her chair, reeling
Calvin and Maggie's arms with her, rocking and moaning softly.
The others keep as still as deer surprised in a clearing. "Oh, my
darling little sister. She has kissed me, Ma, as naturally as in life."

And now Ma (on Maggie's other side) feels her too, feels dear
small hands clasp her shoulders, feels the cold comfort of a presence fleet as a hummingbird. She gasps audibly, and her moist fingers tighten around those of Maggie's left hand. Taffy between Ma
and Leah, Maggie feels nothing at all. She recalls with swift clarity
the night of the first public rappings in the cottage at Hydesville.
She remembers Ma on her knees, interrogating the wronged peddler, her mysterious imperative: *my youngest now. . . .*

What a lot of surprises life has in store, Maggie thinks, if the
dead are to be trusted.

Leah lights the lamp. Shadows flicker and dance, and Kate
smiles from across the table. It's an incomprehensible smile, full of
sorrow and pity and doom and the soft relief of resignation. Maggie
smiles back, though she's tired, too tired almost to relish Katie's
candor.

After that, Ma is successfully converted, "born again," Leah
notes, "as the dear old Methodists used to say."

"How would I deny my lost one?" Ma says simply, honking
into her handkerchief.

"Indeed, we have something to live for," Leah opines, looking
from one dazed face to another, "to hope for in this sacred hour
when each in our humble group is pointed on the path of truth
and duty."

꘠꘠ Leah implements the alphabet board often (which method of spelling out words and sentences is still somewhat ponderous, Maggie thinks, though who is she to say so?), and the next dead relative she pulls from her hat is anything but silent and fleeting. Maggie has no memory of the "revered" old man, as Leah calls him, but his will is unmistakable:

> *You need not wait as I did for that great "change of heart" but adopt the course at once and live up to your highest light. Go where that leads you.*
>
> *My dear children, the time will come when you will understand and appreciate this great dispensation. You must permit your good friends to meet with you and hold communion with their friends in heaven.*
>
> *I am your grandfather, Jacob Smith.*

When Leah shares this doctrine with their circle, Amy and Isaac exchange a meaningful glance.

"You can imagine this affected us all deeply," Leah continues for good measure. "Especially Ma, and brought our souls together in sympathy."

Ma blubbers reliably, and Maggie nods when the Posts look to her for confirmation. What else can she do?

꘠꘠ This latest message does its work. Soon the bell on the door of Isaac's apothecary shop jangles on the quarter hour. Enrapt citizens of every class and background park their elbows on his counter, plead his views, and lobby in turn for an audience with the ephemeral Fox sisters.

To guard the ladies' interests, the Posts appoint four prominent men in the community, in addition to Isaac, to impose order on the proceedings, organize respectable requests, enforce Leah's rules of séance decorum, and guide the broader message emerging from these curious communications.

With the "spirit telegraph" officially open for business, Leah seems more and more in thrall to her own exalted status as high priestess.

Lizzie chides with her big lungs and big teeth and big hands waving in the air (nothing delicate about their Lizzie), "How can you even *pretend* it's done by spirits? I'm ashamed you do such things—it's dreadfully wicked." But her mother doesn't scold or beat her or say, "Don't you dare speak that way to your elders." Leah calls her Doubting Lizzie and treats her daughter, treats all of them, like somewhat feeble-minded minions in need of convincing for their own good.

But the need is hers, Maggie is beginning to understand. Leah needs *them*.

"Listen to this!" Leah waves a sheet of paper at Lizzie, but it's Maggie her eyes fix on before she begins to read. "It's from a woman in Long Island. It came today addressed only to 'The Fox Sisters.' *Listen.* 'Learning of your good work, I was enabled to rejoice that in our spiritual home, love shall be our bond of union. I believe the more our spiritual senses unfold, the better we'll perceive the relations between this and the other life, and our tears for our departed will cease.' What do you think of *that*, Misses Doubting Thomas? There are a dozen more like it in today's post."

"You lead us around like lambs," Maggie complains, unmoved, "and I'm weary of jokes and slander."

But even as she says it, Maggie knows a dam has broken, and that water won't move backward.

❧ At first, the rewards of friendship suffice, but before long Leah is charging a fee for their sittings, usually a dollar a head.

A secondary benefit turns out to be access to the lives of Rochester's fashionable elite, who fancy them an "after-dinner act." Given free rein for hours at a time in wealthy homes as visitors come and go and philosophize, as Leah and the Posts and Eliab Capron and various committee members proselytize in the parlor, she and Kate become spies in service of a lifetime's curiosity.

Enlisting the silk- and velvet-clad children of the house to lead them about importantly by the hand, the girls prowl entryways with massive hallstands. Here are elaborate bonnets and silk toppers on hooks (which they try on, pursing lips and pulling faces in the mirror), expensive umbrellas (which Kate opens and closes, superstition notwithstanding), marble busts on pedestals and brass card receivers on stands (Kate lifts cards with sleight-of-hand when their junior hosts aren't looking, replacing them, once read, with equal stealth). Before, Maggie had only ever glimpsed such lofty hallways from the street.

They steal from room to room, running hands over carved four-poster bedsteads and chintz hangings (at home, the beds have simple iron steads; to dissuade bugs, Leah maintains). The plump mattresses *look* grand, but Maggie is glad to know that when you lie over them, they're no better or worse than the feather beds at home, lumpy as sacked potatoes; though here, of course, one of the Irish girls is charged with shaking them out daily, as Maggie and Lizzie do for Mad Clara. They rifle through wardrobes lined with sprigged and flowered paper, concealing regiments of creamy silks and crinolines, and everything reeks deliciously of lavender.

The wallpaper boasts sophisticated geometric motifs in two or three colors. There are carpets in every room, and each fireplace has its matching shovel-and-tongs set in polished steel. There are fat Persian cats to chase, parlor suites to host musical chairs, fine embroidered cushions to hurl at one another, and monstrous urns to shout echoes into.

Even in parlors and dim drawing rooms, the roaming eye finds *jardinières* (Mrs. Little has started Maggie on a course of French), vases of wet silver sand for flower arrangements and trailing ferns, displays of wax flowers and clockworks under glass, and above all, a dizzying array of tables: whatnots, chiffoniers, console tables, pier tables, sofa tables, occasional tables, work tables. . . . Maggie can't but wonder how ladies regularly traverse well-equipped drawing rooms in full crinoline, constantly at risk of sweeping over *objets d'art*, bibelots, knickknacks, and daguerreotypes.

Maggie would never admit to Leah how much the blasted spirits have changed—broadened—her view of the world and the people in it.

What price weariness.

Leah may not credit the toll the work takes on "the girls," but the others in their circle do.

Katie is acknowledged to be a child in a way that Maggie no longer is, and when the frailest and dearest among them grows despondent and pale with the stress of her labors, the committee determines that Kate must be sent way.

Kind Eliab Capron and his wife persuade Leah to board Kate

with them in nearby Auburn for a time. Some still believe that separating the girls will put an end to it all, free them from their burdens.

"I would ardently wish it," Mr. Capron says, lifting Kate's carpetbag, looking from one good neighbor to another. "Though my philosophical heart holds the same hope you all do."

❧❧ Maggie can't account for how much she misses Kate. It's worse this time than when her sister was shipped on to Rochester ahead of her, and while Kate's cheery misspelled letters are Maggie's meat and bread, they're few and far between. It is no fun wandering through rich people's homes without her. Busy at the Gills' or with chores by day, surrounded by strangers and neighbors every evening, Maggie has little leisure to think or feel. But at night she wakes with humming nerves; the muscles in her legs twitch; she bobs and turns on her creaky iron bed like a hog on a spit, and the hours pass with her sighs.

The truth is harder to see and to serve these days, so she's thankful for her eccentric employer (dare she say friend?). Clara Gill is a beacon of blunt truth but unreliable as solace goes, given her temperament. With no other shoulder to bleat on, Maggie revolts. At the next sabbath, she refuses to participate in any more séances.

"How will we eat?" Leah insists. "How will we pay for those new boots you're wearing? Speak!"

Maggie stares grimly ahead, imagining herself and Kate running hand in hand, bonnets flapping, through David's peppermint fields in spring. Fields pink with blossoms.

"And what of the bereaved of this city?" Leah demands. "All

those hoping for a chance to speak with their loved ones on the other side? What of our dear friends Amy and Isaac? If you refuse to work, it brings shame on them and casts doubt on their other reformist causes."

None of these pleadings moves Maggie, but when Kate's temporary guardian, Mr. Capron, visits with George Willetts twelve days later, and his earnest eyes smile so trustingly into her own as he offers to help make contact with the reluctant spirits, Maggie relents. Perhaps he will take pity and return Kate to her.

Like a weary farm matron sounding the dinner bell, she calls her flock home.

"Rejoice!" cries Eliab as the room echoes with raps. "They're glad to meet us all again."

"It's like the return of long-absent friends." George Willetts's eyes shine with excitement, and Maggie only smiles beatifically. She's right to assume these men will see Kate restored to her. All she need do is ask, and she will ask, when the time comes.

But Leah has seized *this* moment to promote. The sole way to right the wrongs done these young girls in the spirits' name and to silence naysayers and educate the newsmen, she claims, is to introduce the spirits to a still larger community.

Maggie pledges allegiance to this plan but after supper points out, by way of clarification, that a new blue dress will go a long way toward placating the wayward spirits. "I've been looking a bit shabby of late," she notes, "in their view. A bit unworthy."

A more than suitable model just happens to be on show in the newest *Godey's Lady's Book*. A dressmaker is procured and a meeting called at the home of the Posts, during which the spirits advise: "Hire Corinthian Hall."

18 ✢✢ Burning Bright

Because it brings out the deeper highlights in her hair, Clara adopts a gown of rusty gold for the Eland dinner, one made especially for some unspecial affair her aunts schemed up years before. Mary lets it out some at the bust and belly, for Clara is a woman now where before she was otherwise.

She needs do little to adorn such a dress, adding only a simple ribbon choker with a tiger's-eye stone pendant Father brought back from one of his early expeditions. Clara sends Mary away and locks her bedroom door, intent upon ritual or the promise of one, for she has never had cause before to *dress,* to evoke ceremony, to care with whom she eats her dinner.

She stands first outside the fitted and brushed dress like a soul outside a body, contemplating it, turning again to her own bareness in the mirror. She touches her hipbone, lightly traces the slope beneath her chin, trailing down from her collarbone between her small breasts, which are as alert as the rest of her, as if there is indeed a world inside her bones, a wild world of flickering light and tides and waving sea grass.

Always she imagines them together for the first time by the ocean, perhaps because she knows that Will came of age on an island.

Once, when she was a girl on seaside holiday, off doing the lone things she did in real landscapes to amuse herself, Clara lay alone in her makeshift bathing costume on a tidal flat at low tide, surprised by the vigor of that seemingly quiet flow. At a glance, from a vertical distance, there seemed little to remark on. It was a placid ribbon of softly moving water that brought the occasional hurtling hermit crab or spray of seaweed past her feet. But when she lay over and within it, she felt the whole curve of the world beneath, the vast inevitability of the tide, and her body a part of it, purposeful, exquisite.

It's in a place like this that she lies with Will in idle daydreams, never on the barge of a bed under heavy drapes at night. He'll hold her in his gaze and then wash over her like the tide, quietly owning her, inch by inch.

Tonight her face in the looking glass seems a stranger's face, one mysteriously pleased with itself and the universe, pleased with her secret, for she's never had a secret before, has never required one, except her tangled feelings about her mother, withheld to keep others from treading near and over them.

But surely this is different, despite Artemus and his smug cognizance.

Tonight, she knows, Artemus will be busy fretting over guests and likely patrons. Will Cross will hold his own, quietly, and she'll be happy watching without a word across the table. Will his cuffs be crisp? Will his hair curl in that endearing way it does at the ends in the damp (for the menagerie is ever damp, as if the stones sweat dew)? Will he speak with the rough grace and confidence she recognizes or with unassuming shyness? Will those gently crooked teeth gleam in the candlelight?

He'll not hold her tonight, she well knows, or any night soon. Not least because it will be up to her, and she won't spoil the thing with overwillingness. It's understood that the days between them are a dance, a thing fleeting and doomed, like any freedom.

Is it naive to believe they met outside the fray and could remain there? She smooths the not-quite-voluminous skirt over a crinoline petticoat, fingers the pendant at her neck, looking hard into her own flecked eyes, and reminds herself not to trust too much the ease in them. It's as easy to trust a tiger in a cage, she thinks; to admire it for what it cannot take from you.

❧❧ You are weightless, waiting for someone to enter a room, and when Will Cross does, forgoing in wisdom or ignorance the dread half-hour before dinner—that forever of tedium and social rigidity peculiar to genteel society—there is no female of the house to fault him, though Alice looks to want the part.

Recent events have confirmed Clara's long-held suspicion that her aunt covets Artemus (all three aunts covet him, perhaps, but Alice most fervently) for a husband. Twice last week, when Clara called with Father, she found Alice in Artemus's morning room squabbling over tonight's menu with Adele Peat.

The proprietress of London Tavern may be architect of this peculiar dinner, but it was Alice who rallied the downstairs staff when the housekeeper took ill; Alice who called for ice delivery and clean silver; Alice who saw that every crook and candleholder had its dusting. More amazing still, Artemus agreed to retire his garish stuffed baboon when Alice pronounced it "hideous." It now haunts the buttery, crouched glassy-eyed under a sheet, unnerving the maids.

But even Alice's profusion of new candles can't penetrate the velvet-dark corners of the townhouse. Part cluttered *Wunderkammern* with its shelves and cabinets of dried flora and shells and coral, its glass-encased clocks and stuffed fauna, and part wealthy bachelor's refuge, the house is dim as any church, hollow at its scholar's core.

As the butler draws Will's chair, and the assembled rise or look up from their meticulous settings at the edgy young man whose hair, just freed from its secondhand silk top hat, is wispy and alive with static, Clara feels herself rise without aid of her muscles and must grip the chair to stay anchored.

Shyly now, out of context, they face each other across the middle portion of the long table, that part reserved for young, unattached, or otherwise unimpressive guests (Clara has more status than Will for her father's sake, but only just).

Will's eyes find and lose her in an instant, savoring her form with a fine twitch of dimple, measuring the space between them, defining the obstacles, as she has done.

Chief among these is Artemus, of course, grouped with his clutch of leading scientists and wealthy landowners at the head of the table. Alice all but scowls at Will's nod, and Father, a dear, ineffectual presence to Clara's right, only blinks and bobs his head. Father speaks when spoken to in social situations, weighing in softly on points of interest, and tonight he seems overintent on his silver and glassware, as if they might leap from his grasp or otherwise betray him. His memory isn't what it used to be, and the table is laden with a more than usually confounding array of fish knives, asparagus holders, lobster picks, oyster knives, silver epergne, and rose-water finger bowls. Now and again, Clara relieves him of his choice of fork, furtively replacing it with a better one.

Glancing often at Will, she delights in his calculated manners, his easy way of watching and modeling the movements of his tablemates while favoring her with swift, indiscreet looks that all but dissolve her insides. He's a quick study, and she can't train her eyes from him, even when the meal begins in earnest with birds'-nest soup and *tripang*, or Japanese sea-slug, and Asa Buckland's big voice declares both dishes to be "glutinous."

Subscribers of *Bentley's Miscellany* or other journals Buckland contributes to know that the boisterous man *eats* what others only observe. When he had reached the tender age of four, his parents took him fossil hunting, supplied his first collecting cabinet, and fostered his every interest, be it skinning specimens, rat-catching, trout-tickling, or roasting field mice ("never a house mouse, mind," a recent essay cautioned, "though the field variety eats like a lark and makes a splendid *bonne bouche* for a hungry boy"), and his curiosity never waned.

Lord Bartram claims to be experimenting with yaks and American bison on his estate, while Lord Downey has recently stocked his Scottish islands with beaver.

"Thereby killing all the trees for miles," notes Rufus Owen with a sneer, slicing judiciously into his slug.

To Owen's right sits the formidable Marianne Pratt. Like Mary Anning of Lyme Regis, Pratt distinguished herself as a fossil collector at a young age. Also like Anning, she helped support her family after her father's premature death by hawking ammonites to tourists; by her twentieth birthday, she had discovered the fossilized remains of both an ichthyosaur and a pterosaur. Pratt smiles sagely when Lord Downey refuses Owen's bait. No blood yet, but the night is young.

For not the first time that evening, Asa Buckland urges any who will listen to turn over his park to kangaroos.

"And I wonder," adds Bartram, a gentleman zoo farmer with a commanding voice, "have any of you inquired into the capybara?"

The philosophy guiding Bartram and his fellow elite stock-breeders, or so Artemus explained in that afternoon's briefing, is no less than the triumph of human reason over the disordered profusion of nature. The wild world must be subdued, domesticated, trained. His audience, well-trained in its own right, now leans forward in anticipation.

"A sort of monster guinea pig, prolific and possessed of a fair quantity of meat. A good show, I have it, since it feeds almost exclusively on water weeds and other useless nutriment fare."

A young anatomist whose name Clara can't recall sings the praises of the Central American trumpeter bird, which can be trained to manage poultry or herd sheep.

Artemus takes this opportunity to stand up and formally speak to his night's mission, funding his own East Indies expedition and begging his guests' attendance at the sale preceding it. "Mr. Gill, aided by his lovely daughter, is currently hard at work on an exhibit catalog, courtesy of the zoological society, the wild likes of Buckland, and"—he glances meaningfully at Will, who nods in turn—"our lately progressive friend Mr. Cops, who could not be with us tonight.

"Way back when Thomas Bewick was preparing illustrations for his *General History of Quadrupeds*, he had to rely on the capricious nature of collecting. He could do little save wait and hope that some traveling menagerie might spirit porcupine and polar bear to the neighborhood of Newcastle."

Artemus turns as he speaks, considering each would-be benefactor in turn.

"There's something to be said for acquisition by serendipity, as will be credited by our own Buckland—himself known to race the proprietors of beast shows down the Thames. The days of scouring vessels bound from Africa and the Americas in quest of a parrot or a monkey among conventional cargo are not behind us. But it's a method ruled by the whims of the marketplace and by public appetite for exotica. Today, thanks to many of you—men from both sides of the debate—" He pauses, nodding gravely at Marianne Pratt, "—men and *women*, Pratt—a more orderly approach holds forth, one more suitable to the reign."

With a distasteful glance at "Pratt," Alice coyly interjects to ask what debate he means.

Owen explains, speaking slowly as to a child while Alice keeps up a perpetual nod, that the Regent's Park collecting philosophy has two strands. "Landowners see the zoo as an extension of their own interests in domestic animal breeding. They want access to species we might acclimate one day for English parks and tables, species not unlike those indigenous to Britain. Deer and antelope— especially the hulking, meaty eland gracing this table tonight— ducks, pheasants, trout. That sort of thing."

"Come now, Owen," complains Bartram, "patriotism demands some gustatory return for triumphant British expansion! It's criminal that today's Englishmen subsist on the same monotonous diet as their medieval forebears."

"Hear, hear," agrees Lord Downey. "The British empire rivals all in the extent of its possessions yet can't match its neighbors' institutions for the display of exotica from these lands."

"This group," Owen continues, "opposes the naturalists, who would stock and sort creatures of taxonomic interest regardless. Snakes and snails also reflect British domination of the exotic places where nature flourishes, do they not? And why not marsupials from Australia, for that matter? We should acquire for our edification without regard to attractiveness, edibility, usefulness, or," he says sourly, "entertainment value."

"A noble goal," Will ventures, "but will the public support it? I'm told Regent's will open to the masses one day. . . . Tourists in from the country visit the Tower for the thrill. They like being circled by death in all its frightful forms but secure as kittens by a hearth. You see it best at mealtimes. King and commoner alike come for the fiercer animals in their savage and excited state. Will *that* public consent—and subscribe—to be educated by snails?"

Murmuring ensues, but Owen forges ahead sourly: "Yes, well. As far as I'm concerned, a specimen's best moment is just after it buckles down dead. When it might be dissected in the furtherance of comparative anatomy. The society is generous with its carcasses. Be they thrilling or otherwise."

"I have a standing order for the hearts," adds the quiet young anatomist. "And I believe you favor tissue, Master Owen?"

"Diseased joints." Owen sniffs, sipping.

Alice suffers a prim smile and clears her throat, nodding with perhaps too much gusto when the butler offers round bowls of ordinary curried chicken and *ris de veau*. These are seized with relief by all, a respite before the main course of kangaroo ham, Chinese lamb, curassow, Honduras turkey, and eland steaks.

Buckland receives it all with relish. "The steamer's a bit gone off," he reports, "but not bad, for all that." He next saws at his eland with vigor, extending a morsel on his fork for a long contemplative moment before partaking. "While sympathetic to the noble goals of taxonomy, I confess, I'm not above eating even the most exotic symbol of our nation's preeminence."

"And yet, sir," says Alice, "you display such affinity for the other kingdom. I think I have never seen you before tonight without at least one or two animals about your person."

Chewing heartily, Buckland confesses to keeping a dynamic menagerie of guinea pigs, hedgehogs, and adders. "If I meet a fellow who keeps storks, I'm happiest if I can produce from my pockets a frog, or at the very least draw forth a matchbox of little toads the size of beans."

"It's all, on some level or other, to do with gustatory payback, then?" Artemus asks. "Yes, Buckland?"

"I maintain it is."

While Buckland segues to boiled toucan and the rubbery pleasures of elephant-trunk soup, Clara lets her gaze wander to Will again. Buckland's words weave with her longings, screaming now—for Will has caught her out, his own blue stare meeting hers almost rapaciously, too directly, and she is seized with the sweetest terror. Her neck stiffens with the effort to look away. She should most certainly look away. *A fire in a giraffe house resulting in a feast of naturally roasted meat*... She should grope for modesty, look to Artemus or Alice or even Father for a sound grip on that world of muffled voices and clinking glassware, strained smiles or pink lips flapping in the candle glow and white sideburns bobbing along with knowing nods *as white and pleasant to the palate as veal*... But her neck is rigid. She can't blink. Her fork rises mechanically, her mouth working strange flavors and salty longing as his eyes command her. He is reckless. Beautiful. But his raw favor only underscores that he is barred to her and from her. *Armadillo tends toward strong and rank.* Forever and forever. His eyes cut her cruelly and mend again, and he hasn't touched his plate in far too long a time.

When one of the nameless men to Clara's left begins to stir uncomfortably on his comfortable chair, Will finally honors her bewilderment. Lifting knife and fork, he releases her from his dark orbit, but he has upended the room for her, made it absurd, a reeling place of glass and jewels changing the light, of glow exploding.

Clara looks to the far corners for respite but in the leaping shade finds wing and still beak and monkeys poised to swing. The hot curve of a flamingo. Coral in a sinuous vine of shadow. She is struck anew by these artifacts, remnants of lives spent in distant jungles and deep seas. How is it that men will know life better, she wonders, by extinguishing it? What are they preserving, and can the mere suggestion of life suit them?

With a swift, hot glance back at Will, she imagines his honey-flesh beneath the coarse fabric of his dinner jacket. Adam's apple bobbing under the warmth of an unsuitable collar as he chews. Beading sweat and beating heart. Coursing blood. She feels hollow and damp at her center, dangerously adrift. What if Artemus was right and to satisfy love was to relieve a flame with water, retaining nothing? What cruelty to have and to end up impoverished. Perhaps she would do better to be deprived of Will—to preserve him, like a coral or a petrified crane, in the greed of memory.

Like a stranded swimmer in view of shore, Clara finds her way back. *The sole fault of a large red monkey of Demerara is that once skinned it too much resembles a human toddler . . . one is hard-pressed to put knife and fork to it.* Returned to (or from) her senses, she finds half the heads at table bowed in the aspect of troubled prayer.

Alice eyes Buckland sternly, and in a beat or two, he abandons the unfortunate red monkey of Demerara in praise of practical men. His friendship with professional bird-catchers, he says, has exposed him to the benefits of British avifauna. "Wheatears, jackdaws, and young rooks come highly recommended . . ."

He and Will bandy some names about, and Buckland backs his chair up to reach across two backs and thump the younger man's. "Look with what vigor the lad tends his plate. No qualms there!"

Will smiles his sweet, slanting smile. "I'm like to try anything once, as you are, sir." His eyes dart to Clara and away, quickly. "But once bitten, I will think again."

She feels her face flash scarlet, a mistake that fixes Owen's sly attentions on her, though like any gentleman, he addresses them to her father.

"You say your young relation is assisting with Lever's catalog, Mr. Gill?"

Cowed by Owen on his best day, Father swallows hard, his lips shining with grease. He looks with despair at the rose water in his bowl, working his jaw as if a tooth pains him.

Artemus comes to his aid. "Her talents surpass most any man in the field, Rufus. I put my complete faith in her ability to assist her father in this."

Will levels his fierce stare on his host with interest. Does it surprise him, she wonders, that Artemus would publicly praise her work? She feels almost proud of her uncle then—and, in a doomed way, of herself.

Owen, who at one point in the evening complained that he was "much pestered in advanced age" by pious young ladies seeking the privilege of closing his eyes when he dies, now launches into a shameless rant that visibly startles even Alice.

"Ladies are second only to clergymen—" He clears his throat in a way that makes one want to tighten one's hands around it—"as relentless producers of popular natural history books. Brimming with loyal pups and dancing bees and Elephants Who Never Forget. 'O,'" he intones in a cruel falsetto, "'but are not flowers the sweetest line in the God-written poetry of nature?'"

One of the landowners, ignoring his wife's ringed hand at his elbow, argues earnestly, "As a father, I can't but approve of this trend. If every young London beauty will trade the seductions of ball finery and flattery for a boudoir of shells and seaweed, society can only benefit. To gently consider the lilies of the field, how they grow, keeps the female mind pure."

Marianne Pratt, who has assumed an almost impolite silence throughout, now rewards Clara with a nod. "Illustration is a form, perhaps *the* form, of natural history where women uniformly excel. We're *trained* to draw. We study and practice from infancy through adulthood. But if ladies will do more than decorate with ferns and wildflowers, if they mean to know fossils or plant physiology, they'll do well to venture out in the field or stoop over a microscope, not simper in their boudoirs."

This can't but be the last word on the matter, and Owen lapses into a grim silence. With Buckland busy dissecting the flavors on his plate, Elizabeth Owen pipes up, "Boudoirs are all well and good, but pity the naturalist's spouse, won't you?" Her merry eyes flash at her hawk of a mate, and something delightfully elfin in her nature now reveals itself—a formerly hidden something. *As if the mere act of speaking animates her*, Clara thinks, wondering at how invisible people can be outside their element. Would she have noticed Will at all—would he have noticed her?—had they not been each alert for the taking, in thrall to the wild beasts of the Tower?

"Smells are the most persistent problem," Mrs. Owen confides, "to be sure. And the appearance of motley corpses. No sooner has an animal met its demise at Regent's than it shows up on my very doorstep."

Will smiles at Clara, a sad flicker of a smile, and she would breathe him in across the ravaged platters and candlelight, consume him, every atom.

"Last summer when the elephant died was *wondrous* foul. I begged my good husband fire cigars all over the house, and you can't imagine the disaffection belowstairs." Mrs. Owen lightly rests her fingers on her husband's sleeve, and the great scientist's unnaturally thin lips twitch in the effort not to smile.

"It is sometimes very hard to cope when the master calls for the legs of a fowl dispatched for dinner to examine its muscles—or enlists me to look through the microscope at such stuff as the minute worms wriggling in the muscles of a man."

"I declare," Alice laments, screwing up her face, "this is the subject to rival all. Do people of science always take on so at table?"

"You see, then," Mrs. Owen concludes brightly, "it is no field for the faint of heart."

True enough, Clara thinks, her eye falling on Artemus's elaborate antique sideboard, a massive black-walnut construction with a marble slab. It has a curving four-unit base and a three-stage back, and carved everywhere on it are signs of human predation: pouch, gun, bugle, and powder horn; snared rabbits; waterbirds tied together and hung as trophies; fruits, grains, and other signs of harvest and vintage; a shelf supported by alert seated hunting dogs with vacant eyes; and, crowning glory, a dead stag arching over, all—a little temple, a shrine to man's dominion over nature.

Artemus startles her by tapping his wineglass with a spoon. "And to all you stouthearted diners, I tip my hat. We'll keep dessert a simple affair to reward your diligence." The words are hardly out when plates vanish in a blur of sleeve, usurped by platters of candied sweet potato and dried bananas. Cakes. Exotic jellies.

Eager to pick the younger man's brain and compare contacts, Buckland drags his chair over behind Will's, planting himself firmly in the butler's path. Alice looks appalled by Buckland's manners and the white collar stained with orange sauce, the crumb-speckled cummerbund stretched hard over a taut drum of a middle. "That man wants a finishing school," she murmurs, collecting the eyes of the female guests.

This indignant contingent rustles out to the drawing room, leaving the men to retire to the library for smutty stories, politics, and cigars, and leaving Clara bereft.

19 ⁖ A Cunning Imposition

Father is late with the papers, and Clara needs only glance at the prominent notice in the *Daily Advertiser* to understand all that she overlooked in Maggie Fox's mood that morning.

The notice vows, "On Wednesday, November 14th, the citizens of Rochester will have an opportunity of hearing a full explanation of the nature and history of the 'MYSTERIOUS NOISES,' supposed to be *super natural*, which have caused so much excitement in the city and other places for the last two years. Let the citizens of Rochester embrace this opportunity of investigating the whole matter and see if those engaged in laying it before the public are deceived, or are deceiving others, and if neither, account for these truly wonderful manifestations."

It's like a blow—Clara's disappointment when Lizzie and not Maggie comes the next morning. According to the little schedule Father has posted in the pantry at Clara's request, Wednesday is Maggie's day. Lizzie makes better tea, to be sure. Maggie's is ever tepid and filmy, as if the girl can't be bothered to heat the water properly or let it steep, as if her attention just won't hold. No amount of sugar can cure Maggie Fox's tea.

But today (most days, really), Clara would prefer her company. She would like to atone, if she can, without losing too much in the bargain.

Clara is too proud to ask outright about the event, though she creases and recreases the news sheet, the notice shouting like a barker from the page. "'Corinthian Hall is this evening to be the theatre of very new and startling developments,'" she reads again, "'or the exposure of one of the most cunningly devised and long-continuing impositions ever practiced in this or any other community.'"

Lizzie's a rough study—like her mother, reputedly—prone to those exaggerations that benefit her, but she might be relied on in this practical instance.

"You'll be at the demonstration?" Clara asks innocently. The question's abject lack of innocence humiliates her. She hasn't bothered to play ingenue in such a very long time.

Lizzie nods, taking pains not to spill. She replies only after setting down the teapot, rearranging cup in saucer, folding napkin beside plate, and settling the tray in front of her charge (she has to pry away the newspaper to make room for it), which delay gives Clara time to regret exposing her curiosity.

"It's plenty of humbug." Lizzie savors the word, clearly, which has no doubt served her well of late.

"I take it you don't believe in the spirits?"

The girl bristles, stands taller. "I don't suppose *you* do, so why should I? Am I any less wise?"

"Am I so transparent?"

"I wager someone like you doesn't believe much in anything." Lizzie waves at the scientific drawings everywhere. "Except what you see."

"That's very observant of you, Lizzie, but you give me more credit than I deserve."

The girl looks startled, confused even. "Then you'll be there? You'll go to the demonstration?"

"I'll tell you a secret." Clara leans forward, giving tray and table a light shove that makes the girl blink. Everything in Lizzie's youthful aspect confirms it; Clara's interest—this whole implausible dialog, in fact—is deeply suspect. Young Miss Fish doesn't get paid enough to nurse bites and scratches. She'll run screaming from the room if Mad Clara so much as steps toward her.

The girl's jumpiness drains Clara, who slumps back in her chair, nodding thoughtfully at her tea tray. "Send my father to me," she murmurs, "when you go."

"But the secret," Lizzie whispers. "You said—"

"I hardly think my secrets are worth a second thought for a girl like you."

"I'm sure I don't know what sort of girl you mean, but all secrets are worth something. I collect them." She laughs at her own earnestness. "I do."

Clara can't but smile back at her. "I haven't left this house in a great many years is all. I've hardly left this room," she whispers. "I don't remember how."

Visibly disappointed, Lizzie bends down to brush crumbs from the worn oriental rug onto her palm. She folds the fingers closed, lifts her head, and smiles ruefully. "Well, that's no secret, miss, is it?"

⸎ Father does his best to conceal his surprise, though his voice betrays him. "Really, Clara? You'll step out tonight? My *dear*." His words trail off. He'll order them carefully. "Shall I call the dressmaker? Do you have something? Tell me what you need, and I'll enlist Mrs. Bray, who will be pleased indeed to help—"

She holds up a hand. They've been through this before, though past attempts (all failed) were designed to secure his happiness, never hers. Clara can't explain her willingness to venture out now any more than she could her unwillingness before: there's something she needs here, something she must have out. Once and for all. Or die trying.

No, she thinks in answer to Lizzie's question. *I don't believe.*

And how intolerable that's become.

Nodding with pleasure, Father lifts her untouched tray. His narrow wrists seem too frail to manage it. He'll send for Lizzie again, he says, to brush Clara's gown. She'll want a shawl or cape, too, for the walk over. The wind has picked up. Only a little, but it might be a cool evening.

When the latch clicks, Clara rises slowly. She strides to the window, smoothing the curtain aside. A fever of green and brown and yellow assails her. Light and dust. Closing her eyes, she presses a palm to the wall and lets her free hand grope along the sill. Locating the crank, she turns it shakily, and the lifted lower pane admits a rich smell of wood smoke and flattened herbs. She takes in a racket of birdsong—stragglers, moving south or sworn to the feeders—and the bobbing brown of cosmos heads. A chill so promising it begs a hearth fire, though so far autumn has been mellow, barely cool enough, Father keeps saying. Her parent is forever trying to tempt her with weather, draw her magically up and out into a gleaming garden or a fine frost or to view a cat asleep and sprawling on sun-drenched cobbles. He knows her well, but it frightens Clara that she can still begrudge him so little, after so long.

Until the wide-openness defeats her and she begins to tremble and perspire, grope for indoor angles and the anchor of familiar surfaces, Clara stands at the window breathing the new bite of November. She listens to carriages roll by and to the clop of heels and the mewling of cats and to strangers' laughter, and the movement, mewling, and laughter pain her. She imagines dressing with care to walk three blocks and listen for ghosts in a stuffy, crowded auditorium, knowing full well that night will envelop the room and everyone in it with their petty cares and stubborn hopes and doubts and the lie on their lips that they can, perhaps, live forever. The earth will spin, and the cold, opinionless stars will wink overhead, and there will be nowhere to hide but in view of it all—and this, too, pains her. But it can't be helped.

Clara cranks the window closed, draws the drapes, and returns to her chair. Seated again, she feels anything but safe and comfortable. Her back is stiff as pitch, but she can't relax it, can't undo what is so pitilessly being done to her.

"Take care, girl," Clara says into the dim room, speaking to the air, remembering Maggie Fox last morning with tear-streaked face. "The dead are exacting."

20 ❖ Gaping Ears

Her lap is the color of sky and as boundless. Maggie's hands lie modestly crossed over soft blue silk, adrift in dusky sky. Her new dress. Her first-ever store-bought dress, and she can little enjoy it.

She won't look up, can't look up as the doors of Corinthian Hall swing open at seven P.M. sharp, and four hundred-plus citizens and strangers from as far away as Manhattan (the Posts met with a *Tribune* reporter an hour ago) crowd through the single doorway, spilling solemn or tittering into a corridor spanning the length of the building.

They make the floors squeak, these multitudes, their canes and jewels and silky gowns catching the gaslight.

What do they want? Maggie wonders. News of their dearly departed? Signs merely, or evidence to fit their faith? They turn left or right in critical mass, noisily mount steps to the theater on the landing. They flow under lofty ceilings through one of two doors that frame the stage facing a large level seating area with six raised tiers of additional seats behind. They might be ants overtaking a slab of too-ripe melon, and where is Kate? Why is Maggie alone up here with Leah, who looks pale and drawn on the platform stage backed by four Corinthian columns and a red damask curtain? Why should it be Leah when Kate's the one who calms Maggie, fuels her mischief and ambition? Leah only casts a shadow. Pushes but never draws forth.

Maggie does her best to hide in plain sight, in her new blue dress, soft and wide as the sky. She's no philosopher of the divine, like Emanuel Swendenborg, no mystic owned by visions, like Andrew Jackson Davis. She would stare at her hands and let her mind wander and a shallow stance of modesty speak for her here, as at any public gathering, but she feels the crowd craning toward her and Leah, and toward Amy Post and Lyman Grainer, who are also onstage, those gentle guardians, silent wardens of moral order.

Audiences are known to be rambunctious here at the hall, whether they've come for self-improvement or spectacle. Only a few months old and conveniently built behind the busy Reynolds Arcade, Corinthian Hall showcases everything from pugilists to plays, circuses to lectures on mesmerism and the miraculous telegraph. But no one has seen anything quite like this before, and given the controversial nature of tonight's event, Maggie reckons they'll be rowdier than ever.

Just beyond Maggie and Leah, Eliab Capron stands dressed in a dark evening suit and posed nervously at a podium. The audience is in skeptical good humor.

"Order now, good people." To quiet their tittering, Capron clears his throat robustly. "Open your hearts and minds. Remember please that many of the world's great thinkers—Galileo, Newton, Fulton—our greatest discoverers were in their day subjected to ridicule. You have heard tell of a certain loquacious spirit. I, too, was a skeptic, sworn to reason, but have since entertained that spirit under my own humble roof, in my home in Auburn. I invite you. Silence! I invite you to listen for yourselves. The ghost is among us. It is a speaking ghost, proof positive of the continuity of life." He breathes deep, as if the air is too thin. "Friends! Listen."

Faint but distinct raps soon echo through the packed auditorium, disembodied sounds racing along the walls now like tiny hoofbeats, now again like the fall of heavy rain or sleet, and again, much louder if still muffled, like someone beating against window glass with a walking stick, all of which the audience cranes toward with what the papers are bound to refer to as "gaping ears."

As Maggie nervously primps the silk in her lap, hundreds of strangers move in concert, heads swiveling to follow directionally with their eyes. And though they find nothing in the rosy gaslight but each other, the effort draws them together and seems to please them. A collective, good-natured murmur wells up.

But as the sounds assume the novelty of a drone, the bloom in their eyes begins to fade. Eyes roll and hands rise to cup yawns in gloved or ring-clad hands. The more the ghost raps in muffled tones, the more intense grows the mood of mirth and impatience, and Capron has a difficult time drawing them along until at last he suggests, sagely, that a committee be appointed to investigate the phenomenon, find or rule out deception in the matter, and "report not what it is but what it is not."

The audience delegates, through a hoarse volley of nominations and catcalls, a committee of five men to inquire further into the storied notion of communication with the dead.

2I ❦ Agitation's Bride

C lara paces the room, her skirts a hissing drag behind her.
Where is he? This minute.

Having his back thumped vigorously by Buckland? Eluding
Artemus with his eyes? Or does Will know to do even that? Has she
failed him in this? Perhaps he's propped lean and rakish by a window, easily sipping his after-dinner brandy, studying the great men
of science from a corner like some joke on them all. Or just behind
this wall. She passes her hot palm over, flesh raking floral felt, longing for no wall between.

The ceaseless chatter of Alice and Lady Bartram envelops them
like a fog. Marianne Pratt can barely contain her boredom. Propriety will not hold her any more than her stays enclose her sturdy
torso or her cuffs hide the weathered wrists, and were Clara not so
distracted by Will's absence, she might seek out Miss Pratt's society
with relish. She might revel in their apartness and find a mentor, as
Artemus no doubt intended her to. But Clara's too busy being a
lover deprived of favor, and as she circles like an animal, a hard,
rebuking rain begins to knock on the ceiling and windows.

Clara knows this house well—she played here as a child—and slips away into the little anteroom off the hall by a window over-looking the storm-dark carriageway. A pulse of yellow-gray cloud stains the sky, and she crowds against the tall glass and folds moss-velvet drapes around her, hiding like a bee in the heart of a musky blossom. The air is moist and heavy. The panes cool her cheeks. She savors the beat of the rain and lets the other ladies' voices recede like the already distant thunder.

And then Will appears as from nowhere on the other side of streaming glass. For an instant dusk is cut through with something luminous, the last gasp of sun in a sun storm. His frock coat, hat, the hand raised to tip the brim, are all framed in thin, unworldly gold, and then as quickly they aren't, and the air is a gray menace again. *Why are you out there—heading inexplicably away before coffee? How did you know to find me?* But he looks surprised, delighted, advancing cautiously like a child who's spotted a shiny crown on the gravel, one that does not belong to him.

That imperfect smile spilling over his features, he's all dimple and scarred loveliness. One rough hand rises, hesitating, the palm poised in empty space until her own floats to mimic it. (Would she stop it?) She reaches back to scoop the drooping velvet tighter round, settling her raised hand in the outline of his like a small nest cradled in a bigger one, and what a childish thrill. What bliss in that press of cold glass!

The light hurtles away once and for all, and the rain returns with a vengeance, pummeling his top hat and hard-brushed shoulders. He drains the water from his hat brim before flinging the hat onto a shrub. He's wet through instantly, all sodden beauty with rain in his lashes.

Where are you going? she pleads, palms pressing to dissolve the glass and seize him, unmindful forever of chattering matrons primly sweeping crumbs from their laps beyond the walls. *Where are you going? Take me with you. I want your skin your voice.*

He nods.

I want.

Yes.

But he backs away and is gone with a little salute, turning down the lane—a mirage, all brightness in the almost-dark, in his borrowed clothes. There is such a loneliness in his going stance, such self-possession, that she clamps her eyes shut. *I won't look. And when I open my eyes he'll be back.*

But he isn't. The carriageway is still, all shadow but for the wet shine of cobbles. Unbearable, really—such happiness. Who taught her to expect otherwise? She struggles out from behind the drapes, turning toward Alice's treacherous voice with renewed purpose.

But surprises never cease. There's Marianne Pratt, propped like a sentry in the drawing-room doorway. The older woman meets her eyes with a knowing, deeply sorrowful expression, and Clara notes with mounting panic what an expressive face it is. Chiseled, almost manly, it wears the weather, of which it has plainly seen its due.

Pratt—and suddenly Clara feels inducted, entitled to this nickname—glides back into the drawing room with a wry smile. She sits the night long with furrowed brow, smiling periodically from her corner chair, over her teacup, like the old Buddha in the British Museum.

What did she see? What could she have seen? *Do you know me? Would you shame me?* Suddenly Clara sees herself as full of weighty secrets, as a young woman in jeopardy, flayed open. This is a shock for someone so private, unwilling to reveal even the smallest point of pride. Love has ripped her open along a fault line she knew nothing of, and strange that it was there all along, lurking, that potential. She is agitation's bride, and she will wait forever if she has to—and she might have to.

What if she'd passed him by, Clara thinks, staring with dumb adoration into her milky tea, if Father had sent her to sketch in Surrey instead of at the Tower? What if their paths had never crossed? How many people never feel that rift open? Or were *all* people in love always and equally foolish in the privacy of their thoughts? Could it be so common, this uncommon state the poets savor?

It's ridiculous—a world pulsing with undisclosed intimacy! Clara thinks to resist on principal. On the other hand, she's ferociously glad that she isn't one of those who won't know. Whatever disillusionment this yawning state invites, and there'll be no mercy for her in that place left open, she knows, it's better. Better to know.

She touches the glass of another window (how much of her young life has been spent at windows?), her lips testing lightly, instinctively.

I will wait, she thinks. *And wait and wait.*

22 ❧ In a Brown Room

Without alerting the sisters in advance, the newly formed committee decides to conduct its first investigations early the morning of Thursday, November 15, at Sons of Temperance Hall, and to follow up that afternoon at the Posts' home.

Maggie and Leah are delivered as summoned, and the assembled demand a demonstration, forgoing pleasantries. Maggie manages to cast a mournful glance at Leah as they begin. The raps are as brisk and business-like as the committee. Within moments, these eager men with their thick hands and heavy-lidded eyes and stiff lips and salty-gray sideburns have unsettled something deep in her body as if they are trying with their words and eyes to peel off her skin, one layer after another, to get to the core of her, which she herself has never seen and cannot freely offer them.

Questions land at her feet like stones, bouncing back into nothing—for Maggie imagines all around herself a clear membrane like the stuff she sometimes peels from inside a hard-boiled-egg shell, something so light as to be invisible, yet strong and elastic enough to repel, and when one of the men—their names have escaped her; they are all one now, a single great probing eyeball that may as well belong to God—suggests that the sisters be removed to separate rooms, she begins to tremble violently.

She walks with one man's hand lightly at her back—Father or David would take offense at this easy ownership of the small of her back, which handling a lady on the street would quail at, could quail at, as she cannot. No longer.

She meets Leah's eyes as they're separated, directed off into two dark rooms. The men convene first with Leah. Maggie waits alone in a room full of brown—brown chairs lining the wall, a brown counter, heavy brown curtains admitting a sepia light round the edges, a brown-patterned carpet, daguerreotypes of important men with broad brown jaws and proud, watchful gazes—or with Amy, who sometimes comes to see whether she needs anything. Tea? A glass of water? A broadsheet? Is the light too little, too much? Once Amy takes her chin, lifts her head, and, speaking into her shining eyes, says only, "Courage."

By midafternoon, they come to her, bidding her rap, prodding into her thoughts about those who speak to her from Beyond—and where does she think that is? Does she believe in heaven? Will she place both hands folded in her lap, please? Set them on her head? Lift her feet from the floor? She feels her breasts heaving high under layers of fabric, and their eyes lock in the effort not to move with them.

Two members of the committee hold her feet with one hand while placing the other on the floor. They'll later report a distinct jar on the boards though the feet don't move.

Later, when Leah and Maggie are restored to one another, the sounds echo on the pavement, the ground, the walls. One experiment after another appears to bewilder the men, in whose bland yet demanding aspects Maggie detects not merely impatience but a kind of anger. Do they think she's sporting with them? They're not unbelievers, per se, says one. Nor are they converts.

"Take comfort," Leah whispers when the committee removes to a nearby inn for lunch (why she whispers Maggie doesn't know since Amy has gone to fetch them refreshment and it's but the two of them in the still brown room: perhaps the spirits themselves are listening?), "in the fact that we hold them in our hands. Do what I've taught you," Leah urges, "and do it with good cheer."

23 ❖ Further Inquiry

May 1835
London

"Buckland was quite taken with him," Artemus reports slyly after the dinner, as Father and Alice wearily vanish into their respective realms within the house. "But then, he would be. Man of the people and all that."

Artemus, who can't bear disorder, will stay the night in Father's guest quarters while his townhouse is restored to its former austere glory, and Clara hopes he won't keep her from her thoughts and the secret pangs of her own body. She would take her rainy memory of Will to bed directly.

"I don't follow your meaning," she says, setting her umbrella in the stand. Clara savors the good smell of wet horse and leather. She has the sudden irrational desire to escape her uncle's voice and curl up in one of the stalls out in the carriage house as she did as a child, surrounded by straw and snuffling.

"Well, we're talking about a man who befriends every rat-catcher, bird-dealer, and aquarium-stocker in England. He knows the traveling showmen with their mermaids and two-headed song-birds. Why shouldn't he favor your beast keeper?"

"Mine," she repeats absently, and the word revolves in her thoughts like a bee testing sweetness, though she regrets it soon enough.

Artemus strides past, brushing her arm, and his too-placid self-possession troubles her.

"Buckland's never dull," she tries, conscious of the need to repair. "I wish he came to dinner more often."

"A populist," Artemus growls. "Here's a fellow who gives geological lectures on railway trains. He points out evidence of stratification en route through the cuttings—I've seen him do it. When a whale beaches at Gravesend, he's the one they call. Even the country poor know him and send six-legged kittens to please him."

Clara looks at the floor. "Well, what did *you* think of young Mr. Cross, Uncle? What did Father think?"

"Your father is a man of too few opinions, as you know, especially on his daughter's behalf. My feeling is that further inquiry must be made. Were it not for your watchful aunts, I'd fear for you, Clara." He fixes her with a hard, considering stare. "But Alice looks to have it in hand. And your papa consents to retire you all to the country this summer, to his cottages at Mudeford. . . ."

She is careful to seem pleased, bemused. "You know I love the sea. . . ."

He resumes his pacing. "Pratt craves a saltwater cure, I'm told, so I've enlisted her for a fortnight as well. She'll stay on when Alice and the others must to Bath for their holiday with that ridiculous Miles woman."

"I look forward to being well-guarded, then." A wry note might have relieved them in the past, but when Artemus ignores her jest, Clara sinks into a chair.

"You'll leave at once."

At once. I see. "And the catalog? We're so close. I had thought to—"

"I'll oversee the plates myself. I appreciate your work and will ensure the engravers do it justice. It would be too burdensome to transport the stones for your review."

"I could come to London when—"

He shakes his head, almost wincing. "No. I won't have you in London at his mercy."

"You . . . then this is not my father's will . . . but yours?"

He holds a stony silence.

To persist is to risk too much, so Clara veers back. "What of the remaining sketches? You said yourself—and Owen concurred—that the ocelot's tail is too short, anatomically incorrect."

"*Master* Owen."

She blinks astonishment.

"Your manners have suffered of late, Clara. It's no wonder, with the company you've kept. As your father's representative in these things—"

Who made you Father's representative in these things? Not Father, surely. "The hyena needs reworking," she persists. "You know that. Will we compromise now?"

Nothing.

"That's all, then? I should break my brushes over my knee?"

"I'll subtract animals at this point before I'll add them. The printer informs me we've gone over cost. Ordinarily I . . . as you know, my fluid capital is otherwise occupied." He kneels, but at some distance from her chair, and she can't read his looks. Stern? Distracted? *Defeated? Why am I telling you all this?* his eyes seem to say, and why indeed? There may be more, but his confessional air, his aspect of a weakened predator, confounds, and Clara rises abruptly from her chair, rustling toward the rear hallway and freedom.

"Then it was not what you hoped?" She keeps her back to him in the doorway. "The dinner?"

"It was not what I hoped." Somewhere behind her, he clears his throat and resumes pacing. Every bootfall is a feckless thunderclap. *Like a boy*, she thinks, *a little boy deprived of air and sunlight.* "Time will tell," he adds gravely.

Clara turns at the word, wrong on his lips; by some happy accident every syllable rings like Will's name tonight, every utterance. A horse's clop. A nightbird's cry. A bucket of water flung to the cobbles. *Will* an apple tree, silver-leaved, and she the wind, and she hears him everywhere, all around, and she is tired. Too tired to say good-night, though Artemus might require it.

24 ✣ The Subsidiary Committee

How is it possible that five respectable men, after a full day's examinations, can fail to expose two fraudulent females of dubious moral character? What deception, this? What witchcraft?

Audience members rise one after another that second night, like prairie dogs from the earth-dark depths of the auditorium, barking, "Humbug!" and "Expose them!"

Onstage, the lights are blinding.

The hecklers are all darkness.

The crowd elects another five men, an impressive new committee with the vice-chancellor of New York State as chairman. His committee meets with Leah and Maggie on Friday. ("Now don't be alarmed," he whispers, his whiskers brushing Maggie's cheek like a cat's. "I've read Davis's *Revelations*, and I fully believe that spirits can communicate. You shall have a fair investigation." There's something distressing in the way he singles her out, speaking out of Leah's earshot, as if what he has to say owes more to perversion than reassurance.)

But when the chairman is spotted accompanying the sisters to

Corinthian Hall his first night as chief investigator, an outcry ensues; he resigns, is replaced.

The investigation itself is harsh and thorough. The sisters are instructed to stand on a table, and once they're situated, the members of the committee touch, grasp, and peer at their feet, binding their dresses with cord at a point roughly corresponding to what one man later calls "gentlemen's inexpressibles." (He'll utter the phrase, a timely euphemism for "ankles," with a stagy little cough that night to a tittering audience.)

A jeering doctor, moving his stethoscope a graze too freely, listens for movement of Maggie's lungs before moving on to Leah. Maggie shudders. Her stomach takes this opportunity to growl, and she can't but blush at all this indiscretion, involuntary and otherwise. The doctor seems uninterested in her face. None of the men will meet her eyes except as a panel united in judgment, as it were, collectively boring into her.

Through varying tests and techniques, ventriloquism is ruled out, as is machinery.

At length the squabbling second committee departs, no less perplexed than the first. At Corinthian Hall that night, the members relate their findings, or lack thereof, to an increasingly volatile crowd.

The last to testify, a fifty-five-year-old New York State Circuit justice, speaks slowly, as if to a roomful of children: "I was a disbeliever with all my wits about me, on the sharp lookout for deception. With Margaretta seated at one side of the table, the rappings came with a hurried, cheerful sound on the floor where I sat. It was ventriloquism, I said to myself, I put my hands on the table directly over the sounds, and distinctly felt the vibration as if a hammer had struck it. It was machinery, I imagined. But what kind? We debated this at length afterward. Was it a device? How had the teenager and her older sister managed to use it? Where could it be stored, especially since the location of each examination had been secret?"

His shrug does little to contain the mood of the crowd; instead, it incites. He's booed off the stage, and the call for a third committee erupts.

The newly elect characterize themselves as still more skeptical and rudely determined to solve the mystery than their predecessors. One large man with a large voice vows to eat his beaver hat if he can't outwit the sisters.

"And I'll leap over Genesee Falls if this humbug prove otherwise!" cries another, which triggers a great wave of mean laughter that ripples over the crowd and seems to crash on Maggie's head. Everything feels too loud, too rushing-close, and her limbs are weighted, and Leah won't even look at her, won't throw her a line, and she is drowning.

Corinthian Hall is booked again, with the third committee promising its findings for Saturday, November 17. At this meeting, to rule out the possibility of mesmeric currents passing between the sisters and their suspected machinery, the new group has them stand on a table over glass, a known nonconductor of electricity. Likewise, they direct the sisters to rap balanced on feather pillows with their long skirts tied round their ankles.

It is frightening and exciting and sometimes sickening to be touched by all these hot male hands, cufflinks flashing: dark hands, hairy hands, a hand with a gold signet ring, another limp and pale as bread dough. Maggie and Leah are groped, bound, manipulated, and maneuvered as before, but the raps persist, necessitating a new indignity.

The flummoxed committee calls in one of the wives and two

other women to escort them into another room and examine—with the sisters' mortified consent and Amy's rigid, almost secretive nod—their gowns, petticoats, and undergarments. The ladies' subsidiary committee has been instructed to look especially for noisy devices such as leaden balls. Maggie manages not to look at the women but strenuously to divorce herself from their cold, brusque hands. But the thought of the men outside the room in their suits and spectacles and watch chains, tamping pipes and snickering and murmuring God knows what, starts her blubbering.

She keeps it in check at first, gasping almost imperceptibly, reeling herself in like a poked turtle.

But soon Maggie obeys a delicious impulse. She abandons all restraint, propriety be damned, and sucks air into her lungs in great hiccupping gulps, sobbing loudly. This satisfying outburst brings out the maternal impulse in her abusers, who pause in their duties to stroke her stooped back and smooth her disheveled hair.

Hearing cries, Amy storms into the room, demanding an end to the ordeal. Maggie looks at her with love, and, meeting Leah's eyes, is surprised to find them bright with tears. Being manhandled by women seems to have shamed Leah as nothing has before, which will only make her all the more determined, Maggie knows, all the more defiant.

The subcommittee later makes its report to the committee in a certified statement reprinted in the *New York Tribune*. Once again, the women confirm, no evidence of duplicity can be found.

25 ❧❧ The Undiscovered World

July 1835
Mudeford

For a time, the ocean very nearly contains her restlessness. Mornings, Clara sits on the rocky rise overlooking the little beach. Somewhere below, among the soldierly array of ladies' bathing machines, her aunts mince giddily down wooden steps on feet so pale they glow. Cheeks singed pink, they'll plunk doughy selves into the gentle waves and joke hopefully of men in the dunes with telescopes.

Or are they playing canasta on the veranda of the white-washed cottage? From here, the cottage is a glowing gull among a staunch line of gulls on the adjacent rise, perched far from fashionable Gundimore or Highcliffe Castle. Three benign harpies, they'll gossip in vast hats about which quality persons are arrived or conspicuously absent or about the exploits of the aging social adventuress the "Queen of Chantilly," who recently purchased Bure Homage and now entertains poets and peers in her scandalous corner of their little marine village.

Clara sits or wanders without bonnet or parasol, with raised chin. The salt air plays in her poorly piled hair, and she is strange to herself, a muffled tragedy, unrealized. Unresigned. The seabirds pass on their weaving way, dipping and dropping, skimming patient waves, and she is a small figure seen from the sky, poised in her destiny. She feels a fate she can't sort yet, though in another way it shadows her like a thing already past. A memory.

Alice has kept a staunch silence about this abrupt exile, about the eland dinner, and about Will, though once she did inquire with disdain after his health.

"How would I know how he fares?" Clara complained, enjoying her sudden unlikely status as *femme fatale*.

"You *won't* know," Alice retorted, with Lucretia and Tilda nodding and pursing their lips in collusion or confusion or some mood between. "That's as it should be. How it *must* be."

But when the three sisters depart for Bath, and Pratt arrives in their stead with her little terrier, a beady-eyed terror named Bartleby, everything changes.

"Call me Pratt," the new guardian instructs as if it goes without saying, and Clara warms again immediately, uneasily, to this blunt woman assisting a lone female servant with her trunk. Huffing and grunting, the two women wrestle the trunk up the steps as if it's a corpse, and Clara is too stunned to come to their aid or shout for Tom or Mary.

It is a day and a half before Pratt gives her the letter, perhaps weighing the act against Clara's discretion and maturity, or her own. She sends it in—heady sustenance—on Clara's breakfast tray.

Turning the envelope and turning it, Clara feels a hollow trembling begin in her elbows and spread till all her blood hums. She has never seen his handwriting, but she knows this for duplicity. The script isn't decorous but guarded, neat and squat and quavery—all Will isn't. She sets the letter down unopened.

Moving the tray aside, she slips on a tunic and finds Pratt reading her newspaper in a bright chair on the veranda. The morning sun is already high and dazzling, the moppish ball of Bartleby enjoying its warmth from a coarse blanket on Pratt's lap. Gulls wheel past on reckless currents. Clara knows she must be beaming. "Why . . . would you?"

Woman and dog look up, and Pratt's grin is fearsome, over-sturdy, like everything about her.

"*How* could you? is more like. If your uncle knew, he'd have me burned at the stake for a witch—and Bartleby here for a famil-iar." Pratt rubs the sand from her little dog's coat, unmindful where it lands, and he pants in gratitude. "Artemus is a formidable foe. But so be it."

"Why, then?"

"Because I saw your face that night. Because I know what it is to wish and see the wish realized in the face of grave interference. And because, for all my sedentary and matronly airs, I am a roman-tic. I believe in love, though it has eluded me at best not once but three times in my ample life. I also believe in miracles, hobgoblins, dinosaurs—that we find what it is we seek—that far too many seek precisely nothing in this world of God-given curiosities and are re-warded in kind for their trouble."

It's a practiced speech. Pratt has thought hard on the topic, it seems, and Clara is awed by gratitude, by the jolly creases in the older woman's sun-browned face. "I think I love you," she blurts, snatching up one blunt Pratt paw and kissing it, bathing in her guardian's hearty laughter as she steals back to her room, to her prize, like a fox with a fresh bone.

Unearthing his words is a rigorous act, physical. The paper edge nicks the tender flesh by her knuckle—beading blood, exacted payment—and her nerves buzz as an inky landscape spreads before her, an undiscovered world.

Rumor has reached him that a certain clutch of unsympathetic aunts will be removing to Bath, and as he has cause to be in Christchurch on business, he would very much welcome her permission to call, the good Miss Pratt approving, of course. He will meanwhile take rooms, a room really, since he's not, as she knows, a man positioned to take more than one room on any given day (though he has great hopes of altering this sorry state of affairs) at the old smugglers' inn on the Quay, Haven House, respectable lodgings for fine company down from London for the sea air. And will she favor him with a letter if it will not inconvenience her . . . if it can be endured . . . if it will not strain propriety or credulity or discomfit her father to have him call just briefly, of an afternoon, for a stroll along the cliffs, which he's heard are lovely and affording the finest outlook in England.

Come at once, she scribbles, sucking the beaded blood from her knuckle and the ink from her thumb.

❧❧ Desire shapes a world of its own, and only those inhabiting that world, or singed at its edges, are real and present. The rest is a limp dream, a meaningless bustle. The ordinary business of days is a nuisance at best, and at worst cruel distraction. The senses are all, and the waiting—the breathing in and breathing out of absence, the clocking of miles, the maps and charts of mind that lead the lover back like a kite on a cord.

Pratt, silent coconspirator, is Clara's dearest distraction. They walk every morning, sometimes missing tea to stroll on into afternoon. They rarely speak but lift sea lettuce with sticks, poke at irate crabs, or collect mermaids' purses and pleasing stones. Evenings they discourse on all they've seen and stored in mind by day, drinking milky lukewarm tea on the veranda, forsaking lanterns for the moon. The light grows inky, and Pratt with her near-white cropped hair becomes a faint, still glow in her pale summer gown. Bartleby wheezes and dream-yips in the blanket on one or another woman's lap, and Clara is almost content.

How patient they are, she thinks, watching the luminous glimmer of slow waves coming and going below, softly altering shore, leaving a stain of shine. She interrupts a long, dusky silence to tell Pratt how once, as a child, she glimpsed a great fin tumbling in and out of the green. She made a chant in mind that afternoon—*What lives in the curl of a wave?*—a little mantra that repeats to this day whenever she walks alone on shore.

They never speak of the thing itself, that thing approaching like a shadow of wings—Will's visit, so fraught with social peril—or the odd fact of their mutual unconcern. Instead they discourse on curiosity and the consolations of the senses, on art and animal nature, on geology and the anatomy of winkles, several of which they've dissected for viewing with Pratt's compact microscope. Pratt is not one to fashion seashells and ferns into decorative *objets* like other ladies, and everything living finds its way under her blade or ends its days unceremoniously smeared on a plate for study.

Clara even unpacks her folio at one point to sketch. When she asks Pratt's advice about improving her likeness of an albatross, Pratt invokes the Swiss naturalist Agassiz. "Whenever a young man at Harvard applied to be his student, the story goes, Agassiz set before him a fish preserved in formaldehyde. There he left the young man alone, often for hours."

"Did he offer no instruction?"

"'Well, yes. He said, 'Look at your fish.'"

When the letter announcing Will arrives from Haven House, Clara can't order her thoughts, so Pratt corrals them. *Arrive before first light*, she writes, *at low tide when shells and flotsam are at their finest. We'll walk up an appetite.*

Signing off with a flourish, she waves the ink brusquely under Clara's eyes, notes the approving nod, blows on the page a moment, and enfolds the message for delivery.

That evening, they collude like giddy children, and it occurs to Clara as she picks over her dinner that her guardian is as agitated as she is. "Why is it we some of us feel most alive," Pratt muses, "most ourselves, when we are least in accord with what life expects of us?"

"Of which *life* do you speak?"

Pratt meets her gaze with a slow nod. "Precisely."

26 ❧❧ Heaven in the Rafters

Guilty at having sent Maggie Fox away when the girl needed someone to confide in and increasingly curious about the furor in the papers, Clara vows to attend the third evening's proceedings no matter what.

The Posts are family friends. It won't tax Father to secure her a (much coveted) ticket. But he did so Wednesday, he reminds her, only to look in and find her unmoving and immovable in the bleak of corner shadow. When Clara met his patient pleadings—*Are you asleep in your chair, my dear? It's time now*—with steadfast silence, he knew enough not to insist or persist. He leaned without another word to kiss the back of her head, hands behind his back like a man considering a failing vegetable crop. He kissed his daughter's hair and perhaps remembered the smell of her smaller head after a day out hunting butterflies in the warm sun, and the energy that seemed to surge and spray from her bright child's flesh, that invisible halo of promise. He swallowed his disappointment, a chalky bitterness no more forgiving because familiar.

On this day, he agrees only to leave a ticket for her with the admissions desk. "I won't expect you there, but I do hope you'll step out, Clara. I dream of the day."

The click of the door closing, the regret in his voice, the chilly echo of the word *dream,* these rouse her like cannon fire.

Clara has left the curtains slightly open, and branching shadows flash and wave, filling the air with black knives and teeth and nooses. The dark swings round her like a dozen hanged men, boots and all, and she must cover her ears against what comes next: Will's voice, as present and neglected as her hands and feet.

What do you dream?

Rising abruptly, Clara heads to the window. She is all creaking limbs and taut nerves. The shadows reel, and when she yanks the curtains open, half-mad with a kind of relief, she finds, beyond or in spite of the hulking garden and the buildings out back and the gaslit dusk, a peaceful fog of water clutching a little rowboat. The boat is woefully empty, its outline barely discernible in the failing light.

He can't be pleased to be summoned this way again—and from such a far shore—but when she reaches out, as always, the little boat vanishes. The fog is spliced with gaslight. The building's just a building. The cobbles are present, plain, and damp, and the garden is just a garden. Strolling shadows materialize, bending their heads in laughter, heels echoing down the lane.

Clara swipes a hand blindly along the windowsill, scattering shells and dried seedpods—ancient all, save Maggie Fox's birds' nest—remnants of a world that was. She gropes, and her fingers close round the coin, his passage. Though she knows from past experience that the little boat will not be back tonight.

꧁꧂ Corinthian Hall is only three blocks south. Clara has never been inside. She hasn't so much as braved the corner in years. She has scarcely breathed fresh air, and it cuts her lungs. She trembles with ferocity of purpose. Dressed in dark, painstaking layers as much to conceal as warm herself, she itches and sweats under ample clothing. The air is too wide and too windy.

She touches every tree for luck or for balance, leaning for support, breathing hard or failing to, begging under her seized breath for mercy or safety or an end to absurdity, none of which is forthcoming. She's spent a lifetime refusing to plead, apologize, or forgive. Her skills as such are rusty, but she marches on, breathing bravely, placing one foot in front of the other, her flesh raw and exposed and foreign. When others pass, she hides her eyes in her ample shawl and smiles at this stubborn madness—it *must* be madness to make her smile at a time like this—or maybe there's something gleeful in giving up, giving in to it, whatever it is.

The chill coin—a charm, a curse—bites into her palm as couples ride by in carriages. Squirrels quiver and complain on high as she passes. A crow screams at her from a branch, bending its body, but the passing horses comfort her, their soft deep eyes, the *clop-clop* song she always savored as a child living in a London townhouse.

Clara stands an eternity across the way. The queue winds halfway round the block, hundreds of shifting, gesticulating bodies. Slowly, obscenely, the doors swallow them.

When an attendant waves the surplus away, shouting, "Full house!" she breathes deep. Striding over, she tells the man about her ticket.

"I can't hear you, miss. Speak up."

She repeats herself, painstakingly, and he waves her up the steps. "Bill up at the desk'll take care of you."

The desk is many arduous miles away, but Bill does indeed take care of her. "Sarah Gill, you say?"

"Clara. Clara Gill. My father reserved my seat. He'll meet me here."

"I trust he did, miss. It's a sold-out show."

He gropes in a drawer and locates an envelope with her ticket tucked inside, watches as she opens it, gently removes the ticket from her frozen hand, and points her toward the far entrance door. "Go see Mr. Elliott there. He'll walk you to your seat."

Mr. Elliot escorts her through a kind of hell, past row upon dim row of shifting bodies, past eager whispers and craning faces. Father must be delayed over dinner at his club, so Clara waits rigid in her seat with an empty seat on either side. She massages her closed eyelids, unable to regard the sea of waiting faces all around or confront the friendly, presumptuous smiles that only just conceal impatience.

Clara manages her own until Father at last glides almost gracefully into his seat, taking her hands in his, smiling wide into her face with all the gratitude of a frail man in possession of grace. He shakes his head, disbelieving, believing, and his skeletal hands squeeze too tightly.

At first her relief is so fierce that Clara little registers her father's companion. He is a large man but hangs discreetly back, settling on her left only after father and daughter have moved on to mundane matters.

But the day and the event, it turns out, are anything but mundane. "Have you come from the club?" she asks.

"No." Father shakes his head briskly. "We're fresh from the Posts'." He relates in an urgent whisper how rumors have been circulating all afternoon. Faced with threats and otherwise deprived of privacy, the sibling mediums retreated to the Posts' for their own protection. A frightened Margaretta Fox at first refused to attend the evening's demonstration. "Amy vowed she and Isaac would go anyway," Father explained. "'We will sit down quietly,' said she in that gentle, determined way of hers, 'and see how we shall feel about it.' Mrs. Fish agreed to go with them even if it sent her to the stake, and at the last, young Miss Fox relented, too. How she sobbed, poor child, saying, 'I cannot have you go without me . . . though I expect to be killed.'"

With the people seated behind them craning to overhear, Father describes how their party, already numbering some two dozen, gathered bodies and momentum on the walk over. No sooner did the group deliver the mediums and their entourage to the back rooms of Corinthian Hall than Eliab Capron and Reverend Jervis discovered a warmed barrel of tar concealed in the auditorium stairwell.

"The mood is dangerous," Father concludes. Catching his breath, it occurs to him to introduce his companion. The big, ruddy man has a tangle of near-white hair bound back in a leather cord. In general, he seems strange company for Father, Clara thinks. Sven So-and-So looks a very mountain man, bear-like in his worn beaver coat, and his eyes are a strange hazel-green, gold-flecked like her own, attentive but only just. He extends one raw pink paw scarred along the trigger finger in greeting, and his easy smile marks him at once as too reckless for polite society.

Clara stares mutely at the hand until he revokes it but finds, to her surprise, that she doesn't feel awkward in his presence. His pale eyebrows arc in a way that makes him look bemused, and he shakes his head knowingly, as if used to and deserving of such treatment. Straightening his broad back, the man cranes for a better view of Maggie and her elder sister, who've just been escorted onto the riser by their gentlemen supporters.

"Here, then, our Valkyries?" he asks aloud in a vaguely Scandinavian accent, though not necessarily of Clara. It's just a question. He doesn't wait for her to answer it in any case, slipping a small notebook and fountain pen deftly from his pocket.

"You're a reporter?" Clara is startled by the sound of her own voice, so ordinary in so very public a space.

"I write obituaries." He smiles. "Usually . . ."

Of course you do. Sven So-and-So is so large and demanding of ease and cheer that she finds it impossible not to smile at him as the room begins to hum and buzz with urgency. Like everyone else in the crowd, their party of three settles back. Holding her father's hand like a little child, Clara looks up at Maggie, so small and straight-backed at the heart of a mean crowd, and then at the chandelier burning bright above, and feels strangely giddy, thinking the lamp might be the Northern Lights. It might be heaven, though soon enough the room will seem and smell like hell.

After a dazzling show of raps to set the stage, amidst a terrific hush, the final committee files out to make its report.

27 ❧❧ The Earth Between

Before dawn, Clara dons her simplest white dress, airy with a high hem, over a chemise and scant-waisted petticoat.

Pratt's tastes in dress, thankfully, are austere to the point of negligence. While the aunts would make a doll of her if they could—were Clara's opinions on the matter of dignity not so fierce—Pratt cares not a whit what she wears.

Light colors for women are discouraged at the shore, Alice notifies her like clockwork at the start of every holiday, lest they dampen and reveal more than intended. Clara smiles at the idea in the looking glass. She imagines herself licking the salt from her lips. She imagines Will licking the salt from her lips. She tries first one and then another summer bonnet, and in mind they all blow off in a great wind and roll away. Even the one with the spray of silk violets—how she loved that hat when Father brought it from Paris—feels silly somehow, and Clara flings it. She settles on plain and simple straw.

Let her be savagely pure today. Let her scorn all impediment and all that is false. Let nothing draw his eyes from her face or lead him with pattern and brightness other than straight to her.

What an absurd idea, suddenly, women trooping to the seaside in great gigot sleeves and layers of chintz and muslin, armored against sun and wind and the appreciative eyes of the baser sex. Modesty is good and commendable, but is it not a waste of vanity to heap on such clutter?

This mental rant relieves her, for a time, from the all-absorbing loop of lust and anguish that now seems her only honest and desirable state. It's a kind of physical discomfort, a constant ache that radiates out from her middle, and most days she views it with clinical interest, like a surgery patient observing her own guts. There is no eluding it except through busy work of a sort she's not inclined to pursue here in the wilds of Mudeford. Or by sketching it away, and she rarely feels compelled to sketch anymore since her uncle robbed her of a vocation. Artemus reduced her drawing to quaint recreation as quickly as he'd elevated it, and to spite him she's already packed away her crayons and brushes. Clara is aimless as a goat in a carriageway and would sooner wet her hem and dream foolishly and walk, awake in the day, all day.

When she hears Mary call, *He's come up the walk!* she stiffens in her chair. The servants, too—both Pratt's girl, Sasha, and the two from home—are colluders of sorts. They seem curiously roused by the little drama in their midst. Or at least they treat Clara like an unstable queen, a mad duchess delighting in something she can only begin to understand about herself: that she is doomed and won't spare herself or apologize in advance.

Her first sight of him is from an upstairs window. An unfair advantage, intrusive, though she takes a private pleasure in their shared vulnerability, in the endearing way he pauses just so at the steps. When he goes from view, she bolts from her room like a deer.

Clara spies from a shadow at the top of the stairs as Sasha takes his coat, and he stands like a rough and lanky scarecrow at attention, his collar and sandy hair askew as ever. Pratt corners him in jovial greeting, but when Will spots her above on the stair, Clara imagines that Pratt's voice and all the ordinary sounds of the room go muffled for him, as they have for her. There is only the beat of blood in their ears and the echoing stir of the sea beyond. He bows as she walks down. Arriving, she bends at the knee, and because they don't speak for too long a time but only stand there stunned, Pratt relieves them.

"Is the air warm yet, Will? You'll want your coat back? We should away before the tide turns. Walk, walk, children. Don't dally—"

⁜ At the beach, Pratt does not loiter exactly, nor does she keep pace. Soon Clara and Will have moved ahead without striving, and then a deal ahead, and then a great deal ahead. Pratt and Bartleby finally do pause outright—happily, Clara knows—in a tide pool by a rocky outcrop. They fast seem very far away, and when Will notes this, it seems to trouble him. At first he won't look at Clara directly and keeps glancing over a shoulder, as if their chaperone might instruct him.

"She doesn't mind, you know."

"Mind?" he asks stupidly, and Clara smiles, holding her flapping hat brim still.

"In either sense of the word. She isn't much of a jailer, I'm afraid."

They walk a while without speaking, and their hands brush lightly. Fingers grasp and give way, sliding past, uncertain.

But his troubled withholding wears on her. She begins to stride dizzily ahead, to reel and reach for any object in the grit to anchor her. She kicks at groping waves, wetting her hem, and hurls pebbles in appeasement. She is all nerves and swagger, afraid to look at him, and when she spots a dull glow wedged in the sand, a weathered coin, she scoops it up. Turning abruptly, she almost collides with him, biting her lip like a naughty child, holding the token forth on her palm. "Here. For your thoughts . . ."

Reaching for it, he shakes his head. "I can't own them."

"Try."

Locating the windy blackbird of Pratt with his eyes, he takes her balled fist in his hand and flips her forearm. He draws the curtain of her sleeve aside, running the edge of the coin along the fine blue veins of her wrist. Gooseflesh blooms on her arm, but he is careful not to stroke with his fingers, keeping the coin between. His neat fingernails are unclean, but only just, and the veins in his brown hands make her think of maps and rivers.

A wind of sea rose weaves past, and the monotonous waves ease her panic. But there is something dire behind his smile, and Clara damns it for a thief.

He says, "My end will be bitter, I know, and when the reaper comes for me, he'll find this coin under my tongue."

"What reaper?" The sun is shining. Brighter than it ever has. What darkness?

"You and the sea grant my soul its passage, Clara Gill, and I thank you for it."

With a glance toward the speck that is Pratt, Clara retrieves the coin roughly. Taking his cue, she reaches out to trace his lips with it.

If her flesh does not touch his, does not rake and raise tremors, then she will be blameless. The wind riots her bonnet brim, flapping, snapping, and Will reaches to hold it still.

"What do you dream?" he says, and his hard stare, bluer than ever in his summer face, rivets her. He has never been this close.

"My dreams are insensible and ordinary," she admits with a shy laugh, grasping the coin in her fist where it bites into her palm. "A beetle crawling on a leaf."

"I dream of you."

Ha! "I may be naive and at your mercy, sir—"

"Just last night I dreamed of this place. . . ." Will lets go her hat, which sets the brim flapping again. He touches the fabric over his own collarbones, gesturing like a savage painting on strokes for war. "These bones here. The skin all glossy over them. But then they were oars in my hands, or I was holding oars, and I was rowing away in a fog."

Clara reaches to him but checks herself for Pratt's sake. Her fingertips trail over his mouth but settle at her side again, his gaze moving with them. "And how—" she teases, hiding willful hands and the coin behind her back—"with so cropped a view and assuming your answer be chaste, would you know the bones for mine?"

He seems to wince when he says it, eyes darting away: "I've seen you in party dress." He's waving now, but her gaze lingers on his mouth. "Remember?"

Finally Clara turns to find a dark pinwheel on the far horizon, Pratt, with cycling arms, recalled to her duty.

❧ Will returns the next day, and Mary equips them with a picnic basket. All morning they scour the shore, weighting pockets with shells and jagged little spines and sea glass, holding their faces to the sun and wind.

"Pratt, what do you make of Will's pet idea that we're all prisoners but carry around little worlds inside that make us free?"

"You're a philosopher, then," commands Pratt, who will have precision of thought or none at all. "Define 'prisoner.'"

"Well, the pious claim we're prisoners in our very bodies," he ventures, his voice low in the sea wind. "And that death frees us."

"Yes, but what do *you* claim?" Pratt prods. "I hardly deem you unduly pious. Do you presume to call yourself a captive on this earth?" She eyes him sternly, tenderly. "How justify such claim to an African in chains or a woman wed to a brute buffoon for the sake of her day's bread? I trust you've known poverty, as I have, but you are a young man of sound mind and body in a privileged nation."

He laughs. It isn't a hearty laugh, Clara thinks. Pratt doesn't intimidate Will as she does some people—in fact, Clara was surprised and envious to learn that he'd called on her several times since the eland dinner, hoping to win her support. Pratt put him through his paces, and he pleased her enough to be invited back and back again. But favored or not, her challenge seems to trouble him.

"We won't speak of degrees, then. Above and beyond what an unjust world will impose, every person's a slave to choice. We make them, and they make or unmake us in turn." He sets down the basket in the sand, pushes up his sleeves, and turns away from them, toward the waves, adding, "But the world we imagine lives on inside us."

"Like a cancer," Pratt concedes, "but you seem to think little of free will."

He turns back with a grave smile. "I think of little else." He looks at Clara, who can't bear to look back. "Or did."

After they walk a long, not uncomfortable while in silence, Will sets down the basket again and begins gathering scraps of sea wood. Hurling the gray remains of battered ships into the waves with slow grace—and with Bartleby pouncing after like a right wolf—he recounts his childhood and pirates on the Isle of Wight. Clara recalls the smuggler's coin she found in the sand the day before, which rests now in a little dish with her rings and trinkets at the cottage; she must remember to return it to him if his soul depends on it.

In time, they retreat to the dunes for tea, settling out of the wind in a crater of grasses. After eating her fill and flattening her petticoats to lay stout legs before her on the tablecloth, after considering the clouds and waxing about transcendentalists and petrified toads, after slyly assessing her companions' feigned disinterest in her or his own or the other's sun-warmed body, Pratt begins to fidget and lament. The wind is disturbing the sand at her expense. She has eaten too much, and Sasha has forgotten to pack her parasol. "I'm wilting," she complains, "and look at Bartleby, poor wretch. How he perspires under all that mange. I must accost him with a scissors tonight."

She stands with a great heaving sigh, giving her skirts a vigorous brushing. "We'll to the waves again." Pratt marches over the rise with sand avalanching under her steps and her little dog at her heels.

Almost at once, Will assumes the startled expression of the day before. He busies his hands, returning dish towels and crocks and bread crusts to the basket. "Leave those," Clara says—she hopes kindly, for he seems pained, and she can't say why. Now he's brushing at sand fleas. They might be fire ants for all his flailing.

She smiles and turns the smile into her arm to conceal it. She reaches into the deep pocket of her dress, the hidden pocketful of the day's treasure, fondling shells and thorns.

The last of the cherries glint like fearsome jewels in their little wire basket. Bursting out of their skins in the heat. They'll split if she pokes them, and Clara wonders will she do the same should Will reach for her . . . now that Pratt is gone from view . . . now that *they* are gone from *her* view. *We're alone, fool. What keeps you?*

But he only stares, stubbornly, glassy-eyed, toward the sea as the waves, invisible from here, make a monotonous whisper. Her fingers light on rosehips and petals in her pocket, and on a whim she resumes yesterday's game, extracting the softest and pressing it to his cheek. When the limp petal drops, Clara pastes another to the sheen of sweat above his upper lip, where it sticks. He has to look at her now, and what she won't do to keep that helpless smile in his eyes. His whole body seems to sigh.

Playing along, he takes up a pinch of sand and applies it with great concentration to one of her wrists, pushing her loose cotton sleeve up impatiently, pressing and rolling the tiny stones, which leave a white pressure trail in their wake, an edge of sea foam on her bare forearm.

She retaliates with a dainty crab claw, loosening his tie with it, teasing his collar open. The claw clacks along his brown neck, tugs windblown hair, scurries and nips at his ear, breaks.

Agony and genius, this game—whether to spare Pratt or safe-guard Clara's honor—for who will fault them if they keep the earth between, stroking and appreciating with worm-bitten raspberry leaves and tiny sticks and abandoned snails' homes? It's their right, isn't it?—at least this—and tides them over while the invisible tide murmurs encouragement.

In a fit of inspiration, she plucks a cherry from the basket to press against his wrist, staining the edge of his frayed sleeve. When he lifts his arm to clean the bloody mash away with his lips, it takes her breath to watch the muscles in his throat move like the body of a porpoise underwater.

She has to close her eyes (and keep them closed to contain herself) and quick finds his mouth on hers, a greedy ache of heat and cherry sweetness and forgetting. Shadow blankets her, his weight hard and urgent, her own straining to meet it. She makes out his voice between kisses, like the low growl of thunder in hills a long way off: "Someday I'll tell you everything, Clara Gill. Spare you nothing at my expense."

Upending the dregs of the picnic, they're a hungry, clumsy tangle shaping the sand till Bartleby's quixotic barking at the waves recalls them, sending Will over the rise whooping toward the water for relief. He'll swim out so far (full-jacketed and with one rogue shoe on, delighting and alarming Pratt) that Clara half-believes he won't come back, though the taste of cherry tells her otherwise.

28 ❧❧ A Disgraceful Turn

Rochester will be known as a haven for credulous fools!" Josiah Bissel cries from the back of the auditorium. This son of a religious businessman and of one of Rochester's oldest and wealthiest families, together with other leading citizens, has expressed outrage all week—both in the press and behind doors. His minions stand one by one, shouting out of turn.

"Not a one of these committees has been objective!"

"They're packed with spirit sympathizers!"

The real blasphemy, Clara gathers from editorial accounts of the proceedings, is women caring too little for conventional morality. The sisters not only appeared and consented to be debated in a public forum, they allowed themselves to be handled in unseemly fashion by committees.

Watching Maggie up there, stiff and small in her chair on the platform, Clara aches for her. A great deal has transpired since she sent the girl away the other morning. Clara now understands Maggie Fox's quiet determination: It isn't a personal threat; it's an endearing mark of her stubborn character. Maggie won't take no for an answer, and here she is, faced with the biggest *no* of her life, Clara thinks, and about to be lynched.

Each night's audience has expressed its share of impatience, Father whispers, but tonight's crowd is rougher and readier still. They won't even keep quiet for the final announcement, and when it comes—*After three days of strictest scrutiny by means of intelligence, candor, and science . . . acquitted of fraud*—the auditorium erupts in pandemonium.

Stamping and shrieking follow as Bissel and his cronies distribute and light firecrackers, bombarding the room. Father's friend shields Clara from the smoke and din as Father elbows his way up front, where Eliab, Isaac, and the other protective patrons have gathered by the platform. Maggie and Leah wince and turn aside as a heckler accuses the "females"—never has a word sounded so lush and disgusting—of harboring lead balls in their dresses. Maggie slips from her chair and onto her knees, hiding her face in her sister's skirts. Women audience members are being swiftly escorted out of the room as a rhythmic *thump* of boot heels treading in time begins on the wood floor. Certain deep male voices boom over the din: "There's your noise—lead balls. That's what's causing it!"

"Only one way to solve the mystery—"

"Inspect them ourselves!"

"Can't leave so important a task to a women's committee, can we, boys?"

"Hallelujah!"

Father and the others form an unlikely front line, a genteel army surrounding the sisters as the crowd advances and an otherwise soft-spoken George Willetts barks, "Who would harm or discomfit these girls will do so over my dead body!" He mounts the stage, inviting the rowdies up for "investigation"; finally, noting the disgraceful turn things have taken, the authorities intervene, ushering the mediums and their friends out of the smoky auditorium under protection of the police chief.

Clara trails behind jostling multitudes, fearful for Maggie but enervated, too. Her young friend's star can only rise from this low horizon. Notoriety may not suit Maggie as well as she thinks it will—and what will become of that guilelessness (Clara still can't say whether genuine or calculated) that is her chief charm?—but it's too late to mourn for modesty.

The moral objective of that ill-behaved crowd will backfire in the days and weeks to come, triggering widespread publicity. The events at Corinthian Hall, together with articles in the *Tribune* by Capron and Willetts, will stimulate an interest in spirit communication that travels far beyond the confines of western New York.

What can Clara do but suspend judgment a while longer, her arm linked gratefully in Sven So-and-So's?

She's waited this long.

Her escort sees her home. It's a clear night, and the wind has died down. Sven points out constellations in brotherly fashion, and Clara forgives him his assumption that she can't be trusted to tell Polaris from the Dog Star. He's being kind in the way he knows best, and when he deposits her on her doorstep, saying good-night with a stately little bow that mocks his massive frame, Clara realizes with amusement that she's spent a not insubstantial amount of the night with her face buried in a stranger's broad chest and that he smells like horses. She'll do well to forget him with all due haste (and Clara may or may not give Father the satisfaction of a glad report), but it's been an unexpectedly pleasant evening out.

29 ❖ No Choice

September 1835
London

"W hat *is* this?"

Her uncle's fury is a spitting terror. His shadow seems to corner her. As Clara backs away, Artemus—who summoned her there under false pretense, saying he had print proofs from the engraver to share—does corner her, hard against the shelves in Father's library. He is scarcely taller than she, but the unfamiliar nearness of him—a rank threat hitherto concealed in the remote aspect of a gentleman—walls her in. Clara feels books slide behind her back. His breath is hot and spiced from his pipe, the paper trembling in one stern hand.

Clara turns her face away, though he holds the page near enough to cross her eyes. "What were you and Pratt up to out there?" His voice drops alarmingly. "I am betrayed, Clara, and much aggrieved."

She doesn't want to look at it—Will's last missive from Haven House—in her uncle's harsh hand. She will not conjure Will's hand at the ink pot or endure again the sight of his hurried script. It will only grieve her, as it has so often since the day he didn't come and she first had cause to attribute to him a life apart from her. *"You?"*

I know I pledged to come again this morning, Clara, but duty
claims me, and I would not overtax these too-perfect days.
*   Remember me to Pratt, and please ... please ... love me.*
*   Ever,*
*   Will Cross*

"*You* are betrayed?" she gasps, for it's hard to breathe, hard to credit her uncle's nearness without unleashing an immodest torrent of pride and vexation. "Do I skulk and spy among your things? In your home?"

"If you are to flourish under my roof, if I'm to raise you up—a task at which your aunts and father have uniformly failed, I might add—and Pratt, despite her clever nature, is no more than a meddling woman, and a fishmonger's daughter besides, with a fishmonger's virtues—if I am to court a young lady for a wife and not—"

Stunned, she disentangles herself, elbowing her way past to relative safety near the door. "*Wife?* Is it not customary to propose and then presume?"

"I have done." His gaze levels her from across the room. "Your father consents. That is custom, Clara. You live in this world—in this house, with this family. Not here." He rattles the letter. "In a fairy tale with a black end. Have you no shame?"

"You are *not* my family." It wounds him visibly, and she tries not to flinch. "You act otherwise, but this is not your home. I have long been too quiet in my will, perhaps, but you do not know me." Clara shakes her head, shakes away the swell of tears. "You're mad to think I—"

Now he comes at her again like a bull, an old stinking bull, and crowds her back behind the door. He flings it shut, a sound like a musket shot beside them. "I am within my rights. Your elders know it. Even if you do not."

Where is Father? How can Artemus behave this way in her own home? How can he rob her of so much, and so quickly? Had they all retreated upstairs with the shouting?

His voice goes very low and black and all the more terrible for it. Every syllable like a slap. "Did he touch you?"

When she doesn't answer, the knowing sneer returns to his lips. "Do you not see that your Mr. Cross is the furthest thing from a gentleman? The menagerie is closing. He's a young man soon to be without a situation. A scoundrel, Clara, seeking any means to secure himself and . . . " Artemus walks, running his hands along the spines of books as if to train his thoughts. "You know he's been to see me privately? He's been to see your father. To beg for work—and you, beloved, the furthest thing from his lips for reasons I would spare you. What will it take for you to see? Where is all your cleverness now? When it's most required of you?"

She is glassy-eyed. A stone.

"You give me no choice." He grips her forearm hard. "You have robbed me of not only face but mercy. Come."

"Come where, sir?" She plants her heels hard. "Alice!" she howls. "Alice, you'll see to me now for my mother's sake . . . you'll come to me, *Alice?*"

Clara feels a foreboding beyond measure as he leads her out into the hall. Were Death himself arrived to dispatch her, she could not feel more dread. Artemus barks for the carriage, and Mary, drawn wide-eyed into the hall by Clara's shrieking, slinks out to the stables.

❦❦ Clara focuses hard on the drab silk lining in the carriage. The folds form shapes as clouds do. She sees a winking face, a boat with fanciful sails, a leering skull—all in this constricting corner of the world where she crowds in search of safety.

But for the silk folds and the *clop* of horses and the rattle of the carriage wheels, Clara wills the world gone. Should her concentration fail, even for an instant, she'll submit to it. She'll forsake sense and dignity. She's weary with suspense and the exertions of helplessness, weary in a place inside that she's never accessed. *I will not cry. I will not. I will. Will.*

Clara cradles his name for the last time tenderly in her thoughts. The carriage jolts to a stop, and the travelers reel forward, Artemus's arm rising easily to bar her back. He climbs out to speak with the driver, and Clara manages with difficulty to turn her head toward whistling drovers and hawkers, the ringing of bells, the general bleating, crowding, and bellowing of beasts and men.

The street is clogged with pigs and filthy children ankle-deep in mud and blood. At the bright end of an alley she sees the gory slant of slaughtered oxen hung at market. At Mudeford, rain devised a thousand green scents, a salty stew of freshness. Here it greets only foulness. Last's night's makes a putrid stream in the gutters, and a man is spreading straw to no avail, for the road is rutted. The jam is several carriages deep, a maze of bemused horses stamping and shaking their manes over steaming heaps of dung. One stranded party retreats to a nearby public house, laughing merrily. Artemus extends a hand as two dogs collide in a snarl by the alley entrance. "Come down," he barks, assisting her into the muck, which her hem and slippers hasten to drink. "We'll walk from here."

It seems no more ridiculous than anything else this morning that she should be wearing satin slippers—as if they're off to tea and not skirting what must be the edge of the Smithfield live-cattle market. There are many such places, Clara understands pitifully, watching two men lead a drunken woman through a doorway. So many things she hasn't seen or known or done and in her pathetic state doubts she ever will.

Stiff-backed, her uncle strides ahead, turning periodically to hurry her. When his back is turned, Clara finds the flow of her own bewilderment hypnotic, almost soothing, but his expression wakes her time and again.

When she begins to lag, he grasps her wrist roughly, guiding her through the confusion, a religious zealot steering his flock into the sea. Her skins burns from his grip and her throat from pleading, trying to be discreet, as she was taught to be, but the stink and the street noise are terrible, the carts and carriages and whips on horseflesh, the barkers and flung water and swishing of skirts, the *clap-clop* of heels, and she is dizzy reeling with it all, soaked through to her stockings, her skirts dragging through all manner of slop, and now a rat runs out underfoot, sniffing at rancid brick in its haste.

In her panic, Clara half-believes that this man she no longer knows, no longer believes in, will murder her in this maze of rubbish behind the well-lit world, stab her with a knife like some villain in a gothic novel and leave her for the rats.

❧ The pounding of Artemus's fist on the weathered door echoes through the alley. But after that, sound is suspended. Or does the entire world grind to a halt on its axis?

Holding a baby on his hip, Will tries to bar them in the doorway. A curd of spit soils his undershirt. Clara has never seen so helpless a look on any face. He is unshaven and his eyes are wild with all that can't be done or undone; his jaw clenches. In the dank shadows of the room beyond she sees what must be the wife with another, older child clinging to her woolen waist. Hoarsely Will orders them out and wheels on Artemus, who pushes past and into the wretched hovel as if he owns it and has every intention of evicting its residents.

Will releases the child with the same slow grace that he set down their picnic basket on the beach in Mudeford, letting it fend for itself on the floor. For a moment, five pairs of eyes watch the child scrabble like a crab to its mother's ankle, for Mrs. Cross has opted sensibly to remain and hear her fill. These mysterious events concern her, after all, and when Will, gaunt and suddenly raving—a terror, a stranger—lunges at Artemus, the woman watches with patient interest. The children, too, seem more fascinated than anything, and Clara tries to take their lead as the two men jostle and steer one another back and forth across the floor. Despite its slow-motion absurdity, their violence starts Clara trembling. Once she starts, she can't stop. "Not that there's any mistaking it, but tell her," Artemus demands smugly, all but shoving Will to her. "Tell the child now, the whole truth, or I will do it for you."

Will looks up once, into her eyes—straight on, as he's always done before—and seems to deflate. She can see the passion and rage seeping away, leaving him useless, a specter, and when Will closes those blue eyes to her, she knows he will never look at her again, never really look, and the knowing withers her.

His hand shadows his face as if against the sun, and he shakes his head. His raised arm is shaking, too, visibly, and he turns to rest it on the wall, slumped like a pilgrim against the stones of a cathedral.

Clara is so taken by her growing sensation of unreality that she almost pities him apart from her. She feels as though she were high above a battlefield, safe in the clouds and the world a muffled rage of wrath and gunfire below. The air is thin here, but she is calm and somehow free. Everything before was a dream, and in some part of herself that opposes life, that prefers the idea of the thing to the thing itself, Clara is relieved. She won't be called upon to risk so much again. The worst has happened.

The shadows in that plain room (a not untidy room), the bewilderment in that young wife's eyes (Mrs. Cross looks to be a once pretty woman twice her age in woe, swollen-faced and weary to her core), and the vast, round eyes of Will's children . . . all of these bind Clara like a sharp thread. She is afraid to move, afraid this razor thread will mince her to ribbons.

It's only when the child on the floor begins to cry that the spell of stillness breaks and her limbs unlock. To turn away from his slumped back—lean and strong and beloved even in its soiled costume—is a miracle act. But she does turn, and she walks stiffly away, secure in a hollow dignity. She drifts carefully out into the rubbish-brown of the alley.

Back inside, a lifetime past, Artemus is shouting. Will is shouting, too, now, howling with a savagery she can't fathom.

Clara lifts her skirts and runs down the alley and out into the glare of a raucous intersection. Ricocheting through the sinister crowd, she gathers affront and insults round her like a blanket, nearly slipping on the squish of manure and rank vegetables. Finally she joins a group crowding onto an omnibus and jostles aboard, fumbling coins from the little purse in her skirt pocket. She gropes for a handhold with numb fingers, feeling hot and faint and afraid of the clamor in her thoughts, of how her mind is already laboring to distort and deny, to forgive.

Swaying for balance, Clara bites her lower lip, clamping her eyes closed against a dizzying world that will not pause for even this. At the same time, she's relieved the male passengers don't rise or insist on procuring her a seat. No one looks at her at all, in fact, because she is frightening, as all people branded with raw emotion are frightening. She sinks into their aversion with gratitude, and it's like falling backward into snow.

⁂ Vaguely remembering the dance of candle glow and Father's hoarse shouting on the stairs, Clara wakes in her own bed with the doctor departing. Tilda and Lucretia take up the better part of the rose-silk duvet, where they read broadsides with eyeglasses balanced on their noses. Father paces by the window, and Alice gravely inhabits a stool in the corner like a harpy on a post.

Clara lets her eyes focus first on one and then on the other, and this is no easy feat, for the flesh around her eyes feels swollen.

"She's woken," Tilda whispers, expectant, folding the newspaper. She sets it down gingerly, leaning forward.

"Well, let her not wake," Alice says. "Let her never wake again."

"The policeman said fetch him when she wakes," Tilda whispers, and Lucretia rises fog-like, floating out of the room to serve the cause.

"What?" Clara demands.

As if one blunt word might be enough, might appease the desolation that will—that must—devour her. The unfamiliar shrillness in her voice is a blessing. It marks a new and suitably brazen Clara Gill, a fallen woman who will not go quietly.

Let her never wake again? Clara tries to look the question at Alice, but her courage fails. Dutifully she eases up in bed and sits surrounded, like a sickly child. Father lifts her limp hand, and it feels like someone else's hand, or a crab's claw, attached but separate.

"There's been an accident, Clara."

Lucretia and a tiny constable have appeared in the doorway, and the small man sports a big voice. "No accident, miss. Sorry to say. The wife saw it all, and the little ones, bless them. He killed him cold-blooded, beat him to death. I'm sorry to impose, but I need to ask what you saw, miss. How much you saw."

Clara can only shake her head, lick her lips. Thirst is a raging comfort, evidence that her body can, in due course, be given up on.

"Him" would be Artemus, of course. "I saw nothing," she says, and the policeman sighs. But she did see. Something. Their eyes—round and rimmed by gaunt faces—berating her. The eyes of Will's family will ever mock and blame and damn her. She has robbed them. They have robbed her. It's a thieving, bloody world, and now her aunts will be vicious. It will get worse.

Predictably, when the policeman goes, Alice kneels as if in prayer by the invalid's bed. Speaking in the soft voice of a mother reading a bedtime story, though with the constable's bold accents, she reveals the contents of the police report. She relates how many bucketsful of water it took to rinse Sir Artemus Lever's blood off the cobbles; how the perpetrator, William Cross, "'drug him into the alley by the ankles like a lion with its prey'"; how Artemus's head split like an egg with the pummeling. "Your love did that," she accuses in her own voice now, low and terrifying. "Your dear one."

Clara must pay, Alice explains plainly when the others leave the room in exasperation. With her once doting aunts' hopes dashed—and there is no more dangerous animal than a woman doomed to perpetual disappointment—her guardians will, they must, milk this moral lesson for all its nourishment. They have no other *raison d'être* now. Father will look on with the fumbling cognizance of a bat, or not at all. "It must be that you're at my mercy," Alice says jovially, patting her niece's cold hand, and for the first time this morning, of a habit of defiance, Clara meets her eye.

"And Clara, it seems I have none."

❖❖ They spare her at the inquest, more in deference to Arte-mus's standing in the community than anything else. They take Clara's evidence outside the public proceedings. This does little to shelter her reputation. News of her "affair" with Will Cross swells sensationally and travels, together with the larger narrative of the murder.

Father's reputation is likewise savaged, though he grows doddering, perhaps by design, to spite his judgment. What concerns him, or should, is how aimless his life has become without Artemus. It's painfully clear to Clara now that her uncle was not only a part of the family, he was the functioning part, the structure of the thing.

When Clara isn't damning him to hell, she pines for Artemus with a child's pining. The remains of his "family," meanwhile, mope about the townhouse with no purpose, compassion, or hope. The museum catalog comes to a screeching halt as debts mount. Plans for the East Indies expedition, a project Father had looked forward to with his old energy, dissolve. Artemus's solicitor is in Edinburgh when the crime occurs and too beset by scandal upon his return to schedule a timely reading of the will, from which Alice predicts some hitherto unknown nephew or furtive mistress is sure to benefit, at their expense. True, Artemus professed to have no living "family" besides the Gills, but men say many things. "It's what they say in writing that counts."

Tilda alone attempts to be kind to her pariah of a niece, furtively, but it's tempting to poke at a dying animal, and even she complains and laments. A loss it is, and a pity, and a shame. *That* above all: shame will plague them all their days.

There is nothing for Clara to do but sleep. Left to his own devices, Father might have sat by in the manner of quiet consolation, but Alice relieves him sternly: "The child needs rest, Edward. Not stimulation." Minutes are days, and days months. Alice turns visitors, legitimate or otherwise, away at the door. Pratt's hired carriage lingered near the gravesite during funeral proceedings, though she remained respectfully inside. When she came to the house a day later, she received Alice's swift assurance that even were it a fit gesture for her to call, which it wasn't, Clara's headaches were indeed very bad. There's no telling what she says to the newsmen.

Even Will's haunt-eyed wife comes knocking that week, twice, according to Alice, with the infant on her hip and her lank hair and her ruined mind to beg for what reparations might be found. She cares little for an explanation, she tells first Mary and then Tilda at the door, just a few coins. She'll have no memory but the last, which the Gill family delivered and which *her* unfortunate family must account for. Her voice is hoarse with disuse, Alice notes, or perhaps overuse, for as the wife of a malefactor condemned to die on the gallows, she must find herself besieged night and day by reporters and gossipmongers.

Tilda plies the woman on both occasions with a basket of bread and apples, a handful of coins. But when the wretch arrives a third time, with her older child leading an emaciated goose on a rope through the rain, Alice chases the party away with a broom. The youngest, poor child, giggles as if it were a game, while the mother nearly slips on the slick cobbles. But it has to be done. She looks the soul of resignation, Will Cross's wife, a very specter, though it is she who is haunted, Alice assures, by a man yet alive in a Newgate cell. "If not for long. Beside which," Alice adds, swiping her hands together as if to rid them of dirt, "we'll like as not need every coin and loaf of bread we can find before long."

⁂ Two days before the hanging, a letter arrives.

Clara might never have known had the maid not sheepishly hinted as they lay side by side in bed that night for warmth, confessing in full only when Clara seizes a handful of her hair. "Your aunt took it!" Rubbing her scalp, Mary rolls toward the wall, inching away from her abuser.

"Which one?"

Clara knows which one. Mary knows she does and won't turn over, won't implicate herself.

"Where did she put it, Mary?"

"She says she'll sell it," Mary tells the pillow with a shrug, "to the penny press."

Clara rocks on her knees, hidden in her veil of hair, and commences sobbing. Only physical melodrama of this sort—excess and apparent artfulness, her every mood and gesture public and inflated, operatic, ridiculous—suits her existence now. There is no more grace in secret. Gone are the subtle, private maneuverings of a mind and body belonging to her alone. She is owned by all now.

Clara rocks without sound. In the dim of a room full of familiar shapes and shadows, the ornate globe on its stand—a Christmas gift from Artemus—paisley and paint pots and butterfly cases and childhood dolls, the room she has slept in all her life, Mary's bothered breathing is the only honest thing. Snotty-nosed and sick with guilt, Clara strokes the girl's narrow back. "I'm sorry, Mary. Thank you." *Good Mary. Sweet Mary.*

Clara heaves and tosses all night beside her servant like a sleepless sailor, salt-blind, imagining Will in the straw in his cell. There's a pervasive stink of shit and death there, a scuttle of rats and beetles, and there is moonlight. There must be. She leaps out of bed and opens the curtains, but there is no moon.

In bed again, she hums into Mary's hair, the little song about the moon that Mary's mother once hummed to them both. This garbled tune smacks of madness—even Clara knows it—and while Mary is too rigid and unnerved to flee back to her little cot in the eaves, Clara hasn't felt so well in days. She has a reason, and the letter is that reason.

She lies awake, knowing Will is awake, that his ceiling is mossy stone, that his hands and feet are cold. She feels the food churning in his stomach—can he take in food now?—and the blood coursing in his veins, and his spirit writhing, as hers writhes.

Clara kisses her curled servant between cottony shoulder blades, closing her eyes against the heartless dance of shadows.

❧ Lacking a sheriff's order—which benefit admits some six hundred nobles and gentlemen within prison walls for a privileged view—and anxious to observe the effects of an execution, *this* execution, on the public mind, the bereaved family has gratefully acknowledged an invitation to park itself *gratis* in a facing shop window. To supplement their incomes, neighborhood shopkeepers rent out "gallery" seats well in advance for hangings, but the sisters Gill—each of whom, depending on the news source, is rumored to have been Artemus Lever's fiancée—now enjoy a certain notoriety. The murky nature of the crime that brings such shame to his surrogate family has elevated Sir Artemus Lever; he was merely doing his duty as a concerned older male, a family friend, and while Clara Gill suffered an unforgivable lapse in moral judgment, her mentor acted—and died—heroically on her behalf. It must have seemed a fit public gesture (publicity being a pleasing secondary effect) to accommodate this family shamed by association with the villain, redeemed by association with the victim. Immediately after the verdict, some half-dozen competing invitations arrived via messenger from Newgate-area businesses representing a dressmaker, a butcher, an apothecary, and assorted innkeepers. For the sake of comfort, Alice settled on the slightly less fashionable eating establishment nearest the scaffold. It would be a long time before a hackney carriage could get through the departing throng to fetch them out, and Alice had no intention of rubbing elbows with a bloodthirsty mob.

At dinner the night before, she asks Clara outright, "You're sure you won't do your moral duty and see Mr. Cross dispatched tomorrow? There's still room for you to join us, as my brother refuses his seat."

Father stares fixedly at his hands, holding knife and fork, and does not speak. He might be a character in a fairy story, Clara thinks, mute and cursed, slicing not candied sweetbreads but his own tongue on the willow-patterned plate.

"When have you last changed that gown?" Alice persists. "I

can only imagine the state your shift is in. Life may not go on, but laundry must."

Clara turns her face to the wall. "I would speak to you alone, Alice."

The others set their napkins down and file out quietly, which leaves Alice visibly cross; emptying a room is her prerogative.

"I'll have my letter."

"And what letter is that?"

"I heard the messenger last evening. It's mine, Alice. You *must* give it to me."

"Must I?" Alice smiles. "I have every intention of selling it to the press . . . they'll publish it in a little pamphlet and sell it for a pittance, which is exactly how such tripe deserves to be read. *Clara can read it that way, like everyone else*, I thought. But looking at you now, so full of your rights, I'm inclined not to secure you even this much."

The rangy woman is up and moving before Clara can back her chair away from the table. Her aunt strides purposefully to the hearth on the far side of the room, drawing an envelope from her pocket. "You've taken my only consolation to the grave, Clara," she says flatly, extending her arm. "Now I'll send yours to hell."

Clara arrives as the paper flares. She half-believes the flame won't burn—she won't feel it—but she groans as her eyes tear up. Ashes scatter like papery moths, and Clara, grasping her empty hand, welcomes a pain she has no precedent for. "I had no idea you hated me so much."

Her aunt kneels, facing her, as if they plan to play dolls. "*Hate* is too bitter a word, Clara, but if you think I've been blind to the injustice of your . . . good fortune, you're mistaken."

They kneel a while together, and when Alice reaches for the burned hand, regarding it almost tenderly, Clara closes her eyes. She is limp with exhaustion, and until Alice squeezes like a spiteful schoolmarm, just slightly where the hurt is, the familiar bony grasp soothes her. "That will scar," Alice says. "And it won't be the last mistake you make, senseless girl."

Reeling her hand back—it's instinct only; she doesn't care any-more about the pain—Clara looks hard into her aunt's eyes, search-ing for what was, for the family she's lost with everything else.

"Can you have any idea what it's like to grow old?" Alice asks in a cracked whisper, and Clara is surprised to see that's she's over-come with emotion. "Knowing you will never be loved?"

"But you aren't old, Alice."

"Too old for a husband." She looks up, fearsome again, guarded. "I half-imagined Artemus might relent, take pity on me—if not me, then one of us . . . three pitiful sisters without prospects. Instead he looked to you and feckless youth. And look what it cost him." Alice shakes her head lazily. "Fools. Every one of us."

✤✤ Clara kneads the absent letter all night in her burned hand, crying silently. She can't imagine where it comes from—all that water—but then she remembers Mudeford and Will swimming in one shoe with his clothes floating like fins and her breath in his mouth and his fingers trailing smooth stones. There is water to spare, an ocean to draw from.

With her life razed and Artemus's extinguished, why want for mere missing words? Why solve a puzzle proving Will set out to mislead her like a common whore, delude her completely? Or that he didn't. That he was merely thoughtless—he whose thoughts shimmered so, who shared them so openly—or that he wasn't. Did it matter now what message crossed his pen, what words his heart?

Clara rises at dawn to find her bedroom door locked from without. She kicks it with a bare foot, beats on it with her fists, but the answering silence is dire. It defies reason. What time is it? She listens for church bells and, hearing none, lifts the heavy antique globe from its display base. She hurls it feebly at the door, nicking the hard wood. With a *thump*, the world rolls indifferently away.

Clara sinks to the floor in her gray shift, patiently raking her thighs with ragged fingernails. The quiet is deafening, and she fashions a scream. She screams for Father—shut up in his study no doubt, deaf and dumb—and though earnest, her scream rings like a player's onstage. A stark performance for an audience of one, but the alternative is oblivion, so Clara screams again. She screams at the door and out her high window and down into the street until she's hoarse, until neighbors and strangers appear in facing windows to draw their curtains against her.

The streets seethe back at her, bare and silent, shining from last night's rain. Its uneasy rhythms worked their way through her dreams. In one, a fox kit circled its dead mother's breast, racing over and down the still mound, round and around in panic, blood and fur a vivid stain in the snow. In another, she and Will were like children, with Clara arching her back on a swing in the rain, her dress and hair plastered, and Will smiling rakishly from the V of a facing tree.

It's dusk when Alice finally arrives. She unlocks the door, lifts the tray from the hall sideboard, and carries it across to the drawing table, stepping over Clara on the floor. Obscene display! The girl's mouth is open like a panting dog's. Her pretty lips are cracked, and her soiled shift is twisted round her waist, leaving her legs exposed and askew, the thighs striped a brilliant pink.

Crossing to the window, Alice regards the ravaged room. "You must be hungry." She draws the drapes and sits demurely in Clara's reading chair, smoothing voluminous skirts in front of her. She is only mildly mussed after the day's festivities, only slightly wilted, which is more than she can say for her niece.

"But surely you understand . . . Mary didn't feel safe bringing you anything. Your father for obvious reasons can't credit such an outburst. You'll have to behave now, Clara." Alice smiles beneficently, peeling off her gloves. "I have so much to tell you."

But she doesn't. Not this night. Clara is in no state of mind to suffer her words faithfully, and Alice will have suffering.

Clara, for her part, has but one thought, one wish. She'll corner her aunt in the garden or the buttery and take her by the throat and back her hard against brick. *You read it*, she'll say. *YoureadmyletterAlice. What. Did. You. See. There. Alice? Say.*

And for every beat of stubborn silence, Clara will bash Alice's stingy skull against the brick. She'll do what Will did to Artemus, and gladly, holding back just enough for the sake of her aunt's measly life, for the sake of the words. She'll beat her aunt's coifed head against the brick until the tyrant coughs up words like polished coins, buying Clara back her life.

❖❖ But it doesn't end this way, of course. It goes on. Clara goes on, a dry rind timid to her core, though it soothes her to save the bashing-of-her-aunt's-head option by like a nest egg, a trousseau, a jar of jeweled buttons. For now, she'll hear all that Alice has to say. She'll read the newspaper accounts, once each and once only. She'll digest it all impassively. Clara's patience will appall everyone and enrage her youngest aunt, who will dole out her poison over tea in the coming weeks (Father retreating the moment the games begin, his eyes waxing sorrowful, waning blank)."There was much discussion in the streets that morning," Alice will announce over the clatter of wheels when their carriage chances near Holborn, passing in the shadow of St. Sepulchre's, "over whether the victim would hang with his face toward the clock or toward Ludgate Hill. Would he have the rope already round his neck when he came on the scaffold, or would it be fastened on after?"

Lucretia and Tilda temper Alice's commentary with euphemism, of course—it was a quick and peaceful end . . . nary a twitch and no blunders . . . no need for Ketch to tug the young man's legs to ease its coming—but Clara will not be spared. She won't be fooled or repelled. She is a seeker—not that she need seek far with Alice sprinkling barbed anecdotes, ballad slips, and pamphlets about like posies—in quest of what was missing from Will's formal confession, a simple statement of fact published in full in the *Observer*: "Sir Artemus Lever, a far superior man, entered my home with Christian intent that I then, in a confusion of passion, viewed as hostile and unjust, and my rage overtook me." She scours the copious postexecution commentary, lingering especially on the memoirs of Will's jailor. Known in the penny press as "the keeper's keeper," he seemed a kind man and characterized Will as a polite boy who "' loved all and revealed nothing.'" The young man's silences were "'legendary and strenuous.'" He had "'two speeds: utterly still or pacing like one of his former charges in the menagerie . . . 'times I thought he'd pace right up the wall and over the ceiling and down again . . . and I sometimes found him lying at his ease on the floor, staring up into stony space.'"

Will Cross ground his teeth at night and was politely impatient with magistrates and clergy. He seemed "'as like to repent as not,'" his jailor noted, though like all men he "'fastened in the end upon everyone who approached him. They do, you know, 'specially the young men, clinging pitifully and lovingly to whoever happens near.'"

Will labored in his final days on a small handful of letters, disposed of his "'little miserable property of books and tracts that pious or scientific acquaintances had furnished him with,'" and woke at four the last morning to pen his confession, refusing bread and coffee. He "'sighed with the last sunrise.'"

When Clara cannot sift from all this grief what she so ardently desires, what she craves now above life and breath, she puts the whole story of the hanging, its prelude and afterword, violently out of mind, withdrawing instead into words of her own imagining.

She begins to make him up.

She wakes in the night, and fearsome pages unfurl before her, ink-splattered or stained with salt-sweat, written and rewritten on Will's behalf.

> *Dearest Clara.*
> *Clara, dear.*
> *Good-bye.*

No, not that. They weren't ready for that.

Let there be words instead, words everywhere—on the wind, in the crackling fire, deep among the weeds at the bottom of the ocean near Mudeford, way down in the earth where Will now sleeps.

"Alice," Clara sometimes still pleads aloud, her eyes faraway and shining, forgetting herself, "what did you see in the letter? Tell me." *Say the words. Save me.* But her aunt's eyes are sea stones. They are empty shells, roaring in an unknown language. What can Clara do but arrange words herself, place and replace them in convincing combinations?

Dearest Clara,
    Blame me as I will cherish you. . . .

My own one,
    There is a darkness in all of us. Do not doubt it.
But I can't be sorrier that you've owned mine. . . .

Dear Clara,
    How can such promise, such joy, end all promises?
I am dead to you, but I knew you. . . .

Clara,
    I'm yours still. Will the world forbid that?

But they don't convince for long, these musings. How could she fathom a man's feelings at his end? Maybe Will mourned for his young flesh or his infant son, for his mother's hands or his daughter's smile (so like his wife's when they were a new couple about their ease). Maybe it was redemption he craved above all, and Clara is its opposite; how can she presume to know his mind at such a time?

But for herself. If she had Will's words, she could scorn or dismiss them. They would fail in their grave purpose, of course, and she could harden and grow haughty and heal around them.

He can no more fail her now than be forgiven. In the agony and waste of words snatched away, he'll escape her, slip past a riddle, like his song about the elfin prince.

Let me come to you in dreams.

She will never know what he was or wasn't, what she was—to him—or wasn't.

Meet me here beyond forgiveness.

The door will stay open and the wind will wail with his children's wailing, and what words for *that*?

Come sleep with me in the clay, Clara.
And then you will be a true lover of mine.

PART TWO

Fame

To die is different from what anyone supposes,
  and luckier . . .

I bequeath myself to the dirt to grow from the
  grass I love.
If you want me again look for me under your
  boot-soles.

You will hardly know who I am or what I mean,
But I shall be good health to you nevertheless,
And filter and fiber your blood.

Failing to fetch me at first keep encouraged,
Missing me one place search another,
I stop somewhere waiting for you.

· WALT WHITMAN, FROM "SONG OF MYSELF" ·

30 ❖ Mysteries Laid Plain

Father admits Maggie Fox into the room with raised eyebrows and a smile. "I need a magpie," she announces in the doorway.

Laughing, Clara lets herself be smothered in her chair in embrace. She hasn't seen the young spirit medium since last November at Corinthian Hall, when the demonstrations catapulted Maggie's family into the public eye.

Deprived by circumstance of Maggie and Lizzie both, Father resorted—with the widow's intervention—to hiring in some nondescript creature. The tea has improved, but life is a deal quieter, and Clara hasn't exchanged two superfluous words with the new girl, Marta. Nor does she intend to.

Maggie never could take *no* for an answer and has written regularly from various outposts—Albany, Troy, Manhattan—where she and her ghosts have toured. She's also taken to requesting drawings on demand—birds mostly—which, she rhapsodized in her most recent letter, "fascinate me more and more."

Usually Clara does send a drawing, with or without a return letter (she has little to write about apart from Father's declining health, little else to concern her).

"It's funny, this new fascination of yours with birds. When we first met," Clara says with a bemused smile, "not so very long ago . . . you went kicking and screaming to visit your people in Arcadia. You said you loathed the countryside and every tiresome thing in it."

"Well, seasons change, yes? We're just back from the big city, in fact, off to David's farm for a long rest. At least I hope so. I'm longing for it. I like birds," she persists, "because they migrate like me. And they sing for us whether we listen or not. They go goodness knows where into the clouds and speak with the angels, for all we know, and come back again bearing messages."

Maggie sounds very much the guileless child she was before her life was overtaken by the press gang of the new "spiritualism," but she's a child no longer, Clara supposes. Traces of that forthright charm remain, but there's something refined in the girl's presentation, something studied, which proves she isn't guileless at all. Perhaps she never was. Is she world-weary so soon, Clara wonders, or just weary?

"Birds are messengers," Maggie concludes stubbornly. "Like me."

Clara thinks of Sven Holms's reference to Maggie and her sisters as "Valkyries." Sitting across the side table with her sad, strained smile and her dark eyes in her dark silk dress the blue-black of a raven's wings, Maggie might well be one of Odin's choosers of the slain, cheerful banter notwithstanding.

But she is, for better or worse, a young woman in need of a magpie. So Clara gropes the crowded table for her basket of charcoal and crayons, opens to an empty folio page, shuts her eyes, and summons a bird of just proportions.

When Clara opens them again and begins to draw, lifting and

arranging her legs in un-lady-like fashion to employ her thighs as an easel, Maggie watches her every movement without blinking.

"I wish I could have met Mr. Audubon, before he lost his wits, as those who know claim he has. Don't you?" She doesn't wait for Clara to reply but strains with childish joy toward the image emerging on the page. "I fancy when he was young, he looked like our Sven Holms in his ragged skin coat and wild flowing locks. Like Lord Byron with a saddle horse and a rifle. I wish Mr. Audubon had come with those other great men to hear the spirits. I could have shown him your drawings. I'm a fine one for introductions now. Did I say I met Mr. Greeley in New York? He was the first to visit when we arrived at the Barnum Hotel, which isn't to do with Mr. Phineas Barnum, though it's two blocks from his American Museum, which is a big white building full of wonders and you can see it all for 25 cents. We stayed with the Greeleys for two weeks at the end of our visit, and did I say I *met* Mr. Barnum? He's a jolly, calculating person. He invited Katie and me to peer close at his Feejee Mermaid, and it looked to me like a fish or a monkey or a devil-shaped slab of beef jerky. He himself says she looks like she died in great agony. You're missing the green, Clara. Magpies have a hint of green with the blue just here." Maggie points to the floor where her tail would be, grinning impishly as Clara lifts a green crayon from the basket to correct her error. "After this, I'll have a catbird, please, and a woodpecker upside down."

Clara works away, unperturbed. She understands that her young friend is cataloging the experiences of the past few months before her eyes, that Maggie's fitful energy is a kind of reeling back in.

"They wrote a song about us—did I say? A merry song sung on Broadway by Miss Mary Taylor. And there were souvenirs in the shops that read, 'The Rochester Knockings at Barnum's Hotel.'" The girl sighs, as if reading Clara's thoughts. "I've met *so* many people."

"Not least Benjamin Franklin." Clara smiles wryly without looking up from the page. "Long since past."

"You heard about that!"

"Who in all of western New York didn't?"

Swamped with requests even as they were still recovering from the Corinthian Hall debacle, Maggie and her sisters endured an energetic but clamorous regimen of local séances. Clever Leah found a way to impose order and resume ownership of the family's professional life—and of the movement now formerly acknowledged in the press as "spiritualism"—by staging a special séance. Her sisters were magnetized before witnesses and served as intermediaries for the Father of Electricity himself, with the *Daily Magnet* publishing a transcript of the great man's "telegraphed" message from the grave:

> *Now I am ready, my friends. There will be great changes in this century. Things that now look dark and mysterious to you will be laid plain before your sight. Mysteries are going to be revealed. The world will be enlightened.*
> *I sign my name, Benjamin Franklin.*

With a single stroke, Leah succeeded in rallying fans and converting foes, and by winter's end most of New York was in a state of high excitement. Horace Greeley first visited Rochester around this time and declared the goings-on "interesting . . . humbug," though he later ran a front-page review in the *Tribune* of Elias Capron's second-edition pamphlet: "Singular Revelations: Explanation and History of the Mysterious Communion with Spirits. . . ."

By early spring, people in Pennsylvania and New England were forming experimental "circles"—with sporadic interest in spiritualism reported as far afield as Missouri, Ohio, Michigan, and California.

"Speaking of Mr. Holms—" Maggie prompts slyly.

"Were we?"

"Did I mention that he attended my last séance in the city? He was out with some other *Trib* newsmen on a lark. Here's what provoked me to call on you so soon after my return. He spoke of you, you see, while we reminisced about that terrible night at Corinthian Hall." Maggie laughs again, but it's a brittle laugh, jaded—peculiar in someone so young—and Clara is struck again by this strange new blend of child and woman, innocence and cognizance. Maggie it seems is a gifted interrogator, at once giving (forthright to a fault) and guarded. Hidden in plain sight.

Clara frowns, pouring more tea. She's unnerved by the idea of sensible Sven Holms communing with ghosts. His dead wife and baby girl—Father mentioned these in passing—a cholera outbreak in their native Virginia . . . a swift, unspeakable loss.

How can Maggie demean that loss, so many losses? Clara regards Sven as a good man and hardly gullible, and though Maggie's toying angers Clara on his behalf, she holds her tongue; there's no good in driving away her only friend with hasty judgments.

"It wasn't my *first* terrible night," Maggie says.

"Sven Holms sat for you?"

"He did."

Let reason guide the gossips away from Mr. Holms's concerns.

On the other hand, Maggie will be well used to reading the psychological runes by now, catching people out, and she's fixed Clara in that wide, unblinking stare. She's smiling with a great deal too much patience. It might seem odd to abandon the topic now. "I confess," Clara adds, "I don't think of Mr. Holms as the sort to climb aboard a bandwagon. To be—" she pauses, measuring— "susceptible."

"You don't fancy everyone is?"

How blithe, this girl! But Clara has to wonder, in spite of herself.

Even before the Fox women set off on tour in a blaze of celebration and recrimination, the otherwise intelligent residents of Rochester were owning their own "sensitivities," disrupting professional séances with disorderly chants and trance-gibberish, and being frightened out of their beds at night by floating candles and knocking noises. What's more, the dead began acting out all over town. For a time, a devilish river spirit haunted Flour City's waterways, sounding off in buildings near the falls until a scientist remarked on the likely vibratory effects of a dam on the structures in question. "Not *everyone*," Clara notes feebly. "I should hope."

With a sigh, Maggie says, "I saw you with Mr. Holms that night at the hall. My mind wanders shamefully when I'm onstage, and even with all those rude men shouting, I noticed you in the crowd. *There's Miss Gill*, I thought, *a confirmed shut-in, out and about after all this time* . . . but I confess my curiosity soon turned to your burly companion."

Clara stops sketching, drops the crayon in the basket, and massages her temples fiercely. "I'll ask you to sit quietly for a while, Maggie, if you will. If you can."

"Do you still have your headaches? Oh, Miss Gill—"

"I shall not speak to you again, Maggie, until you find out my name and call me by it. Have a care. . . ."

"Miss Clara. I'm sorry I've gone on. I talk all the time—to hundreds of people all the time—and yet I can't talk to anyone."

"I'm well content that you should talk to me," Clara says sternly, "if you'll discuss something other than Mr. Holms."

"I will." Maggie beams, gesturing at the ivory page. "I promise. But you won't stop, please. I'm desperate to have your magpie in the country with me."

"Are there no live magpies in Hydesville?" Clara lifts a crayon tentatively, hiding her smile. "It seems to me that mediums and natural scientists are not so very opposed in spirit. Both have more use for the dead than the living. The zoologically minded, in my experience, would sooner see a bird stuffed and wired to a board than alive in a wood, darting out of view."

"A bird in the hand is worth—"

Clara rolls her eyes. "Your Mr. Audubon labored to solve this puzzle in the field, I know, rigging fresh kills with wire to mimic life in his models. But I remember—as an indulged only girl-child, I often hunted with my father and uncle—it took but seconds for a bird to lose its delicate coloring. Certain black-headed gulls, and some terns and mergansers with white plumage, sometimes had a creamy rose blush or a shell-pink that glowed . . . and this faded instantly, even when the skins were lovingly prepared. The colors in the bill, legs, and feet always seemed to drain away, too, the moment they dried."

"From what do you draw your likenesses?"

"I'm a dilettante with leisure to pick and choose, so I make it a point of drawing live animals. I always have."

"How? As you say, they're forever 'darting out of view'?"

"Yes, that's the trouble. My visual memory's not what it was, I fear."

Maggie looks thoughtful. "What about that monkey you had in the hall out front? Where'd you draw that?"

"Which monkey?"

"That mean monkey. It used to frighten me to death. Lizzie, too. We commiserated often about it. I used to turn it over in its frame while I was dusting."

"Funny you should choose that one. It was a mandrill, and stuffed, yes. My uncle owned it."

"What about the tiger?"

"Tiger?" Clara asks, vaguely alarmed; this was indeed beginning to feel like an interrogation, an interview.

"The one in your old sketchbook." Maggie's eyes scan the room. "I used to flip through while you were dozing. That old marbled sketchbook. Green, I think it was."

Clara feels a dazed willingness to go on, though all morning the conversation has been leading her down maze-like halls and threatening her safety. Why this girl won't leave well enough alone is beyond her. Clara feels reckless when she speaks again, and her voice is hard. "The Tower menagerie. Before it closed. A little zoo in London that at one time belonged to the Crown."

"It's a very pretty tiger. It's my favorite. I know I'm not supposed to say *pretty* or *nice*. A wise teacher told me once those were empty words, and her elocution lessons served me well. I'm an avid student, you know. I have to be."

"Your teacher is pleased to be of use." Clara smiles wanly, the wave of sadness passing, weariness overtaking her. "When do you leave for David's?"

"Tomorrow or Wednesday. As Leah sees fit."

Clara weighs the words. "She's kept you busy, then?"

Maggie's eyes answer for her.

"You claim to be an avid student. What about your studies?"

"Mr. Greeley asked the same thing. He thinks Katie and I are too young to do without, but Katie more so. I'm evidently just old enough to proceed on my path of stupidity. He would make little ladies of us, though we might be chimpanzees for all we're gaped at."

"But isn't that part of the appeal?" Clara ventures. "Maggie. Don't you rather like being gaped at?"

Maggie looks askance, but Clara hasn't the strength to explain herself. "Forgive me." She gestures at the page. "If you'd like me to go on being useful, you'll amuse me by telling of your travels. I believe I read that you were in Albany . . . how fares our capital?"

"We might have gone to Manhattan directly had Mr. Capron his way—he had invitations for lecture-demonstrations left and right—but Ma wouldn't stand for it."

It took some doing, Maggie explains, for Eliab Capron to convince the protective Mrs. Fox to bring the sisters on the road, but his cause was aided by a visit, at roughly the same time, from prominent clergymen investigating spiritual "incidents" in New England. Leah held a special séance, and the ministers were "greatly astonished by the evidence" and proposed that the sisters visit the capital.

After a nervy trial run at Corinthian Hall in April—to test the wind and ensure the stability of the public mood—Maggie, Leah, and Katie traveled with Calvin and Mrs. Fox to Albany, where the elite in droves attended their demonstration at Van Vechten Hall, clamoring to host after-parties in their honor.

But under it all, Maggie acknowledges, were muffled accusations of blasphemy and witchcraft. A "strong army" had to be raised for their protection, which would become the pattern in subsequent cities.

In late May, the sisters left Albany to travel north to the Hudson River city of Troy. "We departed there more or less as we left Albany," Maggie says, "in a flurry of praise and denunciation."

She makes her way to the window and lifts the dried bird's nest. She regards it thoughtfully, then replaces it without comment. "The last thing I'll say on *the other* topic," she begins, and Clara clenches her jaw.

"He's been very sympathetic to us, your Mr. Holms, though he calls himself a 'cheerful skeptic.' He's written two articles, and his views are in line with Mr. Greeley's, I think, whom we girls and Mr. Holms share as a mentor. Mr. Greeley and his wife, Mary, were very kind to us in New York, though I don't mind saying they're strict in their views."

"It isn't the *Tribune* you and your family need worry about, I think, but I'm pleased to learn that Mr. Holms has graduated from the dead beat."

"He'd laugh to hear you say so. He said he lingered so long in that position because he views obituaries as works of art, little gems of biography."

"And so they are."

"He said he likes the dead because they don't write letters to the editor. I said just wait till tonight and hear what they *really* have to say."

Maggie would clearly like to tell Clara about the séance, but Clara won't hear it; Maggie knows that. Thwarted, the girl fidgets and looks at a point beyond the walls. Their visit will soon be over, and in spite of herself, in spite of the almost physical exhaustion Maggie inspires, Clara is disappointed.

"He makes me laugh terribly," Maggie tries, insisting on the last word.

Clara turns her face away, a wave of calm or perhaps emptiness washing over her. "Where will you go next? After your rest?"

"I don't know. I find I can't think so far ahead. It doesn't do to try, with Leah so much in charge." Maggie purses her lips. "Invitations are flowing in from all over." She stands resolutely, pointing to the drawing, which isn't half-bad, Clara thinks, considering how long it's been since she's seen a magpie.

"Let some light in here when I've gone, won't you?" Maggie looks round the room with a sigh. "I've never understood your passion for sitting alone in the dark." Holding the page up at an angle and squinting for effect, she adds, "He's a fine fellow."

Clara can't say whether Maggie means the magpie or Sven Holms, and she isn't about to ask.

31 ❖ A Ghost in the Countryside

Flat on her back in an overgrown meadow at the edge of her brother David's property, Maggie listens to the autumn chorus of cicadas. She breathes in a tangle of goldenrod and bursting milkweed, Queen Anne's lace, pokeweed drooping in gothic hues of eggplant. Everything's riddled with insects and roaring with bees, ringing with the laughter of David's children, who are off staging races, tearing through the fuzz of little bluestem and bottlebrush grass.

Lizzie and Calvin are somewhere by, too. They're all supposed to be out gathering the last of the blackberries. All except poor Katie, who was seized by Leah at the door and enlisted to roll crusts for pie. Ma's staging a big Sunday dinner "like old times." She's in bliss, and Leah's busy by extension and bossy as ever. But also distracted—mulling her next step. *Their* next step, really, for Maggie and Katie are bound to her now in a way that even Lizzie isn't. They've become her bread and butter.

Pa and David have shingled the roof of the new house, which is situated on David's plot. The tangy male smell of fresh-sawn wood, the fullness of family, these seem both familiar and exotic now, and

Maggie is surprised to find that she is more attentive to Leah's voice than to her father's, reflexively. The badge of authority has been handed on, and Pa seems to find his famous daughters both alien and perplexing. He hasn't asserted himself once since they've been here but only mutters inconclusively.

For all her joy in the day, which is bright and fine with the trees along the farm edges beginning to blaze, and for all the laughter of children, and for all her bliss at being in a meadow where the bees are working and she isn't, Maggie can't shake the heady life she and her sisters and even Ma have lately lived in New York City, a world of entertaining and smiling and replying mildly to the most outrageous requests of notable strangers, looking them directly in the eye only when it most mattered, sifting and repackaging their deepest personal secrets.

Their parlor at the Barnum was in a large room opposite the main hotel lobby. Public parlors served as anterooms, and screened visitors were admitted by Misters Capron or Willet or another of their attendant gentlemen. There were a fair deal of Southerners, it being the summer season, and scores of visitors from other cities in the Union and abroad, too, such as the grave old gentleman who thrust forward an envelope of unexceptional appearance, begging the spirits note its contents.

The familiars rapped at length with Leah translating, "A hair from the pate of the dead emperor Napoleon."

The modest triumph in Leah's voice, together with copious tears shed by the elderly Frenchman—who had allegedly sailed with the emperor en route to St. Helena—alerted Maggie that *monsieur* was a hired confederate. Leah rarely discussed such innovations in advance. Her sisters should interpret minor miracles alongside the public, Leah said, so their surprise savored of the genuine. When the task of identifying treasured locks of hair became the rage at table, they would rally.

They held three receptions daily at a long table seating thirty, with advertised hours from ten A.M. to noon, three to five P.M., and eight to ten P.M. The midday session invariably went over, holding them till the brink of dinner, and the later session dragged on till midnight. The tour was well-organized, to say the least, but the days were long, exhausting Maggie in muscle, mind, and spirit, and she knew Kate suffered likewise.

For all the excitement, Maggie's as weary of the living as of the populous dead. Tiresome are those sleepers under the soil (if she props herself up on her elbows, Maggie can just make out the tilting graves in the little meadow plot beyond the neighboring farmhouse) with their power to rouse and compel—though only when she exercises *her* power to raise them to the task. Equally tiresome, though, are family, friends, and strangers with their ever-shifting moods and motives, which Leah now expects her sisters to master on a moment's notice.

What's more, every group outside the main will claim them, yet no one will. Leah, it seems, will court suffragists and Quakers— probably abolitionists and transcendentalists, too, for that matter— if it will serve her family's ends. And it has served, somewhat.

Maggie can't honestly say she understands what distinguishes a Methodist from a Unitarian from a Calvinist from a Shaker, the finer points of that worldly array of -ists and -isms, but she's grateful to Leah for securing her sisters a funny sort of freedom in the thick of it all. Let others cast the new spiritualism in their roaring forges, Maggie thinks, while the Fox girls smile and see the world.

Hearing Leah's shout, Maggie heaves herself up, brushing off her dress. She strolls toward the trees in the opposite direction. It's too early to eat. Leah will want a hand, and Maggie won't give her one. Not today.

She hears a glad shout somewhere by the big willow and veers away yet again, following at a haphazard distance but gaining steadily. She strolls behind, spying on the children who've come down from neighboring farms to spy on the girls who speak to the dead (and who forgot this objective—as children will—the moment they were loosed in fields and woods).

Following with half-interest as they laugh and shove, Maggie lingers, a shade outside their orbit, feeling the ghostly paradox of being at once near and terrifically far away. She could almost raise a hand and tap on a bony shoulder to make her presence known, and she imagines it slicing matter unfelt, unacknowledged. She hears their secret shared laughter and strives toward young beating hearts and lively forms abuzz with the energy contained by flesh.

She lingers, a spectral stranger on the far side of a vast divide, until they catch her out and call to her. The children draw her back to them, reeling her in again, and Maggie gratefully abandons her shield of invisibility. She slips into life as into a warm bath on a chill morning.

With a child clasping either hand—four arms swinging a violent rhythm—and some dozen pairs of short legs marching at her heels, Maggie dreamily inspects the tree line. The brighter stragglers, cardinals and noisy jays, are easy to identify, but the others are too quick and given to vanishing into shade, too wild and swift to study or fix in mind. It occurs to her, too, that all those -ists and -isms are like bright feathers and a common song, a way of saying, *I'm in the club*, or *We're the same species*, but yes: Maggie Fox is a flitting thing, learning and changing, doing and undoing. This is the prerogative of her youth. Is it not? Even Leah seems unwilling to let the world class and tag and tame her, for which Maggie must credit her. Leah has made up her own radical movement to avoid capture.

David and Pa would argue that the Fox family is a clutch of good Methodists, plain and simple. "If you don't stand for something," her brother likes to say, "you'll fall for anything."

But does David really mean, *If you don't stand for something, you'll stand alone*, a dangerous and vulnerable place where widows are burned as witches? Isn't it all—religion, philosophy—about tribes and clans and protection, a common song, an identifiable set of feathers? Who'll watch your back otherwise? You choose something to care about from a dizzying array of works and days, and then you're owned by it.

But Maggie feels dangerously detached, drunk on her own freedom. She doesn't belong in her new life—surrounded by a class of people for whom "ideas" and lectures and silks and stylish hats and velvet casawrecks (like the ones she and Leah and Ma brought back for upstate relations) are commonplace and who find the Fox sisters and their strange "gift" engrossing. But neither does she belong at home in Arcadia under Pa's thumb. The new world is a more *interesting* if less genuine place to while away her days.

Idyllic though these at David's are, Maggie already senses them drawing to a close. It's in the autumn air, in the cry of the geese passing over, in Leah's suspect smile. As Maggie strides, surrounded by children, back up the path to her brother's humble farmhouse, she finds David and Pa high on the roof with their good, grim-lined mouths full of nails and knows that she's leaving home this time, in more than body, perhaps for good.

32 ❦ A Propensity to Run

What's become of the widow? Clara wonders vaguely, helping her father with his collar. The occasion is a conference with his physician, and she's done this since she was a child trained to it by Alice and Artemus, who made it a game: while Father donned shirt and trousers in another room and Mary brushed his overcoat, Clara laid out his brown velvet waistcoat, braces, a necktie or stiff silk cravat, and a pin, saving the best—his silk topper—for last.

Early on, Artemus tutored her in the care and handling of this article, which doubled, he said, as a small pet. Once he even let her model the hat when Alice wasn't looking, and it made a ten-year-old tomboy hold her back very straight and jut out her chin and prance before the looking glass, thumbs in imaginary lapels. "The make is plush sewn onto a stiff flock base of canvas," Artemus told that child Clara, plucking the topper from her head again and rotating it with mock approbation. "Stroke thus—gently, child!—to restore the nap if it's been mistreated, and *always* dry it with a silk cloth. (Our charge, as you know, forgets his umbrella . . . forgets many things.) An economical man never lays his hat down on the crown; always the brim. See you keep the fellow in line."

In recent years, maddened by New York winters, Clara even tried her hand at embroidering flourishes on Father's braces and evening shirts, but her efforts evoked affliction, not gratitude. She had to pick out her stitches like fleas from a pup.

The bell turns her thoughts back to the now she is not inclined to acknowledge.

Marta lets the doctor in, and with scant pleasantries the men vanish into the study, leaving Clara to loiter outside the door.

Sunday dinner last, struggling to hand on a bowl of potatoes, Father complained of being "infirm." Clara refuted him, but she's been playing back the widow's subtle complaints ever since, appalled by her own negligence. Never has Father seemed so small and sly and precious, and Clara would own her failings as a daughter, even solicit Mrs. Bray's advice going forward, but the widow hasn't called in days, perhaps a fortnight. His friend hasn't concerned herself in mother-hen fashion with Father's books and household affairs, hasn't peeked in to see whether "the young lady" would like to step out and take the air. What's more, thinks the young lady with alarm, Father hasn't mentioned Annabel Bray, even in passing.

Called in, Clara settles quietly in a corner chair as Dr. Slotten reviews her father's prognosis.

"You may already suspect that your father's case is of long duration," he says in the soft voice physicians reserve for news calculated to devastate. "Most patients can't even recall when the symptoms commenced."

Clara nods. Many years ago, she first noted the trembling, very slight, in her father's hands and arms, but she would not be able to say *how* many years ago.

"The quaver and reduced muscular power have been ongoing?"

"Yes," Clara puts in softly—and while the doctor doesn't trouble to turn to her, he nods thoughtfully—"but lately, when we walk, he has a propensity to bend his trunk forward, to pass from a walk to a run. It's much worse this week, so it seems he would fly if he could, like a bird with its leg in a snare."

She turns anxiously to Father, who only looks beneficent and knowing. A fat house cat. A sphinx. How dare he sit calmly through this? *How dare you dream of leaving me?*

When her hollow laugh goes unanswered, Clara adds sternly, "His senses, however, and intellect appear quite uninjured."

"Yes, of course, but it's my duty to advise." The propensity to lean, the doctor warns, may become invincible, forcing the patient to step on the toes and the forepart of the feet. In time, it will prove difficult to walk at all. The hands won't answer with exactness to the dictates of the will. Reading and writing will prove impossible.

Clara thinks of Father at his drawing table the other night. She'd come in with tea to find him stooped over a sketch, the magnifying glass trembling violently in his hands, a stream of spittle dangling from his mouth, threatening the page. As she poured, tea flowing over into the saucer, Clara resisted the urge to go to him and wipe his mouth as she might a child's.

As if she had the slightest idea what to do with a child, or an old man for that matter. She was afraid to find the page empty, afraid there would be no marks there. There would be nothing. Only nothing.

Where, she wonders again—a mantra sounding below the doctor's measured doom—*is the widow?* Was Mrs. Bray really so base a friend as to desert Father now? Or has he sent her away? His calm smacks of resignation, and Clara can only stare at her hands on her lap, which seem inadequate to the tasks to come (her thoughts . . . her love . . . all inadequate).

"The mundane particulars of treatment," jests Dr. Slotten, "will only weary our patient, I fear. Shall we leave these to your capable daughter?" Father scuffles out gratefully, and Clara must stay, as if *she* is the patient; and indeed, she now feels herself trembling with foreboding and future grief. The door clicks closed.

Miss Gill should know what to expect.

Her father will lose the ability to convey food to his mouth and must consent to be fed by others.

As the disease accelerates, the trunk will be perpetually bowed, muscular power will be diminished, and tremulous agitation will become violent. The patient will walk only with staunch support, unable to lean even with a stick.

"He'll lose the influence of his will over his muscles, including those of his face, meaning he'll have trouble speaking and withholding saliva. Passing waste will also prove challenging. Stimulating medicine of considerable power may be required, leading to loss of bowel control. You'll note severe shifts in posture, as if he's trying to shock the palsy away, and the result will be constant sleepiness, mild delirium, and other marks of exhaustion."

"And then?"

He manages a thin smile. "These are the stages of affliction as I understand them. It will be too much for you alone. Do you have a trusted servant to board with you night and day? A young lady relation?"

꧁꧂ Clara drags a straight-backed chair to her father's bed that night. She reaches a hand around, feeling his forehead for fever, a mechanical, maternal gesture she can no more explain than prevent.

"Wrong ailment, dear one." He rolls to face her, his hair standing at cheerful attention like a small boy's.

Clara strokes the rogue strands, but they won't lie flat. His breathing seems ragged and his flesh gray. He is unlike himself, laid bare, and she, in turn, feels like someone else. Someone other than Clara Gill: two pleasant strangers strapped together on a sinking boat.

"What's become of the widow?" she tests, trusting him to read between the lines.

"Oh, I sent her away. Busy old hen." He swallows hard, as if it pains him, and Clara thinks how sad, that we can never really know what ails another person, not inside, and how cure them otherwise? "I'll have no nurse but you."

Under the play in his voice, she hears solemn apology and, hating that he should wonder, quips, "You care but little for your life, I see."

He smiles back at her. "You're not rid of me yet."

33 ⊹⊹ Siege in Troy

Maggie isn't one for lengthy analysis but has to wonder how she's come to be here, shut in a wardrobe in the Boutons' home in Troy, New York, in the dead of night, with her effigy burning on a stake outside and lighting up the dry grass, dimming the moon. Here at the mercy of kind near-strangers who are themselves at the mercy of a mob.

The Bouton home is on the outskirts of West Troy near a lumberyard, which Maggie's tormentors have put to good use as a hiding place. There can't be more than five men, but they're everywhere, hurling rocks at the walls. However violent and immediate, their attack feels curiously drawn out by now, almost languid. When Maggie isn't sobbing in terror at sudden new spurts of activity (that hoarse male voice outside, for instance, just beyond the wall, croaking, "Burn the witch!"), she feels dreamy and detached. There in the dark of Libba's lavender-scented wardrobe, she is neither present nor absent; the men might be talking about anyone—they might be *shooting* at anyone. For yes, at least one has fired his shotgun through a window, and while the house is well-barricaded and -garrisoned, the sound of exploding glass curves round the building. When a stray bullet pings against the wood of the wardrobe, Maggie cries out. Libba, beside her in the dark, answers meekly. *Poor thing must be utterly terrified*, Maggie thinks, *and it's my fault.*

Maggie has never considered herself a coward, even apart from her sheltering family. But she is one, it turns out, too timid even to comfort or assist her hosts, now struggling throughout the house on her behalf.

My burden is no longer mine.

This knowledge—of her own failings and her host family's relative bravery—leaves Maggie all the more giddy and thick-limbed, though again her heart has ceased its wild beating. The grim fact of terror is no longer novel. She's had plenty of time to think.

This, it seems, is what freedom *really* is, and what David means when he says, "If you don't stand for something, you'll fall for anything." Fall under, more like—be run down, beaten, trampled, shot, savaged, maimed. There can be no strength without numbers, and no numbers without agreement, and no agreement without a creed or guiding doctrine. *This* is where every -ist and -ism in the world originates, it occurs to her, and suddenly she's bone-weary with not belonging anywhere, with being run out and found out, and what Maggie craves is simple: the safety of numbers. *Take me*, she thinks: *claim me, name me, give me form*, for what she feels under it all is loneliness, deep and abiding. Libba does squeeze her hand from time to time, and the crash of glass is muffled by the door and by the warmth of her fellow inmate, who moves closer instinctively.

Maggie can almost hear Libba's heart in the darkness. Or is it her own heart, acting up again? She has a horrible cramp in her leg but can't stretch to soothe it away; there is nowhere to go, no room to move.

"We are endeavoring for Maggie to go to another place," Mr.

Bouton telegraphed Leah just yesterday. "If she has mentioned its name . . . keep it a secret if you value her life . . . a deep plot is laid to destroy her."

Leah would argue that it's the women of Troy behind the mob outside. She said as much when they left the city under a cloud of ill will the last time, left behind that hateful undercurrent so soon forgotten . . . the "ladies" were jealous. Here were attractive young women displaying themselves before their men, no better than those noisy suffragists with their fanciful attacks on home and hearth.

But it has been much in Maggie's thoughts these days that she and her sisters belong to no movement. There are no suffragists, Methodists, Unitarians, mesmerists, phrenologists, Swedenborgians, abolitionists, or transcendentalists at the ready, none at all but this defenseless young woman beside her, breathing raggedly in the dark like a wounded doe, and Mr. Bouton—one kind, rather harried gentleman—and the few armed citizens he's managed to enlist this week while firing off telegrams to Leah and fending off criminals who would terrorize his family on Maggie's behalf. Where now are the spiritualists and their ever-expanding Summerland? It might just as well collapse on Maggie Fox's head for all the good it does.

Despite the difficulties they had last time in Troy, Maggie made fine friends here, not least Libba, Mrs. Bouton's younger sister. It would be good experience, she argued when Leah proposed other, less desirable plans . . . good in every way for Maggie to conduct séances on her own and build a private audience . . . build her confidence *apart* from Leah and carry her weight. This argument appealed to Leah, as it would.

Where *is* Leah?

Maggie couldn't wait to get away from her overbearing sister—and in fact eagerly accepted the invitation from the Robert Boutons when it came—but now she knows enough to regret that decision. Leah is her rock. Her only ongoing line of defense.

Thump. Thud. The walls are trembling, and nary a spirit in sight. Shovels. Pitchforks. Fists that would tear her shining hair from her blighted head. Somehow the thumping of aggrieved flesh is worse than the graze of bullets, and Maggie starts to tremble again in the dark. The family dog is barking in the hall outside Libba's room, somewhat feebly, and then farther off, in the yard, and Maggie winces at that point to hear it whine. Hit with a stone, poor creature—in the wrong place at the wrong time. On the weaker end.

The Boutons treated her like royalty when she arrived. Their gentle kindness reminded Maggie of the Posts and other beloved friends in Rochester—she and her sisters and Ma have met so many people, and so few of them genuinely have their interests at heart; it's easy to tell when people do—so the Boutons put her immediately at ease. It was the right choice to come, much sounder than Katie's decision to board with the Greeleys.

"Mrs. Greeley is a wretched, unhappy woman," Kate wrote in her most recent letter. "(How I hate her, Maggie! Why did I leave our mother?) The house is as you remember with not a whit of meat or tea or coffee to be had, and though the garden hammock is my friend, what I wouldn't give to look on a curtain or a rug or a smiling photograph! This is a house to rival Mr. Dickens's bleak one—Castle Doleful! Mrs. G. keeps the servants and her husband on their mettle, and the cook has been fired again. We eat only beans and potatoes, boiled rice, pudding, bread, and butter. Spice and salt are *never* tolerated . . . and, woe is me, *never ever* a pickle.

Mr. G. keeps to his office, and Missus has me always rapping after Pickie though I'm faint with hunger half the day."

Maggie recalls these conditions all too well. Mr. Greeley was their cheerful line of defense, and she remembers him fondly, but his manners are rough; he curses like a sailor, perhaps to suit his role as editor of a contrarian grassroots newspaper. In his cream-colored jacket and trousers, with tow-wild hair and light blue eyes, Mr. G. looks unsettlingly like an albino, and both Greeleys are hydropaths—cold water is their religion. Maggie was always chilled in their comfortless home, no matter the weather outdoors. At night, the silence was so deep that she rarely slept through the night. Only the cluster of buildings on Blackwell's Island hinted at how near the city proper was. Broadway might have been the moon.

Maggie avoided Kate's fate instinctively. During their brief stay with the Greeleys the last time they were in Manhattan, she saw that the damaged family wasn't all it seemed; the couple's marriage was not so very different from her own parents' despite its educated and sophisticated trappings, roaring underneath with silence and blame, ready at a moment's notice to be shaken to its core.

But after the terror of the last several hours, she would give anything for Ma's stout embrace or Pa's grimness or Mrs. Greeley's stern airs. Kate might be her heart's companion, but she isn't one for comfort or analysis. Strangely enough, it's Clara—Miss Gill, whose faraway calm seems to say, *The worst has already happened*— that Maggie longs for. There is wise and adequate shelter there, though Maggie won't presume to ask for it.

From time to time, her lower lip trembles. Her hands feel cold and bloodless, and she tries to shift and stretch the stiffness away, but she won't be comforted or depart the lavender-scented dark, even when activity outside dies down, as it frequently does. Libba has stepped out several times to swing her arms and touch her toes, to hiss the dazzled dog in or peek into the hall, where her brother-in-law and the shadowy townsmen stationed throughout the house wave her back.

The ordeal began last evening. Maggie and the three principals of the Bouton household were returning from an event in East Troy in a carriage. To their surprise, when they reached the shores of the Hudson, they found the family rowboat missing. In its place stood a clutch of sinister and shifty men who suggested they try the bridge instead. But the long Troy bridge was remote, "a glorious place for murder," Mr. Bouton whispered to his wife, so they took another route and found themselves pursued. Maggie and Libba were instructed to make a break from the carriage, dash inside, and bolt the door of the bedroom they shared, while Mr. Bouton shielded his wife and managed to get them both inside while firing a pistol over his shoulder.

A servant was sent for reinforcements, who've been holding the fort since. The sun sank and rose and sank again, and now these wretched, patient men—content the candles have been extinguished and that all is quiet indoors—are at it again in earnest, trying and evidently managing to force their way into the house. Boots clamor on the hardwood, and fists begin pounding on the door of the room where Maggie and Libba cower in the wardrobe. "You say your spirits demand that proof of survival after death be given forth to the world?" one shouts, his low, measured voice almost eerie. "The first great lie was spoken by Satan, the father of lies, to Eve in the Garden of Eden: 'Ye shall not surely die!'"

This seething sermon is punctuated almost musically by the flat of a fist beating on board. "'For God doth know that in the day ye eat thereof, then your eyes shall be opened, and ye shall be as gods knowing good and evil.' You shall be God, you say? You *shall not die?* These are the lies of clairvoyants, psychics, and filthy spiritualists!"

Just as it seems certain they'll kick the door to splinters, Mrs. Bouton reaches in and gropes for their hands. "Girls, come!" she hisses. "Papa's in the crawl space." She brushes reflexively at her robe soiled with wood splinters and spiderwebbing. "Hurry!"

They follow, proceeding on hands and knees in the dark. Around the house they crawl like deranged babies, shimmying down into the cellar, then creeping soundlessly out through the bulkhead. Outdoors, they run with frosty breath in web-streaked shifts that glow white in faint moonlight. The earth is a glimmer of frost, and rocks and brambles tear their bare feet and legs.

Maggie and Libba follow the senior Boutons, slipping into a little shack far in the woods beyond the house. "Papa hangs his meat here," Libba whispers as they crowd in together, shivering. Indeed, before Mr. Bouton wedges the door closed again, Maggie sees a buck dangling in the eaves. In the blackness, she's overwhelmed by an awareness of spiders and clay and dried blood, by the musk of a fox denned nearby.

She has never been this cold in her life, chilled to her bones and raw with scratches. As she and Libba huddle for warmth and Mrs. Bouton murmurs touchingly into her husband's chest, Maggie feels sick with grief and pity and guilt to have brought these good people to this state, to have damned them so. She remembers her recent arrogance at David's farm. Did she really imagine she could stand alone and account for herself?

How easy it would be to break down these walls, and would the cold stars help her then?

This fear finds its way to her mouth, and Mr. Bouton insists the small structure is sturdy. "It has to be," he says, "to discourage foxes and coyotes." One misty dawn, he murmurs, he even found a cougar dozing on the flat roof, though the cat fled like a shadow when it sensed his approach.

They pass a long, eerie night in the windowless shack with the dead deer dangling above and voices and shots sounding far off, eventually being replaced by the rasp of dry leaves and the scurry of small animals, by the lonely soundless knowledge of a veiled moon shining on faery frost beyond the walls.

When at last dawn and silence signal them out, Mr. Bouton leads the three women through the woods to the cabin of sympathetic neighbors. Mrs. Bouton whispers of "a striking revival of the old Salem," retreating at once to lie down as the woman of the house follows with a pitcher and basin. Two wide-eyed girls not much younger than Maggie furnish heaps of wool clothing while she and Libba stretch their aching limbs. They dress hurriedly, without a word, trading awkward smiles and anxious looks between them.

And then, abruptly, Maggie must kiss Libba good-bye as Mr. Bouton leads her back by the wrist. Her feet are thorn-addled and bleeding inside the neighbor girl's borrowed boots, and when they arrive at the house, all is quiet, though Mr. Bouton locks every door and boards as many windows as he can.

In due course, Leah arrives in a stranger's carriage. A man with a pistol assists her down, then swiftly and mysteriously signals Mr. Bouton and directs his driver around the house and along the edge of the pasture.

As the carriage disappears from view, the guilty feeling spreads from Maggie's mind to her exhausted body, and she leans against the back of the house to vomit. Leah ducks inside and swiftly gathers her things.

As Mr. Bouton carries their bag back through the pasture to the hidden cart road, Leah explains how the man with the revolver, who met her at the railroad station, also proposes to retrieve Maggie on behalf of her local supporters.

Sure enough, they find the carriage waiting up on the cart road, but Maggie is seized by an unwillingness to go on, paralyzed by the idea that the driver, a man she doesn't recognize, isn't who he seems.

Mr. Bouton reassures, but more to the point, Leah shakes her arm unmercifully, leaning with a cruel hush in her voice. "You will not discomfit these people any more than we already have, Margaretta! Find your strength. You have no business failing after all they've done for you—and no, you won't die, silly child. We've faced worse than that lot. We'll not let them cow us."

As Maggie boards, swallowing back a sob and the rank taste in her mouth, Leah takes Mr. Bouton's hand in both of hers, smiles sincerely, and honors him in her flowery way: "You have passed through the fiery furnace this night, daring to stand before the world and battle for good. Trust that the golden gate of the new Jerusalem will open wide when the time comes, and you'll live long in the memories of children of Earth."

He blushes soundly. "I'll see you safely up to the road."

"You must go now to your family." Leah regards him with stern warmth, and he seems to trust then that she has things in hand. Leah always has things in hand (though the man with the revolver can't but add gravity). Her sister and her host shake hands, and Mr. Bouton reaches up in fatherly fashion to brush the disheveled hair from Maggie's eyes. What a sight she must be!

She can't help it now; a hiccupping sob escapes her. "I'll send the boots back by post."

"Silly girl," he says, echoing Leah's confident barb, "take heart. Your sister and Mr. March will see you home in one piece."

Maggie believes him, though where home *is*, she cannot say. She thinks of running in the night through too-loud, crackling branches, like an animal evading hunters. She remembers the deer in the rafters and the cougar lolling on the roof. Leah, Maggie thinks, slumping back in fond resignation as the carriage bumps and rolls, is like the cougar.

34 ❧❧ The Tiger and the Tattooed Boy

Father's palsy recalls Clara to her work. He can't tame his fingers to his will, he says, and at least one assignment—the agricultural commission requested line drawings for a series of posters and pamphlets promoting the state fair—won't wait. He admits this with downcast eyes. "Would you do me the honor, Clara, of completing the commission? For pay, of course."

She regards him warily, a smile playing on her lips. Their drawing styles are markedly different. Artemus often and shamelessly suggested that Father's best work wasn't his at all but Clara's, and "damn near everyone" knew it. He meant to cheer and encourage her, of course, not demean his friend, but Clara took no joy in rumors, true or false. "Of course. But you're sure?"

"Yes, and we won't explain it in advance. Old Maury will have a surprise."

This is risky, Clara knows. Father's employment has been spotty since they came to this country. To carry one's professional reputation across the Atlantic without also carrying one's personal reputation is no easy feat, and discretion has cost him dearly. He begged no letters when they sailed and would spare his London associates the stink of his troubles.

Father never went so far as to change the family name, and after a brief attempt for his sake at reentry into society in Philadelphia, and subsequent humiliation, Clara ceased to care for society at all. Their notoriety hasn't found its way to Rochester, but it could.

❧ The drawings for the state fair commission are well-received, and together with the stipend, the office of the commission sends a number of complimentary tickets to the state fair and related celebrations at Corinthian Hall.

Clara has no intention of attending the fair, of sitting in a snarl of carriages and hacks waiting to trudge a dusty mile among hawkers and tractor manufacturers and medicine men, but Father pleads, confessing that he's invited a friend from Manhattan and requires her hospitality, her shoulder to lean on in his weak condition, so as not to impose upon the gentleman in question.

It does not occur to Clara to question whom the gentleman might be. Father has friends and university colleagues who stop by en route to his club for dinner. Although more often, and for days at a time, he visits *their* homes in Manhattan or Syracuse or Boston.

This visitor will stay the night, it seems, a domestic occurrence rare enough to agitate Clara, who's all but forgotten the customs (where were women like Alice and Mrs. Bray when you needed them?). She enlists Marta to extend her hours, to cook and clean as needed and make the visitor feel at home inasmuch as possible.

Clara will have enough to do just rallying for an outing.

So to hear the bell and then Sven Holms's muffled voice in the front hall comes as a shock. A swift, anxious pulse aggravates and instructs her, *Rise quickly and see to your hair*. Not, Clara assures herself, because she cares for his opinion of her appearance but because dignity demands it. She won't be taken off guard in view of a mutual friend. Clara does *think* of Sven Holms as a friend, she realizes—grudgingly—perhaps because of their shared association with Maggie Fox; perhaps because she and Mr. Holms are closer in age than he and Father are.

But she doesn't trust her own mind to make the distinction. Wrongly assuming friendship is a social mishap Clara would avoid. She brushes her hair too hard and too quickly, leaving more than a few pale strands in the brush. Would he know or sense that Clara had been discussing—been induced to discuss—him with Maggie Fox? Would he disapprove or otherwise discredit her intentions? What are her intentions?

Clara sits, landing hard in her chair, astonished at her own ridiculousness. She is very nearly convinced that she should not leave her room at all, should perhaps never leave her room again, as was her inclination before Maggie and Corinthian Hall and, yes, Mr. Holms, who so easily walked out with her, musing on the stars.

Her ambition now is to plead a headache, and in fact she does feel a slight one coming on because this is altogether too much to think about, and she resents being invested in a thing without her consent.

A master of polite refusal, Clara has it all worked out, or nearly, when Father arrives in the doorway, hunched and tremulous and the worse for wear, to plead her company in the parlor.

"Our friend has arrived."

"'Our friend'?" Clara frowns for even Father seems to be in league with these questions.

"You remember Mr. Holms, Clara. He'll accompany us tonight and tomorrow as discussed." He sounds almost cross, though not quite. Father has never been outwardly cross with her in all her living years, which seems miraculous considering all she's put him through, all he's endured for her sake.

Did we, she would like to ask, *discuss it?*

Clara holds her tongue, though it occurs to her with terrific distaste that her father may be no better than Maggie Fox in his way, playing matchmaker. This leaves her feeling small and used, like a child locked outside her own busy playroom. But now is no time to speak of it. She's brushed her hair, tidied herself. What good playing coy now? *Feeling* coy.

Father's palsy, which has never weighed on her before—not on her own behalf—suddenly feels intrusive, an imposition. She wants to run her hands along his bony shoulders, smooth him as if he were a rumpled suit that could be simply and swiftly adjusted, make the tremors stop, make him solid again. The idea that he might one day (sooner than late?) be no longer with her . . . no longer on this earth, in this quiet house where clocks tick gently, forgetfully . . . no longer politely and unconditionally available, is unthinkable. Is he contemplating the same unthinkable thing? Perhaps that's what this is about: finding a harbor, providing for her.

The trouble is . . . well. Clara is the trouble. Unfit, unwilling, unwell. *I am not myself.* The time will come, must come, when she'll be called to act on her own behalf.

Father takes her arm and leads her down the staircase, even as he shakes and nearly lurches forward, unable to control his body's urges. Clara hears in mind Dr. Slotten's recent predictions: *Not fatal in itself, perhaps, but the shaking palsy diminishes quality of life to the extreme, leading to grave discomfort in society. . . .*

But Mr. Holms is little changed, and she at least is soon at ease. Marta has already whisked his bag away to his room and brought tea. He wears the same weathered coat, his long hair as loosely and recklessly bound behind as before. He rises too quickly, sloshing tea over the rim of his cup, placing the saucer on the side table (the doily, it seems, is Marta's innovation; such pleasantries don't occur to Clara or to Father). Father escorts his daughter over as though taking a human sacrifice to the slab, and Sven extends two large paws. "Miss Gill." Taking up the single hand offered him (Clara never thought of her hands as dainty before; quite the contrary), he gives it a brisk shake in both of his, not meeting her eyes. "I'm pleased to make your acquaintance again."

"And I yours," she responds dutifully, sitting so that the men might follow and spare Father standing. "Though I confess"—she glances at her culprit-parent—"some small surprise."

"I hope not too unpleasant a surprise?"

"Not at all." Clara feels suddenly cross at having this moment of social awkwardness imposed upon her. They have nothing but tea to offer a caller. Marta won't have prepared a meal, and it will have slipped Father's mind that Clara isn't welcome at his club. And so dinner will be a to-do, a tangle of polite disagreement; herein the difficulty in friendship between men and women.

She tells them they must hurry and dine without her. "Marta has a dish of my favorite soup waiting, but it's no match for hearty appetites. Fetch me before the exhibition, and we'll walk over together."

To her surprise, Father doesn't object or propose dinner at an inn. He nods easily. It is Clara's delusion, then, that she and Mr. Holms share the basis of a simple friendship of their own. It was only an evening, after all, only a walk. The only friend Clara's suffered in Rochester is Maggie, who presses so.

Alice and the other aunts surface in a sick wave of memory with their many social advisings. What rules they enforced! Tortuous prerequisites for every breezy engagement. And in the end, they were overpainted, ill-fated spinsters huddled together for a public execution, swatting beggars and gossips away from their door. Only merry and oblivious Tilda seems to have survived her fall intact, marrying a navy captain and living quietly and for all intents and purposes alone (he was much at sea) in Hampstead with cats and a little garden, the very fate Alice longed for and lost.

In their last years, Alice and Lucretia ran a boardinghouse together near Oxford. The junior scholars kept them busy with their imbibing and cards, forever trying to sneak women of the wrong sort past their eagle eyes. Through it all, they were unwell. Alice died first, some three years ago, and then Lucretia, after subsisting a year in Tilda's care.

Mr. Holms's manner is, as before, open and unobtrusive, and Clara takes her cues from him, smiling occasionally without fear of reproach, slipping into her own thoughts as suits the flow of conversation.

Father laughs more than usual, asking heartily, "So Greeley has you writing this up?"

"Yes, well, just a short filler piece for color . . . mostly about tonight. They've hired another writer to cover the fair in full, all four days."

"I saw Maggie Fox not long ago," Clara ventures when the conversation wanes, watching his face. "She claims you're now officially off the dead beat."

The big man looks bemused. He smiles with shy exuberance, looking away.

"Isn't that what you newsmen call it?"

"Indeed it is. But I've never heard a lady put it that way."

"Clara is a lady in the noblest aspects only." Father smiles cautiously, almost proudly. "Unafraid to venture forth in word or deed."

Mr. Holms seems to note Clara's discomfort with this spotlight and removes his pocket watch, suggesting that dinner must be at hand if they mean to get back for her and make the exhibit.

"Yes," Clara agrees cheerfully, "and Marta will exact revenge if she has to warm my soup twice."

❧ They're not gone long, but it might be hours. Hearing them on the stoop, Clara peers out to find both men red-faced with walking and brandy. They mount the steps carefully, Mr. Holms supporting Father's arm in that easy hulking way of his. They're like a bear and a quivering stork, and she smiles, letting the curtain fall before they spot her.

Clara has already instructed Marta to answer the bell when they come and explain that Miss Gill has been overcome with headache. "When they set out again, you can turn down the beds and go."

The girl curtsied without a trace of irony.

❧ Clara hears them come in after the festival, quite late if the place of the moon is any indication, and they're gravely silent. There is no laughter, as when the three of them sat together in the parlor, but it's for her sake, she knows, this imposed silence.

She lies listening as Father directs Holms to his room down the hall. She turns and turns in her bed, sleepless—usual enough, though the idea of not being free to rise and pace the house for the sake of miles logged restrains her. Clara feels penned in, the opposite of how she normally feels at home—safe and sheltered, tucked away.

She gets up, sits in her chair for a time watching the setting moon, and then—chilly without a fire banked—coaxes herself to sleep again until the birds begin their dawn clamor.

Light seems permission enough to rise, and she does, preparing tea to take back to her room. Passing Mr. Holms's door, she hears nothing and is ashamed by the picture that comes swiftly to mind unbidden, an image of him in his nightshirt, his long hair disheveled like a child's on his pillow. Lacking brothers, Clara has never seen boy or man at his rest—not even her own father—and it has been some years since she has thought to imagine it. Her thoughts have lingered on no living flesh at all, and to let them now is a guilty pleasure.

At breakfast, inquiries are made about her headache, which is a deal improved, thank you . . . and Clara gets an obligatory report on the event at the hall, which though tastefully and impressively decorated with fall fruits and fauna was heavy on blustery speeches made by leading industrialists. Father is very bad this morning, shaking savagely, and as they take the stairs with him between them, arms linked, Father stops on the steps. The carriage has been brought round and waits humbly at the curb. He seems unreasonably stooped under the weight of a thing he can't deflect or control, and his look is helpless. "Clara, I'm afraid I can't. I must rest. You two must go on without me." He looks quickly at Sven, who seems surprised but not unwilling, and back at his daughter, touching her cheek with his tremulous hand. She takes the bony hand and kisses it to try and stop it shaking, willing herself to stay calm as Father sits on the curb, moving slowly like a figure under water. "I must rest. I won't hear of you begging off, Sven, when you have my able boy here and my good daughter to accompany you."

When Clara whispers that she must stay and care for him, he groans woefully. "Please, daughter, do not fuss over an old man. The grief it gives me to have invited you, Sven, and to leave you thus indisposed. Clara, ease your father's mind and his conscience by proving hospitable in his absence."

The younger man helps him up, ducks under his arm, and grasps his shoulder soundly. "Let's get him inside."

They stand on either side of the bed, self-consciously, as Marta ducks between, tucking and murmuring should she summon Dr. Slotten.

"No, no," Father groans. "I'm as fine as I'm like to be today, and the old sod's due at the end of the week anyway. I'll tell him the sad tale then."

꙳꙳ They ride quietly—without discomfort, now there's no longer a bed between—content to be without conversation as traffic mounts well in advance of the fairgrounds, which is situated on the west side of the river opposite Mount Hope Cemetery.

Clara can't but feel grateful to Mr. Holms. Father's condition makes him vulnerable and most of his friends uncomfortable. When he starts twitching, or otherwise loses control of his limbs and features, most men pretend not to see, or make hearty pronouncements of support before clamorously taking their leave. Mr. Holms seems at home with Father's imperfections, like one long since reconciled to his own.

"Thank you," she says meaningfully, sliding the window shade down some to cut the glare. The sun is high and unseasonably hot, the sky the bald, cloudless blue of September. Already she spots temporary shanties erected by hucksters and peddlers at the roadside.

"But why?" He shrugs sincerely. "Look there." He points to a spiral of dust across a distant field, where a tiny figure leads a hulking one, perhaps an elephant, with rope.

The carriage stops and starts in the traffic, inching forward. Clara hears two coachmen shouting overhead that the concourse is a snarl. No alley, lane, or street leading in is relieved of throngs, with the principal thoroughfare ahead a solid crush of carriages, omnibuses, and hacks. Pedestrians are pouring through the entrance gates from every avenue, making it all the harder to pass.

"I'm told Barnum's menagerie will be there," Sven notes cheerfully, "Together with every mountebank in the state."

The word *menagerie* works on her like a dark spell, and Clara settles back in silence, focusing on the wheels, the soothing mechanism of the carriage, now in motion again.

"I hear you sat for Maggie Fox." It's an impulsive thing to say, and she studies her gloved hands in her lap, instantly sorry to have forced him inward, made him flinch. "I'm sorry to pry. She had no business telling me. Maggie isn't thoughtless as a rule, just young, I think."

"She's old for her years, I rate. They both are. Will they be at the fair today?"

"Last I heard Kate was away at school. Maggie's touring with her mother in Philadelphia—"

"I still miss them," he interrupts in a voice low and dire enough to be frightening. Clara understands at once that they are no longer talking about the Fox sisters. "Not every day anymore, not in my sleep and in my bones, as before, but when I don't expect it."

Mr. Holms does not meet her eye; he rarely does—for her sake, the sake of propriety, to spare them both the need to look away. But Clara understands that this is an invitation, a gift requiring reciprocity. Tit for tat.

"My wife and daughter, I mean," he says after a long silence. "I should have explained. I thought perhaps your father—"

She stares at him mutely, no longer trusting herself. The carriage finally jolts forward, entering the dusty, makeshift city of temporary buildings housing the contents of the fair.

"I'm sorry," she says, but her distance startles both of them.

"Haven't you wondered?" He speaks quickly as if to deflect what he feels coming, his own voice more guarded now. "Whether there's anything to it . . . these spirit rappings? Has Maggie never confided—"

"Perhaps you think Maggie and I share more in the way of confidence than we do, Mr. Holms."

He turns and stares blankly out the carriage window. The view is almost obscured by swirling dust, though here and there. as they inch and jolt forward, they glimpse the fairgrounds, some twenty-five acres enclosed by board fence. Yesterday's paper, Clara thinks, described a wide carriage road leading in past massive temporary exhibition halls, the adjacent fields flaunting all manner of tents for the show masters.

There are so many carriages and hacks clogging the roadway that people have begun to abandon them shy of the official entrance, walking the rest of the way, leaving their drivers to fend for themselves.

She watches her companion's jaw working, his ruddy face outright red, and feels chastened but not sorry. She won't be employed to ends not acknowledged. "Forgive me if I've given offense," she says. "I'm sorry for your loss, and sorrier still that I have no insights to share. I lost my mother when I was too young to know the difference. I suppose when Father dies I'll understand how you or any thinking person who has suffered might be . . . susceptible."

"Then you think it's a hoax."

"I'm grateful, Mr. Holms, that you would solicit my thoughts with such attention. Yes," she says. "I do. What I don't know is how willing a hoax. Maggie is my friend, and little more than a child, but she isn't the ringleader, as we know."

He nods seriously as the carriage lurches to a stop. At this distance, the fair resembles recent engravings and copious descriptions of the new temporary settlements springing up throughout California.

He offers his hand as the driver sets out the step for them. The curb is thronged with people, more people than Clara has ever seen, even in the heart of London on market day. Everything in her revolts against leaving the safety of the carriage, but Sven Holms's sympathetic eyes entreat her, directly for the first time, and she takes his hand and steps down into the dusty fray.

She resists the childish urge to close her eyes as they weave among the multitudes. The people move and breathe as one body, vast and implacable, and when Sven leads her off the main drag, ducking into Floral Hall, she's both relieved and redazzled. The air inside is thick with smells and sounds and colors, a fantasy of fragrance and color.

"One of their own relations, their sister-in-law, I think, has spoken against them," he says as he leads her to the unnatural shade of a grotesque artificial oak. This hall centerpiece is decked out like a Christmas tree with sculpted squirrels and birds and rises majestic from a pyramid of false rock, its branches strung with fruit baskets. It seems absurd somehow, illusory, like the people who flow forward in stages to remark upon it. All this makes Clara dizzy if she doesn't close her eyes from time to time. "Did you know that? Mrs. Culver claims Kate told her how it's done. By cracking their toe joints."

"I read the piece in the *Democrat*," Clara responds. She opens her eyes to find him watching her intently. "She's a distant relation—the sister-in-law of their sister-in-law, I think, and a bit spiteful. That argument died down, as did the kneecap theory posed by the physicians. Our rappers resurface again and again because they have a willing audience. Did you know that doctors and lawyers in Buffalo and elsewhere were consulting the spirits before they proposed remedies? It's no wonder community leaders were concerned. It's one thing to promote a parlor game and another to render otherwise sane men feebleminded. I don't blame Maggie or her sisters for their antics. They're supplying a demand and have secured a rather novel way of making a living for themselves. I blame those too credulous to resist taking them literally. Those threatened to their core by it are no better, no more rational."

"But has Maggie denied these claims to you? I find her and Kate, and their elder sister especially, elusive at best."

"So that's why you went to one of her séances? Leah must certainly be wise to the tricks of your trade by now."

"I was sincere. They give you no choice but to judge as others have, from firsthand experience. It's their great talent, this apparent openness, this easy confidence. It's the source of their success, I think. They never flinch from investigation, and it makes them appear sincere."

"Leah is demanding legal recourse over the kneecap business. She's become a fearsome opponent, I think, but an impressive woman all the same."

"In an age of fearsome, impressive women." He smiles. "Were you there in Seneca Falls?"

She shakes her head, letting him intuit from this what he will. *Too damaged too private too tired I will commit to nothing and lose nothing.* "And were your expectations for the séance met," she persists, "one way or another?"

He lifts a prize rose from a tall vase and for an instant, barely an instant, holds it in front of her face, but it's a fleeting gesture; she can't but wonder did she imagine it.

"No." Replacing the flower, he offers his arm again. "I'm prepared to be wrong. If I knew which was which anymore."

They move on to Dairy Hall with its show of grains, butter, and cheese, stroll out among paddocks of cattle and horses, sheep and swine, the stoutest and prettiest in the state and from Canada, too, all vying for prize medals and premiums.

Clara's boots stick in the mud when they must get round people milling in clusters on wooden boardwalks, but she minds very little if it gets her off the throughway.

The fair displays inventions and needlework, musical instruments and daguerreotypes, all manner of fare for the general public. But most of the hundreds, even thousands of people flowing through are farmers, here to inspect perfect stock specimens and labor-saving tools and machines.

The crowds in this section are dense. Almost as one, and without speaking, she and Mr. Holms move for the exit and off toward the carriage road, shielding their eyes against the noon sun.

"The tents beckon!" he calls into the roar and offers his arm again (how easy it is, taking his arm). They dare the dusty road crossing, migrating toward signs for Barnum's Menagerie, jostling with others along a twisting corridor plastered with ads for freaks and wonders. As the corridor opens out into a broad walkway through the menagerie, Clara finds herself overcome by a familiar rank sweetness—the musk and stench of the wild, stopped up like a smoke in a bottle.

They might be the same creatures from the Tower, captured and displayed anew. Their eyes are just the same. Rangy inmates sleep or turn restlessly on beds of soiled straw. The cages are freshly painted, but the paint on the ornate carts that brought them from the train is peeling in bright scabs. Seized by irrational sorrow, a vast, child-sized sorrow (the child she was: naive and brave and hopeful), Clara picks at the fading paint with gloved fingers, chipping and scraping, and sick to think of them—monkeys, snakes, cheetahs—moving and moving on their toy wheels, on their rail cars, never any nearer freedom, and death their sole release. There are things she *won't* think about, things she mustn't think about, and she waves these thoughts away for Mr. Holms's sake. He is merrily striding toward her, hooking his thumb toward the zebra's cage. "Sorry to fall behind. I'm partial to horses, you know, so those fascinate me. Imagine riding one across the western plains. Like a prince from some distant planet."

"Didn't the natives in the south feel so, watching Cortés and his men ride forth on horses?"

"Unlucky vision," Sven agrees, glancing at her glove, now stained with cerulean dust. He looks quickly away again.

Four large board-and-mesh pens mark the corners of the walkway. As they approach the one nearest the exit, Clara makes out a leather boot kicking aside a spent bone. The worn boots—she sees two now, and her head is roaring like the unseen inmate down the row—might be Will's, and the hem of the frayed work pants.

No. Not Will but a squat, pocked boy with blazing red hair and an arrow tattooed over his nose. The boy's stabbing a bale of hay with terrific violence, but visitors flow past without a glance. The pen's wild inhabitant, whatever it is, reclines in corner shadow, covered in straw and shavings. It might be any creature or none at all, a new and undiscovered species.

"She knew my daughter's nickname," Sven says then, and Clara will turn to him, and means to—but that sluggish animal is up on its broad paws now, and the air seems alive with its stirring. It shakes, stretching luxuriously, and the highlights of its coat match the boy's hair. Clean stripes ripple like inky waves over a sinuous frame as it moves, and she feels her fingers remembering, itching to re-create muscular lines on the page.

"She's swooning, mister—" The boy stabs his pitchfork at the air like a pointer, unconcerned as the big cat paces past him. "Give her your arm—"

Clara isn't swooning: It's just a moment's dizziness, she tells her escort; it's the noise and the crowd. Mr. Holms moves her farther out of the flow, but Clara has trouble convincing her legs to go. She is moved and immovable, and, like a foolish heroine in a foolish romance, turns and takes refuge where refuge waits, resting her forehead on Sven Holms's handy chest.

"What was your daughter's pet name?" she relents at length.

Behind her head, she feels his arm move, his hand rise as if to stroke her bound hair, and Clara stiffens and closes her eyes. He checks his hand, as he must, and says in his strong, smiling accent, "We called her Chicken. 'I have a message from Chicken.' That's what Maggie said."

Disguising his anguish, he taps Clara on the nose with an index finger as if she were the little girl in question. "And would I begrudge my child? Would I send Chicken away—even if only the figment of a spirit rapper's fancy or a calculated lie? You seem very sure. Tell me what I should have done."

Clara opens her eyes and manages to turn in his arms again toward the mesh, but his forearms tighten discreetly. He both extends his grasp and locks her in, as if to ward her back from the cage or protect her from what's inside. Whether the tiger or the fierce boy or something else, she can't say. But thus enclosed, she leans back at her ease. Clara can hear or perhaps feel the safety of Sven Holms's heart beating behind her head, on the other side of her skull. With her eyes closed it might be the pulse of the world, and isn't she a brazen thing—reclining on a giant's chest—absorbed in the dull music of his heartbeat? But the crowd pressing through the aisle seems little concerned. People are watching the tiger pace and turn jaggedly, as on a spring, to pace again, circling in a sort of dance around the redheaded keeper, who must smell delightfully of meat despite his barbed bludgeon. The strange dance makes even the fierce boy at its heart laugh, though he keeps his pitchfork poised, and soon Clara and Sven are laughing, too, along with the crowd and the tattooed boy. Even the tiger seems to be smiling, baring all its deadly teeth.

35 ❦ Camellia

Maggie hasn't had much time to *see* the city of brotherly love—just as she didn't exactly *tour* Albany or Troy—apart from this now familiar view of the street below her parlor window, the sweep of carriages coming and going on cobbles, gentlemen and ladies with animated faces and big hats hurrying past in newly excavated cold-weather layers.

It's peaceful here, at least, between sessions. Lunch is a long way off, but Maggie's as warm and fit as a cat on a sunny sill.

Flat against the wine-red velvet of the hotel chair, her hand looks plump and white and freckled. The late-morning light is unforgiving, exposing every subtle stain and pulled thread in the chair's fabric or the weave of the oriental rug. The rug is massive and far from new but nowhere near threadbare, either. Webb's Union Hotel, like most of the lodgings they've taken, is neither mundane nor grand, quite, but somewhere between, and she's come to think of this "between" as homey.

While Ma chatters with one of the hotel maids, Maggie flips through her book of French exercises, closing her eyes and stabbing her finger to a place on the page like a pin to a map. Her world is vast now and requires more than one language to contain it, and though she is no master of foreign conversation, of *any* conversation, Maggie Fox is learning—through slow trial and error and Leah's irascible promptings—to engage others in her person, in her séance tone, rising and falling like a floating feather, in her hands, rising and floating like falling leaves. She is emphatic without effort, making everyone feel like the sole and most singular person in the world.

She's also learned, with intervention from the mothers and daughters of fine families in their circle, to have perfect posture, and Maggie employs it now, hearing the hushed voice of a young man conversing with Ma outside the door. "I beg your pardon, ma'am"—the face belonging to the voice now peeks into the room—"I fear I've made some mistake. Can you direct me to the rooms where the spiritual manifestations are shown?"

It isn't nasal exactly, the voice, but it isn't altogether manly, either. Mannered, perhaps, but in a way that Maggie hasn't encountered yet.

Her tea break is almost over in any case, but she holds her back effortlessly straight. She keeps right on perusing verbs: *je crois, tu crois, il croit . . . nous semblons, vous semblez, elles semblent . . . je hanterai, tu hanteras, il hantera . . .* though it would not be demure to continue her game of stabbing down her forefinger in random fashion. Her mind skims the columns, drifting off to Paris in the rain—or for that matter Tuscany in the sun. Leah says they will see all such places if only they are patient.

"You have found them, sir," says Ma, "the very same. Won't you give the doorman your coat?"

"No, I think not." He peers in again, as if Maggie might be a two-headed calf, a very pretty one at that.

Now that he's positioned himself in the doorway, in fact, he seems quite unable to wrench his gaze away, which is hardly unusual. Maggie seems to have developed an air about her—that newly perfect posture, perhaps, paired with something unattainably mysterious. She sighs, but too quietly for the caller or Ma to hear, leaning forward in readiness.

Maggie is still peeved that Katie has abandoned her again—whisked away to school at Mr. Greeley's urgings—and that Clara doesn't write or answer Maggie's painstaking letters addressed from the bridal suite at Webb's Union Hotel in Arch Street.

Ma leads him over, a young man with gorgeous curls and delicate features. Like his clothes, he's cut from fine cloth, lordly, you might say, though by no means old enough to be a lord and not very tall. He looks like an anxious deer of some arrogant breed and seems as like to bolt as stay. Later she'll learn that the great Dr. Kane, child of a preeminent Philadelphia family, has lately lost his youngest brother to illness, but just now he's another pretty specimen of the male persuasion here on a lark and too polite to ridicule what might prove rewarding.

"Sir." She gives a grave little nod. "Please sit down."

He obeys, making it clear that he is at her service—that is, *obeying*. Rarely does he take his eyes from Maggie, even when he seems not to be looking and is in fact engaging Ma in copious small talk, which he evidently prefers to the patter of the spirits, who dutifully rap out answers to his halfhearted questions about meager matters of faint concern to the living or the dead.

Their caller either lacks imagination or is genuinely bored, and she won't credit it either way. Maggie yawns theatrically into the back of raised fingers.

"You're quite thronged, I understand? It's been in the papers.

I have several friends who have very much enjoyed your . . . yes, well, I feel lucky to have found you at such a quiet hour."

"This is the quiet time," Ma says, nodding importantly. She is clearly taken by this young man, by his airy charm and soulful eyes. "The evenings are fairly raucous. Within bounds, of course."

"Yes, well." He reaches for Ma's hand and kisses it with high gravity, avoiding Maggie's eyes at all costs. "I shall return, then, good ladies, to observe the excitement in the wee hours. I am grateful for your attentions."

⁘ The young gentleman becomes a daily visitor, calling not to consult with the spirits but, as he'll later boast to his inner circle, to see "the fair young priestess of those mysteries."

In time, the stiffness of their conversation wears away. Maggie comes to trust him more, though he little deserves it that she can see. The young doctor is about as genuine as Mr. Barnum's Feejee Mermaid, but his continual presence flatters her. What's more, he sends gifts—books, flowers, sweetmeats—to which Maggie Fox is famously partial, and unfailingly pays the admission fee, never imposing on "friendship." Her attentions are costly, in other words, and his tenacity impressive.

When Ma steps out and the room hums with general conversation, he whispers close to Maggie's ear, leaning suggestively so that propriety obliges her lean away. She has never been breathed on by a man before and favors the sensation rather too well. The doctor seems larger up close, looming, and his smell distracts her. "Excuse me?" Maggie often echoes. "My apologies, sir, but I beg you repeat what you just said."

He takes to calling her "dreamy girl" or "my dreamy girl" and to slipping her scraps of folded paper, affectionate musings, admonishments about the path she is pursuing. *This is no life for you, child. Why aren't you at school?*

During one lively circle, when she feels his eyes on her more fiercely than before—there are a great many men in the room today, far more men than women and all of them young, well-outfitted, and evidently (unacceptably) conscious of some secret between the young medium and the handsome doctor—he hands her a scribbled question: *Were you ever in love?*

Leah would nip this sort of thing in the bud, but Ma is less reliable; she doesn't notice all she should, which sometimes works to the girls' advantage and sometimes not.

Maggie blushes, dashing off her reply, *Ask the spirits*, which she slides under the table in ungainly fashion.

His fingers feel hot, and he reads hungrily, looking up with a furtive smile.

❖❖ When Dr. Kane is away on business, as he often is, he makes a point of remaining present.

Ma hoards one letter from New York until teatime and then reads aloud with a preposterous Cheshire grin, plucking a furred something from the folds of her skirts: "'I could not resist the temptation,'" she reads, "'of sending the accompanying little trifle of ermine, for Miss Margaretta's throat. As I know you to be carefully fastidious as to form, permit me to place it in your hands.'"

How funny, Maggie thinks, inspecting the creature's dead glass eye. Perhaps Clara will draw it.

With the trifles, however, come the sermons. He is a preacher, Maggie jokes to those who know them both. Those who know Dr. Kane well nod; those who know *her* shake their heads gravely.

Returned to Philadelphia, he often attends her twice a day, sometimes thrice, bearing sweetmeats and scraps of poetry penned by his own hand:

A Prophecy
Now the long day's work is o'er,
Fold thine arms across thy breast;
Weary! Weary is the life
By cold deceit oppressed.

Thee shall harrowing care and sorrow
Fret, while journeying to the tomb . . .

For Maggie, this kind concern invokes not gratitude but a crush of unreality. She feels herself playacting at being a woman, pledging something more and more resembling love even as her days resemble one another, blurring past in reckless fashion.

Her duties at the "the spiritual rooms" keep her well-occupied, and he's begun to remark on her self-command and restraint. "You are very coy, Maggie Fox," he says one day. "A curious study."

For a moment, then, she feels herself open out. But reproof lives behind the doctor's ardor. There is a chill under his hot looks always, and beyond his fascination, confusion. "I have learned, Lish"—what he has bade her call him—"this restraint from being continually in the presence of people uncongenial to me. I've schooled myself to reticence . . . but only *just*. Does that explain your 'curious study'?"

He nods urgently. "Yes, and I grant we're more alike than you know, Mag, despite the difference in our stations."

Stung for no good reason, she lifts a hand to waylay him, but he hurries on. His absolute lack of regard for her dignity is refreshing.

"We're the same, Mag—two adventurers in search of undiscovered lands. I know there's an open sea beyond the arctic barrier, a place with mild skies and myriad birds and fishes. I *know* my *way* to it, through Smith Sound, and I'll lead another Grinnell expedition and pursue this belief, against opposition, because it is *worth* believing in.

"But you . . . you delude people who crave their lost loved ones in the spirit world. Perhaps you relieve some of them, but is the lie for their betterment?" He lifts her chin, his eyes bright and zealous. "One quest leads to greatness—the other despair."

❧❧ Maggie is induced to take carriage rides with the great Dr. Kane regularly, always in the company of Ma or another matron, and in this way she manages to take in some of the beauty of this grand old city and the surrounding countryside, though speeches and sermons are the price.

On one occasion, she joins a party, without her mother, to Laurel Hill Cemetery. When Lish helps her down from the carriage, she stumbles at the entrance gate, which troubles him unduly. Wry Maggie begs, "And *who* is the superstitious child now?"

Her escort looks round the sweeping, beautifully tended grounds as if the dead are listening (and perhaps they are) and says, "I wouldn't wish you enter other than in the perfect grace of my good intentions."

Puzzled, she lets him lead her discreetly away from the others to the Kane family vault. There is nothing so beautiful, she thinks, as a graveyard in the mist. The sun never broke through today, and the air is crisp and damp. When he raps his knuckles on an iron door and begins reciting Longfellow's "Psalm of Life," this intensifies Maggie's sense that they are only playacting. She leans back against a damp beech, smiling faintly.

Lish paces, meanwhile, and the tomb hunkers. He speaks with deep feeling of Willie, the young brother who suffered much in the delirium of his last illness, and then turns and strides toward her with alarming energy. Crows are squabbling or harassing a hawk in a tree nearby as Dr. Kane takes her sharply by the shoulders. The bark sits hard against her back, and Maggie hopes the damp won't stain her silks. She blinks up at him, lips parted in perplexity. *You are a stranger*, she thinks, *and I am asleep.*

"You've been a godsend to me, Mag," he murmurs. "Please kiss me."

But he little gives her the chance, kissing her first with thin, wet lips—*the prince waking the sleeping girl*—and roving in her fallen hair with his hands and trembling in alarming fashion.

Then he holds her back by the shoulders. He looks at her intently, waving one elegant hand. "Here will be your last resting place, Mag. At my side."

She stifles a shudder, imagining the worthy Philadelphia dead rising up in every tomb to applaud his dark proposal. He seems willing enough to speak so when no one else is listening, but in mixed company, he's polite as a doorman. Will he say as much to his mother and siblings?

More and more, Maggie feels the people in his life judging her. She's a curiosity to them, mildly interesting at best. It pains her when ladies of his acquaintance come to her sittings with their high eyebrows and learned language. They might be speaking French for all Maggie knows—for all the words echo and bounce and collide in her brain. The *rap rap rap* of ghosts is far easier to decode than the patter of learned ladies.

But Lish is kind to Ma, expressing often his regret that his family is in the bustle of a removal; otherwise the ladies would certainly be invited to visit his father's house.

When they ride out with Dr. and Mrs. Patterson one day to inspect Renssalaer, the Kane country seat, Lish's attentions attract the notice of Mrs. Patterson. When he steps from the carriage, she whispers, "Miss Fox, Elisha loves you. I can see that."

꧁꧂ "Maggie, are you able to feel how sacred, how binding is a promise of this kind? It is a solemn surrender of heart, soul, and life to another."

Here is the caliber of question being put to her. Suddenly.

Almost daily, Lish proposes anew without proposing outright. He seems determined to secure her at no expense to himself, and Maggie can only gaze back at him through a fog of confusion. When did things come to this?

"Think, Maggie, and make no promise rashly. Once made, it must be inviolable. You must promise everything—your whole heart— and sacrifice all other anticipations and prospects."

Extraordinary idea!

But then Ma rings the tea bell, or another carriage full of callers arrives, with Maggie summoned to take her place at table, and the topic is postponed.

Just before she's scheduled to travel back to New York and on to

D.C., Lish offers three rings for her selection. In a panic of modesty, she puts aside a splendid diamond set in pearls in favor of a humbler model set in black enamel. "You will wear this as your engagement ring?" he asks, seemingly in earnest, though it can't be so.

Maggie looks at him with a puzzled, almost pained expression, though she won't name the feeling behind it. It is *no* feeling, really, or none that has tried her before, and she nods vaguely. She smiles vaguely.

He departs before she and Ma do, and books, music, and flowers arrive daily in his absence. On Maggie's last night in town, her surprise is a camellia accompanied by a caution in his ornate script: *Like you, it must not be breathed upon.*

Maggie feels a strange desire to repudiate this, and she slowly, methodically pulls the flower apart petal by petal as if it were a common daisy. *I love him.* As if she were a common farm girl from Hydesville, New York. *I love him not.*

But you are, she thinks, blithely plucking and flinging the velvet petals, *a common farm girl from Hydesville.*

Ma enters, racing toward travesty, and grips her daughter's wrist. "Thoughtless child." With a scornful shake of the head, she collects the vagrant petals, trying to piece them together again. "To have so much and deserve so little."

Maggie sighs. "Oh, but I am weary of Philadelphia."

36 ❧❧ A Singular Status

Leah gave up the cottage on Troupe Street, Maggie explains, when she let the townhouse on West 26th.

It's odd, Clara thinks, to be visiting Maggie in a hotel in Rochester, odd to think of her homeless here at home. But the girl claims to be a "citizen of the world" now, or at least the state of New York. The constant traffic of public séances wherever they go makes hotel life more convenient. She's well-accustomed to it, she says, and, unlike Katie and Ma, actually prefers it.

"I don't mind hotels a bit, but wait till you see the place in Manhattan. You need only step out the door to know it's a neighborhood of first-rate excellence, and the Astors aren't the only millionaires in town, I'll have you know. Everyone's building there. I can hardly believe it when I wake and look out and there's Madison Square Park, all green and lovely. Sometimes we have carriages filed up and down the block when we're home, and we have two maids, a cook, and a housemaid—though no coachman. Leah won't spring for a carriage. You must come visit *very soon*, Clara. I'm weary of your neglect."

Though Leah has married for the third time—to Calvin Brown, their old family friend—Clara thinks the "girls" have something on married women, those hundreds and thousands of young wives and mothers who rise to the ritual of planning nursery, luncheon, and dinner menus before sending them down to the cook; tending to toilet by noon; and turning to letters and tradesmen and dressmakers.

"No one minds a bit," Maggie confides, "or not much if lady friends step out at night unattended for a rump steak with oyster sauce and a brandy and water."

In the London of Clara's youth, gently bred spinsters without support were shipped off to care for needy relations. That, or they advertised as governesses, teaching French and music to spoiled children. They were to be of good cheer, though these works found no acknowledgment in *this* world; a spinster's hope was in the next.

The sort of impoverished women that Alice threatened Clara *could* be if she didn't practice her French or her piano or turn her thoughts toward marriage, hired out as dishwashers in low foul-smelling cellars without windows where meat hung everywhere and people urinated in public. They could also bring home piecework for a pittance, labor over matchbooks and umbrella frames, or take to the street as crossing sweepers. These, like the wretched women who chased omnibuses to sell newspapers, were frequently struck dead by speeding carriages.

Alice reveled in such tales. There were the wretched girls in Clerkenwell who frosted artificial flowers with glass—*objets* sold by the score in West End shops—and earned galloping consumption for their trouble. There were the prostitutes in the Strand and Haymarket, of course, scurrying like vermin in broad daylight with their "captures," retreating to rooms with beds to let.

A far cry from the single professional lives of Margaretta and Kate Fox.

"Oh, but I'm chattering like a magpie." Maggie smiles at this quaint joke between them. She hasn't been requesting birds of late. Too busy, Clara supposes. "What have you been about, Miss Gill?"

Clara makes the mistake of mentioning the state fair—so little else of note has occurred in her life since last they corresponded— and her surprising outing with Sven Holms. It takes an effort to turn Maggie away from the topic once she has her teeth in, and Clara regrets her error at once.

Finally Maggie relents with a bit of one-upmanship, "Well, *I've* met a new friend."

"Hasn't she, though," Katie chimes in from the floor, where she's been lying all this time, kicking her legs back, sorting a jarful of buttons. It seems to Clara a strangely domestic chore, given their itinerant lifestyle. Maggie hushes her affectionately. Will either of these marry, Clara wonders, and what will they make of marriage if they do? What would Clara have made of it had Alice or Artemus managed to impose it? The thought grates, and Clara waves an impatient hand. "Well?"

"I made his acquaintance in Philadelphia." Maggie leans closer in confidence. "All manner of eligible men came to see me rap at Webb's Hotel, and I daresay to flirt a little, but none like this. No one so steadfast. I need your advice, Miss Gill. I've waited and waited to speak with you about it. It's grown quite pressing."

"Honestly, Maggie. *Clara.*"

"Miss Clara, you are the only one we know well with a trace of breeding about you. . . ." She lifts her plump little hand to ward Clara off. "Maybe it's that English air of yours, but all the same, you have me fooled. Now, listen. He's one of *those* men. Quite a catch, I'm told." Whenever Kate or Lizzie is around, Maggie assumes the role of elder sister with a secret—beneficent and whispering.

"He's at least as famous as she is, and richer," Kate puts in, sliding buttons impatiently into piles.

"Rich and reeking of old family," calls Leah from the entrance hall.

Mrs. Brown has an uncanny way of entering and exiting without warning or segue, her voice full of ice and gravel. It's unnerving, and clearly Maggie didn't intend this news for Leah's ears. "Not to mention full of himself and his family and his grandness, too," Leah complains, stepping in. "He's nothing but trouble, and I won't abide him. He's using you, Margaretta. We've talked about such men. We have to take care in our trade. There is no recovering one's reputation. You hear me. I know you do."

The room has grown awkward and heavy. It's the sort of underwater oppression Alice imposed, and Clara half-expects Leah to turn that gray and pitiless gaze on her. There *is* something of Alice in Leah, a ruthless arrogance that Clara cannot trust, but she seems to have her sisters' best interests at heart. Those who feel and say otherwise would not say so to Leah's face.

"Listen." Maggie lowers her voice, turning away from her older sister. She often does, Clara thinks, except when it comes to matters of livelihood. "He says he loves me and that I'm leading a life of deceit. Listen," she says again, digressing, "you'll stay the night, won't you, Clara? Stay a week if you like. We have the bridal suite all to ourselves and another besides."

"I thank you, no. I should get home to Father."

"Mr. Holms mentioned that Mr. Gill was poorly when last I saw him in the city. I'm so sorry for you, Clara."

"We get on." In truth, Dr. Slotten dropped in earlier that morning, fearful that Father's general state of malaise and weakness had advanced to acute pneumonia. For weeks now, Father has been weak and disinclined to do the things he once took for granted. He rarely eats at his club or pays calls anymore. Even their walks, which Clara took to again with enthusiasm after that November night when she attended Maggie's event at Corinthian Hall, have dwindled to nothing. Walking is just too taxing for him, though he sometimes sits by her in the garden while she weeds absently and coaxes new life from the earth, delighting in bees and frost and the mockingbird's taunts. In a funny way, Clara—without husband and respectability—now lives a humbler version of the life her aunts would have wished for her back when she was still an inoffensive child. It's an imperfect life, but vastly improved, and for that Clara credits Maggie. Good, transparent Maggie Fox, who keeps the world guessing.

"Well, we're here until Friday if you can come stay another night. The walls are so thick, you won't hear a thing. Not like some hotels we've worked." She blushes, aware of how it sounds. "The Barnum was a regular sideshow. Maybe you'll even come to a séance. You're one of the few who hasn't cast in her lot. I'd welcome your verdict."

Maggie brushes her hair with long, slow strokes. The parlor has been roped off and closed to the public for their teatime, the endless round of sittings and séances paused. Somehow their constant court of strangers, Maggie's glib musings about technique and the ins and outs of performing, her harrowing tales of "promiscuous visitations" and violence—all of this seems aligned with another, odder character, not the breezy young friend seemingly so incapable of duplicity. *Maggie can't even keep a secret*, Clara thinks. *How would she deceive multitudes?*

"I'll hold my singular status," Clara says. "For the time being."

37 ❧❦ The Unlocked Box

They bury Father in Mount Hope Cemetery on a rainy Monday. Maggie's challenge, her dark eyes, flash before Clara with the minister's rote words. *Though I travel through the valley of death, I fear no evil.*

But I am afraid, she thinks as they stand in a barricade of black—black umbrellas, the cemetery trees damp and black and muscular—*that he will speak. . . .*

Afraid that he won't.

But it isn't Father she means, and in any case, her father is the last person she wants to hear from right now. His silences have damned her enough.

This is real death, Clara thinks with a vehemence that makes her afraid to look over at Maggie and her sisters and Mrs. Fox, who were still in town when Father succumbed to pneumonia.

Real death is not a parlor game but a flat heaviness that weights the limbs, that makes every step a struggle, every breath reproach and violation. It is mold on the morning firewood and a chill that won't go even when the hearth is banked to roaring, even when the familiar quilt is wound full round weighted legs and feet on a stool like a winding sheet. It is the bitterness of herbs in an undertaker's parlor and damp shoes by a hole in the ground and the absence of sunlight and emptiness beyond reckoning. Would they comfort her, these Valkyries among the gracious Posts, and Father's university friends, and yes, even the Widow Bray, who looked meaningfully into Clara's eyes by the gate, wordlessly gripping her two hands? One face *is* missing, that of Mr. Holms, but Clara will not let herself lament the living with the dead.

In her grief and abandonment Clara half-believes that Maggie and her sisters are responsible. They have "chosen" Father, leaving Clara Gill alone in the world just when she had begun to suspect she could inhabit it again. After what she found last night in Father's things, will she ever be duped that way again? She will not.

Father lay all night with the candle burning in the undertaker's parlor, awaiting the sexton at his work and a cold morning's grave. And Clara wandered through his private space, the room that doubled as both bedchamber and library and one she rarely entered except to set a tray and teapot on the table by his sickbed. She drifted in and poked at dusty bookshelves and stuffed birds and flipped unmindfully through trunks of clothing and letters and, at length, found the key with the red ribbon. She unlocked the drawer, Pandora's box, opened it, and realized with something like bitterness that Father must have known he wouldn't wake. He had left the key in the lock for her to discover—a key never there before.

Would she choose now to listen to Father rapping on a spirit table, trying to smooth things over, to justify and apologize for what Clara found in that drawer, to pity and excuse the fresh grief it caused, which eclipsed even her sorrow at her own father's passing? This is most unforgivable of all, worse than his clumsy efforts to shelter and protect her!

What use apology when among Father's musty papers—largely a stack of letters from Clara's mother, chatty missives of no particular import beyond their tender playfulness and easy grace of phrase, beyond the fact of who had written them—was an unopened envelope labeled "For Clara upon my death."

It was not from Clara's mother.

When Alice died, she divided her modest wealth, profits from her boardinghouse mainly, between her sisters. But for Clara she left a letter, one never spoken of, never acknowledged in any way. Father informed Clara when his sister-in-law died, but they had little to say because the very word *Alice* roused a chill between them. Clara understands. Of course she does. He wanted to shelter her. But in making her unworthy of the truth, he robbed her of feelings she should have felt years ago. What she should be done with, she must suffer, together with rage at her father, and so, guilt.

Above all, she blames him now for letting anger be the last thing she felt for him. She slit open the letter addressed to her with an almost paralyzing certainty. Her fingers fumbled, and her thoughts bent against her like a strong wind. But she opened it.

Clara,

As predicted, you will find me at the end of life suffering a certain dejection and small torment over my treatment of my only niece, my sister's daughter—and grief at the girl's willful failure to secure my affections. But here I entrust to you the contents of the letter written by your unfortunate paramour. His words were few and strange, easy enough to recall even this far on. I doubt you have cause for solace so long after the fact, and your father will bristle at my meddling, but it can only soothe me on my journey to be rid of them, so I bequeath to you these dying words of William Cross:

You are my world in little.

38 ❧❧ The Cords of Love

When he isn't on hand, the Preacher is little in Maggie's thoughts. Accordingly, he keeps up a steady stream of letters and gifts to remain where he is not.

She's hardly reinstalled at West 26th Street, feeling hollow and somehow chastened after Mr. Gill's rainy Rochester ceremony, when the barrage resumes.

Does darling Maggie fail to answer, writes Elisha, because she's forgotten her friend, or does her new life so consume her that she can imagine no other? Dr. Kane is now en route to Baltimore to lecture before three thousand people and then on to see the great men of Washington. Then—there is no rest; he must toil for his enterprise—to explain the arctic expedition to the scientific bodies.

When Maggie doesn't reply, he writes to Kate. When they aren't rapping for the public, the sisters spend a deal of time comparing letters. Kate is more protective of his feelings than Maggie is, and Lish feels no hesitation in entreating her: "Kate, why did you let that fickle, wicked Maggie forget me?"

News of a dinner given at the Revere House by Mayor Seaver

of Boston for "a few select friends, among them Dr. Kane" follows, and Maggie is struck by how unimpressed she manages to be.

Kate waves about the bill of fare that Lish has taken the liberty of including, reading his words aloud with gusto: "Here is a specimen of a good dinner to feast the eyes of my friend"—Kate pauses, pleased to exclude Maggie for the sake of controversy—"*Miss Kate. The service was of gold and glass.*"

"Braggart," Maggie says.

Kate balls up the parchment, laughing, and stuffs it into her bodice. Soon they're squabbling and beating one another with cushions, all delicious fun until Leah and Calvin walk in, stiff in their opera clothes. They married out of practical imperative while Calvin was gravely ill—"He wants to bequeath me his name," as Leah, that great romantic, put it—but they're as tedious now as any proper match.

"Well, then," Cal teases, "aren't we thick as thieves."

Maggie sprawls shamelessly on the cushions on the floor, but Kate clambers to attention, smoothing her dress and slouching so as not to draw attention to the incriminating lump in her bodice.

Calvin, who has never favored one side over the other even for his wife's sake, hangs his overcoat and heads to another room.

"What are you two about?" demands Leah.

"About?" There is no more impenetrable innocence than Kate's. Stalemate. Leah can only sigh.

The letters arrive daily, often more than one.

When I think of you in your humble calling and of myself with my toiling vanities and cares, I feel only that I am about to leave you, and feeling this, how very much I love you. I am a fool for this, yet I know you have some good reason for not writing. Keep this from Mrs. Brown, our own One-Hundred-Eyed Argus. Do you ever walk out alone?

But leave he doesn't, instead lamenting Maggie's life, "dreary with the mysterious workings of the spirit world," and perhaps it is—just so. But it's her own dreariness, not to be disparaged except by her.

You must try, Maggie, to do your duty in this world, be true to your loves and yourself. You have a good heart, but practice in anything hardens us. A time will come when you will be a hardened woman, gathering around you victims of delusion. I would put forth my arm to save you, I would be to you and your sister that which, from a gentleman in my position, you will never have again.

She must also send a letter to Girard Street at Philadelphia stating how her hours are filled, the names and character and appearance of the servants, and word of when she will see him. He'll arrive in New York on Friday and, with permission, will call Saturday evening.

Or does she know Satler's Cosmoramas in Broadway near 12th Street, on the right-hand side going down? If she and Kate will walk past at exactly four o'clock on Saturday afternoon, he'll be there. The cosmoramas are a sort of picture gallery, he notes (as if she were a child), visited by the first and best ladies. If Maggie and Kate do not like to walk past, they might proceed into the picture room and amuse themselves looking at the paintings until he arrives. He'll be there at four precisely and wait until half-past.

Maggie does see him once or twice in passing, though not in the covert manner he suggests; they are never alone, nor does he reveal "his hand" in mixed company.

It's almost a relief, then, to board the train for Washington with Ma, to sit quietly by the sooty window—Maggie always takes the window—and to watch the world chug past, laundry blowing on lines, horses in the fields, the big towns rising and sinking from view in a blur of waving grass and mud roads and general stores and wind-weathered stations.

Governor Tallmadge procured lodgings for them at a Mrs. Sullivan's house, where many officers are known to stay. Maggie has no doubt that Lish knows this fact and is appalled by her profession:

How does Washington come on? Many beaux? Many believers? Many friends? Answer these questions, wicked Maggie!

How disgusting is this life, to be discussed in the papers. I need not be so proud, for I am no better than the rappers. When I think of you, wasting your time and youth and conscience for a few paltry dollars, and think of the crowds who come nightly to hear the wild stories of the frozen north, I sometimes feel that we are not so far removed after all. My brain and your body are each the sources of attraction, and I confess that there is not so much difference.

The more proper Maggie is in restraint, the more ardent are his advances. When she relents, even a little—confessing affection born of his persistence—Lish rebukes her.

He insists on code names in telegraph messages—"Cousin Peter" or "F. Webster." The meddling world would think it strange that a grave man of science should write thus to a character like her. But where Dr. Kane loves he confides, and where he confides he does not think of caution. Maggie *will* be careful of him and his reputation.

He would rather die than injure hers.

The laces will come to you by express—one, an underhand-kerchief of Honiton, with sleeves to match; the other of French work, for morning wear. Do be careful and dress well about your neck and arms. Tell Kate as soon as I get back to Philadelphia I will send her a real appliqué. My sister got one, and they are a very rich character of lace.

Is it any wonder that I long to look—only to look—at that dear little deceitful mouth of yours?

Kiss Miss Katie for me, and tell her she owes me a letter. She is worth two of you. Bye-bye.—Preacher

Though she reads them with more interest now, Maggie rarely answers Lish's letters. She can't but feel that every word she writes is under study, under siege.

But when news arrives in Washington that her friend has taken ill, she does write, urging "Cousin Peter" to telegraph with news of his health. She is uneasy about him. This very afternoon, in fact, she went out shopping and was so put out that she lost her way and was obliged to ask a lady to direct her. Once safely indoors again, she told General Hamilton that she did not like Washington at all, and the general joked that no young lady could ever lose her way in Washington unless for an *affaire du coeur*. Would Maggie deny this charge?

᪥ Oh, laments the good doctor—but he has forgotten himself, his high calling, and let himself down to love. There is nothing he would not do, in spite of his public duties and the adulation of the world. His thoughts revert constantly to Maggie Fox. At the very dinner table of the president, he thinks of her. But does *she* comprehend him? Not at all. She holds him too cheaply. "You love me, Mag, but not enough. It is not in your nature."

Perhaps, thinks Maggie—with more self-judgment than usual—Lish is right, and their time together will be as a dream once he embarks on his arctic expedition. Perhaps she lacks the depth of affection to be worthy and will end up with only a sad conviction of all she has lost.

Were you a pure, simple-hearted, trusting girl, Maggie, you would love me—not the soft, half-affected milk-and-water love you now profess, but a genuine, confiding affection. I am nothing but a cunning dissembler to you now because you view me with the suspicion that your intercourse with the world—your world—has forced upon you. You flatter yourself that this is penetration, *and that you can read motives and character.*

You do not love. Believe me, Mag, I can tell when it is present, and you do not. I rather like you for this, because if you were entirely artful and selfish you would pretend to love me for the sake of your interests.

Leah's unceasing commands and machinations have made it difficult to remain in the same room, and Maggie's own interests are beginning to emerge, though they do not clamor or assume, any more than Maggie does.

"You're a dear fluttering bird," writes Elisha from his sickbed far away. "But don't you miss the warm kiss of 'Cousin Peter'? That trusted friend and master who leads you to better ways by the cords of love?"

39 ❖❖ The Carriage Ride

Sven Holms has a carriage waiting for her by the curb. "Maggie is busy overseeing plans in your honor," he says, stepping down as the driver lifts Clara's small trunk. "So I volunteered to fetch you home. It's good to see you again, Miss Gill, though I wish at a better time. I'm so sorry I wasn't at the funeral. It was a grief to find the telegram waiting on my return from St. Louis. You received my letter?"

Clara nods, lowering her head. She thanks him sincerely and lets him lift her and her mass of black crepe into the carriage.

"Are you well?" Climbing up across from her, he seems nervous or agitated, though the seeming passes quickly.

"Yes," she admits. "Enough."

"Will you ride for a time?"

When she nods, Sven signals the driver with his knuckles and settles back comfortably, long legs pulled close, his big knees almost touching hers as they roll forward.

Clara has been to this city only once before. It reminds her of London, but only for its boisterous crowds. The idea that any novelty—the arrival of a steamer, a snatched purse, a celebrity sighting—might rivet hundreds and thousands of people in the same moment overwhelms her. A relief, then, to be up in the carriage, set off from the continual flow of coats and cloaks and patterned gowns, whiskers and spectacles, hats and bonnets—from all those bright faces and hurrying feet that make it feel like a gala day. In fact it's a day like any other, a day in Manhattan, and now that she's safely removed, Clara enjoys the kaleidoscopic motion, the flood of sensation.

"Have you spent a deal of time here?" he asks.

Clara admits that she knows the city principally through books and newspaper accounts.

Sven orients her quickly, pointing out St. Paul's and City Hall, the Astor House—all six granite stories of it: "Bigger than any hotel in your London or in Paris, we're told. Over there is Barnum's—and now we'll sit for a time in the traffic. East past the museum is the newspaper district where I work; the laundries and shops of Chatham Street; and beyond that the Bowery with its shows, saloons, and tenements. Far north is Five Points, where the lowest of the low live, hungry and cold in cellars and garrets."

Craving a look at Barnum's fabled American Museum, Clara leans to wipe the steam from Sven's breath off his carriage window. Her nearness seems to embarrass him, which embarrasses her, though she keeps her thoughts on the street outside. It swarms with carriages, mule carts, and people—all creaking and shouting and braying. Someone plays a trumpet, though she can't pick him out in the crowd.

"We bear the blame, I guess."

Clara snaps to, regretting her lack of attention. What possessed her to travel, she wonders, to venture out at a time when she has so little—even less than usual—to offer companions? "'We'?"

"The *Trib*, I mean," Sven explains. "And the *Herald*, the *Sun*, always pointing out the differences: rich and poor; us and them. But it's just steps that separate the two. Lower Broadway, Greenwich Street, Park Place—these were all fashionable blocks not long ago. Now they belong to the tradesmen and tourists . . . the rich just keep fleeing by degrees above Bleeker. The faubourgs are all in Madison Square now."

"Yes," Clara agrees. "Maggie takes great pride in her family's residence there."

"You'll be uptown soon enough," he jests, "but Broadway's better than a hurly-burly village fair, full of showmen. You have minstrels and giants here, quack doctors and tooth-pullers, wild-animal trainers and tiny men and gypsies. But nothing tops Barnum for sheer nerve. Look at all those flags, and he put in the first Drummond lights in the city. Every night the limelight shines from the Battery to Niblo's, and there's a band on the balcony. He'll have wagons rolling all over town plastered with advertisements. You won't have seen anything like it."

Clara never has, she thinks, taking in the vast transparencies depicting countless species of animals (many of them life-sized) that decorate the building.

They sit quietly for a time and not uncomfortably until Mr. Holms says, "Your father confided in me in his last weeks. We exchanged several letters, and I found I had a great many . . . questions."

These words seem overburdened, suggestive, and Clara feels defiant in the face of them. "I'm sure I don't wish to know"—her voice cracks, betraying her brittleness—"what Father had to confide."

He nods but seems compelled to go on.

Clara adds briskly, "And if my father's confidences concern me, I'm sure I don't wish to share them."

There is no more to say. Mr. Holms is henceforth silent, and she won't look at him again, staring instead out the sooty carriage window at the urban blur, which blooms green as they approach Madison Square with its spacious row houses and mansions.

He deposits her grimly on the Fox doorstep, lifts his hat, and heads gallantly away again.

Perhaps now, she thinks, *you've had your fill.*

40 ❖ Easy to Love a Ghost

After a brisk tour of the new townhouse that would dazzle if Clara weren't so weary and detached, the restless Maggie calls for their warm-weather gear again and leads Clara—who drags her mourning crepe like broken wings—outdoors for sightseeing.

"It will do your spirit good," Maggie insists on the marble steps.

A very pale Calvin strides to the curb to hire a carriage, standing by to help them up. He blows up a kiss as they roll away, a hulking, cheerful man, credulous and loving, it would seem. As he recedes from view, Maggie confirms the rumor that he married Leah on his deathbed. "A false alarm, thankfully, for Cal's nearly *always* on his deathbed."

Clara can't long forget the crater Father has left in her life.

"We love him all the more for it, every minute, and he really shouldn't be out of bed today."

Clara sits back without comment, prepared to wait for whatever her troubled friend will say or confess.

They *clip-clop* along for a time, passing sumptuous private residences and grand hotels, stopping just shy of what could be an

Italian Renaissance palazzo, five stories high and cut of brilliant white marble.

Carriages clog the curb ahead, and the building's facade boasts huge cast-iron pilasters and plate-glass windows. A brass-buttoned porter in blue races out to assist them down, escorting them in the shade of a parasol to the entrance. A shifting mass of smartly dressed women, all ribbons and silk and the latest Paris fashions, flows past on either side, but not *only* women, Clara notes. Plenty of men promenade up and down Broadway, from conservatively dressed businessmen to dandies with curling mustaches, patent leather shoes, and pegged trouser legs.

"At night," Maggie whispers as they glide inside, "it's like magic here with the streetlamps and windows blazing and all the carriages and omnibuses with their colored lamps . . . a wide river made of light."

The inside is airy and opulent with a domed skylight overhead and a large central court. Clara has never seen a shop like this, even in London or Philadelphia—with wares displayed on polished mahogany counters and shelf after marble shelf of goods, each neatly and conveniently tagged with a price.

"There's no bargaining here," Maggie cautions, lifting an Italian glass paperweight, rotating it gingerly in her gloved hand. "Too vulgar," she adds under her breath, wrinkling her nose. She sets the treasure down again.

"Well, I thank you for sparing me certain humiliation." Bending back her head for a view of the skylight, Clara blinks into the white glare as a seagull coasts over, backlit and brash, a small assurance in this crowd of pawing, chattering consumers. There are clerks everywhere, bending and measuring, nodding smiling heads.

Clara catches her breath and moves closer to Maggie, her anchor. "And how is your Dr. Kane?"

Maggie lights up at that, slapping down a much-handled fur muff. "This is what I've been dying to speak with you about. You'll meet him tonight . . . if he's well enough and if we can get away without Leah latching on (Lish calls her Argus for all her many eyes). He and Mr. and Mrs. Greeley have proposed a carriage ride to show you some of the city. I've invited Mr. Holms, too . . . I hope you don't mind . . . he's of that circle. I know it's a breach, but you're well enough now? To have society?"

"Have I a choice?" Clara smiles. What she doesn't do is mention her awkward conversation with Mr. Holms in the carriage or the subsequent heaviness that has lined up with all the other weighty things inside her ribs—so many crowding there, like mindless cattle against a gate, like shoppers swarming Stewart's Emporium.

"I daresay," Maggie dares. "You and he seem more alike than ever. Even in your relative seclusion."

"I appreciate your earnestness, Maggie, but I won't perish if you fail to find me a husband. Father left me well-provided-for." This is not strictly true, of course, but no matter.

"Then you'll stay in Rochester?"

"I may. But I have a tolerable aunt left in London. With grand-children in need of a tutor."

Maggie sighs wretchedly, moving toward a shelf of crystal. "A governess! And for family? Oh, Clara, don't!" she blurts. "Won't you *ever* marry? What's so terrible in that?"

"It's the mind's way," Clara puts in almost thoughtlessly, staring with Maggie at a glittering tray of tiny crystal figures, nymphs and unicorns. (The world in little has grown large of late. Clara feels herself a flooded landscape, and she will drown in her own excess if she doesn't open the dam from time to time.) "To hold fast some-times to what it shouldn't. To settle into a kind of loop." *A noose,* she thinks. "I loved someone once—"

"I know."

"*How* do you know, Maggie?" Feeling suddenly unwell in the bright light among all these strangers, Clara takes Maggie's arm and leads her lightly toward the exit. Maggie goes willingly enough but will not answer, not yet. Her face is closed and thoughtful, and Clara wonders whether that is the face she wears for her séances, an *I have gone inward* face. It's already tedious again: Maggie knowing everything and understanding nothing. Such a long time has passed.

Remarkably, there is no porter at the ready on the curb, and Maggie insists they forsake a carriage and brave the omnibus in-stead. "I have one more place to show you," she says. "Somewhere I know you'll like."

They board at the next block, and the men make way for them. As the omnibus haltingly passes beyond the settled fringes of the city, approaching what Maggie calls "the only building in town that puts Stewart's to shame," Clara prompts, "*How* do you know?"

"Everyone likes the Crystal Palace—"

"How do you *know*," Clara adds in a voice low and dark, "that I loved someone once?"

Maggie shrugs. "I just do."

Clara regards her friend with a sigh and something like sus-pense. Perhaps it will plague her always—this past life that now seems to belong to someone else, someone with a heart and a con-science. Perhaps it will outlast even the illusion that she might be-come an ordinary middle-class American émigré and tend her garden and draw her pictures and possibly recover her courage and play the clavichord and fall in love and have babies. It's too late for most of this, surely, but the garden and the pictures she has tasted and would keep. "Do you, Maggie? I almost believe you. And now I will ask you to let the subject lie."

For some blocks now they have been bouncing past coffee-houses and grog shops and saloons, not to mention peep-show postings for live alligators, model-artists, and three-headed calves. At 40th Street, the conductor cries, "Crystal Palace!" and they jerk to a stop on a crossing.

"Did you know there was a field here once, right here?" Maggie asks, stepping down with Clara at her heels. "I read about it—and did you know that General Washington's troops were chased across that field by jeering redcoats?"

"Jeering, were they? Is this when I fall to my knees and surrender for the king?"

"No, Miss Clara, but do feast your eyes."

Clara obeys, taking in what must be many thousands of tons of iron supporting tens of thousands of panes of enameled glass culminating in a massive dome.

They pay their admission and roam without speaking past shimmering fountains and glaring clusters of gaslights. Illuminated are all the wonders of the age, from guns and clocks and scientific instruments to fire engines and Fresnel lighthouse lenses. It's a humbling experience and leaves Clara emptied out. By the time they take refuge in a tea shop hours later, her lower back is a knot and her heels are blistered. To know that throughout this tireless city, machinery is pumping water, sewing buttons, setting type, finishing wood, refining sugar, rinsing gold, and churning out ice cream is no consolation at all.

When the tea arrives, she and Maggie toast, gingerly clinking china cups. Tea has never seemed so refreshing, and Clara sips hers slowly, closing her eyes. When she opens them again, Maggie's gaze, liquid-brown and bright, full of shifting reflections, is intent on her. Clara wishes she could pull down the window sashes, or better yet roll into a ball like a hedgehog, spikes bared.

"I told you that Mr. Holms came to one of my séances in Rochester," Maggie begins, pausing to read her companion's expression. "What I didn't say was that your father came as well. You never thought he would, would you, such a reticent man? It's no wonder you are as you are. But he came for sport with Sven and that apple man from Canada, a few scientific friends from Newark. After they made the appointment, Leah inquired."

Disturbed by the emphasis Maggie places on the word *inquired*, Clara sets down her teacup and settles back, adjusting her rasping ring of crepe.

"Inquired?"

Maggie leans forward to compensate, neglecting a smear of butter on the tablecloth, which will stain her lace undersleeve. "As Leah must if we're going to engage or entertain, you see, or inspire the spirits to their accustomed level of loquaciousness. No one seemed to know much about Mr. Gill, however. About either of you. Except that you were originally from London."

Clara feels a seizing in her gut, though Maggie keeps her voice low, and gazes hard at a point above the young woman's head, at a gilt-framed painting of a secretive-looking woman with a small child on a cushion by her feet.

"As I told you before, they'd had a lot of brandy by the time they got here, the men. And, well . . . your father's wife manifested, of course. Your mother."

Clara winces, shaking her head. "Of course she did, Maggie. Perhaps your new beau is right. A bit of shame might serve you well. But there's no shame to speak of in your profession, is there?"

Reaching, Maggie tries to shush her with a forefinger and is undaunted when Clara jerks her head away. "Your father was overcome, Miss Clara. He said he'd failed you. He'd failed you both, and that you might never love anyone again or know what your parents knew together before—"

"Before," Clara echoes, her voice cold and absent. "I can't say there is any *before* where I'm concerned. Only after. But I'm sure dear Mother's ghost told you all about that."

"—Before what comes inevitably to us all and between us. He said this young man you loved was taken from you unseasonably. That was your father's word, not mine, *unseasonably*, and that you mourned 'somewhat more than usual.'"

Relying on old habit, Clara begins to massage her temples. There is something stirring in there, though it isn't a headache, some gangly dragon. "And I suppose you have my beloved's ghost and Father's all ready in the wings, Miss Fox, all scrubbed and ready and calculated to amaze."

The idea of Father standing at her back with that old sheepish look on his face—Maggie patiently interpreting his palsied raps—holds little lure for Clara. He wasn't able to speak of it then; why would he be able to speak of it now, and to what end?

Maggie takes the accusation in stride, and her expression is so fresh and unassuming that Clara forgives, as she always has, the girl's relentless needling.

Maggie pays the bill, and they rise together as if on cue, walking out into the sunlight and bustle.

Clara imagines for a moment strolling thus with the mother she never had, as the mother she'll never be. She indulges herself in the idea, a moment's fancy, that Maggie *is* her daughter, a slightly wayward daughter with a sound heart and a shortage of common sense. "What joy can you possibly find," she complains, "in dredging up hardship in other people's lives for a few red cents? Or worse, for mere amusement since Lord knows I don't pay for the service. Is our friendship worth so little to you? I'm not one of your parlor-squatters."

Maggie only smiles, waving for the omnibus. While they wait to board, she holds her hands demurely behind her back. "I'll take you to the book stalls over by Astor Place—I know you like to read—but mind, there's smut in every one of them, hidden away. Nothing here is as it seems."

❧❧ They are still debating when Lizzie admits them into the imposing entryway of the townhouse. Lizzie wasn't home when Clara first arrived, and Clara accepts her embrace without question or hesitation as earnest Lizzie follows them in, affixed to their combative tone.

The rooms smell delicious, of cinnamon and stew and autumn vegetables. "We have an ace cook now," Maggie pauses to say under her breath before resuming almost playfully, "But I won't be distracted, Miss Clara. Answer me this: with a man like Mr. Holms in the world, a good and pleasing widower with much to offer of an earthly nature, and well-disposed to you, don't you tire of loving a ghost?" She leads Clara by the hand to a sofa. "It's easy to love a ghost."

"Love is not easy, no matter. I expect you're too young to know that, despite all you've seen of the world in your brief life."

"No." Maggie lowers her voice conspiratorially. She lets go of Clara's hand and sinks back into the cushions. "But don't you crave to touch someone and be touched, to be *loved*?"

"I suspect she means with a capital 'L,'" Lizzie, at the window, puts in with exasperation, letting the curtain fall.

"That's what ghosts miss, you know," Maggie insists. "The fullness of food in their bellies . . . heat and damp and blood and saliva and the brush of skin against skin. They miss smells like these"— she gestures in what must be the direction of the kitchen—"and the taste of salt and wine and bread pudding and ripe tomatoes."

Maggie says all this as if it were the most natural thing in the world to be in possession of such knowledge, and that chills Clara. It calms her, too.

"She's ranting again," Lizzie puts in, pursing her lips.

"How can they not?" Maggie asks softly. "But do you remember when they moved all the graves from Buffalo Cemetery to Mt. Hope to build the hospital? I walked out back and stood all that morning while the workmen dug up the graves, laughing and spitting tobacco the while, their chains clanking and earth spilling away and everything ripe. It wasn't ghouls and worms that met me; it was the good, rich smell of a garden, and I felt more pleased with my body and all its gifts. But I knew they didn't smell it. They didn't feel what I felt. I thought, surely if I was ever going to feel their presence, understand them, I would feel it then, as their sleep was disturbed. I've been to dozens of graveyards over the years. I've gone to the dead so that I might get from them some little token. Nothing ever came of it—nothing. I've been in graveyards in the dead of night. I've sat alone on a gravestone that the spirits of those who slept underneath might come to me. I've tried to obtain some sign. Not a thing! No, the dead shall not return, nor shall any that go down into hell. The spirits will not come back. God has not ordered it."

"Are you telling me truth, Maggie? Is this the truth you would set down for posterity? If so, a great many people deserve to hear it."

Maggie rallies brightly. "No. I mean only that in the sense of personal satisfaction, I've had little. I've felt and discerned and rapped and reported, but underneath I don't *know* anything. I've studied ferns as they sprout and unfurl and yellow and shrivel and die. Elisha would have me be certain, but what is certain? Is a ghost any more improbable than a fern or a giraffe or the progress of water from cloud to ocean to cloud again, or of a moth emerging from a cocoon? You're a student of nature. Answer me."

"There are observable scientific principles behind these phenomena, Maggie—a basis in fact."

"You can explain that water moves about the earth and worms become moths and giraffes have spots, but not *why*. Why all the fuss and busyness if it isn't going to *mean* anything? And why shouldn't death mean something, too? Why shouldn't the dead mean something? Who says heaven is a strange and separate place? Do you know a very well-schooled lady in Philadelphia gave me a book by a Frenchman, one of your great thinkers, who said, 'All nature is resurrection.' The fact is, the only thing we know is that we don't know much of all there is *to* know. Katie and I give people pause to think. That's all."

"You're meddlers," Lizzie accuses, "to be sure."

"People pay me to meddle," Maggie snaps, as if her niece had spoken out of turn and spoiled something otherwise propitious.

"And I do it well. Whenever Lish comes round—you be quiet, now, Lizzie, and don't parrot these things that pass between us. I can't trust you to save my life—I can't but think what it would feel like to be his wife, to lie in his arms at night and wake up there in the morning with the sun shining on us through pretty embroidered curtains."

"Embroidered by somebody else," Lizzie puts in, threading her needle and squinting. "Thank you very much."

"It's a happy sentiment." Clara accepts a cup of tea from the hovering chambermaid. "But hardly credible."

"Not to mention," Lizzie puts in, "you're getting so plump on rich hotel food, you'll have gout before you know it like some fat French prince—those short arms soon won't get about you. He's an elfin thing, your preacher."

"Hush, Lizzie."

Lizzie snorts in ungainly fashion and turns back to her mending.

"And I take it your ghosts have told you all this? What they crave?" Maggie's coy expression as she sips her tea saps Clara's patience. "Will you never tire of this charade, Maggie? What would you say if I asked you outright as your friend? Do you or don't you? Can you or can't you?"

"I never answer those questions, Miss Clara. Not for anyone. My family's livelihood depends on it. Besides which, there's altogether too little mystery in this world, don't you agree? I mean, what's so terribly wrong with not knowing for certain one way or another . . . and believing anyway? It's what the majority of people prefer. Every religion is fueled by faith. It's not a crime, you know. I'll put the same challenge to you that I do the others. The same one

Leah always poses. Attend a séance. Come and see for yourself. What are you afraid of?"

Seeing Clara's eyes, Maggie looks away, apologetic. "Forgive me. It's too soon. But one day you will. You'll come and make up your own mind."

"My mind is quite adequately made up, thank you." Clara stares hard at her young friend, so coy and invasive, torn it would seem between mindlessly hurting and clumsily healing. "What do you want, Maggie? I've asked before and never had a satisfactory answer. Whatever your supernatural gifts or the lack, your intuition is uncanny. But wouldn't this . . . empathy of yours better serve the living? The dead need not concern themselves with it. In another time you might have been a midwife or—"

"Or a witch?" Maggie challenges, her eyes flashing.

"I meant that all this, paired with your easy, confident manner and a certain innocent air, has granted you income and independence. This I understand, but why seek unwilling converts when plenty already want what you have to sell? I can only deduce that you do and *must* believe in this farce you've perfected. That you no longer know real from imagined."

Maggie smiles infuriatingly. "I've heard it better said by great rational men who just as quickly came nibbling out of my hand. What I *think*," she says crisply, "is that it doesn't matter what I think. It matters what I *do.*"

Clara can only sigh. "Then what do you want from me?"

"What I want right now, more than anything, is to know something about love. Do I love this man who comes to me in such openness? I *don't* know, and yet he says I must. He says I must be certain or release him unconditionally."

Lizzie pulls a great exasperated breath. "Well, can't *I* have him, then? Maybe Katie can win him over. He's too good to squander. Mama will come round in time."

"Leah loathes Elisha," Maggie confides, "because he insists I give up rapping."

Clara's intrigued. "And will you?"

Maggie leans forward again, as if with a secret, and Lizzie sidles over on her knees to eavesdrop on the answer. "I have done. For two weeks now . . . And he's quite pleased with me and means to send me away to the wilds of Pennsylvania with my French lessons and more besides—to live and learn with some elevated and pious family—to be educated and become a lady—to be . . . when he returns from his expedition to the Arctic . . . Mrs. Elisha Kent Kane, his wife."

Lizzie gasps, and Clara isn't sure whether to congratulate or interrogate. She knows enough about the famous young explorer, a dashing, exotic figure and a favorite in the popular press, to doubt his sincerity. But she knows enough, too, of Maggie's ingenuity and charm to fear for this union. He might be in earnest, but there must be more to the story. Maggie's eyes, in any case, are gleaming with a sort of fever.

"But then this came," Maggie says, "just today, before you arrived and we had our walk. Look here."

Maggie thrusts into Clara's hands a carefully scripted letter from First Lady Jane Appleton Pierce, who recently suffered—in horrific fact, *witnessed* with her husband—the loss of their only remaining child, an eleven-year-old boy, in a violent train wreck. *You are cordially and most urgently invited to visit the White House to ease our minds, so eclipsed by this heartless tragedy, with your work of mercy. . . .*

"The White House!" Lizzie cries out. "That's a first—"

"And a last, no doubt," agrees Clara.

"I leave on the morning train for Washington. Mother will travel with me. The First Lady has offered to come to *me*, but I won't hear of it. You'll manage here for a day or two without me?"

Clara nods. What should she tell the girl? *Take care?*

An education would serve Maggie well, certainly, even if things don't work out with the young explorer, but how to stem this tidal fame when the waves keep lapping? Should she advise Maggie to go to him unconditionally? The idea that Clara might have advice about love is not only ludicrous but cruel. She's by far the less experienced of the two, and so she lifts the girl's hand without a word, kissing it in sisterly fashion. Let her be quietly supportive. Let her be quiet.

41 ❖ In the Region of True Spirits

To rap or not to rap, Maggie thinks loftily, raising her teacup to her lips, pleased with herself for remembering her Shakespeare. Paraphrasing the bard opportunely is what the well-bred do, it seems, and Maggie is a breed in the making: Dr. Elisha Kent Kane's soon-to-be retired original spirit-rapping phenomenon. *That is the question.*

Her adventures in the capital dispatched over tea, she would like to lead Clara out of the ordinary clamor—demand a private audience—but Maggie's already imposed on her friend enough. Clara had to cope here alone while Miss Fox called at the White House, and even now she's navigating teatime—Kate and Lizzie bickering over jam, Ma assaulting a stain on her sleeve with a napkin, Calvin calling from his sickbed upstairs, Leah rattling her news sheet—with grace and good cheer.

Watching Clara endure, Maggie considers the canary in its cage across the drawing room. The parcel arrived earlier that morning with a letter and news clippings from Lish, and she's has been struggling to keep her own counsel ever since. But whenever Clara looks up and meets her eyes across the table, Maggie knows she can't, she mustn't, make this decision alone. It's too important.

If it can be argued that Leah and Lish are at war for her soul—and it feels just so to Maggie, at least some of the time—then it can also be argued that Clara Gill is the one objective soul in their circle. Clara has opinions about the spirits, certainly, but keeps these separate from her opinions about Maggie. If only *Clara* would make the decision, then Maggie could trust it. But Clara won't, and Maggie can't.

The maid, having seen to Cal, begins clearing as Kate and Lizzie lure Ma and Clara over to the birdcage. Leah and Maggie watch the others poke their fingers in through polished brass and whistle softly at the canary hopping from bar to bar. Maggie takes no joy in the little bird. She knows too well what it stands for, why Lish sent it.

She's been trying never to be alone with him, the better to weigh his proposals, but after Clara stepped down to follow the Greeleys in to dinner last night, Lish held her back and kissed her in the carriage. It was a fine, deep kiss (if only he knew what sway he held before his words unworked the spell), and she paid the established price for it: a sermon.

"Mag, listen. You were born for better things than to entertain strangers at a dollar a head, but you and your sisters have led everyone by the nose at the spirit table." He held her roughly under the chin to keep her eyes level with his. "Can you now agree *to be led*—to give up the novelty of this frivolous life of excitement for the hope that one day we'll be together? How will you get by without celebrity sitters or investigative committees?"

She didn't answer his barrage of questions. He didn't mean her to.

"And if you *don't* do as I ask, who will help you remember while I'm gone at sea? Please, Mag. Say only that I can meet you and your mother at the boat, as we discussed—and again Thursday at the Union Hotel to take you to Mrs. Turner's."

"My friend from Rochester has lost her father," she objected firmly, waving at the carriage door, which was still ajar. "Clara needs me. And I can't say how long our visit will last."

Smoothing her skirts, Maggie looked away from his too-dark gaze, and that was that. Until this morning.

She kneads the letter in the pocket of her gown as if to reshape its contents. Like her brother-in-law Calvin, wrote Lish in a shakier hand than usual, her preacher now found himself indisposed. He woke in a grave state, and his physician has ordered him to bed for at least today.

There's nothing so unusual in that, Maggie thinks unkindly. Lish has weathered rheumatic fever and related illnesses on and off for years, but the words do chasten.

Always respect sickness, Mag. No one in full health can realize the awful prospect of a sudden fall into the dark regions of true spirits. *I won't be here forever. You* won't be. *Make of your life what it may be, what it should be. Make it your own."*

But will it be, Maggie wonders, her own? Any more than it is now?

Leah rules with an iron fist, equating what they do with a public service, but their shared life is in many ways an easy and prosperous one. It would take more courage to *stop* rapping, which must support Lish's notion that to give it up is the better choice, the nobler one.

The time for disbelief is past, yet his plans for her seem unreal.

I trust you've held your resolve, Mag, but if you need more evidence . . . you've seen the Herald *of this morning? There is an account of a suicide, which causes some excitement. Your sister's name is mentioned in the inquest. Preacher encloses an opinion piece, likewise of interest, from the* Daily National Intelligencer *brought to his attention by a concerned party.*

The editorial condemns spirit rapping as a delusion that preys on the weak-minded, out of place in an age of reason and progress. The "disgusting theme" and "imposture," its author claims, is still "marring domestic happiness and filling our madhouses with its victims." A lecturer in Richmond, Virginia, put forth precise figures: 573 have been confined to asylums in the United States, and 17 have committed suicide on account of spirit rapping.

The Fox sisters have faced censure almost since the beginning, but never has Maggie felt her own doubts—apart from Lish or any other influence—more keenly. Almost as soon as they got back to Manhattan, Leah reinstituted their former grueling schedule of sittings and séances. But Maggie, distracted by images of Clara aloof in the rainy cemetery with bowed head (or alone in that big empty house, in the silence of her garden room, with all those animal eyes staring from the walls) couldn't concentrate. She followed Leah with puzzled eyes, wincing at her sister's grating, familiar voice, at Leah's monstrous sense of entitlement. For the first time, it dawned on Maggie that she doesn't really *know* her sister. She certainly doesn't like her.

She's entrusted her future to a stranger, and alongside Clara's level counsel, Leah's every word and deed appear oppressive and absurd. Even dear, wry Kate seems insubstantial these days, an automaton going about her spectral chores without question, without a will.

May your bird sing sweetly and be a glad companion in the relative wilds of Pennsylvania. Fly you must, the Preacher's letter urges, *away from it all.*

Oh, but this is a tiresome lover, always talking and writing, always thinking and pledging and prodding. Always intruding on her thoughts. At their best, Maggie's thoughts are as transparent as windowpanes, a place from behind which to view the world; they reflect the world only as shadows reflect form—and with as much bearing—yet she is not thoughtless.

She looks up at the ring of women around the birdcage and finds Clara looking back at her, concern on her face.

Maggie smiles faintly, meaningfully, mumbling her excuses. She hopes Clara will follow her out of this room so frivolously transformed by chirruping. Whom else can she confide in? Ma will know soon enough that Maggie won't rap again. Kate will accept but without understanding. Leah mustn't know, not yet. The world is not *out there*, after all, on the other side of Maggie's glassy thoughts; she lives in it, and she is wasting. This is a tedious decision, but Maggie must honor it for the opportunity it is.

She lifts the *Herald* that Leah left lying on a wing chair, thumbing through. At the same time, her mind thumbs through faces and voices—the friends and strangers who attend the Fox sisters' sittings in droves—for that which is now lost. A suicide. She folds the news sheet open neatly, smoothing it with her palm as she reads.

His name means nothing. He is nothing, whoever he was, nobody now. Except to someone: a lover, perhaps. A mother.

She looks up in anguish, afraid Leah will come instead of Clara, Leah who is too serious even to peer in at a little bird and delight in her family's laughter, Leah who is always thinking. The drawing room next door is alive with the raucous pealing of a brainless little bird. *Think, Maggie. Think.* She sifts the words again, Elisha's, the newspapers', words and words and words, doing her best to concentrate on what's real beneath their stern surfaces. When she looks up, she finds that Clara has been standing in the doorway—for how long, Maggie can't say—and her friend speaks her name, a question.

Maggie's unsteady hands let slip the pages. Having to stoop and struggle in crinoline layers to lift them from the rug again calms her, as rigorous motion always does; it's one reason Maggie likes rapping so much; it's a physical act that claims her full attention.

"Mrs. Pierce cried in my lap," she says at last, and her voice rings too loud, even aligned with the noise in the next room. "Did I tell you? The First Lady of our nation wept in my arms."

Clara looks back at her, expectant.

"We've seen all manner of places, my sisters and Ma and me. We've sat with judges and generals and doctors. I was a farmer's child, Miss Gill. I milked the cows—up to my ankles in dung." Maggie pauses, holding out her hands absently, studying them with her head tilted before crossing them over her chest with a sigh. "Kate and I made it about as far as the well each day, or to market if we were lucky. I met my very eligible husband-to-be at a séance in a fine hotel with a chandelier. For all that's dubious in it, rapping made me someone."

Clara steps forward but without reaching, without touching her. "*You* made you someone. And now that you have, you can be anyone."

"Were that true," complains Maggie. "If we could be *anyone,* then you'd be a famous artist."

"I mustn't want it badly enough." Clara smiles ruefully. "Besides which, you've already lived above the rules."

"Some would say below them."

"People say all sorts of things, Miss Fox."

42 ❖ Poised to Do Good

H e's forever marking me full of deceit and every vile sin, and I confess I miss the spirits already, who are always pleased to find me as I am."

Maggie's view of Dr. Kane seems to shift erratically from moment to moment.

The doctor has commissioned a portrait of his beloved so that he might bear it away to the Arctic as a token, and with noontide and tea long since past, his beloved's patience is wearing thin.

"*Why* mapping the frozen wastes is a morally superior endeavor I can't say I understand. He does his best to explain, and I nod my head dutifully, but I don't *really* see why freezing to death in the frozen wastes is more noble than rapping for strangers night after night." Maggie plucks a piece of lint from her sleeve and blows it away without breaking her pose. "We both make sacrifices. But he would see me sacrifice my calling for his sake. Has done. Would I ask as much?"

Clara suspects, after yesterday, that Maggie is less an anxious bride-to-be today than a woman torn between two versions of her future. To give up rapping will be to give up a part of herself. It's clear that Dr. Kane cares more about how the rapping will affect his standing than about whether or not it's real, and Clara is almost annoyed to find herself arguing in his favor. "But you must see the difference, Maggie. There's the good of proving a thing, of arriving at a certainty. Your view, your *calling* . . . would have us back in the Dark Ages with all it assumes."

"I don't have a view, Clara; that's my trouble." She waves her arms expansively. "I have all this and no view to speak of, no certainty. Of this I am certain. I'm a vessel. They speak through me."

"Maggie. You can't believe that after all this time. What you said yesterday . . ." Clara glances toward Signore Fagnani. ". . . about your *debt* to the profession, what it's secured for you . . . this I understand. But the truth—"

"God, I'm weary of sitting here. I have a kink in my neck." Maggie stretches, arching her back, and Fagnani tut-tuts.

Artists, it would seem, are as invisible as servants.

"May I hold up the book, at least, sir? May I read to Clara while I wait this interminably long while? I know your heroic employer means to march my image across the frozen seas on his back, past gaping Inuit men and walruses with their long tusks, on the path to rescue the lost, but must I suffer for his ambition?"

"Yes, yes," the painter insists. "Read . . . please. Anything that will occupy you. This is a serious matter, madam, a great man's passion. You should count yourself lucky."

"I shall if you say so, but it's *you* being paid—isn't that a crude observation! *Naughty* girl." She laughs for shame, and her two companions join her in spite of themselves.

"Coquette." The artist winks wryly at his subject, who pouts in turn.

"*Undine* is the story." Maggie holds up her book in theatrical fashion. "Of a *very* naughty sea nymph and the handsome knight who would make a lady of her." She leans sideways, toward Clara. "The Preacher, that's my pet name for Lish . . . better known as *Dr. Kane* . . . pleads, the dear hypocrite, that I should take up German and write him smutty letters in that venerable language . . . but things end poorly for Undine . . . because this is a German tale, after all." She slaps the book shut. "I've read it already, as you can see, Clara. I suppose you have read it as well?"

"Every word," Clara concurs, "with careful attention to the themes."

For most of the afternoon, the light has been fine and bright, and every now and then Clara has stood at the painter's shoulder, murmuring pleasantly until he turned and fixed her with that sleepy Italian stare of his. Just when she's as weary of the inactivity as Maggie, in breezes Dr. Elisha Kent Kane, bowing with a flourish.

"We meet again, Miss Gill. Lovely to see you, and thank you for keeping my dear girl company during this trying time." He kisses the nape of Maggie's neck, and Clara smiles at the ground as Maggie waves him away.

They met after dinner last night, when Maggie convinced her mother that Clara was sufficiently "mature" to be her chaperone, and that she and another friend would take one carriage while Mr. and Mrs. Greeley took another. Sven Holms, stung no doubt by Clara's earlier treatment, sent apologies.

Kane isn't a tall man, to say the least, and Clara finds his height, or lack thereof, distracting. To meet his eye, she has to look down. Given his large stature in the world, all she's heard and read about him—he's a brave and somewhat reckless man given to dangling over the lip of volcanoes and otherwise placing himself in harm's way—his actual stature distracts, and it takes a moment to adjust her expectations.

"I'm so very tired of this, Lish," pleads Maggie. "Can't I break for the day and we'll resume tomorrow?"

"There are too few tomorrows before I am at sea, pet, and—" His air waxes serious; this is a teaching opportunity, evidently, and Clara, who would not wince at his condescension, turns away.

"I don't fancy *you'd* ever sit still this long," Maggie interrupts, "unless you were ill—"

"I've often been ill, as you know, desperately and lately. What's more, I served as a navy doctor, which can't but demand patience, as any seaman's life does. Patience is the lion's share of a human education, Mag. Understanding the rigors of time is key to success in any endeavor. Don't you agree, Miss Gill?"

Clara tilts her head, smiling noncommittally. In her experience, failure requires as much patience as success.

Maggie shifts and smiles sullenly at Signore Fagnani, whose lip curls in a confined smile. "The light has gone for today," he pronounces, and Kane takes Maggie's hand with a shrug. Offering his arm to Clara, he escorts the ladies out to his carriage.

Clara has never spent so much time in a carriage as in the past few days in these crowded New York streets. But this will likely be their last outing. Certainly it will be Clara's. Very soon, if her resolve holds, Maggie will depart for Crooksville and her lady's education. Soon after, Kane will leave for the Arctic, heading a much-publicized expedition in search of the missing Franklin party. Clara will remain in the city a while with Kate before returning to Rochester and an empty house, at which time she'll tuck Sven Holms's calling cards in the drawer for official documents in Father's old desk, locking it with the key on the ribbon.

43 ❧❧ Once in a Penny Newspaper

It was a setback, to be sure, slipping off to D.C. to rap for the First Lady, a difficult and moving experience that Maggie can't find it in her heart to regret.

All the same, she has made her *final* decision even before Lish takes her hand at Calvin Brown's wake, in the room with the corpse lying. Seeing Cal this way, a still husk, only confirms her choice.

In a public and binding proposal, Lish now vows to make her his wife as soon as he returns from the polar seas. "I will be true to you," he says, and Maggie glances up and across the coffin in time to see Leah grimace and roll her red-rimmed eyes, "until I'm as the corpse before you."

Frowning at the widow, Maggie returns his pledge, and the days that follow are chaos. She helps with Cal's arrangements, conspires with Ma, and bickers with Leah over why she will not do her duty and fulfill the sacred tasks entrusted to her. But Maggie must also visits schools with her betrothed and learn what constitutes a suitable wardrobe.

Once they have Cal in the ground—and his soul en route to

that glorious Summerland that he, more than any of them, came fervently to believe in—Leah is less desolate than belligerent. It doesn't take much to convince Ma to let her own apartment blocks away with Katie.

Lish's days are as chaotic as Maggie's with lobbying for funds; inspecting recruits; dashing off telegrams and letters; pricing supplies and rounds of beef for his crew; running Maggie around to schools and the milliner; and conferring with her guardians, the Turners, his aunt, Mrs. Leiper, and Cornelius Grinnell, who will see to Maggie's expenses in his absence. If Lish is satisfied with her re-education when he returns, they'll marry. But until then, they won't announce their engagement, and Elisha's brother Patterson will quell rumors and safeguard the family name.

In late May, Lish escorts Maggie and her mother as far as Philadelphia. They stop at the Girard House and sup together for the last time in years, and when they kiss good-bye under the vast hood of Maggie's spring cloak (with Ma inspecting nearby blooms for disease), Maggie feels a genuine, disabling anguish.

That night, it wakes her with heavy paws on her chest, and after a melancholy breakfast, Ma leads her out to the carriage engaged by Dr. Kane for the purpose, and they are conveyed eighteen miles into the country.

The drive is four interminable hours, and this may be the fulfillment of Elisha's dearest wish; it may be that his own aunt will be on hand, at Maggie's disposal; it may be that she'll emerge from the experience as a worm does from a cocoon, all festooned with grace and learning; but none of this reassures her. On the contrary, Maggie feels panic as they arrive in that small manufacturing village on Ridley Creek; panic as they stop before the home of the Turners, a peaceful, unpretentious house ringed with picket fence and fronted with flowerbeds; panic as they follow the coachman and her trunk up the walk.

Ma, who's trying not to cry, enthuses about the abundant shade and the lovely piazza entrance thick with honeysuckle and roses, and Maggie lets this cheer her since Ma seems to need it so much. But when her mother shakes Mrs. Turner's hand and returns to the waiting carriage, looking very small and dear and urbane in her new mantle, Maggie's panic mounts. She thinks of the empty birdcage in the hotel room—Maggie misses the little creature terribly and now regrets letting it escape down the hall.

Lish soon sends word, though, that he has recovered it "with a reward," and that Mrs. Walters will send it on posthaste, together with other neglected treasures, by early boat. They will be in Chester, care of Sam Smith, Tuesday afternoon.

"By then, Maggie dear, my little bark will be plowing the trackless sea. . . . Let us live for each other."

❧❧ On May 31, 1853, Lish sets sail for the Arctic, and when the exiled Maggie thinks of him now it is with sorest tenderness. She supposes it a sisterly love, a blend of gratitude and regret and resentment. Bothered by his pomposity, she took him for granted, and now she must follow her fiancée's movements in the news like everyone else. She must suffer a restlessness and boredom so acute it will wake her in the night when the rural silence roars. It doesn't make sense to be here without him.

Dr. Grinnell reports that the expedition "went off beautifully," with every man in town at the appointment hour. "They'll pause at St. John's, Newfoundland, for fresh meats," he writes. "We may expect to hear from them in about a fortnight."

Lish's last letter—*Am not I your heart?*—posted from New-foundland, imagines her under the shade of a drooping chestnut, "startling the birds with your tokens of the spirit world." It's a letter full of high sentiment and a nostalgia Maggie is too young to recip-rocate, but she clings to Dr. Kane's last words because they are, unless and until he returns, last words:

Once in the mornings of old, I read in a penny newspaper that for one dollar the inmates of another world would rap to me the secrets of this one: the deaths of my friends; the secret thoughts of my sweethearts; all things spirit-like and incom-prehensible would be resolved into hard knocks, and all for one dollar. "Strange!" I thought, "so much for so little. All this for one dollar. I'll go and see them."

With that, I went alone to a hotel, and after the neces-sary forms of doorkeepers and tickets, I saw the "spirit." . . .

Feeling every bit the specter, Maggie begins to people her "im-proving" world with spirits to keep her company (and perhaps for spite). These help her through tiresome recitations with the dour governess. They stand by as summer supplants spring, and stroll in the meadows with her. It saddens Maggie, in a way, that she has no mind for country pleasures anymore. They're an urbane lot, the spirits she conjures in doorways or spots in the fields of Crooks-ville, the sort of well-dressed multitudes you might observe on a rainy city street. The rhythms of New York will not desert her, and her only consolation is the little canary, which sings as it ever has with its whole small heart, despite the bars containing it.

One sunny morning Maggie takes her tea by the window and happens to glance into the cage with the light just so. Squinting, she notes a small patch of brown feathering just under the darting bird's tail. Since her bird *has* no brown—it's yellow through and through—it stands to reason that this is *not* her bird recovered "for a reward" but an imposter. The likeness is there, and it's a perfectly pleasant bird; furthermore, Maggie knows it's childish to feel put out by so small a betrayal—kindly and expediently meant—but she feels it anyway: a roaring, irrational child's rage.

Marching out to the garden with the cage extended at an awkward, swinging angle, she plunks it down on the garden table, slides up the gate, and coaxes the little bird out onto her knuckle. *At least one of us should do as we please*, she thinks, and before she can cry, "Farewell," the bird rises like a piece of yellow silk taken on an updraft. It is gone instantly, into the dazzling summer trees. She won't see it again.

Mrs. Leiper, Lish's aunt, occasionally calls on or for Miss Fox, inquiring after the progress of her studies. In her fine, musty drawing room, she asks in a subdued voice, "How do you fare with your piano?"

She asks Maggie to play for her, and Maggie replies with an unhappy crashing, tears streaming down her face. From this, Mrs. Leiper concludes that homesickness has adversely affected Maggie's health, and she advises Mrs. Turner to give her leave to visit friends in New York. "It would be prudent, I think."

Not long after Maggie arrives into the care of her friend Mrs. Willetts at Clinton Place, she takes ill.

A gentle tug-of-war continues all the while Lish is away—there are no more letters after the first, and his return is regularly delayed—with Maggie absconding from and returning, chastened, to Crooksville.

During one such "vacation" at Clinton Place in October 1854, word at last reaches Maggie that Elisha's ship has docked safely in Washington and is expected in New York the following day. She telegraphs Clara in Rochester and tries to silence a foreboding born of silence.

I love him.

I love him not.

She, at least, no longer wonders.

44 ❧❧ Dovekies and Greenland Belles

C lara heard the guns, a hero's welcome, in the carriage traffic on the way from the canal drop to Clinton Place. Her driver confirmed that Kane's ship had entered the bay.

By now, the ship would have long since docked. It would have been unseemly for Maggie and her family to meet Elisha with the others—his friends and family and adoring public—at the wharves. Both his brother Patterson and Mr. Grinnell had made that clear, apparently; so Mrs. Willetts's parlor swarms with agitated women. There are six in all, with only Leah conspicuously absent, and Maggie has been pacing all afternoon.

With darkness coming on, Clara feels as Will must have felt, flanked by hungry cats at feeding time. There is a dangerous energy in the room, for none among these vigilant women can say whether Elisha will honor his promises or not. No one knows who Elisha will *be* after years adrift in the frozen wilds, much less how he will behave toward Maggie.

To distract from a disappointing and possibly, as the hours tick past, devastating reunion, Katie reads aloud from a report in the *Tribune,* skimming the text and mumbling in a way that makes Maggie visibly twitch. When she isn't commanding Kate to stop, Maggie is begging her to speak up and enunciate, and Clara smiles at this. Her lessons with Mrs. Turner must have taken, after all.

"'They saw an immense number of whales and dovekies,'" Kate reads. "Oh, listen! Here's Lish: 'In the harbor of Leveley/North Greenland,' he says, 'every night while we remained there, Sundays included . . . we had balls and parties and passed the time very pleasantly. Imagine a ballroom full of Greenland belles, dressed in seal skins, moccasins, and breeches, ornamented with gay-colored leather, and dancing to music of melodious fiddles. . . .'"

Maggie locks her sister in a fearsome look, and Clara worries she'll lunge at her.

"'Melodious fiddles,'" the girl croons. "Oh, that's plush. That sounds like our Lish, doesn't it? Isn't that his own dear voice?"

"Kate, please," begs Mrs. Willetts. "Can you not see that your sister is put out?"

"Yes, well. We can feel sorry for ourselves, or we can consider poor Toodles, the dog. 'The sole survivor of a pack,' it says here, 'Toodles had a narrow escape when the starving men nearly shot and ate him. Had not one of their party chanced upon a seal . . .'" Kate sighs happily, reading on in silence.

"How is he?" Maggie asks when several uncomfortable moments have elapsed with only the sound of Kate's rattling news sheet. "Don't they say? He's in sound health?"

"'The safe arrival of the intrepid navigator and his brave crew,'" reads Kate, "'will to-day send a thrill of thankfulness,'"—she flaps her lips silently, locating a dramatic reentry point—"'The fame of Dr. Kane is in the sacred keeping of his country.' Here, wait, Mag. Listen about the men. 'Every one was stout and rosy, and as no razor had marred the beards of the mariners since their departure from these shores, every face was covered with a sturdy growth of hair. . . . Dr. Kane himself wore a beard of patriarchal proportions.'"

Maggie seems little soothed by this news but turns on her heel, pacing back the way she came. Clara thinks to rise and go trap the girl in her arms, force a respite, but it would be a fool's errand.

Mrs. Fox and Mrs. Willetts are adamant. They won't let Maggie stir out, though Clara thinks it would be good for the child to walk. As the evening wears on, Maggie's agitation grows terrible, tyrannical. No one speaks. They are fresh out of theories, and even Kate is resigned to a silence that threatens to consume them all. They wait. Midnight, and still nothing. Nor has he arrived by noon the next day.

"Doesn't he *know* you're in New York?" complains an exasperated Kate at last. "Send another letter."

Mrs. Willetts prepares a dispatch to Grinnell, and Clara and Mrs. Fox succeed in wooing Maggie home to rest. No sooner is she settled in her mother's apartment than Mrs. Willetts arrives to alert them: a carriage bearing Mr. Grinnell pulled up moments after they left Clinton Place. Grinnell came in Dr. Kane's stead, for the young explorer was stricken with rheumatism and beset on all sides by unhappy relatives and friends. Though anxious to call, he couldn't. Not yet.

Mr. Grinnell then requested all letters addressed by Dr. Kane to Miss Fox, which he knew to be in Mrs. Willetts's keeping. "'Surely,' the gentleman insisted, 'were the young lady here, she would place them in my care without hesitation.' I didn't, of course, Margaretta. They're yours to do with as you will. But this is a bad business."

Leading Clara by the hand, Maggie retreats abruptly to her room. She settles Clara in a wing chair by her bed, smiles wanly, and climbs under her covers. Clara hums softly in her throat because it seems the thing to do, as does reaching out tentatively now and then to rub Maggie's back—the many blankets heaped upon it, that is—until her friend manages to sleep.

The bell wakes her about nine the next morning. Stretching the stiffness from her back, Clara hears Dr. Kane's voice in the hall downstairs and jolts to, hurriedly locating a morning gown in Maggie's wardrobe. A nudge sees the girl out of bed, and Maggie slips into her gown, making two swift turns round the room, padding in bare feet. Smoothing hands over her tangled hair, she already looks the part of a woman scorned but electric also, expectant.

"Where is Miss Fox?" Dr. Kane pleads downstairs, noisily and somewhat pitifully.

"Don't let my mother in, will you?" Maggie murmurs, lifting Clara's two hands. "Or Mrs. Willetts. I don't want them here. I want you to stay—so I can speak to him. They'll consent to that."

Clara nods, distaste rising in her throat. It is both too much to ask and the least she can do.

"Abovestairs," Mrs. Willetts repeats, "completely broken down," and in the gruff voice of a man long divorced from society, he demands an audience, over and over until the voices of the elder matrons and Kate converge and calm him, and soon footfalls sound on the stairs.

When her mother knocks, Maggie attends her in the doorway with a wave toward Clara, who drifts to a chair in the corner, claiming shadows. Mrs. Fox looks skeptical but nods her consent, holding the door open for the doctor, who looks both gaunt and more swollen in the face than when last Clara saw him.

Maggie and Elisha stand stubbornly apart. It seems a long time before she says, her voice flat, "I've never seen you in your naval uniform."

Does he look a stranger? Does the uniform remind her of his life apart, Clara wonders, of the gulf between them? Their intimacy is humbling, and for a moment Clara looks away. She can't but notice, though, when Kane backs Maggie against the wall, entreating and kissing her clumsily and repeatedly, missing her mouth as she twists away. She can almost see Maggie sinking into his familiar smell, reshaping herself to his shape, relaxing out of herself. She can almost remember the feeling, and for the benefits of Mrs. Fox and Mrs. Willetts in the hall, Clara clears her throat loudly.

Maggie steps back, and his apologetic eyes follow. He is under siege, he says, in a voice almost too low for Clara to hear—from all sides—and must beg from her a letter . . . to satisfy and relieve his mother . . . stating that their relations are merely friendly and fraternal. "Maggie, please. Forgive me this weakness. "

She stares at him for a long time. Finding her voice, Maggie shakes her head firmly. "No. I won't make it easy for you."

"It is anything but easy."

"So you say." Looking flushed and small, Maggie thumps him feebly in the chest. It's a silly gesture, tender somehow, and when Lish does nothing she tries again, but this time he catches her fist, holding it in two careful hands. Maggie pulls free, and he draws the parchment from his overcoat pocket.

"Where is your beard?" she accuses, backing away as if from an attacker. "That great huge beard of recent legend, and the seals and the lonely dog, lately doomed, and the dovekies and the Greenland belles? They are as unreal as you are."

Maggie lurches for the letter, walks it over to the desk, and smooths the page flat. "You have never been real." She dips her pen and signs.

45 ❖ High Enough

In the end Dr. Kane could neither leave Maggie Fox alone nor honor his vows. The couple resumed their relentless dance: Elisha advanced and retreated, and Maggie, a constant subject of rumor and recrimination, grew increasingly sensitive to disapproval. Clara retreated back to Rochester, to her quiet life, and in this way a year passed, and another.

Clara lives so quietly these days, in fact, that she all but forgets the sound of her own voice. As Father's modest trust dwindles, she begins to compose letters to Aunt Tilda in London, compose and recompose and then burn them in the hearth fire. The sight of burning pages, black ink coiling to cinder, still makes her stomach clench, but faced with starvation, Clara supposes Tilda the lesser of evils. She alternates this absorbing activity with adding and subtracting drawings from the worn-soft leather portfolio Artemus gave her on her nineteenth birthday. Is she brave enough to circulate it? Father never made a secret of his associations, and she knows as well as any artist who should see her book, but where to begin, and how to weather the pity of would-be patrons?

She sits sketching among crows and blue jays and chipmunks in the garden, feeding them peanuts so they fill her trees and tip her feeders and make a perennial, much-loved racket.

Her dreams in those quiet days are astonishing and full of animals: mangy tigers and quarrelsome magpies; Mettle the African grey; her first dog, Hound; Pratt's little terrier, Bartleby. The feral marmalade cat that comes and goes on ancient paws, but there are no people apart from Marta, that shadowy girl who tidies and serves tea, and eventually Clara realizes she can't afford Marta anymore and has to let her go. And then only Amy Post calls, once a week or so to pray with Clara (or by her, or for her) and see that she isn't too thin or too addled.

Sometimes Clara wakes sweating in the night with a noose round her neck, but more often now her mind works its way backward, craning for a version of Will untainted by time and circumstance. She lives only to hear his voice, which so often intrudes with the clarity of dreams that it's difficult, these days, to tell waking from sleep.

When memory allows, Clara constructs a labyrinth around herself with only Will's voice to lead her from end to end and back again (she often wonders, *Back to what?* Reality? Who would have her believe after all these dogged years that William Cross wasn't real?).

In the aimlessness of not knowing, not caring for tomorrow, Clara has wound and unwound and rewound yesterday—or that part of it that pleases her—and on the morning of the day when Maggie Fox unexpectedly returns, Clara happens to notice the dusty oriole's nest on her windowsill. It has become, over the years, her favorite object in the room, and today when she lifts it, Will is there, speaking with such ease in the electric air of memory that it takes her breath.

You would have loved Tom.

For a moment, that's all he says. Back in the menagerie, with or without Mettle on his shoulder, Will scattered stories like seeds wherever he stepped or raked while Clara sat sketching the animals. She remembers this story well and with fondness: a fatherless boy being led wide-eyed about Smithfield Fair on his brothers' shoulders . . . and then high into the treetops by his mentor, the old gypsy "seller of nesties."

Held aloft now by his voice, Clara understands for the first time her dream on the night before he hanged. In the dream, it was raining—a hard, warm rain—and Will was a child, watching her gamely from the high branches of a facing tree. She was a child, too, a little sodden girl on a swing with wet hair flung back, pumping her legs, trying to get high enough to reach him.

Understanding that he will never go forward again, only back, is a glamour of its own, and Clara is sinking gladly into memories and smallness.

She has forgotten the house and the tax man and the sound of the front bell and the harsher sound of knuckles rapping. It is only when she hears Maggie's knowing voice outside the glass of her window, not a yard away out in the garden, when she hears those plump knuckles rapping to her like the spirits rapping, rapping her awake—that Clara returns to the here and now, and she isn't sorry.

She's delighted to lift the curtain and find her friend, that ghost-girl whose red ribbon is wound through a perfect brittle bird's nest on her windowsill, and she rises stiffly.

"Here I am!" sings Maggie in the doorway. "Muddy boots and all. Embrace me!"

Clara obeys, moving slowly like a body underwater.

Breathless, Maggie relates how Elisha is finally gone away again, sickness and all, to England, but first he gave Maggie a diamond bracelet from Tiffany's and took her to the opera at Niblo's and had her ambrotype taken and proposed to her in front of the Fox matriarchs, and strangely enough, she loves him better than ever and more surely—now that it's like as not too late, for what has he really left her with but jewelry, gloomy forebodings, and a stack of envelopes lined with muslin and directed to himself care of Bowman, Grinnell & Co., Liverpool?

"So you really must have me in for tea, Clara. I know I should have sent a card first but I can't be bothered, not today. I can't bear it, any of it, and I must be entitled to rest my head on your shoulder and weep because the world is a pitiful place, and I am pitiful in it."

Clara leads Maggie by the small of the back, indoors and into the pantry, where they prattle and fix a tray and retreat with it to Clara's room, to the best light in an otherwise dim house, that small, bright island in a sea of hushed, unused rooms and ticking clocks.

Apologies are made, tea dispensed, silences explained. For a time, they nibble wordlessly at sloppy bread-and-butter sandwiches.

"And your calling?" Clara asks finally. "Your pledge not to—"

"He won't return," Maggie says bluntly. "I know it. I've always known it somehow, that Lish and I were doomed to be just what we've always been and no more. I've mainly kept my promise not to rap, and when rarely I break it—when someone needs me to—then I'm discreet. He'll never know, and not knowing won't hurt him. But enough about that," she says at last, brushing crumbs from her lap. "I told an untruth before in the doorway. You don't look well at all. You look a fright."

Turning her plate this way and that in bony fingers, it strikes Clara with brutal absurdity that just below a thin crust of earth the world over lie countless millions of bones doing what bones do, a ceaseless dance of decay and regeneration. Thinking vaguely of Sven Holms's calling cards in a drawer locked with a key on a ribbon, card-paper yellowing to the color of old bones, she looks up and all but whispers, "Rap for me, Maggie?"

46 ❖❖ Passage

Meddlesome as ever, Maggie invites Sven to the séance, though he seems quietly mortified by the sight of Clara, refusing to look up when the maid admits her into the parlor. He does not acknowledge Clara in any way until she sits across from him at the little side table and touches his sleeve to show that she would value it.

"Are you to participate in the séance, then?" She lifts her chin in the direction of the adjacent drawing room from which voices and laughter issue.

When he says he will not, Clara is powerfully and unexpectedly relieved. She would not have him see her in whatever state she'll find herself in. She is more frightened than ever of what she might see and hear, of what she might not hear. Clara has already removed her gloves and, resting her wrists on the table, rolls the coin from one absent finger to another like a magician or an illusionist, passing its heat from hand to hand.

"What is that?"

Realizing, she flattens her palm over it.

He continues to look the question with his eyes.

Clara leans forward, her voice low, for she will not arm the rappers with this or any other detail that will help them disappoint her. "A coin for the dead."

Mr. Holms tilts his head, still questioning.

"For the boat crossing," she says, "as in the old stories."

Ah, yes, blooms in his gold-flecked eyes, and spontaneously Sven Holms lays his hand briefly over her fingers, lifting it again in apology. His smile is equal parts warmth and sadness. "Good luck, Miss Gill."

"You'll be here? When it's over?"

"Would it suit you?"

Clara can't trust herself to know. She feels her throat stop up, feels the coin burning a brand in her palm. The little boat is bobbing in the fog of her thoughts, and she can only wonder, will that stubborn ghost come and board it? She nods consent.

"Then here I'll be." Sven crosses to a plush chair by the window, lifting a book from a facing table and pretending to read.

"It's upside down, Mr. Holms."

His expression is sheepish and comical, and they share a smile. Sven settles back, his big, booted feet propped on a dainty damask footstool. He lifts the heavy drapery and looks out at a darkening street. "I'll wait here, Miss Clara."

Maggie opens the heavy curtain separating the parlor from the drawing room and, smiling, waves Clara in. "There you are! I thought you wouldn't come."

Clara approaches obediently, avoiding the eyes of the dozen or so people already milling about inside.

In contrast to the cheerful parlor without, this room is large, windowless, and somehow cool and stuffy at the same time. It's a room Clara never ventured into during her previous visits. Maggie never offered it as part of the standard "tour," and no wonder; it's an unremarkable room, apart from the massive oval séance table—its mahogany top rubbed and scuffed and scarred—ringed round with hard chairs, and a vast wall mirror in an ornate oak frame.

Clara notes one other exit besides the curtained doorway as well as a wide folding screen, painted black and positioned near the rear wall (this Clara makes a point of peeking behind the moment Maggie resumes mingling—in search of hidden doors or associates or covert supplies), and two side tables. One supports an oddly respectable-looking tea service and the other a gas lamp (one of only two in the room) and a pair of tall funnels fashioned of stiff brown paper, which Maggie identifies as "speaking trumpets."

The walls are of neutral color and, apart from the mirror, boast only two pictures, one a painting of clouds from which a lurid-colored face emerges, the other some kind of geometric puzzle. Guests mill, craning politely forward, their hands behind their backs, to study these gilt-framed images or pace the spartan room wearing vague, distracted faces. Or they cluster in uneasy pairs and small groups, whispering over teacups.

Clara has done her research and supposes that at least two people in the room are "confederates" hired by the mediums to assist with various cues. Studying the scattered group with kind uninterest, she settles on two merry student types, self-proclaimed "skeptics" who at the moment are amusing themselves with the speaking trumpets, pointing the long funnels at each other's ears, murmuring through the tubes in hoarse, assumed voices like giddy boys. For a moment, their antics even jeopardize the shaky tea table until Kate levels the young men with a look (learned from Leah, no doubt) and they slink off to join another of their party, who's smoking meditatively in a corner.

Her turn about the room completed, Clara settles in one of the only free chairs along the wall, where she can't but overhear the hushed conversation of a trio nearby—a jocular, big-bearded man and two overdressed women, a petite thing called Florence, Clara deduces, and an unapologetically dour Mrs. Sewell.

"My cousin claims to have sat with a famous medium in Edinburgh," says the petite woman. "Do you remember Morris's little pantomime, George?" She turns to her friend again. "Cousin fairly channeled him, this noted Scots mystic."

The dour woman only lifts her chin in what might be a challenge. *And?*

"'Nightly,' Cousin mimicked, raving in the fashion of the gentleman-medium, 'when an esteemed matron took her place for dinner, she tipped the table to settle a burning question: *Dear Charles, may I have fish today?* If the table tipped a *yes*, she answered, *Thank you, dear Charles: I thought I might, for I felt a strong desire to* have *fish for dinner*. If the table tipped *no*, it was *I thought not, Charles! I felt one of my chills coming on, and fish is dreadful for me when I have my chills.'*

"'Domestic imbeciles!'" barks the petite woman impersonating the cousin impersonating the Scottish medium. "Charles, of course, was the lady's dead husband."

The jocular man laughs in recognition, and even the dour woman seems intrigued. "It must be true," she says for all in the room to hear, "that the majority of the questions and pleas for intervention from the spirits can only be base or material. We're a race trained to the average, yes? Aligned always to the most probable event? Miss Fox, has this been your experience?"

Discoursing with a group across the room, and perhaps taken off guard, Maggie looks up. Poised professionalism blooms on her face in place of intellectual panic. Witnessing this transformation, Clara—who has spent her life courting the improbable—wonders whether, in the end, true mystical experiences can be communicated at all.

"Am I meant to suppose, Mrs. Sewall," Maggie replies, "that you don't care for fish?"

In the fading laughter, Kate begins leading people quietly to the table, both singly and in pairs. "We'll begin in a few moments," she announces over her shoulder, "and once we do, please refrain from wandering in and out of the room. Subdued conversation is preferable to weary silence—you're all doing a capital job in that regard—and you should feel free, though it may be at odds with your character, to dance, sing, or gesticulate . . . yes, I'll say it . . . as the spirit moves you."

There is another flurry of nervous laughter. Mrs. Sewell, though, seems restored to her former mood and leans toward her companions. "But are not mediums like this *accountable* for the good matron and her fish? Is it not a kind of dependency for some? My nephew, an 'artistic' young man, claims it's 'better than opium,' and there are few decisions he is willing to make without first consulting . . . *them.* But in truth he is consulting *her,* the paid medium, is he not?"

Clara surprises herself by speaking up, though less out of conviction than a chilling sense of isolation. She can feel Will's presence in the room, which is no more strange than suddenly becoming aware of the sound of her own breathing. But here and now, she doesn't welcome it.

You would've loved old Tom.

Not like this.

It's a long tale devised to keep you.

Clara would sooner know the difference. She would know, and not confuse anything.

Shaky now, she feels a need to venture in among these others, whoever they are—who question as she does, who doubt as she doubts. The women swivel round and regard her with warm surprise; the man smiles openly.

"I suspect it's a bit like other forms of mass communication," she says. "We owe so much of our understanding of the world to artists reporting from the field, for instance, but before their news reaches the public, the journeyman engraver must step in and do his work, interpreting the journalist's or artist's intent. There is always a middleman—" Clara looks up at the sisters, busily situating their flock—"or -woman, as the case may be. To read the runes."

"True enough," responds the guest named Florence. "And let us say that mediums and spirit manifestations are *not* what they seem, there are still real mysteries that beg attention. There are forces beyond ourselves that we must acknowledge. I heard once of a Mrs. Morton in Bangalore, for instance . . . do you remember, George?"

George nods.

"The lady woke oppressed by the idea that something was wrong and saw then her young sister-in-law at the foot of her bed. The girl was in nightdress with her hair loose around her and one thick lock cut off at the temple. The apparition stared intently, then faded away, and in due course a letter came notifying Mrs. Morton of her sister-in-law's death en route from South Africa to England. Tucked inside the letter was a lock of the woman's hair."

The exacting Mrs. Sewell turns to Clara as a sort of sister-in-arms, awaiting her reaction, but Clara has let her mind roam. Like a billion bones lurking under the earth, the ghosts haunting the edges of other lives do not concern her.

Maggie and Kate seem to have the other guests settled, so Clara rises with a nod, and the other three vagrants follow. Each hovers behind a chair, and when Kate nods approval, Florence's husband assists the ladies one by one.

Only Maggie remains standing.

"Those stationed on either side of my sister or myself should feel free to position a forefoot over the medium's toes," Kate says, glancing meaningfully at Clara, "and I trust we have no person of a strong magnetic temperament present?"

I am sorry, Clara Gill. Your attentions fish words from me I'd never sensibly part with.

Kate instructs those who haven't already done so to remove their gloves as Maggie turns off the gas in the side-table lamp. "You'll find the room well-ventilated," she says, "but chill. We find frostiness is best."

As Maggie strides over, easing into the last empty chair, Clara feels terror and excitement and such solitary anguish that she believes the others must see into and pity her.

You've watched a hawk hunting in a field . . . the way it veers and tips, and you know death is there—you feel its wings beating?

Just before Kate dims the remaining light, Clara notes how red and strong both sisters' hands are—strong enough to tilt tables and make other mischief, surely—and it dismays her to think that a friend might deceive on this point around which every tendril of her life revolves.

You pity the soft little thing in its sights, but the fact is you're cheering the hawk.

Clara lays down her coin, her palm resting over it briefly, then follows the lead of those around her, extending her arms, accepting the grip of warm male fingers on either side. Maggie, somewhere to the right, seems to snap to then. "Won't Mr. Holms join us?" she asks, craning toward Clara. "I thought he meant to sit in."

Heavy with foreboding and sorrow, Clara says, "No, Maggie. He'll wait outside." She closes her eyes a moment, breathing to steady herself.

You're far from mercy, but it takes your breath, don't it? There's beauty in it.

She's read that three confederates often sit together to free the hands of the person in the middle for arranging phenomena and would rule out this possibility (nor will she abide either sister slipping out to answer "the call of nature" or to fetch smelling salts or to otherwise cast doubt upon the proceedings). "May I ask, Maggie, that you sit on my right, with Kate on my left?"

Kate, who never had the respite from these duties that Maggie enjoyed thanks to Elisha, has aged noticeably in the years since Clara saw her last. Her voice—wearily objecting, citing the rules of order—so recalls Leah's (which, for Clara, recalls Alice's) that it chills Clara, but it also steels her resolve. "I need this much assurance," she insists. "Please, Kate. Maggie? I need to believe in the outcome. Whatever it is."

One of the boy-skeptics asks (with perhaps too much innocence), isn't it customary to alternate male and female? To do with the energy?

A flicker of something—steely resignation—passes between the sisters, nothing strangers would notice. Maggie nods first, and then Kate, who rises to change seats with the gentleman on Clara's left. Her fingers are cold.

Maggie whispers to the man on Clara's other side, and they too swap places.

It might be a silly precaution, Clara thinks, having the sisters each in reach, in view as much as possible, in listening range. She will not be fooled if it can be helped, and it can't be. But she won't rest without the truth or its next-best shadow, and there must be no softness for the sake of ease.

"Do not break the circle at any point," instructs Kate, "nor will we, unless the invisibles sound five raps to call for the alphabet board. They require all of our energy combined to manifest."

Kate turns down the last remaining lamp, and as the flickering shadows lengthen and eclipse her vision, there does seem to be an unusual energy in the room, something born of collective expectation, embarrassment, skepticism—whatever it was that drove each of them here.

It is a darkness she can't fathom, full of strain, and Clara holds tight to Maggie's fingers.

They were oars in my hands, and I was rowing away in a fog.

"If one of the party grows drowsy or mesmerized, lapsing into a trance or contortions, do not fear," Kate says softly, and suggests they begin with a prayer or a song.

Florence suggests "Power of Love Enchanting," and Kate launches in, adapting the hymn to feeble spiritualistic musings as the others straggle behind.

"I have often found," interrupts a nasal elderly lady at the far end of the table, "that the music used to evoke a sympathetic atmosphere at séances can be tedious. Perhaps we might try, 'We Won't Go Home Till Morning'?"

After a ripple of nervous laughter, one of the skeptics says, "You, madam, are of the crowd termed *jolly dogs*—we who want congeniality over solemnity at our séances. I'm all for trying, 'For He's a Jolly Good Fellow' on the grounds that it's a tune the whole company knows."

To the delight and titillation of all at the table, the spirits seem to agree. A reeling ruckus sounds at the base of their chairs, as of someone running round and round the table, dragging a stick over the chair legs.

That jolly-good tune is tossed off, and several others, more or less discordantly, and it's a treat to hear the dour Mrs. Morton doing her best at the other end of the table. Clara's own tongue is a cold stone in her mouth, and her heart beats hard when raps break out under the table. Then comes a sort of auditory rippling or racing up the wall and down again, all of which invokes in her not gratitude or alarm but an obliging fascination, a ridiculous desire to concentrate harder than she ever has before, to penetrate the mystery as hundreds of clear-minded men and women before her have failed to do. She's heard the theories, all of them: the sisters pop their kneecaps . . . hire detectives . . . crack the joints in their toes . . . bob apples on strings. But the infamous "rapping" is first like a thunderclap in the brain and then like the fairy clamor of tiny booted feet racing up and down the walls.

There is appreciative chatter at the table, but on the heels of this promising beginning comes what must be the least credible part of the evening—or that which most calls attention to itself in Clara's mind as an act. Near the center of the blackened screen is a peephole, evidently, some eighteen inches square. Luminous faces appear there in fast succession, shining and fading and shining again: a ghostly-looking child; a woman with a strange leaden look in her eye; a plump, mustachioed face with opera glasses. There has to be a hidden entrance behind the screen, Clara thinks, and having failed to spot it, she wonders what else she has failed to see.

Dour Mrs. Sewell seems to agree. "Oh, have on with it," she complains. "This is child's play," at which critical juncture one of the skeptics (none too quickly, Clara notes) springs from his seat and strides over, knocking down the screen theatrically. His groping meets with no one and nothing, of course, and he returns to his seat all huff and verbal shrug.

Maggie takes this as an opportunity. Indeed, she points out, spirit faces no longer interest her as a medium. She always seeks vainly the lineaments of her own departed friends. "But," she cautions, "there are many on the other side—most unknown to us— just as there are multitudes flowing ceaselessly past in the street outside."

As if to punctuate this comment, a glowing hand reaches out of the void to touch Kate's hair. Clara leans to watch the luminous limb cast its faint shine on the young medium's face. It seems to rise and fall in the dark, stroking her cheek with tapered, light-stained fingers, disheveling and lifting her hair before bobbing and floating, an aimless, manic little figure on the air.

For a moment, this performance has the desired effect, but Clara fast recalls that spirit hands are one of the least difficult of counterfeit phenomena. A long black kid glove stuffed with pliable substance, coated in phosphorescent paint, will do, either worn by a confederate or concealed under a medium's skirts and attached to her foot somehow when the call comes to take the stage.

Picking up on Maggie's show of weariness, Kate admits to shaking spirit hands "as unconcernedly as I do those of my own acquaintances in the street," which reminds Clara of the coin on the table, of her futile objective. In her mind's eye she sees it there, glowing with the stain of her longing.

My end will be bitter, I know, and when the reaper comes for me, he'll find this coin under my tongue.

Clara looks up and round abruptly in the darkness.

Had Will known all along? So many of the things he said rang with a kind of finality. Had he held back from her not because he was morally obligated, as a married man, but because he saw reflected, in Clara, his own end?

But the world we imagine lives on inside us. . . .

The world in little was the only world she and Will could have known together, the only one available to them. Would he make the choice to love her again, knowing now how it would end? Would he take it all back if he could?

Clara feels curiously numb and content in the chaos. All around, sitters are being knocked on the head with speaking-tubes and assailed with cushions.

"Rest, rest, perturbed spirit," Kate croons, while some at the table, those not favored with spectral brutality, shift in their seats and complain.

"Have a care what you wish for," Maggie warns, "or you'll get a bucket of water over the head. It's happened before."

Clara almost acts on the urge to go, preserving what's holy in her anguish, but would an evening's amusement harm her? Would it harm Will? The levity in the room might have pleased him, and in any case, the real issue seems to be the shifting nature of her perceptions: amusement, expectation, astonishment, despair, scorn . . . impossible to know *how* to feel as events unfold, what to believe, and fighting the urge to believe for the sake of ease, for the relief it brings, has made for a trembling kind of tension in her body. She's a bound spring, a wound clock, a poised mechanism, and from somewhere perhaps within her erupts a sudden whistling and chirping as of an invisible bird circumnavigating the room, the light swooping of a bird (or a bat?) caught between the walls, which of course sets some of the ladies shrieking.

Clara closes her eyes hard against this distraction, and indeed the hysterical ladies are quickly silenced, and when Clara opens her eyes again she finds that the bird has dissolved into beautiful little phosphorous lights, sometimes two floating together—resembling eyes—sometimes many more than two, darting together or drifting about the room in stately fashion.

Maggie gives selected sitters leave to break the circle ("slowly, please") and reach for them; those chosen report with awe that the lights are unlike glowworms, which are easily captured with stealth; instead the reaching hand passes through them.

"Link hands again," Maggie commands, and Clara sees the little lights reflecting in the looking glass on the wall, though she cannot make out the edges of that mirror or much else in the darkened room; she almost hates to think that the phosphorous oil often found in fraudulent mediums' kits might be behind this pretty display.

The bird was a fine innovation, Clara thinks—Maggie's, no doubt—and Clara *is* trying to think, to complete this experience in rational fashion, but Maggie is gurgling and swaying beside her now, speaking in a strange, faraway voice. "I have a message," she says, shuddering, "from Teresa," and one of the men across the table gasps. *A message from Maria . . . a message from a man in a sailor's cap, a man who drowned . . .*

Hypnotized by this voice—her friend's, a stranger's—Clara feels, without fanfare or warning, the briefest brush of hands cradling the back of her head. She shudders, her child's grip on Maggie's fingers tightening. Kate's hold is firm as the hovering hands stroke and lightly cup Clara's head. Lips brush her hair, a whisper of a touch, and she trembles violently.

You and the sea grant my soul its passage, Clara Gill, and I thank you for it.

Ecstatic with panic, Clara tries to wrench her hands away, but Kate holds firmly. Maggie, too, holds on with the severity of the dead. The raps resound, intent and clamorous, though Maggie's hand doesn't jar in the slightest; there is no telltale twitch. Apart from their grip on her fingers, nothing in the physical aspect of either medium alters in the slightest.

Clara would like to accept it—peace or relief or whatever Maggie and Kate and also Sven, in their goodness, are trying to offer her. But there is something untold in all this, a thought that penetrates the faraway drone of Maggie's voice.

Given the choice, Clara *would* repeat it, all of it, even with full knowledge of the consequences. She would court death between them always because what little life she has lived, she lived with Will. And all these years, it seems, a monstrous guilt has lived undetected in the shadow of grief because she cannot, even for his sake, regret *them*. What seems obvious now, as Maggie speaks his name in the darkness, is that love cares little for choice. It won't be willed away, and there is no shame in wanting what's impossible. Having it is another story—someone else's.

Duty claims me, and I would not tax these too-perfect days.

"I have a message from William," Maggie repeats, the strangled intensity gone from her voice, "from Will. But he says he can't stay."

Clara twists her hands free from her neighbors', and with that, the room seems to drain of whatever collective energy formerly animated it. She gropes the tabletop in front of her. "The lights—"

"He can't stay—"

"Turn up the lights. Please, Maggie."

The other séance participants murmur and lean. In a moment, oil lamps bloom with light. The table is bare. The coin is gone, and Clara swivels away from the others in her chair. Doubled over, she begins to rock and moan softly as Maggie rubs her back, embracing her from behind, holding on hard, like a mother.

In a few weeks, Maggie's bold explorer and ailing preacher will meet his end in Cuba. Within weeks, the words *I can't hear you, Lish . . . I can't hear you* will echo through her every thought, a blight on her mind. Within months, she'll commence drinking herself to death.

But Death will take its time, leaving her leisure to recall this night and how she intuited the very slight movement of the heavy curtain separating the outer parlor from the séance room and seemed to glimpse the dim silhouette of a giant; how she felt rather than saw his swift approach, his stealthy, hulking presence behind Clara's chair; how he lingered there for the length of a heartbeat— touching her perhaps, this object of his large affections (how Clara's grip tightened on Maggie's fingers!).

Maggie will replay her astonishment that Sven Holms should stage a visitation in the Fox sisters' stead, manifesting without Maggie or anyone else to prompt him, without permission or apology or technique, sliding Clara's strange token soundlessly from the table and gliding away again like a fog.

Maggie will remember "Clara's séance" in vivid detail and never speak of it. The Preacher's silence stubbornly refutes it, the years eat at her like lye, but Maggie will persist in believing—as she ever has in the fuzzy privacy of intuition, in the dark sanctity of her heart—that anything is possible. Not probable, perhaps, but possible.

When Sven Holms vanished from the séance room that night, sliding away like a true shade, Maggie had to smile. He'd made an ordinary miracle of devotion, and after that, nothing would startle Maggie Fox in quite the same way again. Not even the force of Clara's subsequent emotion. In the presence of grace, while Katie lit the lamps again, Maggie smiled into her friend's disheveled hair, and it was abloom with electric light, with stardust.

꙳꙳ When Clara can contain herself enough to walk with straight back past the others, straight out to Sven Holms, who's still reading in his chair—the much-discussed collection of poems by Mr. Whitman is now right side up in his bear's grasp—she extends her hand.

Sven takes it without a word, rising clumsily, and together they walk out and down two flights and into the clamorous city.

Clara holds fast to her friend's hand, and though she can't see the constellations for the city lights, she knows they are there. This, too, is a world in little, this busy place beneath the stars, and she remembers that last night with Pratt on the little cottage porch in Mudeford, that waiting night when the world seemed large indeed and full of promise, and that night is not gone.

Acknowledgments

I drew heavily on primary sources for this fictional account of Margaretta Fox's life, notably the letters attributed to Fox and to Elisha Kent Kane in *The Love Letters of Doctor Kane*, as well as Eliab W. Capron & Henry D. Barron's *Singular Revelations: Explanation and History of the Mysterious Communion with Spirits, Comprehending the Rise and Progress of the Mysterious Noises in Western New York, Generally Received as Spiritual Communications* (Second Edition) and Leah Fox Underhill's memoir, *The Missing Link in Modern Spiritualism*. I also consulted contemporary studies, especially Nancy Rubin Stuart's *The Reluctant Spiritualist: The Life of Maggie Fox* and Barbara Weisberg's *Talking to the Dead: Kate and Maggie Fox and the Rise of Spiritualism*, which cast light on exaggerations and distortions in the earlier sources.

Other books I owe a debt to are *The Tower Menagerie*, by Daniel Hahn, *The Table-Rappers: The Victorians and the Occult*, by Ronald Pearsall, which offered many wonderful historical anecdotes, and to Henry Mayhew for his timeless portrait of a gypsy seller of "nesties" at Smithfield Fair.

Thanks too to Writers & Books of Rochester, NY, and the Gell Center of the Finger Lakes; Larry Naukam, Head of Local History and Genealogy at the Central Library of Rochester and Monroe County; Cynthia Howk, Architectural Research Coordinator at The Landmark Society of Western New York; to Ellen Bourne, Lisa Goodfellow Bowe, Jill Grinberg, Courtney Wayshak, and everyone at Unbridled Books, most especially my editor, Fred Ramey, whose level counsel kept me on the rails.

14